The Spirit of This Covenant

For Miss Vickie —

Congratulations on your
retirement, and happy reading!
If you enjoy this one, check
out my other novel, Remembering
Miss Addie.

12/5/2014

The Spirit of This Covenant

Lamar Wadsworth

Writers Club Press
San Jose New York Lincoln Shanghai

Writers Club Press
an imprint of iUniverse.com, Inc.

For information address:
iUniverse.com, Inc.
5220 S 16th, Ste. 200
Lincoln, NE 68512
www.iuniverse.com

ISBN: 0-595-16804-3

Printed in the United States of America

The Spirit of This Covenant is a work of fiction. While there are passing references to actual historical figures, all of the characters are fictional, and any resemblance to actual persons, living or dead, is coincidental. Likewise, all of the churches, associations, and schools in this novel are fictional. They, like the characters, exist only in the author's mind, where they are exceedingly real.

The Author

The author acknowledges the quotation of portions of the following hymns and gospel songs:

"You Can't Do Wrong and Get By" by Lethal A. Ellis, copyright 1929 by R. E. Winsett, copyright owned by Sacred Music—A Trust, Kendallville IN, heirs of the R. E. Winsett Music Company. Used by permission.

The following songs are in the public domain:

"A Child of the King" by Harriet E. Buell

"The Church's One Foundation" by Samuel Stone.

"Children of the Heavenly King," by Caesar H. A. Malan, refrain by John Cennick

"Rescue the Perishing" by Fanny J. Crosby

"Higher Ground" by Johnson Oatman, Jr.

"Just As I Am," by Charlotte Elliott

To all the many friends who read my manuscript in progress, offered constructive criticism, and more than anything else, offered encouragement. If I try to name all of you, I will certainly miss somebody.

Thanks to Harry Gordon for the cover photo of Hill City Baptist Church at Hill City, Georgia, and to Missy Wadsworth for the photo of author. Thanks to Clark Riley for editing and formatting.

We moreover engage that when we remove from this place, we will as soon as possible unite with some other church, where we can carry out the spirit of this covenant and the principles of God's Word.

—From the covenant of
Clear Springs Baptist Church

I

It had been just over a month since Mike Westover endured the ritual known among Baptist preachers as "facing the hiring squad." He had preached at his wife Karen's home church in Williston, Alabama for the pastor search committee from Harrington Baptist Church in Harrington, Georgia. Afterward, he, Karen, and daughter Asalee went out to dinner with the committee. The chemistry seemed right, and they felt as though the interview had gone well, but committee chairman Carl Baxter was hard to read. They parted with a check to cover their expenses in coming down to Alabama and with Carl's promise, "We'll let you know something soon." With that, they bade quick good-byes to Karen's family, threw their things into the car, and made the nine-hour trip back to their home near Mid-Atlantic Baptist Theological Seminary. Mike and Karen had to work the next day, and Asalee had school. Asalee was asleep by the time they got out of Williston, and Karen followed shortly afterward. They slept most of the way, and Mike drove the trip straight through.

Two weeks earlier, his faculty advisor, New Testament prof Paul Kerns, stopped him in Leland Hall to tell him of his conversation by phone the night before with Carl Baxter. Dr. Kerns had been one of Mike's reasons for choosing Mid-Atlantic. When Dr. Kerns visited the Baptist Student Union at Rullman College, Mike was impressed by his scholarly acumen. He liked Kerns' dry wit, unassuming manner, and unpretentious spirituality. Dr. Kerns seemed to recall some anecdote about every student he had taught in his almost forty years at Mid-Atlantic. Dr. Kerns told Mike, "I don't think anything I said will hurt your chances."—a classic Paul Kerns understatement. He had received the Kerns imprimatur. That evening, Mike received the call from Carl Baxter, inviting him to preach a trial sermon at Harrington Baptist Church.

In this last semester of Mike's Master of Divinity studies, his photograph and biographical summary had been included in the paper that the seminary placement office sends to churches, associations, and state conventions all over the country. Karen helped Mike create the most impressive looking resume possible without inflating his credentials and experience. Asalee helped stuff envelopes and lick stamps. Ever since Karen had gotten pregnant this time, she had been nauseated by the taste of adhesive on stamps and envelope flaps. Asalee thought it tasted yummy, so that worked out well. They sent out well over a hundred resumes to people and places known and unknown, but it was not the paper from the placement office or the flurry of professional-looking resumes that led to the appointment for Mike to face the hiring squad.

Mike thought back to that early morning phone call from Brother Woodrow, the pastor of Luckett's Creek Baptist Church, Karen's home church in Williston, Alabama. He had just gotten in from his night job at the Holiday Inn near the seminary campus. Karen had left for work in time to drop Asalee off at school on her way. Mike had managed a light schedule in this last semester of seminary, so he did not have a class until 11:00. Looking forward to a two-hour nap, he stretched out on the sofa. Wallace, the dog of uncertain ancestry that Asalee named after the chairman of deacons at Mike's student pastorate, was ready for a nap, too. He

had been awake while Karen and Asalee made noise fixing breakfast and getting themselves ready for their day. He had done his
business out in the yard. He had disposed of the scraps from
breakfast and the leftover milk in Asalee's cereal bowl. Finished
with all responsibilities until evening, Wallace needed a nap as
badly as Mike. He curled up on the rug in front of the sofa where
Mike had stretched out. Both of them were drifting into twilight
sleep when the phone rang. Wallace hated the sound of a ringing
telephone even more than the sound of Karen's hair dryer. Mike
grabbed the phone as soon as he realized that the alternating *rrring-
WOOF-rrring-WOOF* was not a part of his dream. The person on
the other end took off talking before Mike in his semi-awake state
could say "Thank you for calling Holiday Inn East. This is Mike.
How may I help you?"

"Brother Mike! Bless your heart; glad I caught you at home! This
is ol' Woodrow Bentley down'n Alabama. How're you doin', Son?"

Mike didn't see how anybody could be that exuberant at eight
o'clock in the morning. By the time Brother Woodrow got around
to breathing, his familiar voice had awakened Mike sufficiently
for him to respond coherently with "Fine, Brother Woodrow.
How're things in Williston?"

"Mighty fine, son, mighty fine. The Lord's treatin' us better'n
we deserve, Amen? Think y'all could make a trip down here so
you can preach for me on the eighteenth? Some folks from just
over the Georgia line at Harrington wanna come hear you."

Much to Wallace's chagrin, Mike was now too excited to take a
nap. He was up, talking on the phone. He called Karen at work
and told her. That was easy. Four months pregnant with their
second child, Karen was looking forward to Mike's graduation and
a call to a full-time ministry position. She had been discouraged by
the lack of response to all the resumes they had sent out, and this
was their first solid lead on a call to a church. Likewise, the call to

Dr. Kerns' office was easy. The hard call to make had been the one to Wallace Coggins.

*   *   *   *   *   *   *   *   *   *   *   *

Wallace and Estelle Coggins had treated Mike and Karen like their own children during Mike's two years as pastor of Clear Springs Baptist Church. Asalee was another grandchild to the couple she knew as "Papa Wallace" and "Mama Stell." When five-year-old Asalee ran up to them at church that Sunday, full of excitement, telling them about her new puppy and the name she had chosen for it, Wallace's eyes welled up with tears. He told her that was the highest compliment he had ever received, and he asked for a photo of Wallace the Dog to carry in his billfold. Wallace the deacon chairman never missed an opportunity to show off the picture of the "great-granddog" that bore his name.

Estelle died back in January, very suddenly, from a cerebral hemorrhage three months after she and Wallace celebrated their sixty-third wedding anniversary. Wallace was devastated. One minute she was sitting at the kitchen table talking with him over breakfast; the next minute she was dying in his arms. Wallace dialed 911, and the paramedics came very quickly, but Estelle was dead when they arrived. The sudden passing of "Mama Stell" had been Asalee's first experience in dealing with death. At the funeral, Wallace asked Karen and Asalee to sit with the family while Mike conducted the service. At the graveside, Mike handed his Bible to Karen and took a seat with the family. Karen was taken aback when Wallace asked her to do the graveside service and committal. She told him that she wasn't a preacher, that she wasn't ordained, and that she had never done anything like that before. Wallace said he knew all of that and it didn't make any difference. He said Estelle thought a lot of her, and he thought it would please her. It was the hardest thing Karen ever did, but it helped her deal with her own grief. Asalee tried to comfort her Papa Wallace that day as she took his hand and walked with him behind the casket from the church outside to the cemetery at Clear Springs.

Clear Springs Baptist Church has stood for over 140 years at a rural crossroads in Sanders County, Virginia where Clear Springs Road crosses State Route 116, about thirty miles from the seminary, surrounded by family farms with pasture land and fields of tobacco, corn, and soybeans. With about 65 members, it was viable but not large enough to support a full-time pastor. Always served by seminary students, Clear Springs considered getting young ministers off to a good start to be an important part of its mission.

The older people could remember back when the preacher rode the train down on Saturday, spent Saturday and Sunday nights with a family in the church, and caught the train back on Monday morning. Estelle Coggins said, when she was a young girl, her father and Mr. Jess Walker were the only ones in the church who owned automobiles. Estelle said her father used to go every Saturday to meet the Southern Railway local at Coley's Station and pick up the preacher. Mr. Walker would take him back on Monday morning. Some of Estelle's happiest memories were of that weekly trip with her father. As a young lady of eighteen, she still looked forward to going with him. Her mother hoped and prayed that she would develop a romantic interest in Edgar Renshaw, the young single seminary student who was then serving Clear Springs.

Estelle said that, one Saturday as her father was getting Preacher Renshaw's luggage, she asked her uncle, the station agent, if he knew the name of the handsome young man firing the engine on that local train. Mike and Karen laughed until their sides hurt, listening to Estelle tell about the lecture she got from her mother about how unbecoming it was for a proper young lady to climb up into the cab of an engine to flirt with the fireman. Estelle's father was more understanding. He continued to take her with him on the weekly run to pick up the preacher, and he and the preacher started having longer conversations with Uncle Parker at the depot. Long skirt notwithstanding, Estelle learned to mount an engine with the agility of a squirrel scampering up a tree. Estelle's mother finally gave up and told her to wear old clothes when she went over there so she wouldn't get coal dust and grease on her good dresses.

Wallace said the engineer on the local did his part, too. "Ralph told me he'd take care of oiling around when we got to Coley's Station, and he'd take his own sweet time doing it. Jim Berry was flaggin' for us. He'd climb up on the tender and top off the canteen for me. They both told me to stay on the engine with Estelle. Ralph used to tell people that since his fireman started courtin' Parker Williams' niece, he had the best-lubricated engine on the whole division, said he figured Southern Railway could afford a little extra alemite in the interest of romance."

Mike remembered sitting in the living room with Wallace the morning Estelle died. Wallace took down the faded picture of engine 1092 from the mantle and brought it over to him. A smile broke across his leathery, tear-stained face as he told Mike, "One Saturday morning, we were stopped at Coley's Station. Ralph was oiling around, and Jim was puttin' water in the tender for me. Estelle mounted the engine. Right there in the cab of that ol' ten-wheeler was the first time we kissed. 'Bout three months later, same thing, same engine. Ralph was oiling the valve gear while we took on water. Estelle was up on the engine with me. It was the day before her nineteenth birthday. That's when I asked her to marry me, right there in the cab of the 1092. Preacher Renshaw married Jesse and Eunice Walker's daughter Beulah. Preacher Renshaw did baptize me, though, and he performed mine and Estelle's wedding."

Remembering that conversation and many more since, Mike knew that Wallace was having a hard time dealing with his wife's death. Not until she died did he realize how much he had depended upon her. He told Mike how Estelle used to tease him, saying it amazed her to no end that a man who ran steam engines for a living couldn't boil water at home. All four of Wallace and Estelle's children lived within twenty miles of Wallace's house, but he said he hated to impose on them. They all worked during the day, and Wallace had given up driving after dark. What helped Wallace more than anything was when he started volunteering in the pediatrics unit at Sanders County General Hospital. He liked to read and tell stories to the children, and it did his heart good to meet people who had never heard about the time he was called for the Presidential Special. Wallace relished telling about that trip, about giving Harry S. Truman the fastest ride he ever had on land behind engine 1404, and how ol' Truman slipped through the fingers of the Secret Service when they pulled into Danville and climbed right up on the engine with him. Wallace said his fireman was on the ground checking the lubricators and he was working the injectors when he felt somebody looking over his shoulder. He turned around, and there was the man from Missouri standing right there on the deck of his engine. Mike had seen the note, handwritten on White House stationery that Wallace received from President Truman.

A smile came across Mike's face as he thought about the eighty-six year old retired engineer visiting children in the hospital. The administration had given up any hope of getting Wallace to wear navy slacks and a light blue blazer like the other male volunteers. When Wallace went to the hospital to read and tell stories to the children, he put on his old hickory stripe overalls and cap. He would have his big shiny open-face Hamilton pocket watch that he inherited from his father, the one with the old style Southern

Railway "arrow" logo on the back, in the bib pocket of his overalls and the watch chain draped across his chest, and he would tie a red bandana around his neck. The crowning touch came when he dug out a pair of goggles that he wore back when he worked on steam engines. He gleefully took them to his optometrist and had them fitted with his current prescription bifocal lenses so he could use them when he read to the children. Wallace was still hurting deeply over Estelle's death, but Mike was confident that he would do all right and help others in the process.

It wasn't just Wallace that Mike thought about as he pondered how difficult it would be to leave Clear Springs. Carol Richardson, a thirty-six year old divorced mother of three, had just undergone a radical mastectomy last month after the lump in her right breast turned out to be malignant. Mike remembered the fear in Carol's eyes when he saw her at the hospital the night before her surgery. She wondered whether the surgery and radiation treatments would get all of the cancer and whether she would live to see her children grown. Until she found the lump in her breast, it had never occurred to her that she might not. She thought about the history of cancer on her mother's side of the family and wondered whether twelve-year-old Megan and nine year old Jessica carried the gene that would predispose them to develop the same insidious cancer. Carol's background as a high school biology teacher equipped her well for asking questions that neither her friend Dr. Mary Kate Sessions, her oncologist, nor her pastor could answer with absolute certainty.

Mike and Karen visited Carol on the Sunday afternoon after she came home from the hospital. Carol told them about Bill leaving her in 1985 when Bill Junior was fourteen months old. Then, at the next church business meeting, Lester Halstead stood up and said he didn't think a woman who was separated from her husband ought to be teaching the church's young people in Sunday School.

He said he thought Carol ought to step down for the good of the church. Carol said that she kept her emotions in check long enough to say that she would resign so as not to cause dissension in the church or be an unwholesome influence on the young people in her class. Then she ran outside sobbing uncontrollably. Her parents, Russ and Joan Ayers, her sister, and her friend Linda Trimble followed her out. They were all sitting on the front steps with her, trying to console her, when Lester came stomping out of the church, face red as a beet, looking like his blood pressure was high enough to blow the top of his head off, muttering something about finding himself a church that believes the Bible. Russ started to grab Lester and fight him, but Carol told him to let him go. Lester got in his truck, slammed the door so hard that the glass shattered, raced the engine, and tore out of the church parking lot slinging gravel every which way.

The state trooper's timing, Carol said, was truly providential. Had he topped the hill on 116 a split second sooner, he would have plowed into Lester and killed him. The trooper had to slam on his brakes to avoid a collision. Russ pictured Lester's head mounted like a deer hunting trophy on the wall at the state police barracks in Canfield and imagined the man with the Smokey Bear hat telling his fellow troopers, "Yep, I bagged that ol' boy one Wednesday night out on 116, right in front of Clear Springs Baptist Church." Lester was pulled over on the side of the road, his lap full of dime-size fragments of shattered glass, dealing with the irate state trooper. The front of the church was bathed in blue light, and Carol's racking sobs had been replaced by a look somewhere between complete bewilderment and mild amusement when Wallace Coggins came out to tell them what had just transpired.

Wallace said that Lester made a motion to accept Carol's resignation. After a long deathly silence, Preacher Clark looked over at him and said, "Brother Lester, your motion dies for lack of a second." Then Michelle Halstead, Lester's fifteen-year-old niece, stood up and said, "I'm a member of this church and I'm in Mrs. Richardson's class. May I say something?" Preacher Clark told her she certainly could. Michelle said that Mrs. Richardson had taught her at school and at church, and that she was one of the best teachers she had ever had. She said that she thought the church should ask her to take back her resignation and keep on teaching. Preacher Clark asked Michelle to make that in the form of a motion, that the church ask Carol to withdraw her resignation. Wallace seconded Michelle's motion, Preacher Clark called for a vote, and Lester cast the only negative vote. The church hung Lester Halstead out to dry. Wallace told Carol, "As chairman of deacons, on behalf of the church, I'm asking you to withdraw your resignation for the good of the church." Those last words, "for the good of the church," echoed the words Lester used in making his original motion. Carol appreciated that gentle touch of humor. Her mascara all streaked and running down her face, flanked by her parents, her sister, and her lifelong friend, Carol came back into the business meeting. A hush fell over the room as she announced in a voice hoarse from the racking sobs of five minutes before, "I withdraw my resignation." Carol said that when Preacher Clark saw her surrounded by people hugging her, he said, "Carol, you've got your job back." Mike knew the church that stood by Carol Richardson when she was going through the separation and divorce would stand by *Deacon* Carol Richardson as she faced her cancer.

Mike smiled as he thought about the way Carol Richardson and Linda Trimble became deacons, and how Clear Springs almost got kicked out of the Sanders County Baptist Association during his third month as pastor. It all started when First Baptist Church in Canfield chose Mary Kate Sessions to be a deacon. Mary Kate, who grew up in Clear Springs Baptist Church, was a family practice physician in Canfield. Her parents, Arthur and Maude Sessions, were in failing health. Maude was confined to a wheelchair, and Arthur gave up driving after he crashed his car through the door of the Ledford post office. Arthur called Russ Ayers to ask him if he would take him and Maude to Canfield on the Sunday morning that Mary Kate was to be ordained. Arthur said he'd never given much thought to a woman being a deacon, but Mary Kate was his only child, and it would mean a lot to him to participate in the laying on of hands. Russ said he would be glad to take them and, since he too was a deacon and had known Mary Kate all her life, he would like to participate as well. When Russ told the other deacons that he would be gone that Sunday, Joe Norris said he thought it would be good if they all went over there to help ordain Mary Kate. They all went. Clear Springs called off services that day because the whole church wanted to go. They met at the usual hour for Sunday School and car-pooled sixty-one people over to Canfield for the 11:00 ordination service at First Baptist Church.

At the next deacons meeting, Russ Ayers said, "I got to thinking after we went over to Canfield to help ordain Mary Kate. Fellows, we've only got five deacons in this church. Poor ol' Arthur's so frail and feeble, crippled up with that rheumatoid arthritis, he can't be active, so that leaves four of us. I'm fifty-nine, and I'm the youngest man in this room 'cept for the preacher. I think it's time we ask the church to choose a couple more deacons, and I've been thinking, ever since we helped ordain Mary Kate, maybe we ought to consider some of the women in this church. What do you fellows think?"

Mike just sat back and listened. Wallace spoke up. "Isaiah Mathis used to work with me on the railroad, best fireman I ever had. They put him to firing for me when I first made regular board engineer. He had a lot more seniority than me, nearly as old as my father. Ol' Isaiah taught me more about runnin' an engine than any other man on the railroad. Best air brake handler I ever saw. A lot of times, 'specially if we were runnin' at night, I'd take over firin', let him run the engine. One time we come through Canfield 'bout three o'clock in the mornin'. Isaiah was runnin' the engine. He had that ol' Ms4 hooked up so tight you couldn't tell which side was exhaustin'. The stack sounded like a jet when he opened up the throttle comin' off Chaney Creek trestle! Never saw a man handle an engine any better, but the railroad said a colored man couldn't be an engineer, would'n even let Isaiah take the test. Disqualified 'im on 'count'a the color of his skin, an' hit wad'n right. What I'm gettin' at, Russ, is I see it the same way you do. If we disqualify women just because they're women, the way the railroad disqualified ol' Mathis 'cause he was colored, the church is not any more Christian than the railroad."

Joe Norris and Wayne Ethridge were men of few words, but they were nodding in agreement with Russ and Wallace. Wayne added, "I know one thing. My wife and daughters are a lot better than me when it comes to visiting shut-ins and folks in the hospital."

Like Wallace admiring Isaiah Mathis' artistry in running an engine, Mike was in awe of the consummate skill with which four country church deacons had handled an issue that could get a preacher killed in a lot of places. Almost as an afterthought, Wallace asked Mike, "What do you think about it, Preacher?" All Mike had to do was say, "Fellows, I agree with you." The deacons recommended that the church choose two new deacons, and that women as well as men should be eligible. There were no dissenting votes. When the ballots were counted, the church had chosen Carol Richardson and Linda Trimble, the daughter of Wayne and June Ethridge. After prayerful consideration, both agreed to serve.

At the ordination council, Carol and Linda each presented a clear, compelling Christian testimony. Carol's divorce was never mentioned. If anyone had made an issue of it, Mary Kate Sessions, who came over for the ordination council of her two lifelong friends, had seen bruises on Carol's body that were not consistent with a fall down the stairs. She had met her at the office late one night to sew up her busted lip. Russ Ayers knew about his former son-in-law's philandering. Linda Trimble could have broken her silence about the times she had rebuffed Bill Richardson's unwanted advances. But none of that ever came up, because nobody said anything about Carol being divorced. Wallace set the tone for the council when he said, "Carol and Linda, you've been coming to this church since nine months before you were born. If we don't know you by now, we never will." The ordination service was held the following Sunday, and Mary Kate came back to deliver the charge to the candidates.

The issue of *The Religious Herald* with the report of Carol and Linda's ordination came out the week before the annual meeting of the Sanders County Baptist Association at Bolton's Chapel Baptist Church. It was Mike's first time to attend a Baptist association or convention meeting of any kind. Mike didn't grow up in the church. He became a Christian in his second year at Rullman College, after he started dating Karen.

On the Sunday before the association meeting, Wallace called Mike and the deacons together for a short meeting between Sunday School and worship. He said he'd heard that, since no other church in the association ordained women and the Southern Baptist Convention had gone on record against ordaining women, some folks were planning to stir up a stink at the association. Wallace said Ed Halstead had called to tell him that the pastor of True Gospel Baptist Church, and Lester Halstead, who had joined True Gospel, were planning to challenge the seating of Clear Springs' messengers on account of the women deacons.

It intrigued Mike that the tip came from Lester's brother. Ed never was much of a churchgoer. Decoration Day, Easter, and

Christmas—that was about it. He came to see his children baptized. His wife Barbara, who was Linda Trimble's sister, and children Michelle and Kevin came every Sunday. Even though he rarely came, he cared about the church and appreciated its ministry to his wife and children. Ed didn't profess to be a Christian, but he once told Mike that he wouldn't talk to a dog the way he had heard his brother talk to his wife and children. Ed said he didn't know what the fuss was about anyway, said he'd known Carol and Linda all their lives and thought well of both of them. Ed told Wallace that Lester was the one egging Billy Fite on—not that Billy Fite really needed anybody to egg him on. Brother Billy's last name, pronounced like "fight," suited him nicely.

Mike asked the deacons what they thought the church should do. They agreed that the only thing they could do with any degree of integrity was to stand their ground without apology, put it in God's hands, and let the association do whatever it chose to do. Carol and Linda said they would take personal leave days from work in order to be there. Linda said she thought the association ought to at least see their faces and see what awful monsters they were before they threw them out. She said that, as long as she had worked at the Farm Bureau office and as long as Carol had taught school, a lot of folks should recognize them.

✶　✶　✶　✶　✶　✶　✶　✶　✶　✶　✶　✶

Karen had to work, it was a school day for Asalee, and Karen needed the car. Mike caught a ride down to Sanders County with Greg Nash, the pastor at Bolton's Chapel. They lived a few doors apart in the Seminary Court apartments. Greg's church was hosting the meeting, and Mike's church was in danger of being kicked out of the association, so they both decided to miss a day of classes and work to be there. As Greg headed his old Toyota south on the Interstate toward Sanders County, they made small talk about seminary life and about their respective churches. Mike had no idea how Greg felt about the ordination of women. If Greg knew anything about Carol's and Linda's ordination, he didn't say anything about it. Mike told Greg that the ink was barely dry on his ordination certificate and that he had never been to an association meeting before. Greg said that it was his first time, too. Mike asked Greg if he knew of anything unusual in the way of business that might come up. Greg said all he knew was that, as host pastor, he was supposed to get up at the beginning of the session, welcome everybody, tell them where the rest rooms are, read some Scripture, and pray.

Mike was sleepy. When Greg exited the Interstate and headed east on the two-lane road toward Bolton's Chapel, the sun was in their eyes, and that made it worse. Mike reclined the passenger seat and closed his eyes. He was awakened by the sound of tires rolling across crusher run gravel as Greg turned into the parking lot at Bolton's Chapel Baptist Church.

It was 8:50 by Mike's watch, another hour and ten minutes until the meeting was to begin, but the parking lot was already filling up. Greg headed over to the fellowship hall to see how the preparations for the noon meal were coming along. It was a clear, crisp October morning. The weather report they heard on the way down said that it was supposed to be around sixty-five degrees by mid-day. They would be able to use the large outdoor tables built for dinner on the grounds, which would expedite things considerably.

Mike was pleased to see a huge urn of steaming coffee and boxes of Krispy Kreme donuts that the men of Bolton's Chapel had put out for the benefit of those arriving early. He spotted Wallace and Estelle in the coffee and donuts line and went over to greet them. Wallace was still a big, robust man with a strong grip and a booming voice. "Mornin' preacher! Don't worry, all of our folks're gonna be here. If we get throwed out, we get throwed out together."

As Wallace was speaking, Russ and Joan Ayers' Plymouth Voyager turned into the parking lot. Clear Springs was entitled to ten messengers in addition to the pastor. Russ and Joan, Carol Richardson, Sharon Chambers, Linda Trimble, and Linda's husband Wesley climbed out of the van. Wayne and June Ethridge came in right behind them in Wayne's Ford Ranger. After they all had a chance at the coffee and donuts, they followed Mike into the foyer of the church and took their place in line at the registration table. After registering and picking up their ballots, they made their way into the high-ceilinged white frame church and took their seats on wood slat pews made long ago from heart pine by some local carpenter.

The woman at the piano was playing *Jesus, Hold My Hand*, embellished in gospel quartet style with fancy runs that would defy conventional notation. John Hobgood, the minister of music at First Baptist in Ledford, was more accustomed to a Moller pipe organ than a clunky old upright piano tuned a half-step flat, and he was accustomed to *The Baptist Hymnal* rather than the manila-bound *Stamps-Baxter's Favorite Songs and Hymns*. All his musical training had been with round notes. He almost developed astigmatism looking at the small print and the oddly shaped notes. Songs that were lively and energetic were easy to find; songs he knew well enough to lead were not. John searched the book for a lively, energetic song he knew, and found it just in time to begin the meeting promptly at 10:00, leading the congregation in singing *When We All Get to Heaven*. Mike pondered the irony of singing about all of us going to heaven while some of those present were plotting to disfellowship Clear Springs.

Greg Nash had never spoken to more than thirty-five people at one time. He walked up to his pulpit and looked out over the crowd. Every pew was packed. All the chairs in the aisles were taken, and people were standing around the walls. Greg welcomed the messengers to Bolton's Chapel, and there were a few chuckles at his weak humor about hoping that everyone present would be back for Sunday School and worship next Sunday. After telling the people where to find the rest rooms and telephone, he opened his Bible and read Ephesians 4:29-32,

Let no corrupt communication proceed out of your mouth, but that which is good to the use of edifying, that it may minister grace unto the hearers. And grieve not the Holy Spirit of God, whereby ye are sealed unto the day of redemption. Let all bitterness, and wrath, and anger, and clamor, and evil speaking, be put away from you, with all malice; and be ye kind one to another, tenderhearted, forgiving one another, even as God for Christ's sake hath forgiven you.

Greg's few remarks and his prayer were timely and in the right spirit, but Mike knew that some were already running ahead, chomping at the bit, to get to the first order of business.

The enrollment of messengers was usually a perfunctory housekeeping matter. After the welcome and invocation, the moderator would call the meeting to order and recognize the clerk, who would call the roll of the member churches of the association. The messengers from each church would rise and respond "Present" when the moderator called the name of their church. On that day, however, there was nothing routine about the enrollment of messengers.

Claude Bradley, a small wiry man in his sixties with wavy steel-gray hair and piercing blue eyes, had been pastor over at Coley's Station since 1965. A Sanders County native, he grew up in Bethel Number One church. Always a bivocational pastor, he owned and operated the True Value Hardware in Ledford, and his wife had taught third grade for many years at Clear Springs Elementary School. A much-loved man, he was finishing his second term as moderator.

Felix Marshall was in his twenty-third year as clerk of the association. In his early seventies, he still kept himself trim and fit.

He had been the postmaster in Ledford for many years. An avid amateur historian, he had an appreciation for good records. Felix took superb, detailed minutes, just on the long shot that someone a hundred years down the road might want to know what was said and done at the one hundred and fifty-second annual meeting of the Sanders County Baptist Association.

Claude struck the top of the pulpit with his gavel and announced, "The one hundred fifty-second annual meeting of the Sanders County Baptist Association is now called to order. I recognize our clerk, Brother Felix Marshall from the First Baptist Church in Ledford, for the enrollment of messengers."

Felix stepped up to the pulpit and adjusted his glasses. "I will call the roll of all the churches holding membership in the Sanders County Baptist Association. If you are the pastor or a duly elected messenger from your church, please rise and say 'Present' when I call the name of your church. Atwater Baptist Church."

"Present."

Mike listened intently as the names of the churches were called in alphabetical order and the messengers responded. "Bethany. Bethel Number One. Bethel Number Two. Bethlehem. Bolton's Chapel. Carson Creek. Central Avenue. Clear Springs..."

Mike and the messengers from Clear Springs rose as one, called out "Present," and sat down. Brother Billy Fite and Lester Halstead had made it a point to park themselves on the very front pew in the center section, directly in front of the pulpit. Coley's Station was the next church in alphabetical order after Clear Springs. Felix just managed to get out the first syllable of "Coley's" when he was cut short by Billy Fite springing up like a jack-in-the-box calling out "Brother Moderator!"

Claude Bradley was patient with most people and tried to treat everyone kindly, but he intensely disliked Billy Fite. He reminded himself often that God only requires us to love all people, not to like them all. Claude's eyes rolled like an odometer turning 100,000 miles. It was exactly nine minutes after ten in the morning, and Brother Billy had already wearied him more than a long day at the hardware store. With an unmistakable note of disdain, he said, "I recognize Brother Billy Fite, pastor of True Gospel Baptist Church. What in the world is it, Brother Billy?"

"I move that we refuse to seat the pastor and messengers from Clear Springs Baptist Church be..."

"Second!," shouted Lester Halstead before Brother Billy could finish his motion, and scattered voices, including all of the ten male messengers from True Gospel were saying, "Aye."

Thundering above the voices of his allies, Brother Billy continued, "because Clear Springs has ordained two *women* as *deacons.*" One could not miss the surly tone of voice in which he uttered the words *women* and *deacons.*

Claude didn't have strong feelings either way on that issue. He was well read enough to know that it could not be reduced to a conflict between those who believe the Bible and those who do not. He and his wife were patients of Dr. Mary Kate Sessions. They had the highest regard for her, and they had congratulated her on her ordination. Claude knew Linda Trimble, since she had worked about fifteen years at the Farm Bureau office in Ledford. He knew Carol Richardson by reputation. Carol had taught Claude and Ruth's grandson Curt at Sanders County High School. When Curt was chosen for the Governor's Honors Program, he named Carol as his outstanding teacher. Claude was a gentle soul with no appetite for controversy. It was out of character for him to be furiously pounding his gavel, shouting "Order! Brother Billy, you are out of order! Sit down, Brother Billy, you are out of order!" Some said it was the first time they ever heard Claude raise his voice.

No amount of gavel-pounding and calling for order would silence Billy Fite until he got in his last words. Shouting above Claude's efforts to rule him out of order, he added, "And one of those women is *DIVORCED!* Clear Springs ordained a *divorced woman deacon!*"

Brother Billy sat down and patted perspiration from his forehead as Claude reiterated, "Brother Fite, you are *OUT OF ORDER!* A motion to challenge the seating of messengers from any church will not be entertained until the clerk finishes calling the roll of all the churches and makes a motion to enroll the entire body of messengers. You can make your motion then as an amendment to the clerk's motion to enroll the messengers. You can, but I wish you wouldn't. Brother Clerk, please continue with the roll call of the churches."

Brother Billy and Lester sat fuming as Brother Billy waited to be recognized for his postponed moment of glory. Although Claude handled the situation well, Brother Billy had caught him off guard, and he was not going to let it happen again. He was thinking and praying as Felix finished calling the roll of the twenty-three churches of the Sanders County Baptist Association.

"Ulmer's Ferry. Westside. Brother Moderator, I move that the pastors and duly elected messengers who have answered the roll call of churches, along with any pastors and duly elected messengers from the member churches who may arrive later in the day, constitute the one hundred and fifty-second annual meeting of the Sanders County Baptist Association." There were numerous seconds to the motion.

Claude stepped up to the pulpit and said "We have a motion and a second to enroll the messengers. Is there any question or discussion?"

Again, like a jack-in-the-box, Billy Fite sprang to his feet. He almost got his mouth open before Claude could say, "Brother Billy, come on up here so everyone can see you and hear you."

Brother Billy strutted up to the pulpit. "Thank you. Thank you, Brother Moderator. It breaks my heart to say this, but one of our churches, one of our historic old churches, Clear Springs Baptist Church, organized in 1846, has departed from scriptural practice by ordaining two *women*, Sister Linda Trimble and Sister Carol Richardson. One of our fine godly men at True Gospel Baptist Church, Deacon Lester Halstead, used to be a member at Clear Springs. He left there heartbroken a couple of years ago because he realized even then that the church was drifting toward liberalism. It is from Brother Lester that I learned the shocking information that one of these women, Sister Carol Richardson, is divorced from her husband. Now our beloved Southern Baptist Convention adopted a resolution in 1984 saying that women, to preserve the divine order of submission, should not serve in leadership roles entailing ordination. Clear Springs has committed an abomination in the sight of God, having their ordained men lay their hands on the heads of two *women!* Let me ask you, Brethren, how in the world can a *woman* be the husband of one wife? And one of these women, Sister Carol Richardson, is not even the wife of one husband! She is divorced! What kind of example is she setting? The demise of family values is destroying America, I tell you..."

Billy Fite was getting into his preaching cadence when Claude cut him short. "Brother Billy, I'm sure you have a point. Please get to it."

Brother Billy looked as though Claude had backhanded him. Quickly regaining his composure, he said "Because Clear Springs Baptist Church has deviated from Bible teaching and sound Baptist doctrine, I move that the association refuse to seat the pastor and messengers from Clear Springs Baptist Church."

There was a smattering of seconds, the loudest from Lester Halstead. Claude stepped next to Billy Fite, put his arm around his shoulder, and said, "Brother Billy, I said that I wished you wouldn't make this motion, but you did and you are within your rights to make it. If we take this action, we're going to do it in the right manner and in the right spirit. Is the pastor of Clear Springs, Brother Mike Westover, present?"

"I'm here, Brother Moderator," Mike responded as he stood up.

"Are Deacons Carol Richardson and Linda Trimble present?"

Carol and Linda indicated their presence, and Claude Bradley asked them all to come to the pulpit. Turning to Mike, he asked, "Brother Mike, is it true that these women are in fact deacons ordained by Clear Springs Baptist Church?"

"Yes, it is. We ordained them about three weeks ago."

Turning to Carol, Claude asked, "Deacon Richardson, I apologize for putting you on the spot like this and having to ask you something that really is not any of the association's business, but is it true that you are divorced?"

"Yes, I am divorced," Carol answered in a strong, confident voice, "and my church is well aware of the fact and the circumstances of my divorce."

Claude turned to Brother Billy and said, "You know, Brother Billy, in dealing with a matter like this, I like to make sure we have our facts straight. Now Brother Billy..." he paused for emphasis, "I know you believe the Bible to be the inspired, inerrant, infallible word of God. I've heard you say so many times. Am I right?"

"Amen, Brother Claude, if we all believed that, we wouldn't be having problems like this in the association, Amen?" Brother Billy answered gleefully, unaware that Claude was tightening the noose around his neck.

Brother Billy always carried his twenty-pound ordination Bible in the most conspicuous way possible, so Claude took advantage of the opportunity to say, "Brother Billy, would you be so kind as to step up to the pulpit and read to us from Matthew eighteen, verses fifteen through seventeen?"

Billy Fite knew what the passage was before he turned to it, and he realized precisely the point that Claude was making at his expense, but he had no way out, graceful or otherwise. He had just walked into Claude's skillfully set trap, and there was no going back. All he could do, as he turned various shades of red, was to start reading,

Moreover if thy brother shall trespass against thee, go and tell him his fault between thee and him alone: if he shall hear thee, thou hast regained thy brother.

But if he will not hear thee, then take with thee one or two more, that in the mouth of two or three witnesses every word may be established. And if he shall neglect to hear them, tell it to the church: but if he neglect to hear the church, let him be to thee as an heathen man and a publican.

As soon as Billy Fite finished reading that passage, Claude said, "Now turn over to James the fifth chapter, verses nineteen and twenty." Billy read obediently,

Brethren, if any of you do err from the truth, and one convert him; Let him know that he which converteth the sinner from the error of his way shall save a soul from death, and shall hide a multitude of sins.

Claude turned to Mike and said, "Seeing as how Brother Billy's heart's breaking to pieces over what y'all did over't Clear Springs, I'm sure he went out of his way to go see you and talk to you privately before bringing this to the association. When did he talk to you in private?"

"He never did. Today's the first time I ever saw Brother Billy."

Claude continued, "That's about what I expected. Brother Billy, there's room for honest people who love the Lord to come to different conclusions on whether to have women deacons, but the verses you just read, that you say you believe to be inspired, inerrant, and infallible, are as plain as it gets. Since you did not follow Scriptural procedure, you are completely out of order in trying to bring this matter to the association. Now sit down, and I don't want to hear another word from you about this at this annual meeting. Do you understand?"

* * * * * * * * * * * *

The rest of the morning went smoothly. At lunch, Wallace called Claude over to him and told him, "Brother Claude, you ran that meetin' as smooth as Isaiah Mathis runnin' an engine." Linda said that Claude's handling of Brother Billy was nearly as good as when Lester pulled square out in front of that state trooper. "Only thing," she mused, "Brother Billy didn't get any points against his driver's license."

* * * * * * * * * * * *

Mike thought of many other reasons, many other people, many other ministry relationships that would make it hard to leave Clear Springs, but he knew it was time to make that move. He made the call to Wallace and told him that he would be preaching in view of a call to Harrington Baptist Church. Wallace gave his blessing, wished him well, and told him to call and let him know something as soon as he knew the outcome of the vote.

Mike had asked Heather Simmons to supply for him at Clear Springs the Sunday he preached for the committee. He had heard her in a preaching class and in chapel when she was chosen to receive the James Towers Memorial Preaching Award, and he was quite impressed with her. She eagerly accepted the invitation, the first such invitation she had received in her two years at Mid-Atlantic. She was well received, so Mike told Wallace that he would invite her back the Sunday that he preached the trial sermon at Harrington.

2

It was drizzling rain when Mike, Karen, Asalee, and Wallace the Dog left home early Saturday morning, but it cleared off about two hours into the trip and turned into a warm, pleasant mid-April Saturday. They stopped to see Mike's parents on the way to Harrington and ate lunch with them before continuing the trip. Wallace enjoyed riding in the car and presented no problems as long as he got to walk around a little at the rest stops. He slept peacefully most of the way on his old beach towel, next to Asalee on the back seat of Mike and Karen's 1980 Ford Fairmount station wagon. Mike's parents agreed to baby-sit their granddog until Mike, Karen, and Asalee could retrieve him on the way home. Denham, Georgia, where Mike grew up and where his parents and sister live, is just beyond the halfway point on the way to Harrington. They arrived in Denham about eleven o'clock and resumed the trip a little after one.

The visit with Mike's parents, though brief, was a good one. Knowing that the Baptist ministry is not the most financially secure profession, they were not entirely supportive of their son's decision to leave his position as an industrial arts teacher at Maddox County Central High School, uproot his family, and go to Mid-Atlantic Baptist Theological Seminary to prepare for a vocation in ministry. Grady Westover had hoped that his and Julia's only son would come into the family business and take over when Grady got ready to retire.

Charles Westover, Grady's father, opened Westover Automotive Machine Shop in Denham in 1926. Like his father before him, Mike grew up around the business. By the time he was in high school, Mike was turning and balancing crankshafts and doing precision machine work on engine blocks and cylinder heads. When Mike was 15, Grady gave him the '59 Ford pickup, a retired shop truck, that had been sitting behind the building for three or four years. It ran when it was parked, but it burned oil badly. Mike saved the money he earned working around the shop and bought a wrecked '68 Ford three-quarter ton with a good 390 engine for $300. He sold the rear end, transmission, and other parts off the '68 for enough to pay for the parts to do a first-class rebuild on the 390. The 390 went in the old shop truck, and Mike built the six cylinder that came out of it and swapped it for some body work and a paint job. He drove that truck all through high school, college, and the years he taught school in Denham. It received other improvements along—custom wheels, tinted glass, and a plush leather seat from a wrecked Buick LeSabre. Grady, who would have had that truck hauled off for junk if Mike had not wanted it, bought it back from him for $3000 when Mike and Karen were getting ready to move to go to seminary. It had an appointment with the sign painter as soon as Grady bought it back. Lettered with the name and phone number of Westover Automotive Machine Shop, it did some shop duties, but mostly it became high school transportation for Mike's sister Amanda.

During the three years Mike taught school in Denham, he picked up some extra work on Saturdays and in the summer months at the shop. Westover's was one of the few shops still set up to pour Babbitt bearings, so they did quite a bit of engine work for people restoring antique cars and trucks. Grady had four machinists working for him, so he was able to concentrate on jobs that really interested him. He worked almost exclusively on antique and high performance engines. Even though they were only in town a little over two hours, Mike walked with his father down the hill to the shop to see the straight-eight Packard engine he had just finished for a man in Atlanta and the oddball Willys-Knight sleeve valve engine belonging to a customer in North Carolina that was waiting for him to start on Monday morning.

When they got back on the road, Mike told Karen that, if there had been more time, he would have put on some coveralls and helped his father tear down that Willys-Knight engine right then. Mike said it was the first one of them he had seen, and Grady had told him that he had not seen many of them. "Knowing Dad," he commented to Karen, "that engine'll be apart by the time Mom gets Sunday dinner on the table." It was probably due to the brevity of the visit, he told her, but it seemed worth noting that he and his father didn't get into an argument. "Daddy never got into his usual rant about my foolhardy vocational choice, and he didn't badger me about moving back to Denham and coming into the business with him. Dad said that Grandpa Westover said the sleeve-valve Willys-Knight was the sorriest engine ever made by human hands, said they gave a lot of trouble when they were brand new." Mike said his opinion of the sleeve-valve Willys-Knight was a little more charitable. Even if it never was a good engine, at least it facilitated a conversation with his father that did not escalate into an argument.

Karen told Mike that she enjoyed the time with his mother and sister, talking about the anticipated move to Harrington and about being pregnant again. Asalee was really excited about her mom's pregnancy. She liked to feel the movement of the baby inside her mother's body, and she told her grandmother about it as though she thought her grandmother knew nothing about such things.

Julia Westover told her daughter-in-law that she had started going to the Methodist church in Denham with one of her friends whose husband had died recently. Julia's friend and her husband were long-time members of Denham United Methodist Church, but she found it hard to go back to church after her husband's death. Julia grew up in Talmadge Street Baptist Church in Denham, but she dropped out when she was in high school and had not been in church on a regular basis since. Grady never was a churchgoing man, so there was no incentive for her to become active in the church after her marriage. Julia said that she really surprised herself when she told her recently widowed friend that she would go to church with her and sit with her if it would make it easier for her to go back. Her friend accepted the offer, and Julia said that she had gone with her friend every Sunday for the past two months. She said that she thought her friend would be able to go alone now, but that she was no longer going just to help her friend. She said she was going for her own sake now, and that Mike's sister Amanda had started going with her. The worship services and the sermons, she said, were starting to make sense and mean something to her. She told Karen that she had started reading the Bible and praying for the first time in years, and that she was probably going to join the Methodist church.

✶ ✶ ✶ ✶ ✶ ✶ ✶ ✶ ✶ ✶ ✶ ✶

"Wake up, Hon. We're in Harrington. Mike! Wake up!" Karen had pulled the car under the canopy of the Comfort Inn in Harrington, and she was calling Mike and shaking him, trying to rouse him out of his deep sleep.

"Momma, I know how to do it. Let me get him up," Asalee volunteered as she crawled on the floorboard under the back of the fully-reclined passenger seat, reached around to the side of the seat next to the door, and pulled the lever on the side of the seat, causing the seat back to spring forward, catapulting Mike's limp body into a bolt-upright position. Mike awoke to the sound of Asalee giggling and calling "Wake up, Daddy!" right in his ear.

"We're in Harrington, Hon, let's get checked into the motel," Karen repeated. "You've been sound asleep since we got out of Denham. Asalee imitated the snoring noises Mike had been making moments before.

Mike had worked the 11-7 shift the night before. Karen and Asalee had everything packed and ready as soon as he got home from work. They quickly loaded the car and went through the drive-in at McDonald's for breakfast on the way out. Mike had insisted that he was wide-awake, and he drove the first leg of the trip to the home of his parents in Denham. Julia had cooked enough dinner for a barn raising. Mike was stuffed from the big meal, and being up all night was starting to catch up with him. He gladly accepted Karen's offer to drive the rest of the trip.

Mike got out of the car, yawned, stretched, and walked stiffly into the lobby and up to the registration desk. He told the clerk that he had a pre-paid reservation for Westover, party of three, two adults and one child. Asalee followed her father up to the registration desk and reminded him in a stage whisper that could have been heard by anyone within fifty feet, "Daddy, there's really four of us 'cause Mommy's pregnant." The desk clerk laughed and said, "That's OK, Sweetheart, there's no extra charge for pregnant mommies at Comfort Inn."

Mike and Asalee went back out to the car and told Karen the room number. He and Asalee loaded their belongings onto a luggage cart and took it up to the room while Karen parked the car. The desk clerk had given Mike a message to call Carl Baxter as soon as they got into town. Mike waited for Karen to get to the room and then made the call.

"Joyce'll have our dinner ready about 6:30," the voice on the other end of the phone said. "Instead of me trying to give you directions, since you're new to Harrington, it'll prob'ly be better for me to come get you. The first settlers in this area were some folks who got off in this holler, couldn't find their way out, and decided to stay and make the best of it. Anyway, if I come get you, I can show you how to get to the church in the morning. I'll be there to pick you up about 6:20 if that's OK. It's about ten minutes from the Comfort Inn to our house."

Mike indicated to Carl that those arrangements would be fine. Mike, Karen, and Asalee would have preferred to have a pizza delivered to the room, spend a leisurely evening together at the motel, and make an early night of it, but they were at the mercy of the hiring squad. They would be on display and subject to inspection until mid-day on Sunday.

"Do Mr. and Mrs. Baxter have any children?," Asalee asked after her father hung up the phone.

"I'm not sure," Mike told her, "Do you remember, Honey?"

"I think they have a daughter in high school who is still at home, but I'm not sure. There are seven people on the committee, and they all told us about themselves and their families. It's all melted and run together. So we'll just have to wait and see when we get there. I'm sure they are nice people and that you will like them, Asalee."

Asalee didn't seem so sure. She picked up on Mike and Karen's lack of enthusiasm for the evening's plans and their apprehension about being on display at the Baxters' home. It was only a quarter after four, another two hours before Carl Baxter would pick them up. They took advantage of the opportunity to unwind for a little while. Karen stretched out on the bed and elevated her feet on a couple of pillows, and Asalee curled up next to her. Mike staked his claim on the recliner. With the television on ESPN for background noise, Mike opened his Bible, reviewed his sermon notes, and mentally walked through tomorrow morning's sermon.

* * * * * * * * * * * *

Asalee was grumpy and fretful as Karen brushed through her hair and replaced the cheap plastic barrettes with a pretty bow. She would have preferred the jeans and the Ninja Turtles sweatshirt she wore on the trip to the dainty dress in which she was now attired. As she put the finishing touches on Asalee's hair and clothes, Karen gave her a crash-course review of all the manners she had been taught since her birth six years ago, March 27, 1984. "Asalee, there's one thing you must remember," Karen intoned solemnly.

"What's that, Mommy?"

"You know how Daddy and I tease and joke a lot, calling pulpit committees 'hiring squads.' It's OK for us to call them that when it's just us, but we can't ever say that in front of them. Do you understand?"

"Yes, Mommy."

With a tone of pretend sternness in her voice, Karen cut a glance toward Mike and added, "That's very important, isn't it, Mike? We don't say 'hiring squad' in front of the committee, do we?"

"Of course not, Hon."

* * * * * * * * * * * *

The desk clerk called precisely at 6:20 to tell the Westovers that Carl Baxter was waiting for them in the lobby. Mike, Karen, and Asalee met him, and he directed them to his maroon Crown Victoria. As he drove away from the motel, Carl said, "Well, welcome to Harrington, such as it is. Nice town, I think. Good schools for your little girl. Been here all my life except for when I was in the Army and won that all-expense-paid trip to Viet Nam. I'm going to take you by and show you the church so you'll know how to get to it in the morning. You take a right out of the motel parking lot like we just did, go down here to the first traffic light, where you see that Phillips 66 on the corner, and turn left." As he made the left turn, he continued the running commentary, "This is Peyton Street. Here we are now. You'll see the church up ahead on the right as soon as you turn onto Peyton Street." Carl swung into the church parking lot, made a quick U-turn, and headed back out. As he turned left at the light by the Phillips 66, he said, "Now we're back on Martin Luther King Boulevard. Used to be Monument Avenue before they changed it. Most people still call it Monument Avenue. You need to know both names so you'll know which street people are talking about. So how was the trip down here, Preacher?"

"Not bad. A little rain when we first started out this morning, but it cleared off by mid-morning. We stopped by to see my parents and my sister in Denham on the way down. That's about the halfway point. We ate lunch with them and visited a little while before we got back on the road."

"Actually, I'm the one to ask about the last half of the trip," Karen interjected. "Mike was snoring by the time we got out of Denham, and Asalee and I had to wake him up when we pulled into the motel."

"Like I was saying," Mike continued, "the last half of the trip was as peaceful as it gets. I worked 11-7 last night. If nothing else, working full-time and going to school has taught me to sleep anywhere, anytime I get the chance to catch a few Z's."

Carl headed the Crown Victoria west to the edge of town and turned onto a narrow county road. "This is Freeman Valley Road My mother was a Freeman, one of the first families to settle in this area. Right after you cross this little bridge, our place is up on the hill. First driveway to your right after you cross the creek."

"Hi, come on in," Joyce Baxter called out. A true southern woman, she hugged Karen even though they had never met before. Bending down to hug Asalee, she asked, "And what's your name, Honey?"

"Asalee Nicole Westover."

"That's a pretty name, Asalee."

"Thank you. ma'am," Asalee responded precisely as she had been coached.

Mike started to explain that Asalee was his grandmother's name, and that it was a fairly common name in the south at the turn of the century, but he stopped himself as he remembered where he was. He reminded himself that he was in a place where shopping carts are called buggies, where people with aches and pains are stoved up, and where everybody has at least one elderly female relative named Asalee.

Asalee seemed to warm up to Joyce, and she learned that Joyce would be her Sunday School teacher if they moved to Harrington. An attractive woman in her mid-forties, Joyce had a bubbly personality, and she enjoyed entertaining in the spacious country home that she shared with her husband, eighteen-year-old daughter Samantha, and a lethargic Irish setter named Bullet after the dog in the *Snuffy Smith* cartoon strip. Like his namesake, Bullet was the kind of dog you nudge with your foot every couple of days to make sure he is not dead. Asalee took a liking to Bullet, and Joyce seemed really sweet like Mama Stell.

Carl blended into the woodwork and let Joyce introduce Samantha, their older daughter Jenny, and Jenny's husband Eric Latham. She told them that Eric, the band director and choral music teacher at Harrington High School, directed the music at the church.

The Westovers followed Carl, Eric, and Jenny into the great room as Joyce and Samantha finished putting dinner on the table.

Mike commented on the Baxters' attractive home with the wide plank floors, exposed beams, and huge rock hearth, fireplace, and chimney. Carl, a building contractor, told Mike that he bought and tore down an old cotton warehouse up at Rome that was built before the Civil War. The beams, he pointed out, were eight by twelve heart pine, and all of the flooring throughout the house was inch and a half thick chestnut. He said that the house was framed in the post and beam method, the way the Amish people up in Pennsylvania build their barns. "Got plenty more of the big beams and chestnut flooring out in the barn," he added. "We just poured the foundation for Jenny and Eric's new house. We'll use some of it there. The rest of it's for when Samantha gets married and her'n her husband get ready to build." Mike knew enough about construction to admire the workmanship in Carl's masterpiece and appreciate the scarcity of beams cut long ago from old growth pines and flooring sawn from trees now nearly extinct.

Asalee noted that Jenny was wearing maternity clothes, and she facilitated a conversation between Karen and Jenny by blurting out, "Mommy, look! She's pregnant too, just like you!" Karen and Mike turned every conceivable shade of red. Jenny, Eric, and Carl thought it was hilarious and took no offense. Eric and Jenny, married four years, were eagerly anticipating the birth of their first child, and Carl and Joyce were looking forward to their first grandchild. Jenny was a little further along than Karen. Karen found out that she was pregnant the week that Estelle Coggins died back in January. Jenny was due in July, and Karen was due in September. Karen took a liking to Jenny and asked her if she would recommend the obstetrician she was using, since she would need to get connected with one as soon as they settled in Harrington if the church called Mike. Jenny wrote down the doctor's name and phone number, and Karen put it in her purse. About that time, Joyce called them to the table, and Carl asked Eric to say grace.

* * * * * * * * * * * *

Mike didn't like to be up late on Saturday night. He had his sermon prepared, but sometimes preparing the sermon is easier than preparing the preacher to preach it. Mike kept stealing furtive glances at his watch, and he saw the erosion of the time that he had wanted to spend reviewing his sermon, meditating, and praying, but the Baxters were gracious hosts, and it was impossible to make an early night of it. Mike was able to talk at length with Eric and get a feel for how it would be to do worship planning with him. Eric had brought a bulletin with the next morning's order of service, and he and Mike went over that. It was about 10:30 when Carl Baxter took the Westovers back to their motel.

Mike stopped by the desk on the way in to request a 6:30 wake up call. It was well past Asalee's bedtime, and she was starting to get fussy by the time they left the Baxters'. All three Westovers were ready to call it a night when they got to the room. Asalee missed her bed and her room at home, and she didn't like going to sleep in a strange place. She got out of bed and crawled into bed with Mike and Karen. Five minutes later, she was dead to the world. She never knew when Mike picked her up, put her on the other bed, tucked her in, and got back in bed with Karen.

Mike slept soundly while he slept, but he was wide awake at 4:00, two and a half hours before he had planned to get up. Karen and Asalee were still sleeping soundly, and Mike wished that he could. He lay on his back staring at the ceiling for a while. Then he turned over on his side and put his arm around Karen. With his head resting on her shoulder, he could hear the slow, steady beating of her heart. He closed his eyes, listened, and tried to go back to sleep, but it was no use. About 4:15, he got up, took a shower, washed his hair, and shaved.

Mike remembered to call the front desk and cancel the wake up call. He was glad to see the little two-cup coffee maker, pre-measured packet of coffee, and two styrofoam cups. Keeping the volume low so as not to wake Karen and Asalee, he surveyed the gamut of early morning television programming before settling on an old *Andy Griffith* episode, one that he had seen so many times that he almost had the script memorized. He watched it while he sipped his first cup of coffee. Then he poured himself a second cup. If Karen wanted coffee when she got up, he would go down to the lobby where they serve the continental breakfast and get her some. With the second cup of coffee in hand, Mike turned off the television and settled down in the recliner with his Bible and sermon notes.

Before they left home, Mike had tucked his dog-eared copy of Bruggemann's *Praying the Psalms* inside the back cover of his Bible. He found it to be one of the few books he was motivated to read more than once, one that had been immensely helpful to him in cultivating the discipline of prayer. Mike aimed the reading lamp away from the beds where his wife and daughter were sleeping and read for the umpteenth time some sections of Bruggemann's book that he had highlighted. He had almost passed up the book because of its diminutive size. He ended up buying it because of the author's reputation. His Old Testament prof, Dr. Gordon Corrie, had introduced him to Bruggemann's weightier and more scholarly tomes; Mike had stumbled across this little treasure on his own.

As he pulled back the draperies and saw the sun coming up over a distant ridge, Mike thought of the nineteenth psalm's description of the sun rising and the psalmist finding in the warmth and light of the sun an apt analogy for the law of God. As the sun's heat helps to cause seeds to germinate and spring to life, so the law of God revives the soul. As the radiance of the sun makes it possible to see clearly, so the commands of God give light to the eyes. Mike opened his Bible to that familiar psalm.

As he pondered the psalmist's prayer, *May the words of my mouth and the meditation of my heart be pleasing in your sight, O Lord, my Rock and my Redeemer,* and as he offered that prayer up as his own, Mike thought back to decoration day and homecoming back in August at Clear Springs. Arthur Sessions was having one of his better days, and Mary Kate had driven over from Canfield to bring her parents to church at Clear Springs. Dr. Gordon Corrie had served Clear Springs when he was a student at Mid-Atlantic back in the late 40's, and he had married Evelyn Coggins, Wallace and Estelle's oldest daughter. Mike invited him to come and preach that day. Before Dr. Corrie got up to preach, Mike called on Arthur to pray. A hush fell over the church, and Arthur's voice rose with such strength and clarity that it did not seem possible for it to be coming from a frail, sickly man. Mike had often thought of something Arthur said in that prayer, "Lord, reign in the wanderings of our minds, that we might center our thoughts and affections on Thee." As he had done with the psalmist's prayer, Mike made Arthur's prayer his own as well.

By seven o'clock, Mike had mentally preached through his sermon four or five times. It was time to wake Karen and Asalee, and time to put on the new suit, shirt, tie, and Florshiem Imperial shoes purchased for the occasion. Mike's mother had sent a gift certificate from J. C. Penney's when she learned that Mike was going to be preaching the trial sermon. The sermon was as well prepared as it was going to get. He wondered if the time would ever come that he would be completely at ease about his sermon when it was time to get ready for church on Sunday morning.

Mike, Karen, and Asalee went down to the motel lobby for the continental breakfast. It was good to get at least this one meal by themselves. While they were eating, Mike told Karen and Asalee how pretty they looked. He was not just saying it to make them feel good. It was the truth. Karen was normally a poised, confident woman. On this Sunday morning, she felt insecure about her looks and the clothes she had chosen for the occasion. She seemed to believe Mike when he told her how pretty she looked, and she relaxed about as much as a pastor's wife can on the Sunday morning before a trial sermon.

Asalee, normally a playful, mischievous little girl, was quiet, subdued, and clinging close to her mother. She would have preferred to be at Clear Springs. Only four years old when Mike was called there, she had little memory of any other church. Joyce Baxter was really nice, and the other people she met last night seemed nice too, but she didn't know them very well, she was about to meet a whole church full of people she didn't know, and she was scared. Usually, she was not a picky eater, but even her favorite Peanut Butter Cap'n Crunch cereal did not appeal to her. She clutched the new birthday doll that she named Estelle and wished that Mama Stell and Papa Wallace could be in this strange new place so she could sit with them. Of course, she knew that Mama Stell was with Jesus up in Heaven, so she couldn't be there, and Papa Wallace was a long way away at Clear Springs, so he couldn't be there either.

3

Elaine McWhorter, a member of the pastor search committee, knew the manager of the Comfort Inn where Mike, Karen, and Asalee were staying. When she made the reservation for them, she arranged a late checkout for them so they would not have to rush and get packed before church. Sunday School started at 9:45. It was 9:20 when they left the motel. *Turn right out of the motel onto MLK Boulevard, which most people still call Monument Avenue, go up to the first traffic light at the Phillips 66, turn left onto Peyton Street, and the church will be on the right.* It was 9:25 when they pulled into the parking lot. Mike parked the car, and he and his family got their first daytime look at Harrington Baptist Church.

This was Harrington Baptist Church in Harrington, Georgia, but it could have been any one of hundreds of other churches in hundreds of towns from Maryland to Florida to Texas. It was a cookie cutter design from the church architecture department of the Sunday School Board in Nashville—a red brick shoebox auditorium with a white-columned portico, five stained glass windows on each side, and a fiberglass steeple, joined at the back by a two-story educational building. Before setting foot inside the building, Mike and Karen knew what to expect. Luckett's Creek in Williston and Talmadge Street in Denham were built from the same plans about the same time, in the early 1960's. There would be a center aisle and two narrow outside aisles. On either side of the entrance foyer, which most Baptists couldn't find if you called it a narthex, there would be a room that could be closed off with folding doors to make Sunday School rooms or opened for additional auditorium space. The pulpit platform would be small and cramped, bracketed by cubicles for the piano and organ. Mike would feel as though he were standing in a box to preach, just as he did when he preached at Luckett's Creek. Brother Woodrow was not one to stand still in one spot behind the pulpit while preaching. There was not more than two and a half feet between the pulpit and the partition separating the pulpit area from the choir. It always amazed Mike that Brother Woodrow could preach in such close confines. It was hard enough for him, and he didn't move around as much as Brother Woodrow.

It would be, as Yogi Berra said, "*deja vu* all over again" to walk into the building at Harrington. The baptistry would be directly behind the choir. There would be seating for twenty-six in the choir, two rows of eight and ten on the back row. On the first floor of the educational building, there would be a fellowship hall that could be divided into four classrooms with the use of folding doors. There would be a narrow hallway, some small classrooms, a kitchen, a pastor's study, restrooms, and a nursery on the first floor. There would be a water fountain at the mid-point of the hallway, right beside a little teller's window into the tiny office for the Sunday School director. Upstairs, there would be two large classrooms that could be divided with folding doors. The next two doors to the left off the upstairs hallway would open into assembly rooms containing a lectern, folding chairs, and an upright piano that had not been tuned in thirty years. Off each assembly room, there would be two postage-stamp sized classrooms, one for boys and one for girls. Access to the dressing rooms and baptistry would be to the right off the upstairs hallway.

Mike had only used an indoor baptistry twice. Bethlehem Baptist Church, about three miles from Clear Springs, had let Clear Springs use their baptistry on Sunday afternoons a couple of times when it was too cold to baptize in the creek. When the weather was good, Clear Springs baptized in Chaney Creek over on the back side of Wayne Ethridge's farm.

Mike remembered his first baptismal service at Clear Springs, which was the first one he ever did. He had just been called there as pastor, following Logan Clark. It was the Sunday of Labor Day weekend 1988, the temperature was in the nineties, and the humidity was so bad you needed gills to breathe. Chaney Creek originates at the springs for which Clear Springs was named, and the baptizing place on the Ethridge farm is about half a mile downstream. Dr. Corrie, the one who recommended him to Clear Springs, had coached him on the fine points of baptizing in the clear, icy waters of Chaney Creek. "All you have to do," Dr. Corrie said, "is put them under. You don't have to worry about bringing them back up. Straightway they come up out of that water!"

Megan Richardson, Jason Chambers, Jeremy Norris, and Melanie Echols were being baptized that day. Russ Ayers and Joe Norris were assisting because it was Mike's first baptism, and each of them had two grandchildren being baptized that day. Russ and Joe had towels draped around their necks to dry the faces of the candidates after they were baptized. Russ helped baptize his grandchildren Megan and Jason, and Joe helped with Jeremy and Melanie.

It always intrigued Mike that some people who rarely attend regular church services will come to an outdoor baptism in an out of the way place over on the back side of the Ethridge farm. He remembered one in particular who was at that first baptismal service, Linda Trimble's husband Wesley. Wesley was a deputy with the Sanders County Sheriff's Department. A genial, easygoing man, he was well-respected in the community and among his fellow officers. Although he bore the name of the founder of the Methodist movement, Wesley did not grow up in any church, and he came to church with Linda only on special occasions. For years, Linda and others had prayed for Wesley's salvation. That day, Wesley was scheduled to go on duty at 4:00. He came to the baptismal service in uniform, complete with badge, gun, holster, nightstick, and handcuffs. As he watched the baptisms of Megan, Jason, and Jeremy, hot tears began to trickle down his face. By the time Mike and Joe baptized the last candidate, Wes was on his knees weeping unashamedly. Linda and her parents, Wayne and June Ethridge, were kneeling beside him. Wallace called out to Mike from the creek bank, "Stay in the water, Preacher, you might have one more." Karen began singing the familiar words of *Just as I Am*, and others joined in. As they were singing, Wes arose from his knees, unbuckled his heavy black belt with all his police equipment, and handed it to his father-in-law. He took off his shiny black shoes and his socks, and waded out into the water in his crisply pressed uniform. Mike and Joe baptized him, badge and all. As Wes was drying his face with the towel Russ handed him, he saw his and Linda's eleven-year-old son Nathan, tears streaming down his face, taking off his shoes and socks. Wes waded over to the creek bank, took Nathan's hand, and led him out to the deeper water where Mike and Joe were standing. Joe stepped back and said, "Brother Wesley, there's nothin' in my Bible that says you have to be a deacon to help with baptizin'." Still dripping from his own baptism, Wes helped Mike baptize Nathan. Miss Bertha Mullinax, who never left home without a loaded camera, got some good pictures, and Carol Richardson wrote an article about the service. It made the front page of *The Religious Herald*.

As Mike walked toward the church building at Harrington, he knew that he would thank God the rest of his days for that incredible baptismal service. The spontaneity and freedom of the Spirit they had that day on the banks of Chaney Creek would not be likely to occur with a baptistry up behind the choir, accessible only from the second floor hallway. There was little chance that anyone would get up from a pew bolted to the floor, climb over people, walk down an aisle, and find his way through the catacombs to get to baptismal water. Mike wondered whether that might be a parable of sorts about other things, and whether he would have anything like the degree of freedom in this place that he had at Clear Springs.

* * * * * * * * * * * *

"Karen! Mike! Asalee!" Elaine McWhorter called out as she hurriedly made her way across the auditorium in order to hug all three Westovers. "Welcome to Harrington!" Elaine was in her late thirties, married and the mother of two girls, thirteen and ten, and a seven year old boy. A legal secretary for a small two-partner law firm in Harrington, she served as church clerk and taught seventh and eighth grades in Sunday School. She called and motioned to her husband Jerry, who was coming into the auditorium from the educational building, prepared to lead the opening assembly for the adults in a few minutes. "Jerry, come here! I want you to meet the Westovers!"

They exchanged pleasantries, and Jerry commented, "Elaine sure does speak well of you folks. It sounds to me like you're just what this church needs. We need somebody young and energetic to bring young families in, hold the interest of the young people, help us build up the youth group, you know what I mean? Just between us, our former pastor, Reverend Reynolds—good man, don't get me wrong, nothing against him personally. I liked him, but he was here sixteen years. Stayed too long, I think. He was not very far from retirement, just couldn't draw the young people, if you know what I mean. His kids were all grown…Well, like I said, I've heard good things about you, Preacher, and I'm looking forward to hearing your message this morning." Jerry shook Mike's hand again and excused himself, explaining that he was Sunday School director and needed to get around and make sure all the teachers were present.

Joyce Baxter had taken Asalee and escorted her to her Sunday School class while Jerry was talking to Mike and Karen. A number of mostly older adults were coming into the auditorium for opening assembly. Mike felt a tap on his shoulder and turned around to see a woman in her seventies who appeared to have stepped through a time warp. The only times Mike and Karen had ever seen a woman wearing a pillbox hat with the fishnet veil over her face, and the only times they had ever seen a woman wearing gloves to church in warm weather were in old movies and photos made before they were born. Yet, they were definitely not on a movie set. There were no cameras, and there were no antique cars in the parking lot. The hat, veil, and gloves were part of this woman's dress code for church, and Karen suspected that she was judging her harshly for not being similarly attired. "Are you the new preacher we're going to hear today?" the woman asked. Before Mike could get his mouth open to answer her, she continued, "You certainly are a young man to be a pastor, Reverend Westover. I'd hoped the committee would bring us someone older and more mature, more settled and more experienced. I'm troubled that they would bring in someone fresh out of seminary with so little experience." Without appearing to breathe, she continued, "Oh, forgive me, I forgot to introduce myself. I'm Geneva Millican," and, as she turned to the short balding man who stood meek and mute at her side, "and this is my husband Roland. We've been members here since 1939. We certainly miss dear Reverend Reynolds. What a marvelous man! I don't believe anyone will ever fill his shoes. Such an inspiring preacher! Oh, and his wife Earline was such a dear. She was Womans Missionary Union director for the association, you know, and a wonderful hostess, always entertaining at the parsonage..."

Although she had said or done nothing to give this woman any basis for forming an opinion of her one way or the other, Karen nonetheless felt that she had been weighed in the balances and found wanting. With a six year old child and a new baby on the premises, Karen didn't plan to be always entertaining at the parsonage. She imagined this woman glaring with equally stern disapproval upon Asalee's normal six-year-old exuberance, expecting her to be a miniature adult rather than a normal child. Geneva Millican would have died in a fit of apoplexy had she seen Karen and Asalee dancing and singing in front of the chimpanzee cage at the Birmingham Zoo the previous summer.

Karen had not been able to choose her week of vacation from her job at the advertising agency. She had to take the week they gave her, and it was a week that Mike was tied up with summer school classes and unable to get off from work. She decided to make the best of it and have a very low-budget mother-daughter vacation with Asalee. They rode the bus to Anniston, where Karen's sister-in-law picked them up and drove them to the home of Karen's parents, Harold and Margaret Owen, in Williston, Alabama. Karen borrowed her mother's car, and they got an early start the next morning, arriving at the Birmingham Zoo before the gates opened. They stayed until closing time. Karen had not been there since she was ten or eleven. Asalee liked the zoo as much as Karen had when she was a little girl. As she watched Asalee laugh and skip merrily along the pathways through the zoo, Karen's first impulse was to tell her to settle down and behave. She resisted that urge because there was nothing about Asalee's behavior that needed correcting. Karen realized that she was witnessing something holy, the pure Edenic delight of a little girl reveling in God's creation. It occurred to her that none of the other people in the zoo knew her, and none of them were likely to see her again, so she decided she didn't care what they thought. She took Asalee by the hand, and they both went running, skipping, and laughing through the Birmingham Zoo. Whenever anyone gave them a disapproving look—as though they thought Karen should act like an adult and make Asalee behave—Karen and Asalee would look at each other and burst out laughing. Sometimes they laughed so hard that they got dizzy, they gasped for air, their hearts pounded, and they had to sit down and catch their breath. "And Yes," Karen imagined herself telling Geneva Millican, "Asalee and I sang and danced in front of the chimpanzee cage, and God loved every minute of it. And No, I didn't scold her when she kissed that sheep in the petting zoo." It was unlikely that a twenty-eight-year-old woman with a six-year-old child and a baby due in September would measure up to Geneva Millican's expectations of a pastor's wife. Karen could not be Earline Reynolds, and she was not going to try.

Mike wondered just what he could do about his youthful age. He was born October 19, 1961. He would be twenty-nine in six more months. He could not make himself age any faster, and he would not if he could. Granted, his ministerial experience was limited to a two-year student pastorate at a little country church thirty miles from the seminary, but he wished Geneva Millican could know the richness of those two years. Clear Springs had taught him every bit as much as the seminary. Clear Springs was not equipped to teach Hebrew and Greek, but it was not Mid-Atlantic Seminary that taught him what to do when a much-prayed-for man starts weeping and falls to his knees on a creek bank at a baptismal service. No seminary class or textbook taught him what to say from the pulpit on Sunday morning hours after a drunk driver, the nephew of one deacon and the cousin of another, killed the son of one family in the church and the daughter of another family in the church on their way home from the senior prom at Sanders County High School. There was no seminary class on how to officiate at one's first funeral in a high school gym packed with grief-stricken adolescents whose presumption of immortality had been called into question. Mike's resume was accurate as far as it went, but it didn't mention the baptism of Wes and Nathan Trimble who had not planned to be baptized that day. It didn't mention that he had helped ordain Mary Kate Sessions, Carol Richardson, and Linda Trimble before the ink was dry on his own ordination certificate. The resume didn't mention being with Jim and Becky Echols when they identified Jim Junior's body at Sanders County General Hospital, driving from there to Canfield Regional Medical Center at 5:00 Sunday morning to be with Mark and Teresa Ethridge when they made the decision to take Kimberly off life support and donate her organs, and then driving back home to pick up Karen and Asalee and get back to Clear Springs in time for the morning worship service. The resume mentioned nothing about the long conversation with Wes Trimble about how it felt to get the call to notify Jim and Becky about the wreck, drive them to the hospital to identify their son's body, and then get the call to transport Tommy Ayers from the emergency room to the county jail after he was treated and released. On Mike's resume, things like "helped Wes baptize his son," "helped Wallace bury his wife," and "prayed with Carol the night before her surgery" were all subsumed under *1988-Present: Pastor, Clear Springs Baptist Church, 65 members, annual budget $56,000.*

Likewise, all the information the committee included in the packet of materials about the church appeared to be accurate. Two hundred and twenty-one members, average Sunday School attendance 112, annual budget $97,000. The church was debt-free except for a $12,000 note they had taken to resurface the parking lot last summer. The board at the front of the auditorium indicated that last week's Sunday School attendance had been 134, but last Sunday was Easter, and the previous Sunday's attendance had been 116. Last Sunday's offering had been $2,837.42, but then again, last Sunday was Easter. Their beloved former pastor, Harry T. Reynolds, resigned in October after a sixteen-year ministry at Harrington to accept a Home Mission Board appointment to start a new church down on the Gulf Coast. Harrington was a small west Georgia town, population 3,832 on the 1980 census, county seat of Mintz County, population 17,441. All of that was ostensibly true, but Mike knew that there were many untold stories underlying those facts, just as there were many untold stories underlying *1988-Present: Pastor, Clear Springs Baptist Church, 65 members, annual budget $56,000.*

During the Sunday School hour, Karen talked with the musicians, and Mike wandered around, observing what he could. In the back hallway across from the water fountain, he paused to look at the eight-by-tens of the church's former pastors. He looked into each face and noted names and dates. John C. Beckett, 1887-1889 and again from 1892-1896. Philip J. Nestor, 1889-1892. E. L. B. Hamilton, 1897-1903. Bartholomew Lang, 1904-1917. John Leland Walters, 1918-1940. A. C. Lancaster, 1941-1941. Mike wondered what happened. Did Lancaster die, have an extramarital affair, embezzle church funds, or get caught in some act of moral turpitude? Did he—such a handsome, energetic-looking man of perhaps thirty when the photo was made—despair of any possibility of filling the shoes of the late great Dr. Walters? Definitely, there were some untold stories. Whatever happened, it was a part of the corporate memory of the church, and it would figure into the events of this day. W. Edward Brown, 1942-1949. Lawrence D. Carson, 1950-1956. James M. Decker, 1956-1958. Franklin B. Seals, 1959-1964. Walter W. Grant, 1965-1972. Harry T. Reynolds, 1973-1989. More untold stories, and more people who remember.

Mike had never met Harry Reynolds, and he had never talked to him. He doubted that Reynolds was as flawless as his admirers claimed or as flawed as his detractors asserted. Mike presumed Reynolds to be a man who had found grace in the eyes of the Lord, one who delighted to see people come to faith in Christ and grow in Christian maturity, a man with strengths and weaknesses who was neither deserving of credit for all the church's strengths nor deserving of blame for all of its weaknesses.

* * * * * * * * * * * *

Courting Karen had been easier, but Mike observed that dealing with a hiring squad was not unlike courtship. Just as Mike and Karen had tried to present themselves in the best possible light when they were courting each other, they did the same when they faced the hiring squad, and they knew that it was reasonable for the committee to present the most positive picture they could of their church.

The call to Clear Springs had been more like an arranged marriage. Dr. Corrie at the seminary, Wallace and Estelle Coggins' son-in-law, had preached at Clear Springs some in the summer of 1988 after Logan Clark graduated and took a church in Tennessee. The deacons asked Corrie to recommend a seminary student who might be interested in the church. He gave them Mike's name, and Wallace called that evening and invited him to come down and preach. After he preached, the church voted unanimously to call him. They never saw his resume because he didn't have one. All they knew was that he was a Master of Divinity student at Mid-Atlantic who came recommended by Gordon Corrie. That was all they needed to know. The trial sermon, such as it was, was a formality. Mike had preached a total of seven times before that day—three times for Brother Woodrow at Luckett's Creek, twice for Dan Jordan at Talmadge Street in Denham, and twice in Dr. Leggs' homiletics class at the seminary. If his first sermon at Clear Springs had equaled the superb preaching of Dr. Corrie, it would not have improved his chances. If that first sermon had been a disaster, it would not have diminished his chances. Mike was called to Clear Springs because Gordon Corrie, who had never heard him preach and had only had him in a first year Old Testament survey class, vouched for him. Wallace trusted his son-in-law at the seminary. The church trusted Wallace. It was a done deal.

Today was different. Mike was now accustomed to preaching every Sunday at Clear Springs. Nevertheless, preaching in a different place, knowing that people would vote for or against him on the basis of a single sermon, was not like preaching on a normal Sunday at Clear Springs. Karen was over by the piano with Eric and Jenny. She had been singing along as Jenny played a medley of familiar hymns. At least, they were familiar to Karen. She grew up in church, Mike didn't. He was still discovering hymns that were familiar to everyone but himself. Karen had taught Mike to read music, and he could sight read well enough to fake his way through anything in the *Baptist Hymnal*. As much as he enjoyed hearing Karen sing—he would never forget her singing *Rock of Ages* and *Amazing Grace* at the service for Jim Junior and Kimberly—he had pretty much tuned her out this morning in the last minutes of the Sunday School hour as he sat on one of the front pews mentally preaching through his sermon one last time. His concentration was broken by a gentle touch on the shoulder and a deep, resonant voice saying, "Brother Westover?"

"Yes. Mike Westover." Mike took the man's outstretched hand and asked, "And you are?"

"Bob McKnight. Been looking forward to meeting you. I've heard good things about you. I've been interim here since Harry Reynolds left. I pastored thirty-four years in this association before I retired in '84, the last twenty-one years at Valley View, west of Harrington like you're going to the Alabama line. Great ministry, wish I could've stayed 'til Jesus comes. Harrington here has been my eighth interim. I've been as busy as I ever was as a full-time pastor. I've had a good time here, but I'm ready to move on. They need to go ahead and call a pastor. The pastor at Lakeside's leaving the end of this month, and they've already approached me about being interim there. I look forward to hearing you preach, and I'll be praying for you."

Bob impressed Mike as warm and genuine. Some quick arithmetic told Mike that he had to be in his early seventies, but he didn't look it. He was well over six feet, a big man but well-proportioned. His dark wavy hair had only a few touches of gray around the temples. Bob McKnight was the kind of vigorous, energetic man who would be dead within six months if he tried to retire completely. The conversation with Bob helped Mike more than further mental rehearsing of the sermon.

The Sunday School classes were dismissing, and people were coming into the auditorium from the educational building. Others who had not been there for Sunday School were arriving for worship. Mike guessed the auditorium would comfortably seat two hundred, and it was starting to fill up. Karen sat beside Mike on the front pew. Sensing how tense he was, she reached up and gently massaged the back of his neck. That felt good. Asalee was sitting with Joyce

Baxter. Joyce told Karen that Asalee had boasted to the Sunday School class that "My daddy is going to preach today and you're going to like him because he's the best preacher in the whole world," and Karen wished that there was time to tell Mike that Asalee vouched for him. Joyce said that she would vote to call Mike on the strength of Asalee's recommendation. The seven members of the hiring squad took their seats on the front pew with Mike and Karen. It was eleven o'clock, time for the service to begin.

As Jenny played the prelude, the choir members filed into their places behind the pulpit railing. Their greenish-gold polyester choir robes screamed "1972! 1972!" The only good things that could be said about the choir robes were that they matched the baptistry curtain made from the same material, and they harmonized with the seventies-vintage gold carpet.

Aside from the awful polyester choir robes, Mike and Karen were favorably impressed with the music. The hymns were not the ones Mike would have chosen, but the people sang enthusiastically. The church had a new-looking Yamaha baby grand piano. The instruments were in tune. Jenny and organist Jean Brinkley played well. Eric did a good job directing the choir. The anthem, a simple *Glory Songs* arrangement, was nicely done.

Mike's mind wandered to Clear Springs and Heather Simmons. As Carl was coming to the pulpit to introduce Mike, Carol Richardson would be coming to the pulpit at Clear Springs to introduce Heather. The Sunday Heather supplied for Mike when he preached for the committee was the first time Carol had been back in church since her surgery. She almost didn't come that day. She was not feeling all that well, and she felt awkward about her appearance. She told Mike and Karen that she was glad she made the effort, because Heather's sermon was particularly helpful and encouraging to her. When Carol learned that Heather would be preaching again, she asked Mike for her phone number. Carol called and invited her to come down on Saturday and spend the night in her home, and she asked Wallace to let her introduce Heather. Mike only half-way listened to Carl's introduction. He was breathing a prayer for Heather and for himself.

* * * * * * * * * * * *

"Well, how do you think I did?" Mike asked Karen. Carl had escorted Mike, Karen, and Asalee back to a classroom on the first floor of the educational building to wait while the church voted and the deacons counted the ballots.

"You did fine, Hon. I could tell you were a little nervous when you started, but anybody'd expect that. I feel OK about it." Mike was never entirely satisfied with any sermon he preached, but he appreciated Karen's affirming words.

"I told everybody in Sunday School they were going to like you because you're the best preacher in the whole world,": Asalee added matter-of-factly and then, in the same breath, asked, "How come they made us go back here by ourselves? Did we do something bad?"

Asalee's innocent question provided a much-needed moment of comic relief. "No, we didn't do anything bad, or at least if we did, it looks like we did it together and got in trouble together," Karen replied.

Just then, Carl opened the door and said, "Well, you didn't get a unanimous vote like I'd hoped, but it was a good vote. A hundred and thirty-one for, seven against, and two abstained. That's well over the required two-thirds. It's getting so you hardly ever hear of a unanimous call anymore."

Even as Mike was wondering who the seven negatives and two abstentions were and whether he might eventually win their support, he heard himself tell Carl, "I'll accept the church on that vote."

"Well, let's go tell the church that you accept," Carl said as he escorted them back to the auditorium where the congregation was waiting to hear the outcome.

* * * * * * * * * * * *

Mike, Karen, and Asalee felt as though their right arms were going to fall off from shaking hands with all the people in church at Harrington. Asalee had a crick in her neck from looking up to talk with so many adults who towered over her. Hiring squad member Susan Whitmire, a fifty-three year old widow with grown children who worked for the Department of Family and Children Services, was ahead of them in her car, and Mike and his family were following her to the Old West Steak House for dinner before going back to the motel to pack up and check out. Susan had the keys to the parsonage, and they were going to look at it on the way out of town.

4

It was about 3:30 Sunday afternoon when the Westovers bade goodbye to Susan and began the trip back home. The gas gauge was down to a quarter of a tank, so Mike stopped to fill up before getting on I-85. Seeing a pay phone at the edge of the gas station lot, he pulled over to it after paying for the gas. "I want to go ahead and call Wallace, let him know how things turned out," he explained to Karen and Asalee.

"Daddy, are you crying?" Asalee asked, although the answer to her question was obvious.

"I guess I am a little," Mike admitted. He was going to be the new pastor of Harrington Baptist Church, but that meant leaving Clear Springs. He loved Clear Springs, and he was only beginning to realize how deep his roots were there, but the whole idea of going to seminary had been to prepare for ministry as a full-time vocation. He was frustrated by the lack of time to devote to the work at Clear Springs. Carrying a full load of classes, working a fulltime job, and serving the church had been stressful. He saw so much more he could do at Clear Springs if he had the time, but one of the things he would miss about Clear Springs was a group of people accustomed to student pastors who lived thirty miles away and had other responsibilities. Many of them had learned to do some of the things that a full-time church would expect the pastor to do.

Mike was thinking specifically about the way the church ministered in the aftermath of the wreck that killed Jim and Kimberly. The school brought in crisis counselors on Monday after the accident, but many of the students turned to Carol Richardson. Some asked questions of a profoundly spiritual nature and asked Carol to pray with them. Carol was amazed that so many turned to her. She was taking it pretty hard herself. The drunk driver who killed Jim and Kimberly was her cousin on her father's side. Kim's mother was her cousin on her mother's side. She had known Jim and Kimberly since they were babies, and she had taught both of them. She was not an outsider to the grief of those who sought her out.

Two girls who talked and prayed with Carol on Monday made public professions of faith at Clear Springs the following Sunday. Since Carol was the one who led them to faith in Christ, Mike asked her to present Tycina Nichols and Jennifer Cline to the church. When Carol presented them that morning and asked the traditional Baptist question, "What is the pleasure of the church?," the rolling-thunder voice of Wallace Coggins called out "Movewereceive'em"—all one word, just as he had said it for many others. Kim's mother, fighting back tears, said "second," and the vote was unanimous. Mike was concerned that some might not want to accept Tycina because she was black, but she was received as warmly as Jennifer.

The following Sunday, Jennifer came to church with a new Bible her grandmother had given her. Mark and Teresa noticed that Tycina did not have a Bible. They invited her and Jennifer home with them for Sunday dinner and gave Tycina the Bible they had given Kimberly the previous Christmas.

Carol helped Mike baptize Tycina and Jennifer. He and Linda Trimble had since baptized Tycina's younger brother Tyrone.

Tycina's and Jennifer's boyfriends had recently started coming to church with them. Tycina's mother came on the Sundays that she did not have to work. Mike knew that he could take no credit for any of this. It was from God, brought about through the ministry of the people at Clear Springs. Mike was not afraid that Clear Springs would fall apart when he left. He only hoped that he would do as well as Clear Springs.

While Mike was making the call to Wallace, Karen went inside the convenience store to get Cokes for herself and Mike and a carton of chocolate milk for Asalee. Asalee clung closely to her father at the pay phone, listening for the familiar, comforting voice of her Papa Wallace.

Wallace picked up on the second ring. "Hello, Wallace Coggins." Retired from the railroad twenty years, he still answered the phone as though it might be the dispatcher calling him for one more run.

"Brother Wallace, this is Mike..."

"Hey, Preacher. I've been sitting here hoping you'd call. Just got home a little while ago. I went over after church and ate dinner with Gordon and Evelyn, but I didn't stay too long. I wanted to get on back in case you called. How'd you come out?"

"OK. They voted right after church. I didn't get a unanimous call, but it was a pretty strong vote, a hundred and thirty-one for, seven against, two abstained."

"I expected you'd get a unanimous vote. Are you going to accept it?"

"I already have, Brother Wallace. I told them that May 27 would be my last Sunday at Clear Springs and that I'd start there on June 3. I'm going to resign next Sunday. It's going to be the hardest thing I've ever done."

"I expect you won't be the only one shedding tears. We sure do hate to lose you. I've gotten pretty attached to you and Karen and

Asalee, especially after the way y'all holp me when Estelle died. Estelle thought the world of y'all, too. Of course, I reckon we've gotten along all right with every preacher we've had. Got along so well with ol' Gordon Corrie that he ended up being our son-in-law. I have to admit, though, I never had a dog named after me 'til you come along. All of us'll miss you, but the time comes that you have to move along where the Lord's leading you."

"Thanks, Brother Wallace. How'd everything go at Clear Springs this morning?"

"We had sixty in Sunday School, more'n that for preaching, about seventy-five, I guess, real good preaching attendance. The young lady who filled in for you, Preacher Simmons, brought a fine message. I admit it's different to see a woman in the pulpit, but she's a good preacher. Looks like we might have to deal with ol' Lester and Brother Billy again, on account of a lot of people are tellin' me they think she'd make us a fine pastor. You'll be hearing from Carol soon's you get home, 'cause she told me this mornin' how much she enjoyed havin' the preacher spend the night at her house last night. Her kids've really taken to Preacher Simmons, 'specially the girls. Carol said she felt like she'd known Preacher Simmons all her life."

"Sounds good to me. I'll look forward to talking to Carol and Heather. Glad to hear we had such a good service this morning. Lord willing, I'll see you Wednesday night. Guess we'd better get back on the road."

"You kids be careful traveling. What time'll you be gettin' home?"

"Probably about middle of the day on Monday. We're going to stop and spend the night with my folks. Karen's off tomorrow, we're going to let Asalee miss a day of kindergarten, and I don't have to work at the motel 'til 11:00 tomorrow night."

"OK, Brother Mike. See you Wednesday night. Bye."

Mike hung up the phone and walked back to the car, Asalee still clinging to him like Velcro. Mike took the Coke that Karen handed him as he got in the car, and Asalee took her chocolate milk. Mike started the car and headed down the ramp onto I-85 north. As soon as she finished her milk, Asalee curled up on the back seat and went to sleep. Karen tuned the radio to a classical music station, took off her shoes, and reclined the seat. They were some distance down the road before she asked, "What'd Wallace say?"

"Said he hated to see us leave Clear Springs, but he understood and wished us the best. Said we had a good service this morning, about seventy or seventy-five for preaching. He bragged on what a good message Heather brought, and he said a lot of the people want to call her as pastor."

"You think they will? We came pretty close to getting drummed out of the association over the women deacons."

"I don't know. They'll call her if Carol and her kids have anything to do with it. They were telling Wallace how much they enjoyed having Heather spend the night. Meg and Jess've really taken to her. I'd like to see it happen. She's an excellent preacher, but a man who can't preach a lick'll have an easier time getting called to a church. We'll just have to wait and see. By the way, what'd you think about the house?"

"It's not one I'd pick if I had a choice, but it's OK. It's got three bedrooms, so Asalee can have her own room and we can fix one room as a nursery. It's more house than we need, but we'll grow into it. I know you like having that enclosed garage so you can work on the car. Just one thing that bothers me, something Carl said when he pointed the house out to us last night."

"About it being a good neighborhood, no blacks close by?"

"Yeah, I had to bite my tongue. You know what I was thinking about?"

"About the way Tycina and her family have been accepted at Clear Springs?"

"That crossed my mind, but the first thing I thought about was the Ogunlajas from Nigeria at the seminary. You remember them, don't you?"

"Oh sure, Moses Ogunlaja. Did a Ph. D. in New Testament, Dr. Kerns' fellow. He's back in Nigeria, teaching at the seminary. Good guy, I liked him a lot."

"I don't remember if I ever told you about this. The first day we put Asalee in daycare at the seminary, when I went to pick her up. She was all excited and happy, saying 'Mommy, Mommy, look at my friend Miriam.' Miriam was the Ogunlaja's little girl, same age as Asalee. When I knelt down to speak to her, Asalee took her hand, held it up to my face and said, 'Mommy, look at her pretty skin!" I did, and Asalee said, 'Feel how soft it is, Mommy,' and I did. She was so dark, a beautiful little girl. When I picked up Asalee every day, she and Miriam hugged like two little old ladies. They could've been the poster children for race relations Sunday."

"So you wonder how Harrington's going to handle a preacher's daughter who thinks black is beautiful?"

"I guess so. Then I was thinking about back when I was Asalee's age. You remember Alberta and Roscoe Wills, the older black couple who came to our wedding?"

"Sure. You told me that Mrs. Wills used to work for your family."

"Mmhmm. I remember Alberta showing me some pictures of her granddaughters, and I said they were very pretty little girls. I told Alberta I thought she was pretty, too. My brothers were about thirteen and eleven at the time. Rob and Bill overheard me, and they started teasing me and calling me 'nigger lover.' I told them I did love Alberta, and I didn't care who knew it. She was always kind to us and treated us well. She'd always listen to me, and I could tell her anything. I liked to hear her tell the stories the old people in her family told her when she was a little girl. She would've been pretty to me because of that, but she was a pretty woman. She must've been in her mid-fifties at the time, but her skin was soft and silky smooth, just like the Ogunlaja's little girl. So, if Asalee thinks black is beautiful, she comes by it honestly."

"She really meant a lot to you, didn't she?"

"She did. I took Asalee to see Alberta and Roscoe when we went down to Alabama last summer. You know how Asalee is most of the time, a little shy around people she doesn't know. She acted like she'd known Alberta and Roscoe all her life. I guess she'd heard me talk about them so much, she felt like she knew them. Alberta still had the little school pictures I gave her when I was a kid, right up there with all the pictures of her children, grandchildren, and great-grandchildren. I gave her a picture of the three of us, and she put it right up there with all the others. They hugged us as we were leaving, and Alberta laughed and asked me if I still thought she was pretty. I told her she's one of the most beautiful women I've ever known. She's got to be close to eighty, but her skin's still soft and pretty, just like I remember when I was a little girl. I hope I'm that pretty when I'm her age."

"Don't worry, you will be."

"Good answer. Now you said there are some things that bother you about Harrington. We've talked about one thing, and it bothers me, too. What else?"

"Oh, I don't know," Mike answered. "That's it, mostly. It's a lot different from Clear Springs. Some of it's hard to put my finger on. How do you feel about it?"

"Well, their expectations of a pastor's wife are different. Clear Springs is used to the pastor's wife being a young woman with children and a full-time job. Harrington's used to somebody with grown children who's home all the time, always entertaining at the parsonage. It's not that I don't like to entertain. You know I do. But I'm not about to let our house be another fellowship hall for the church."

"Something else," Mike added. "Harrington's used to the pastor living around the corner from the church. Clear Springs is used to the pastor being thirty miles away at the seminary. Speaking of living around the corner from the church, I hate hearing the house we're going to live in referred to as the 'pastorium' or the 'parsonage.' Those '-age' and '-orium' endings sound like some kind of institution, a place to send pastors when they crack up. 'Poor Brother Westover,' Mike intoned with mock solemnity, 'just completely flipped out. The guys in the white coats put him in a straightjacket and took him to the pastorium.'"

"Yeah, and you're not the only one who's being committed. We're all being committed to the pastorium."

"That's what we need," Mike mugged facetiously, "more committed people serving the Lord. Anyway, maybe I can put my finger on some of the other stuff that bothers me. There are some serious turf battles going on in that church."

"Oh, you mean like the woman, I didn't get her name, who met me when I went back to look at the nursery. She looked me up and down and said, 'I see you're pregnant.' The way she said it, it sounded like she thought there was something wrong with that, like I needed to explain that it's OK, I'm married, and my husband's the father of the baby. Then she said, 'Just understand, this nursery's mine and I don't want anybody messing with it.'"

"And you told her…"

"I promised her that no matter what else I did, I'd never mess with that nursery as long as she was alive. I told her I was going to mess with the music ministry and, if the church had a computer with the capacity to do graphics, I'd mess with that, too. I assured her that her nursery was safe. I told her I planned to keep the baby with me as much as I could, because I was going to breast-feed the new baby like I did Asalee. She looked at me plumb appalled, as though there's something unnatural about nursing a baby, like I said a dirty word when I said the word 'breast.'"

Mike egged Karen on a little. "I know you didn't tell her what you felt like tellin' her, because I didn't see anybody hauled out on a gurney. Go ahead, tell me what you felt like telling her."

"I felt like telling her, 'yes, I said the word breast! I've got two of them, and they work so well for nursing babies, you'd think God made them for that very purpose.' If she'd still been standing, I could've told her that you like them, too."

"Whoa! If you'd told her that, there would've only been six negative votes, and you would've been free to mess with the nursery. That would've finished her off."

The Sunday afternoon traffic was light as Mike followed I-85 through downtown Atlanta. Asalee was asleep in the back seat, and Mike and Karen's conversation was making the trip go by quickly for them. As they crossed I-285 on the north side of Atlanta, Karen asked, "So what turf battles do you see going on, besides the nursery? I don't think that's much of a battle since nobody's fighting her and I don't plan to start."

"Well, Carl implied that he and the deacon chairman, what's his name, Frank Brinkley, didn't get along too well. It's a turf battle between Carl as chief head hunter and Frank as chairman of the *board of* deacons. Frank introduced himself to me this morning as 'Franklin A. Brinkley, Chairman of the Board of Deacons of Harrington Baptist Church,' like that was all part of his name. He's miffed because he wasn't automatically on the hiring squad. Got two deacons, Ted Coleman and David Groves, on the committee, but Frank still feels slighted. He thinks the hiring squad ought to report to the deacons instead of reporting directly to the church. He wants the deacons to run the church, and he wants to run the deacons. He clearly expects to be my boss. A lot different from Wallace, that's for sure. And what was the older woman's name, the one who thought I was too young?"

"Geneva Millican. I'd like to forget, but I can't. I know she would've been happier if I'd looked more like June Cleaver. I'm not going to entertain at the parsonage enough to suit her. She's not going to be happy with me when I don't make it to all the WMU meetings, and she won't be pleased to discover that Asalee acts like a child sometimes."

"Yeah, and what about her poor husband Roland. Never saw a man look so cowered. All he needed was a dog collar and a leash."

"I'd go easy on the sympathy for Roland. He picked her out. Nobody put a gun to his head and made him marry her."

"Maybe so, but I still feel sorry for him. I like what Brother Woodrow used to say, that some people won't be happy in heaven 'til they find something to complain about. I know we've got negative, critical people at Clear Springs. Myrtle Norris could be a pain in the rear if you let her, and Jim Echols was sore for a while because the church didn't choose him to be a deacon. Every church has some like that, but Clear Springs doesn't let them run amuck. They made an example out of Lester Halstead, and it put the rest of 'em on notice."

"You're right, but a lot of churches are as cowed down to people like that as Roland is to Geneva, and it's their own fault. As soon as we finished that conversation, such as it was, I decided I'm not going to make this woman happy no matter what I do. I won't do anything on purpose to antagonize her, but I won't break my neck to make her happy."

"It's not worth it. I doubt I'll make her happy unless I figure out how to suddenly make myself thirty years older. I hope Harrington keeps her reined in like Clear Springs does Myrtle."

Karen was giggling like a thirteen-year-old, "Honey, talking about Myrt, you made me think of something funny. You remember when we first went to Clear Springs, Myrt was doing the bulletins. Remember the first Sunday you preached there, how tickled I got right before you got up to preach, when I read in the bulletin, 'We welcome all the visitors in our mist today,' and I could just see this fog rolling in, enveloping all of us, visitors and members alike. I thought it was just a funny typo until the same thing happened the next two Sundays. I took Myrt aside and told her the word she was looking for was 'midst,' m-i-d-s-t, that a 'mist,' m-i-s-t, is a fog. She still got in a huff over it."

"Myrt can get in a huff pretty easily. Doesn't take much. She's not my favorite person, but I can't say she ever caused us much trouble. The church knows she's been that way all her life and probably won't change. Clear Springs doesn't let her build a following and become a thorn in the preacher's side. I hope Harrington does as well."

Mike eased into the right-hand lane of I-85 north as they approached the exit for Denham. Karen reached over the seat to nudge Asalee, who had been asleep most of the trip. "Wake up, Az, we're nearly to Nanny and Pop Pop's." Asalee slowly began to stir, rubbed her eyes, pulled herself up in the seat, and asked, "Where are we, Mommy?"

"Almost to Nanny and Pop Pop's," Karen repeated. "I bet Wallace has missed you and been pining for you. He'll be one happy dog when he sees you. Good thing you got a nice long nap. Wallace'll be ready to run and play 'til dark. Nanny'll have a good dinner for us, and we're going to spend the night with Nanny, Pop Pop, and Aunt Mandy."

"Can I sleep with Aunt Mandy in her room?"

"It's OK with me if it's OK with her." Karen liked Mike's sister, and Asalee had missed her greatly when they moved for Mike to go to seminary. Amanda had a special affection for her only niece.

Asalee didn't really need Santa Claus, the Easter Bunny, or the tooth fairy—she had her Aunt Mandy.

* * * * * * * * * * * *

"Well, Son, how'd it go this morning?" Grady asked as he helped Mike get the suitcases from the car.

"Pretty good, I reckon, Dad. They voted to call me and I accepted. We'll be moving the end of May. June 3 will be our first Sunday. Seems like a nice town and a good church."

"That's good. I've been through Harrington a few times. Don't know anybody down there. Son, I need to do some apologizing. I've been hard on you about this. I don't mean to be. I just know how some of these churches around here chew up preachers, and I hate to see you get into something like that. I have to admit, though, Clear Springs has treated you all right."

"Yeah, they have, Dad. I've enjoyed Clear Springs, and I learned as much or more there than I did at the seminary. They've been good to us. Leaving there'll be the hardest thing we ever did, especially for Asalee. She's the princess of Clear Springs."

"Well, Son, I hope this'n down at Harrington'll be just as good to you. If they're not, there'll always be a job open for you at the shop as long as I'm in business, and you'd make more than you'll ever make pastoring a church. I'd like to have you back. I never had to recheck your work. I'm braggin' on myself in a roundabout way 'cause I taught you, but you're as good a crankshaft man as I ever saw. That 390 you built and put in that ol' shop truck when you were in high school still runs like a top. I've done nothing to it but oil changes and tune-ups."

"It's hard to mess up a 390 Ford, Daddy. That was a decent running old motor before I built it. Speaking of motors, I guess you've got that Willys-Knight torn down by now."

"Haven't touched it. It's just like it was when you saw it yesterday. I know you figured I'd have it tore down by the time your Mama'n Mandy got home from church. I was of a mind to do that when I got up. I put on my coveralls and drank a cup of coffee about 6:30 this morning. Then I went out on the patio to smoke me a cigarette. Since your Mama quit smoking, she can't stand to smell 'em in the house. I lit up like I do every morning, same brand I've always smoked. It tasted awful! I didn't take more'n three or four drags on it. Every puff tasted worse than the one before. I threw it down, went back in the house, got another cup of coffee, and walked down to the shop, thinkin' I'd be back to normal by the time I got the head off'a that Willys-Knight. I unlocked the shop and turned on the lights, all set to start tearin' it down. It was strange is all I can tell you. I stood there sippin' my coffee and lookin' at it. I just didn't care anything about startin' on it this morning. I tried to smoke another cigarette, like to've choked to death, tasted worse'n the one before it. So I come back up to the house, took a shower and shaved, cooked breakfast for your Mama'n Mandy'n ate with them. Son, I don't know what's goin' on less'n the Man Upstairs is gangin' up on me. I lose my best crankshaft man when you leave to go off up yonder to seminary. Then that little church called you, and your Mama'n me an' Mandy made the trip up there to see you ordained, first time I'd been inside a church 'cept for weddings and funerals since I was a kid. Then, we've been up there a couple times to Clear Springs to hear you preach. The times I heard you, you talked plain English, made good sense, and I ended up thinking about some of the things you said. Then your Mama starts goin' to the Methodist church with Ann Raines after her husband died. 'Fore long Mandy started gettin' up and goin' with 'er..."

"Now Daddy, you're not about to tell me you went to church this morning, are you?"

"Well, I reckon I'm tellin' you just that, Son, 'cause that's what I did. I didn't go with them to Sunday School. After they left, I paced around the house, tried to play with Asalee's dog, but ol' Wallace just wanted to sleep, wouldn't have anything to do with me. I put my suit and good shoes on, got in my truck, and drove down to the Methodist church. You ought to've seen the look on Julia'n Mandy's faces when I walked in and sat down beside 'em. I was thinkin' it was a good thing me and all the guys in the shop took that CPR course at the fire department last year. I thought I was gonna have occasion to use it. Ann looked like she was gonna go right on up there and join up with ol' Jack when she saw me."

Heretofore, it had been useless for Mike to talk to his father about matters of the spirit. Even after starting to church herself, Julia had let Grady alone and let him go his own way. Mike's past efforts to talk with his father about such things had ended on an angry note, with Grady telling Mike in no uncertain terms that he wanted to be left alone about it. After telling Mike to leave him alone, he would go get a can of beer from the refrigerator and light up a cigarette. In the body language of Grady Westover, a beer in one hand and a cigarette in the other meant, "Subject closed." Now Grady was the one who had brought the subject up. Mike embraced his father and said, "Daddy, that's wonderful. I'm so proud of you."

"Now don't go gettin' ahead of yourself, Son," Grady cautioned. "All I did was get up and go to church this morning. I'm not gonna make a fool of myself. I'm not sayin' I'll be there every Sunday. I still got my tickets for Daytona and Talladega. And I'm not saying I'm gonna join the church like your Mama did this mornin'. All I'm sayin' is I'm glad I went this mornin', reckon I'll go back next Sunday. So, to answer your question about the Willys-Knight, Lord willin', I'll start on it first thing in the mornin'."

5

As he drove across the Veterans Memorial Bridge into Riverton, Virginia, Mike remembered the first time he drove across it, at the wheel of a U-Haul truck with everything they owned in the back and Karen and Asalee following in the car. Riverton and the apartment in Seminary Courts had been home for three years now, and Mike crossed the Veterans Memorial Bridge daily, but, crossing it on this particular day was a surreal experience. It was just after mid-day on Monday, and they had only been gone since Saturday morning, but it felt as though they had been gone for years, as though they were passing through a place they had lived a long time ago, so long ago that Mike found himself thinking consciously about how to get onto Morgan Avenue, go past the seminary campus, and make the left onto Edwards Street to get to Seminary Courts. Pulling up in front of 1703-A Armstrong Circle, it felt as though they had been gone so long that someone else, someone they did not know, perhaps someone born since they left, should be living there now.

Karen looked forward to moving out of this cramped apartment with its tiny closets, massive cast-iron radiators, ugly metal kitchen cabinets, 1930's vintage bathroom fixtures, and dirt-color carpet. Yet, there had been good things about life in Seminary

Courts. Karen felt safe letting Asalee go out to walk the dog or play without having to watch her every second. Most couples in Seminary Courts had children, and they knew each other's children and looked out for them. If Asalee were to fall and skin her knees at the other end of the block, the people down there would take care of her. She or Mike would do the same for another seminary student's child. Having been brought up in a safe environment, Asalee was a fairly confident six-year-old, but she was afraid to get into too much mischief because the news about it would get home before she did.

Most seminary students lived on a tight budget, just as Mike and Karen did. Surveying the cars parked on their street, Mike recognized some fugitives from the scrap metal crusher whose lives he had extended. In return, other students and their spouses had helped Mike and Karen with everything from babysitting to income tax preparation. Lisa Carraway, a student in the school of church music, annually tuned Karen's piano in return for a tuneup on her car.

Mike got Saturday's and Monday's mail from the mailbox while Karen checked the voice mail. There was not much mail—a statement from Karen's obstetrician, a letter from Karen's parents, and an envelope with the return address of I. M. Coggins. Wallace and Estelle's son Matt was the treasurer at Clear Springs. A road foreman of engines for Norfolk Southern, his work often caused him to miss church services. Yet, he was vitally interested in the church, generous in his financial support, and he was there with Sarah Beth whenever he could be. At church the previous Sunday, Mike told him to take the pay for the supply preacher out of his paycheck since he would be at another church preaching in view of a call. When Mike opened the envelope, he saw that the check was for the full amount, and he read the hand-written note enclosed with it:

Bro. Mike—

Some of us chipped in a little extra to pay Preacher Simmons for pulpit supply. I didn't want it to come out of your pocket. Hope everything went well for you Sunday in Georgia.

Matt

Mike was touched by the kindness, but it hardly surprised him. This was typical of the way Clear Springs took care of its pastor, and he knew that the church had been generous with Heather as well.

"Mike Honey," Karen called from inside the apartment, "couple of messages for you on the voice mail, one from Carol and one from Heather. Both of them say they can't wait to talk to you about yesterday at Clear Springs."

Mike took the phone from Karen, punched in the number for the voice mail, and listened. "Brother Mike, this is Carol. I can't wait to talk with you when you get home. I'll call you this evening when I get in from school, before you have to go in to work. We had a wonderful weekend with Heather Simmons. My kids and I love her, and she's an excellent preacher. We hate to see you leave, but if you do, I hope she'll be our next pastor. She'd be so good for Clear Springs. I'll talk to you tonight. Take care." Mike listened as the voice mail continued with the next message. "Mike? Heather Simmons. Thank you for inviting me back to Clear Springs. I enjoyed preaching there, and I had a delightful time with Carol and her children. Call me as soon as you can. I'll be working at the library, main circulation desk, until 6:00 this evening. I'll get a bite to eat, should be back to my room by 6:30. I can't wait to talk with you about this weekend. Bye."

The sound of two happy women on the voice mail confirmed Wallace's report that it had indeed been a good Sunday at Clear Springs. The conversation with Carol would have to wait until evening when she got in from teaching school. Heather couldn't take personal calls while she was working at the seminary library, so Mike decided to just drive over there. The circulation desk was not very busy on Monday afternoons, and Mike was eager to talk with her about the weekend at Clear Springs.

*   *   *   *   *   *   *   *   *   *   *   *

"Mike," Heather called out in her best library stage whisper. "How'd it go for you down in Georgia Sunday?"

"Pretty good. They voted to call me and I accepted, so we'll be moving right after graduation. Seems to be a good church. Got your message on the voice mail and decided to come over here and talk with you in person."

"Better be careful talking to me here," Heather cautioned only half-jokingly. "Since Sturgill took over, the walls have ears. It's not a good idea to act like you know me. We women preachers are all a part of the godless secular feminist agenda to destroy the home and family. Or so Sturgill says."

"I'll take my chances. I stopped and called Wallace on the way home yesterday. He said you were very well received, brought a good message, and a lot of the folks have their hearts set on calling you as pastor."

"I know Carol and her kids do, but I don't know if it'll work out. I'm afraid to get my hopes up. Been there, done that, it hurts. But I had a wonderful time with Carol and her kids. I feel like I've known them forever. Carol's a beautiful person, been through a lot, doing a super job as a single parent. If we hadn't needed to get up for church on Sunday morning, we could've talked all night. I'm the first woman preacher Meg and Jess ever saw, and they're quite fascinated with me."

"So I hear. I had two excited women on my voice mail when I got home, you and Carol. Carol's chompin' at the bit to talk with me when she gets home, and she left enough of a message to tell me that she wants to talk about calling you as pastor."

"Carol's not the only one who's got to be convinced." Heather cautioned. "But, if they want to call me, the answer's yes. I'd take Clear Springs in a heartbeat. It's a great little church. Everybody who talked to me spoke well of you and Karen. They hate to see you leave. They paid me a hundred dollars just for supplying."

"Doesn't surprise me. Clear Springs has been good to us. I hear the horror stories from some of the guys, and I can't believe how good we've had it. I'm not saying you won't run into problems. We did, and you will, too. But the church'll support you and do right by you. I can count on my fingers the times I'd preached before we went down there. They didn't call me for my preaching ability, though I think I've improved in the time I've been there. Dr. Corrie's the one who recommended me to Clear Springs. He served the church when he was a student back in the late 40's, married Wallace and Estelle Coggins' daughter."

"Small world. I didn't know Corrie had connections to Clear Springs."

"Oh yeah, he and Clear Springs go way back. Corrie can tell you anything you want to know about the church. He and his wife visit from time to time, and he's been interim pastor a half dozen times. Wallace's wife, Mrs. Corrie's mother, died back in January, and we had her funeral at Clear Springs. Estelle was a sweet lady. I wish you could've known her. Wallace is as good as they come. He's really been a mentor to me, and I expect he'd be the same to you. I hope they call you. You'd be good for the church, and they'd be good for you."

"Thanks, Mike. I hope it works out, too. I appreciate you inviting me down there to preach. By the way, how is Corrie about women preachers?"

"He's OK about that, and he knows about you preaching there yesterday because Wallace had dinner with the Corries after church. Corrie's one of the good ones."

"I liked Corrie when I had him for Hebrew and for Old Testament Survey. He called on me as much as the guys in the class, always gracious and respectful. I felt like he was OK about women in ministry, but I never talked with him about my call to be a pastor."

"You'd find him supportive. We both know he has to be careful with all these yahoos running around with concealed tape recorders. But don't worry, Corrie won't blackball you. Besides, it'd be hard for anybody to blackball you at this point. You've made a very positive impression on your own, and for what it's worth, I think my recommendation carries some weight. Wallace told me that anybody who comes with my endorsement is all right as far as he's concerned. You have my endorsement."

"Thanks, Mike."

"I'll be praying, and I'll do all I can to help you. If it works out, I hope it'll be as good for you as it's been for me. Wallace joined the church in 1926, and he speaks well of every pastor they've had in the last sixty-four years. All seminary students. Some of 'em had to be turkeys, but you'd never know it from talking to Wallace."

"I was pleased to see that you have a couple of women deacons. Carol told me how that came about, and how y'all nearly got booted out of the association."

"Yeah, we were the first in the Sanders County Association. Mary Kate Sessions, who grew up at Clear Springs, was ordained at First Baptist in Canfield a little while before Carol and Linda were ordained, but Canfield's in the Broad River Association. Sanders County Association's probably a little more conservative than Broad River, in fact I know it is. After we ordained Carol and Linda in '88, First Baptist in Ledford, the biggest church in the association, ordained some women deacons, and they ordained Carolyn Williamson who has been minister of education there since Abraham was in Ur of the Chaldees. So, by the time the association met in '89, we weren't out on a limb by ourselves."

"Well, Mike," Heather mused, "we might be out on that lonely limb again if Clear Springs calls a woman pastor. How do you think the association'll handle that?"

"Don't know. If Claude Bradley hadn't been moderator when the challenge to our messengers came up, we might not be in the association now. Jerry Langley, pastor over at Mountain View, is moderator now. I don't know him all that well, but I know he's pretty conservative. I know he wouldn't be real happy to have a woman pastor in the association. As to what he'd actually do, I don't know. Nobody raised a stink last year about the ordinations at Ledford First, probably because that church carries half the budget of the association. Since nobody's raised the issue on his watch, who knows how Jerry'd handle it. It got ugly enough when Billy Fite challenged the seating of our messengers, but it would've been worse if Claude hadn't been such a good moderator. Claude's no liberal, but he's fair and decent. So, to answer your question, there'll be opposition in the association, and some of it'll be ugly. How it'll come out, there's no telling. I quit making predictions a long time ago."

"What about your director of missions?"

"Jeff Dowridge? He's a promoter of whatever cometh down out of Nashville. Hard to pin him down. He agrees with everyone privately and stands with no one publicly."

"Oh well," Heather sighed. "All of this speculation is premature. They haven't called me, and there's no guarantee they will. No need to worry about what the association might do about something that hasn't happened. The church'll probably want to look at a lot of candidates before they settle on one. There are a lot more seminary students looking for pastorates than there are churches looking for student pastors. I'm not going to get my hopes built up just because I had a good time supplying down there."

"Heather, I'm not in a position to promise anything, but your chances of being called are better than you think. When I was called there two years ago, Dr. Corrie was serving as interim. He gave my name to Wallace—why Corrie thought of me, I'll never know. Wallace called and invited me to come down and preach two Sundays. The second Sunday, they voted to call me. They didn't look at anybody else. Clear Springs goes about choosing a pastor the same way I went about choosing a wife. I didn't collect resumes of eligible women, narrow it down to a short list, or anything like that. Karen and I met in an American Lit class our freshman year at Rullman College, and we connected. We started dating, and we decided we didn't need to look any further. We've got another case of love at first sight down at Clear Springs. Talk to Corrie and see what he thinks. I need to get home, talk to Carol, eat a bite, and catch a little sleep before I go in to work. I think it's yours if you want it."

Heather said that she wanted Clear Springs more than she had ever wanted anything, and Mike promised to keep her in prayer and up to date about what the church was doing. He bade her a good evening and drove back home, stopping on the way to pick up a few items at the Shop'n'Save.

As Mike worked his way through traffic, he was praying. It was not a prayer asking God to do anything, since God already seemed to be doing plenty. When he asked Heather to preach for him the Sunday he preached at Luckett's Creek, he had no idea it would go this far. It bothered him to see a preacher of Heather's ability have so few opportunities to preach. She had never once been invited to preach at her home church. Mike could not rectify that injustice, but he could give her a place to preach one Sunday. He didn't need to ask permission to invite her, since the church always left it up to the pastor to secure a supply preacher when one was needed. He figured that anyone who got upset about it would get over it since it was only one service, and the church wouldn't give him any grief about it since he was about to leave anyway. He had been overwhelmed at the strong favorable response to Heather. Wallace said he had heard no complaints. If Wallace didn't hear any, there weren't any. Mike's prayer was simply an acknowledgment of God's amazing work in progress. He kept thinking of the Psalmist's words, *the Lord has done this, and it is marvelous in our eyes.*

* * * * * * * * * * * *

"Honey, the phone's for you," Karen called as Mike came in the door. She was fixing supper, and she had picked up the phone in the kitchen. "It's Carol. I've already been talking to her. Carol, here's Mike. Tell him what you just told me."

"Hey Carol, got your message on the voice mail, and Wallace told me about his conversation with you. Sounds like things went well while we were gone."

"Well, we did miss you. Don't think we didn't. We're really going to miss you when you graduate and move down to Georgia. You've been a wonderful pastor, and I'll always love you and your family. But yes, Mike, this weekend went *very* well."

"Tell me about it."

"Well, I told you how much I enjoyed Heather the first time she was down here. You know, I'm thirty-six years old, and that was the first time I'd ever heard a woman preach a sermon. I almost didn't go that day. I didn't feel like going. I was still getting over the operation, and I felt like I'd been run over by a Mack truck. I didn't know who was going to preach, and I wasn't worried about it. I knew you'd get somebody. If I'd gone by my feelings, I would've sent the kids on with Mom and Dad and stayed home to rest. I felt bad, and I was self-conscious about the way I looked, but the Lord told me, 'Carol, I know you feel lousy, and I know you're worried about how you look, but go ahead, get up, get ready, and go on to church. If you do, I'll make you glad you did.' Megan was so sweet, helping me get dressed and helping me with my hair, because I was so sore and it was hard for me to lift my right arm. The doctor hadn't released me to start driving again, so the kids and I rode with Mom and Dad. It hurt something awful getting in and out of the van. Daddy had to help me. But I'm so glad I went. As soon as the people at church, especially the kids in my Sunday School class, saw me and hugged me, I realized I wasn't disfigured in their eyes or God's eyes. Heather preached from the story in Luke about the crippled woman Jesus healed on the Sabbath, excellent message. Mom and Dad took us all out to eat after church. I felt so much better coming out of church than I did going in, and I enjoyed talking with Heather while we ate. I was so excited when I found out she was coming back, more so when she accepted the invitation to spend the night at our place. It feels like I've known her all her life, and my kids love her to death. Bill Junior went to sleep about eight o'clock, but the girls and I would've still been talking with Heather when the sun came up if we hadn't needed to get up for church. I finally chased the girls to bed about 11:30. I'm so glad my girls had that time with Heather. Megan had been storing up so many questions since the first time Heather preached. I had no idea how many questions were rolling around in her mind. Heather got to our house about 3:00 Saturday afternoon, and the questions didn't stop 'til we went to bed. After the questions Meg asked her, Heather's ordination council should be a piece of cake. Meg asked her about her whole life, when she became a Christian, how she knew God wanted her to be a preacher, when she preached her first sermon, how she went about preparing sermons, everything you could think of. Heather brought another fine message yesterday. Mike, I hope we can get her to be our next pastor. She'd be so good for us, and we'd be good for her."

"I just talked to Heather this afternoon over at the seminary library. She enjoyed Clear Springs and being with your family as much as you enjoyed her. I don't know which one of you is more excited."

"Glad she enjoyed herself. She's welcome at our place anytime. I've never been more comfortable with a guest in my home. She's a lovely person, no pretense, just as down-to-earth as she can be. I'm doing pretty well getting my strength back, but she was so sensitive to me not being a hundred percent just yet. She helped get supper on the table Saturday night, and she and the girls told me to rest while they cleaned up the kitchen. Bill Junior pitched in and helped all he could, too. I just kicked back in my recliner and listened to them. It sounded like they were having a party in there, but the kitchen was spotless when they got through. Mama and Daddy had us up to their house for dinner after church. They're as impressed with Heather as I am. I didn't know how Daddy would be about considering a woman pastor, but hearing her preach, seeing the effect she's had on my kids, and talking with her has been enough to take care of any reservations he may have had. He took me aside up at their house yesterday, and he had tears in his eyes. He said, 'Carol, honey, I don't see how the Lord could make it any plainer unless He starts writing on the wall. We'll miss Brother Mike, but it looks like the Lord's already sent us the one who's right for our church.' I told him that was almost word-for-word what Linda said to me after church. Daddy said he figured Linda was already chewing on Wayne's ear, said he'd talk to Joe, Arthur, and Wallace between now and Wednesday night. Bless their hearts, Meg and Jess buttonholed Daddy and Wallace at church and told them that they want Preacher Simmons to be our new pastor. Do you think she'd take Clear Springs?"

"I know she would."

"In that case, we need to work fast. It'd be great if she could start the Sunday after you leave. Wallace called and told me that the church in Georgia called you and you'd be resigning this Sunday. It'd be good, after your resignation, if the deacons could present a statement of appreciation for your ministry, say that we believe God's already led us to the one who should be our next pastor, and announce that we'll vote the following Sunday on calling Heather. You think you could come down early Wednesday night, about 6:00, if the other deacons agree?"

"Sure, as far as I know."

"Good. Now go on and get some sleep before you have to go into work," Carol said in her most motherly tone of voice. "I'll call Wallace and the others, and if they're in agreement, I'll call Heather to see if she can come. I'll call Karen back and leave word for you as to what we're doing. You just say a prayer and go to bed."

Karen was also reminding Mike that he needed to get some sleep before time to go to work. It was about seven o'clock when he finally stretched out on the bed. He should have slept from exhaustion, but there was too much adrenaline circulating. His mind was racing, and it took him a good hour and a half to go to sleep. He heard Karen answer the phone. Glancing over at the clock radio, he noted the time was 7:45. He heard enough of Karen's end of the conversation to know that it was Carol calling to tell him that the meeting was on for Wednesday night.

∗   ∗   ∗   ∗   ∗   ∗   ∗   ∗   ∗   ∗   ∗   ∗

Arthur Sessions' body was painfully knotted up with rheumatoid arthritis, he was nearly blind, and his wife had been disabled by a stroke, so he didn't get out much. Nonetheless, the other deacons kept him informed and sought his input on anything of significance. When Carol called him about the meeting with Heather, he told her that he was in favor of calling her, and he said he wanted to come to the meeting if somebody would stay with Maude. Joan Ayers and the Richardson girls stayed with Maude, and Russ took Arthur to the meeting. At Megan and Jessica's suggestion, Maude and Joan joined them in praying for the meeting in progress. Joan later observed that the girls didn't stop with talking to Russ and Wallace.

After Linda opened the meeting with prayer, Wallace asked all the deacons to introduce themselves to help Heather get names and faces matched up. Then he said, "Preacher Simmons, I've been a member of this church since 1926 and a deacon since 1938. I've known every pastor we've had in the past sixty-four years, and I've gotten along fine with all of them. I got along so well with ol' Gordon Corrie, he married my daughter just to have me as his father-in-law. Got along so well with Brother Mike that his daughter named her dog after me. So, if you become our pastor, I expect to get along fine with you, too. This church has been served by seminary students for over a hundred years, and we've never run off a preacher in the sixty-four years I've been here. The Lord showed me a long time ago that part of the purpose of this little church was to help young preachers get started right. I don't know how long it'll be 'fore the Lord calls me on home. I'm eighty-six, so I don't expect it to be a whole lot longer, but as long as I'm here, I'm here to help you and work with you the best I can. I don't speak for anybody but Wallace Coggins, but I think you'd make us a fine pastor."

"The only problem I saw," Linda Trimble began, "has been taken care of. Wes commented to me after the first time you preached here that he'd never noticed how tall our pulpit is! We could barely see your head above the pulpit. So, when we heard you were going to preach here again, Wes came down here with Ed Halstead and built that little platform to raise you up about six inches."

The laughter about the platform put Heather more at ease. "That platform really did help, and I didn't know who to thank for it. That big old pulpit wasn't built for somebody 5' 1"."

"And I guess y'all noticed Ed was in church Sunday with Barbara and the kids," Wayne Ethridge added. "Ed's my son-in-law, Heather. It's gonna take you a while to learn all the family connections..."

"Amen," Mike quipped, "I'm still learning."

"Me too," Linda added. "I'm kin to myself three different ways."

"Anyway," Wayne continued, "Ed's a good ol' boy who needs to know the Lord. Couldn't ask for anybody to be nicer. He's good to my daughter and their children. He knows how to do a little bit of everything, plumbing, electrical, carpentry, you name it. He's the first one to help anytime we need something done down here at the church, and he won't take a dime."

"He came to my house Christmas morning to fix a busted water pipe," Arthur added, "and he wouldn't let me pay him anything. Said he was glad to help us."

"Doesn't surprise me," Wayne noted. "That's just the way he is. He just never was brought up to go to church. But, like I was saying, he was here with his family Sunday, and I couldn't help but notice he was paying close attention to the sermon. He told me after church that he was glad he came, said he got a lot out of the sermon. Only thing I'm concerned about, Preacher Simmons, is what're you gonna do, little as you are, when some big ol' boy like Ed gets saved and wants to be baptized."

Heather didn't need to respond to Wayne's point of concern because his daughter Linda, who was sitting next to him, gently touched his hand, looked him in the eye, and said with the most dead-pan serious expression, "Daddy, right there's one of the reasons we let big strong men like you be deacons, too."

When the laughter subsided, Carol added, "You know, Wayne, you did bring up a good point. Brother Mike started the tradition of having deacons help with all the baptisms, and I think it's a good idea. You'll never know how much it meant to me to help baptize Tycina and Jennifer, and it was the happiest day of my life when Brother Mike told me that he wanted me to baptize my daughter Jessica, and he would assist me instead of the other way around. So, Heather, we baptize in Chaney Creek, a real pretty place over on Wayne's farm, unless the weather's too cold. In that case, Bethlehem Baptist Church, about three miles from here, lets us use their baptistry. We always have deacons help with baptizing, so it won't be a problem if you get to baptize Ed Halstead."

"I never thought about it until Brother Mike asked me to help with his first baptismal service," Russ Ayers said, "but it sure meant a lot to me, especially when I helped baptize two of my grandchildren. It meant nearly as much to me as when I was baptized. I'm glad to help with baptism anytime."

"Same here, Preacher," Joe Norris added. "You're welcome to ask ol' Joe here anytime you need help baptizin'. Nothin' I enjoy more."

A silence came over the room as Arthur Sessions spoke up. "You know, at one time I'd a' said 'no' if you asked me about a woman being a deacon or a preacher, 'specially a preacher. At one time, I wouldn't a' been too keen on a woman being a doctor, either. But the Lord opened my eyes, showed me where I was wrong about some things. My daughter had her mind made up from the time she was six years old that she was going to be a doctor, and she made a mighty good one. The church over't Canfield asked her to be a deacon, and I sure couldn't refuse to help ordain my only child. I'm glad I had part in her ordination. She's made one of the best deacons I ever saw. That brings me to you, Preacher Simmons. I didn't get to hear you in person, but Linda brings Maude and me a tape of the service every Sunday, and you preached two good messages. I think you'd make us a fine pastor. Maude and I can't come to church as much as we want to, but we'll pray for you and support you the best we can."

"That's all I could ask for, " Heather responded. "If I become your pastor, I'll look forward to visiting in your home and getting to know your wife. Carol told me that Mrs. Sessions was her first grade teacher and taught her at church, too. Carol said she was a superb teacher, and that she had a lot to do with her decision to become a teacher. I want to get to know her."

"Well, you'd sure be welcome at our place, and I know Maude'd be pleased to meet you. She really put her whole heart into teaching, loved doing it. After she retired, she substituted and tutored children who need extra help 'til that stroke put her in the wheelchair. You could tell how much she loved to teach, and the children could tell it. Anybody could see that the Lord meant for Maude to teach like He meant for birds to fly and fish to swim."

Russ Ayers had mostly sat and listened, his listening skills having served him well through thirty years of working with the farmers of Sanders County as county agent. Russ picked up on what Arthur said and continued his train of thought. "And just like anybody can see the Lord meant for birds to fly, fish to swim, Maude and Carol to teach, and Mary Kate to be a doctor, Brother Mike and Preacher Simmons, I think anybody ought to be able to see that the Lord meant for y'all to be pastors. At one time, I wouldn't've been in favor of a woman pastor, but the Lord's opened my eyes to see some things. Preacher Simmons,…"

"I'd just as soon you call me Heather. I'm not much for titles."

"Heather, er, Sister Heather," Russ continued, "You've preached here twice, and you brought fine messages both times. You wouldn't be able to preach like you do if the Lord hadn't given you the gift. The Lord wouldn't give you the gift and then tell you not to use it. You've been in my home, and you're as down-to-earth as you can be, but what opened my eyes more than anything was seeing the way you connected with those two granddaughters of mine. Carol, I don't know if you know it, but your girls've already cornered me and told me they want Preacher Simmons to be our pastor."

"They cornered me, too," Wallace added.

"Megan and Jessica made quite an impression on me," Heather observed. "Megan especially. Not often you find a twelve year old head-over-heels in love with the Bible like she is. Both girls have a very mature understanding of the Christian faith for their ages. Carol, you and others in this church have taught them well. After the questioning I got from Meg and Jess, my ordination council should be easy."

"Speaking of that," Mike noted, "if the church calls you, and I expect they will, we'll need to call for your ordination. Where is your membership now, Heather?"

"First Baptist in McMillan, Tennessee. I've mostly attended Woodland Park while I've been in seminary because it's close to campus, but my membership's still in the church where I grew up."

"Then as soon as the church votes to call you, we'll contact them and ask them to ordain you."

"Good luck. My home church recommended me to the seminary only because they thought I'd get up here and marry a preacher or go into early childhood education. They figured I'd come to my senses, realize that God meant for me to be a preacher's wife instead of a preacher. I've never been invited to preach there, don't expect to be in this lifetime. When I was sixteen, when John Hathaway was pastor, I went forward on the invitation one night during a youth revival and told Brother Hathaway that God was calling me to preach. He looked bumfuzzled and didn't know what to do or say. He told the church that I was rededicating my life and rushed me back to my seat. Then, he and the evangelist came to our house the next afternoon and told me that God does

not call women to preach. He told my parents I was very confused, and suggested that they get me some counseling. He's not
there now. Kevin Stone's there now. He's more conservative than
Brother Hathaway, got his heart set on being president of the state
convention, maybe even SBC president someday."

"Would that by any chance be the same Kevin Stone who went
to Mid-Atlantic, pastored this church back in the early 70's?"
Wallace asked. "His wife's name was Emily, his daddy was a conductor on the Mobile division."

"Sure sounds like the same one. I never knew he served this
church."

"He sure did. I knew he was somewhere down in Tennessee.
Small world. Get me his phone number and I'll call him in the
morning. Hardest three years of my life when Brother Kevin was
here. Had to go three whole years without making a wisecrack
about the Mobile Division. We used to say Southern Railway
never scrapped obsolete equipment, they just sent it to the south
end of the Mobile division. They had the world's largest operating
railroad museum 'til the diesels came. I had to go three long years
without cracking a joke about it. To make matters worse, my boy
Matt was promoted to road foreman while Brother Kevin was
here, and I had to cut out all the road foreman jokes. It like to've
killed me, worse'n tryin' to quit smoking. Had to go mighty hard
on those limb-dodgers down on the Knoxville Division during
that time."

* * * * * * * * * * * *

It was about 10:30 Thursday morning, and Mike was walking
out the door to go over to the seminary campus when the phone
rang. It was Wallace. "Well, Brother Mike, I talked to Kevin
Stone. He's not the same Kevin Stone who pastored Clear Springs.
He is, but he's not, if you know what I mean."

"Acted like he never knew you?"

"Yep. All the times him'n his wife and kids ate dinner at our house, and all the good times we had shootin' the bull about Southern Railway. He baptized three of my grandkids. I remember when he first come to Clear Springs, he was driving a '56 Ford with four bald slick tires, front ones wore down to the cord, you could nearly see the air in 'em. I was afraid he was gonna get killed, kill his wife and kids, or kill somebody else drivin' that car like that. I handed him my Sears charge card, told him to take that car to Sears and Roebuck, put four new tires on it. I didn't mind one bit, still glad I did it, thankful Estelle and I could afford to do it. But I don't reckon any of that counts for anything. Like to've never talked my way past his secretary. I asked to speak to Brother Kevin, and she said she'd see if *Dr. Stone* was available to speak with me. When I finally got through to him, he acted like he couldn't wait to get rid of me, 'specially when I told him why I was calling. He said Heather's a fine young lady, but she's sadly mistaken if she thinks God wants her to be a pastor. Said the SBC spoke to that issue very clearly a few years ago, and no woman'd be ordained at First Baptist in McMillan, Tennessee while he was pastor."

"So what'd you tell him, Wallace?"

"I told him I thought it was the church's place to decide things like that, and he said, 'no, it's my place as God's appointed ruler of the church. The church is not a democracy,' he said. So, I told him he needs to take the word *Baptist* off'n the church sign. I told him we sure didn't want to stand in the way of him gettin' to be president of the convention. I apologized for bothering him, told him I knew his choir was bigger'n our whole church, but our little church could ordain a preacher as good as his big church could."

"I'll get word to Heather. The way she talked last night, I don't think she'll be disappointed."

Wallace told Mike that it sounded that way to him, too. "That's one thing that's really impressed me about this young lady. She's only been down here three times, and you can tell she loves us with all her heart. I expect she'd rather be ordained at Clear Springs, and it'll do our church good to get to ordain a preacher. If Clear Springs has ever ordained a preacher, it was before my time." Wallace, who had been at Clear Springs since 1926, loved to tell tall tales about how far back he could remember. He once had Asalee believing he could remember back before they put the river through Riverton. It had hurt him to be snubbed by Dr. Stone, formerly known as Brother Kevin. More than the personal affront, it hurt him for Clear Springs Baptist Church to be slighted. The hurt was assuaged by the excitement he felt over the anticipated ordination of Heather Simmons at Clear Springs.

6

One good thing about Mike's night job was that he usually had a few hours during the night when the front desk was not busy. The manager had no objection to him bringing work in to occupy himself during the hours that the job required little more than being present and awake. Mike used the time for sermon preparation, reading, and study. On this night, he allotted the dead time to writing the most difficult thing he had ever had to write, his resignation as pastor of Clear Springs Baptist Church. Five or six attempts ended up in the wastebasket before put together the version that read,

April 29,1990

Dear Church Family,

It is with much sadness that I submit my resignation as pastor of Clear Springs Baptist Church in order to accept the call to become pastor of Harrington Baptist Church in Harrington, Georgia. My resignation will be effective at the conclusion of the service on May 27,1990, and I will begin my ministry at Harrington on June 3.

Karen, Asalee, and I thank you for two of the most blessed years of our lives. I have often heard Brother Wallace Coggins say that part of the reason the Lord put this church here was to help young preachers get started right. You have certainly done that for me.

When I came here, I had preached a total of seven times. I had never officiated at a baptism, Lord's Supper observance, wedding, or funeral. Not only was I new to the ministry, I was a relatively new Christian. If I have been a good pastor to you, it is because I have been greatly helped by your love, prayers, encouragement, and cooperation.

Pray for us as we pray for you. May God continue to bless and multiply the ministry of Clear Springs Baptist Church until Jesus comes again.

In Christ,
Michael Grady Westover

He proofread it one last time, placed it in an envelope addressed to church clerk Sharon Chambers, and put it in his briefcase.

* * * * * * * * * * * *

Wallace was right. Heather had not gotten her hopes up that First Baptist in McMillan would ordain her. She was elated, not only at the prospect of being ordained, but at the prospect of being ordained by Clear Springs. When the deacons met again Wednesday night, Wallace told them what Dr. Stone—formerly known as Brother Kevin—had said. Mike told them that Heather said she would rather be ordained at Clear Springs anyway. Russ said Maude Sessions told him that Clear Springs had ordained two ministers, Lemuel Dixon in 1859 and Josiah Hunter in 1874. The deacons agreed it was high time they ordained another one.

Wallace appointed Carol to write a letter on behalf of the deacons, expressing appreciation for Mike's ministry, to be read following Mike's resignation on Sunday. Wallace said that he would present the recommendation that the church vote the following Sunday on calling Heather Simmons and ordaining her to the ministry.

Linda suggested that Mike invite Heather to preach on the Sunday of the vote, and since that would be communion Sunday, that Mike and Heather jointly officiate at the communion service. Mike asked the deacons if they thought Sunday afternoon May 27, his last day, would be a good time to ordain Heather and install her as pastor. They all agreed, provided the date would work for her. Upon returning home that night, Mike called Heather to confirm the date.

*   *   *   *   *   *   *   *   *   *   *   *

Asalee crawled up in Karen's lap and said "Mommy, hold me" when Mike unfolded the letter of resignation after he finished the welcome and announcements. As he began to read it, Asalee held tightly to her doll named Estelle. Karen pulled Asalee close to herself, cradling Asalee's head between her breasts the way she had often done when Asalee was much younger. Barely six years old and on the small side for her age, Asalee still liked to be held and cuddled. As Karen gently rubbed her back, Asalee closed her eyes, rested in her mother's comforting embrace, and tried to ignore everything but the familiar sound of her mother's heartbeat. Sitting between Wallace Coggins and Marie Jernigan, with Marie gently holding her free hand, Karen felt a comfort not unlike the comfort she was giving her daughter.

Fourteen years in the classroom at Sanders County High School, and about that many years teaching ninth through twelfth grades in Sunday School, had made Carol comfortable talking in front of people, but on this occasion her voice was breaking with emotion. "Wallace asked me to make this presentation on behalf of the deacons," she began. "He said, 'You're real good with words, Carol.' Most of the time I am, but these words I am presenting on behalf of the deacons were very hard for me to put together. Pray for me, and bear with me. I cried as I wrote them, and I will cry as I try to deliver them. First, I present this letter from the deacons of Clear Springs Baptist Church to the deacons of Harrington Baptist Church:

Dear Colleagues,

We commend to you our pastor, Brother Michael Grady Westover, who has recently accepted the call to become the pastor of your church. He, his wife Karen, and their daughter Asalee have been with us for two very blessed years. We have gotten close to them, and it is hard to let them go.

Because we are a small church near Mid-Atlantic Baptist Theological Seminary, we have traditionally been served by student pastors. Brother Mike is the forty-second seminary student to serve this church. Getting young ministers off to a good start is an important part of our mission. We would like to keep the Westovers forever, but that would be selfish. We send them to you with our blessing and the prayer that they will be as good for you as they have been for us.

Brother Mike is a man of unimpeachable integrity, a faithful preacher of the word of God, and a devoted pastor. Karen is a delightful person of many talents whose musicianship, teaching ability, computer skills, and ability to relate to all kinds of people have greatly strengthened this church. Asalee is a bright, playful, energetic child whose presence here will be missed greatly. We do not know what God has in mind for her, but we know that it will be good.

We pray that Brother Mike's ministry at Harrington will be long and fruitful, and that your association with the Westovers will be as blessed as ours has been.

The Deacons of Clear Springs Baptist Church

"This letter" Carol continued, "is signed by each of our deacons: Wallace Coggins, chairman, Carol Richardson, secretary, Russell Ayers, Wayne Ethridge, Joe Norris, Arthur Sessions, and Linda Trimble."

Carol paused to sip some water and dab the tears from her eyes before she continued. "Bear with me. This is hard. I wouldn't be standing up here, and I wouldn't be serving as a deacon had it not been for Brother Mike. While the Southern Baptist Convention has sought to limit the ministry of women, our pastor has affirmed the spiritual gifts of all of us, men and women alike. Most Baptist churches exclude both women and divorced people from deacon ministry. When you asked me, a divorced woman, to be a deacon, I was taken aback. Brother Mike's encouragement was one of the ways in which the Lord led me to say 'yes,' and I'm glad I did. Serving as a deacon has been one of the richest blessings to ever come my way."

"During Brother Mike's time with us," Carol continued, "Clear Springs has experienced both joy and sorrow. Seeing people saved, and seeing saved people grow toward maturity in Christ has been the greatest joy. If I live to be a hundred, I'll never forget that incredible unplanned baptism of Wes and Nathan Trimble. The accident that killed Jim Echols and Kimberly Ethridge was the most devastating thing this church has experienced in my lifetime. It would be a hard thing for any church, but it was especially hard for a small church with intricate family ties. Kim's mother is my cousin. So is the drunk driver who killed her and Jim. Yet, we saw God do some beautiful things in the midst of that horrible tragedy. The donation of Kim's organs extended life or restored sight for a number of people. Jennifer, Tycina, Tyrone, and Marie became a part of our church family. Brother Mike Westover and Clear Springs Baptist Church made a powerful impression on the students, faculty, and administration of Sanders County High School. Through joy and sorrow, Brother Mike, you've been there, walking with us, ministering to us. I'll never forget your ministry during my recent bout with cancer. You gave me the most blessed gift when you let me baptize my daughter Jessica, and you assisted me instead of the other way around.

"I was ten years old when Brother Steve Kane baptized me at the same place we baptized Jessica," Carol continued. "I knew what I was doing even at that age. I've known the Lord as a real presence in my life as far back as I can remember, but I know the Lord better than I did because of Brother Mike's ministry and the challenges that he has put before me. I speak for the deacons, but I also speak for myself and my family when I say, Mike, Karen, and Asalee, we love you, we'll miss you, and we pray God's best for you."

"Even in leaving us," Carol concluded, "Brother Mike, you've shown concern for the future well-being of this church by introducing us to Sister Heather Simmons. At this time, I am going to ask our chairman of deacons, Brother Wallace Coggins, to present three recommendations from the deacons. Brother Wallace..." Carol sat down next to her children on the pew behind Karen and reached over to hug her as Wallace came up to the pulpit.

"Preacher Simmons has made quite an impression on me," Wallace began. "She's only been down here three times, twice to preach and once to meet with the deacons, and you can already tell she loves us with all her heart. Brother Mike invited her to preach the first Sunday he was away, not knowing how a woman preacher would be received. If there's anything negative to be heard, I'm usually the first to hear it, and I didn't hear anything negative. Sister Heather's a powerful preacher. Many of you have spoken to me at church or called me at home to tell me you think she'd make us a fine pastor, and I agree with you. I'll tell you what impressed me more'n anything. Megan and Jessica Richardson talked to me and told me how much Preacher Simmons had already meant to them and told me that they want her to be our next pastor. When nine and twelve year old children care enough about something to sit down with me and tell me what they think, I sit up and take notice.

"The deacons met with Preacher Simmons Wednesday night," Wallace continued. "Megan and Jessica, along with their grandmother, stayed with Maude Sessions so Arthur could come to the meeting. Arthur could've just sent word that he was in favor of calling Preacher Simmons, but he wanted to be there and meet with her. He's crippled up so bad with that rheumatoid arthritis that Brother Russ had to put his arms around him and pick him up to put him in the van. While we were meeting with Preacher Simmons, Megan and Jessica told Joan and Maude they wanted to have a prayer meeting. Those girls didn't stop with talking to the deacons!"

"At the deacons meeting," Wallace concluded, "we agreed that Preacher Simmons would make us a fine pastor, and we don't see how the Lord could make His will much plainer. Our bylaws say that a vote on calling a pastor has to be announced a week ahead of time. The deacons are unanimous in making the following three recommendations to be voted on next Sunday at the conclusion of the 11:00 service:

1. That Clear Springs Baptist Church call Sister Heather Clarice Simmons as pastor, with her duties to begin on Sunday, June 3, 1990.

2. That our pastor be authorized to call an ordination council for Sister Simmons at 6:00 PM on Saturday May 26, 1990.

3. That Clear Springs Baptist Church ordain Sister Heather Clarice Simmons to the Gospel Ministry and install her as our pastor on Sunday afternoon May 27, 1990.

Preacher Simmons will be with us again next Sunday for the benefit of any who have not had an opportunity to hear her. The deacons encourage all members of Clear Springs Baptist Church to be present and vote next Sunday. Carol's already made the presentation on behalf of the deacons. She's a lot better with words than I am, and she's better at gettin' up and talkin' in front of people. I'm just gonna say, as chairman of deacons, Brother Mike, it's been a pleasure to work with you. I'll miss you and Karen, and I'm sure enough gonna miss Asalee. I'll never forget how y'all holp me when Estelle died. I love you all and wish you the best. You'll always have a place in my home, my heart, and my prayers." As he spoke, Wallace motioned for Karen and Asalee to come up to the pulpit. With tears running down his face, he embraced all three Westovers and repeated, "I love you. I always will. God bless you."

* * * * * * * * * * * *

The auditorium was packed the following Sunday, and the church voted unanimously to call Heather Simmons as pastor. Arthur and Maude were having a better than usual day, and they called Russ to ask him to bring them to church. Russ took Wes Trimble with him, and they left during Sunday School to go get them. They arrived about fifteen minutes early for the worship service, so Heather was able to meet Maude and talk with her and Arthur before the service started. She hugged them and thanked them for making the special effort to be there.

There was a jubilant spirit in the church when Wallace announced the result of the balloting, sixty-three in favor, none opposed, none abstained. After he announced the outcome, Joan Ayers stood up and said that there would be dinner on the grounds May 27. "We need to show our new pastor how this church does dinner on the grounds. All of us need to bring a plenty. We'll have a lot of visitors, and we need to be prepared."

Heather rode down to Clear Springs with Mike, Karen, and Asalee that day. It was a little after 1:00 before they got away from Clear Springs, and they had an invitation to the home of Gordon and Evelyn Corrie for Sunday dinner. Mike and his family had been to the Corries' home a number of times during his tenure at Clear Springs, and Wallace had a standing invitation. Wallace had traded his old Chevy Citation in on a new Chevrolet S-10 pickup the day before, and he wanted to show it off to Gordon and Evelyn. Asalee rode with Wallace in the truck, and Mike, Karen, and Heather followed them in the car over to the Corries.

Gordon and Evelyn Corrie live about halfway between Ledford and Riverton in an elegant late nineteenth century farmhouse they renovated. The son of a master cabinetmaker, Dr. Corrie grew up around his father's shop. He and Evelyn had done most of the work on the house themselves, and it had been featured in *Southern Living*.

Evelyn, like her mother before her, enjoyed growing flowers. After Estelle died, she promised Wallace that she would take care of her mother's cherished rose bushes and flower beds. Evelyn had set out tulip bulbs at her house and at Wallace's, and brilliant red and yellow tulips were in full bloom at both places.

Gordon and Evelyn had also renovated the carriage house behind their home as a guest house. Ever since Estelle died, Evelyn had been after Wallace to give up his place and move into the guest house. Wallace thanked her kindly but declined the offer. He said that there were so many memories stored up in his old house and so many of Estelle's touches that it would be hard for him to live anywhere else. He explained that Estelle came to see him in his dreams every night, and he just slept better in the house and bed they had shared since they built their house in 1934. Evelyn told him that she was afraid they were going to find him dead down there one of these days. He told her that, given the fact that he was eighty-six years old, it was likely somebody would find him dead before too many more years, and if it was all the same to everybody else he'd just as soon be found at his own place. He told his daughter that dying was the least of his worries, and that he'd been telling the Lord ever since Estelle died that he would be content to go any time. The last time Evelyn started in on him about moving into the guest house, he sat her down and said, "Evie, I love you and Gordon and appreciate your kindness, but I don't want to hear another word about that guest house unless I get down where I can't do for myself. Right now, the only thing I can't do for myself is grow flowers, never could do that, so I appreciate you taking care of Mama's rose bushes and flower beds, and I do 'preciate Matt and Sarah Beth's boys keepin' the grass cut for me. Now if you find me dead down at my house, it'll be all right. I'm saved and ready to go. Evie, I've done lived so long some of my friends in Heaven prob'ly think I didn't make it. Now leave me alone about movin', and go easy on the lamentations when I die. When you find me dead, just call Billy Gresham down at Gresham Brothers Funeral Home and tell 'im to come get me. Everything's paid for. Give me a Christian funeral at Clear Springs Baptist Church and bury me next to the only woman I ever loved." Evelyn had not mentioned the guest house to him since.

* * * * * * * * * * *

"Evelyn, I want you to meet one of my students, Heather Simmons," Gordon Corrie said as he introduced Heather to his wife.

Evelyn hugged Heather. "Welcome to our home, Heather. I hope this is only the first of many times you'll be with us. All of you are smiling, so it looks like things went well."

"Oh yes, very well!" Heather replied.

"Unanimous," Wallace added. "Good crowd, not one vote against her."

"Well, congratulations, Heather!" Gordon Corrie said. "I guess you've heard by now that I pastored Clear Springs when I was a student. I was there from '48 to '51."

"Mike told me, and he said you've been interim several times over the years."

"Yes, I have, and all the good things you've heard about the church are true. I know it's hard to believe any church can be *that* good, but Clear Springs really is. I had a good experience there, and I've known the church forty-two years. We know everybody there, and we get down there from time to time. Of course, Evelyn's kin to half the church."

"I really am," Evelyn laughed. "Gordon's not exaggerating. My mother was an Ethridge. Wayne's my cousin. His daddy, Uncle Charlie, was Mama's brother. Grandma Ethridge was an Ayers."

"Yeah," Wallace quipped, "Linda Gail Ethridge, married Wes Trimble, says she's kin to herself three different ways."

"And I could tell her two or three more she doesn't know about," Evelyn added. "Come on in the dining room. I was just getting dinner on the table when y'all drove up."

Dr. Corrie returned thanks and then, in the same breath with which he said "Amen," continued the conversation with Heather, "So where are you originally from, Heather?"

"McMillan, Tennessee."

"Down on the Memphis Division," Wallace added. "Now I can't make wisecracks about the Memphis Division."

"If Southern Railway goes through a town, Daddy knows about it," Evelyn laughed.

"I know where McMillan is," Gordon said. "Preached a revival down there, must've been in the late 50's or early 60's, before your time, Heather, at First Baptist in McMillan."

"That's my home church," Heather replied. "Mother grew up in the church, so she was there at the time. My father's from Nashville. They married in '62, and I was born in '66."

"You're making me feel old as Methuselah," Gordon laughed. "One of my students, Ray Holman, was there back then. Who's there now?"

"Dr. Holman married my parents. Kevin Stone's there now. I don't know him all that well. He came about the time I went away to college."

"I knew him. He was at Mid-Atlantic in the early 70's, pastored Clear Springs. I'd lost track of him, didn't know where he was."

"I called him about requesting Sister Heather's ordination," Wallace picked up the thread of conversation. "Like to've never talked my way past his secretary, acted like he didn't have the time of day for me, worse'n a general superintendent on the railroad. When I told 'im what I was calling about, he said Heather was a fine young lady, but she's certainly confused if she thinks God's called her to be a pastor. He said no woman'd be ordained at First Baptist in McMillan, Tennessee while he was pastor."

"Oh boy, this is gonna be good," Dr. Corrie cackled. "What'd you tell him, Papa?"

"I asked him, 'shouldn't that be the church's decision?' and he said, 'No, it's my decision as the divinely appointed ruler of the church. The church is not a democracy,' so I told 'im he needed to take the word *Baptist* off'n the church sign. I told 'im I realized his choir was bigger'n our whole church, but our little church could ordain a preacher as good as his big church could. I told 'im we didn't think Sister Heather was the least bit confused, that she seemed pretty clear-headed to us. I apologized for bothering the great Dr. Stone and promised to never do it again."

"*Doctor* Stone my foot!" Gordon Corrie hooted. "A lot of those boys're more interested in having 'Doctor' in front of their names than they are in getting a legitimate degree and learning a little bit in the process."

"I read his bio when he was called to McMillan," Heather commented. "His doctorate's from Gulf Coast Institute of Theology. I think that's the name of the school. I'd never heard of it."

"And for good reason," Dr. Corrie explained. "Nothing but a post office box and a rented office suite somewhere down in Florida. Lots of those boys get their doctorates there. Kevin Stone's not all that conservative unless he's changed a lot since I knew him. Sounds like he's just ambitious, probably got his heart set on being state convention president."

"I think you're right," Wallace commented. "He was all right when he was at Clear Springs, good preacher, church did all right while he was with us. Anyway, we don't need his help. We're going to ordain Sister Heather at Clear Springs. It's been 116 years since we ordained a preacher, so it's high time we ordained another one. That ol' boy we ordained in 1874's gettin' some age on him."

"Dr. Corrie," Heather began, "I'd be honored if you'd be on my ordination council and participate in my ordination."

"It'd be my pleasure. Dr. Sturgill won't be pleased, but I'm sixty-four years old, so I don't have a whole lot to lose."

Karen spoke up. "Heather told us on the way over here that a whole bunch of people are coming up from Tennessee for her ordination."

"Eighteen the last I heard," Heather reported. "I called Mom and Dad. I knew they'd want to come, and my sister, and my brother and his wife and their two children—I knew they'd all come. That's seven right there. My grandmother's eighty-two, not in the best of health, so I wouldn't've thought about her coming, but she said she wouldn't miss it. That makes eight. When Dad told the other deacons that Dr. Stone refused to present the request for my ordination to the deacons, they were not happy. Four deacons and their wives are coming, so Dr. Stone may have a mutiny on his hands. Two of my closest friends all the way back to first grade are coming. Dad's driving his van, and Lance Robison's driving his motor home."

"That certainly speaks well of you, Heather, that so many people would want to come up here for your ordination," Evelyn commented.

"Thank you, but I think it says more about the church than it does about me. The church is not as conservative as Dr. Stone would have you think, at least not the whole church. We've just had some pastors who were more conservative than the church. John Hathaway was there all through my middle school and high school years, and I was a thorn in his side. Testimony time—I've known I was going to be a pastor as far back as I can remember anything, though I learned early on not to say that's what I was going to be because people were quick to tell me that girls can't grow up to be pastors. I was baptized when I was eight, and I knew even then I was going to be a pastor. When I was in the tenth grade, we had a big youth revival, some hot-shot evangelist they brought in. One night when the invitation was given, I went forward and told Dr. Hathaway the Lord was calling me to preach. As we'd say down in west Tennessee, I might near stopped his clock. All the color drained out of his face. He turned white as a sheet, looked like he was going to die and go on to glory, told the church I was rededicating my life and rushed me back to my seat. Dr. Hathaway and the evangelist came the next afternoon to talk to me and my parents. They told me they were sure I meant well, but God does not call women to preach. They told my parents I was very confused and suggested they get me into counseling."

"How'd you handle that?" Dr. Corrie asked.

"My parents and my grandmother were wonderful. They told me, if God was calling me, God would make a way. I still took it pretty hard, though. I cried myself sick for a couple of days. I felt devastated. I didn't go to any more revival services. When Sunday morning came, I told my parents I didn't feel like going to church, and they didn't push me. They just went on and left me at home.

After they were gone, I was lying in bed, crying, feeling sorry for myself. The Lord spoke to me as clearly as He ever has and said, "Heather, you're my child, and you know my voice. Are you going to listen to the people who laughed at you when you were a little girl and you said you were going to be a preacher? Are you going to listen to Dr. Hathaway and that evangelist he brought in? Or are you going to listen to Me?" I decided I was going to listen to God, and God gave me some people who believed me, took me seriously, and supported me—basically this group of eighteen people coming up for the ordination service."

Asalee had been listening with rapt attention to Heather's every word. "Preacher Heather! Preacher Heather!" she piped up. Her animated gestures looked as though she was trying to flag a train.

"Yes, Asalee, I'm sorry we've been doing all the talking and haven't let you get a word in edgewise. You look like you want to ask me something important."

"Preacher Heather," Asalee asked in her most grown-up voice, "Did you know any women preachers when you were a little girl?"

"No, I didn't, Asalee. I thought I was going to be the first one. The first woman preacher I ever met was when I was in college. Her name was Olivia Harris. When I was in college, I'd go home on weekends, go to church with my family, and leave after dinner to go back to Pendleton where I was in school. I'd usually get into Pendleton about 4:00 Sunday afternoon. One Sunday as I was coming into Pendleton, the Lord spoke to me and told me to turn down that next little side street, and I did. It was a narrow little street that went through a really rough, poor section of Pendleton that people called Birdtown because all the streets were named for various kinds of birds. There were run-down narrow little houses on both sides of the street, broken down cars up on blocks in some of the driveways. Most of the houses looked like they hadn't seen a paintbrush in years. All of a sudden, I came upon one of those old houses that was freshly painted, white with bright blue trim. The ground around it was spotless, and there were flowers planted along the sidewalk and around the front porch. I got closer and saw that somebody had built a little steeple on top of it, with a home-made wooden cross. Up over the porch, there was a sign that said *Bluejay Street Baptist Church*. I stopped and got out of my car. I saw another sign on the wall beside the front door with a schedule of services. Down at the bottom, it said *Olivia Harris, Pastor*. I stood there for the longest, looking at that sign, tears running down my face."

"How come you were crying, Preacher Heather?" Asalee asked with a puzzled expression.

"Oh, I wasn't sad, Az, I was happy. Sometimes people cry because they're happy. It was a happy kind of crying. I kept reading that sign over and over, telling myself I'd never heard of a man named Olivia, and I knew why the Lord told me to turn down that street. There was an evening service at 6:00. I looked at my watch, and it was 4:30. I drove on to the dorm, unpacked my car, freshened up, got dressed for church, and drove back over there. My heart was pounding. I didn't know what to expect. I just knew it was a Baptist church, the pastor was a woman, and I had to meet her and hear her preach. There were about twenty people there that night, and they made me feel so welcome. It was the first time I'd seen black and white people in church together. Olivia looked like the grandmother in a Norman Rockwell painting. The covers of her Bible were held together with duct tape. I thought I'd just slip in, sit on the back row, observe, and slip out after the benediction, but Olivia came over and introduced herself to me before the service began. She said their pianist was sick and asked me if there was any chance I could play the piano. I told her I wasn't the best, but I could play hymns, so I played the piano for them. I was so excited when Olivia came up to the pulpit, opened her Bible, and started to preach. She was a good preacher, brought an excellent message that night."

"This was in Pendleton, Tennessee?" Dr. Corrie asked incredulously. "Tell me about this woman."

"Well, I found out she hadn't been preaching long, just a few years. She told me that she first felt the Lord calling her to preach back in the '40's, right after the war, when she was a young mother with two small children. She didn't publicly acknowledge her calling until after her husband died. She'd been active in another Baptist church in Pendleton, taught Sunday School, sang in the choir, served as WMU president. The church didn't know what to do when she said God was calling her to preach. The church and her family acted like she'd gone off the deep end. She knew no church was going to let her preach, let alone call her as pastor. It occured to her that nobody has an exclusive right to the Baptist name, so she went into Birdtown and started a church. She'd driven a school bus for thirty years, and her route went all through that community, so she knew all the children and their families. There was no church in that community, and nobody was in a big hurry to start one. Olivia knew the man who owned about forty of those old shotgun houses that he rented out. He was a member of the church Olivia left. She went to his real estate office and told him she wanted to rent one of those houses. She must've laid a guilt trip on him big time, because he rented the house to her for a dollar a year. All though college, I went to church with my family on Sunday morning and rushed over to Pendleton to go to Olivia's church on Sunday night. I preached my first sermon at Bluejay Street. My last year in college, Olivia started having some health problems, and I filled in for her a lot. She died about a week before I moved up here to go to seminary, and I conducted her funeral. We had to have the service at the church Olivia left, because no other church in town was big enough to hold the crowd."

"Wow! She really had an impact on you, didn't she?" Karen observed.

"Yes, she did. Amazing woman. When she was sixteen, she had to quit school and go to work in the cotton mill to help support her family. She got married at seventeen and had three children by the time she was twenty-one. She got her GED at sixty-four and took classes at the community college until a couple of months before she died. Her church wasn't affiliated with any association or convention. If anybody asked her what kind of Baptist she and her little church were, she'd always say, 'just plain old Baptist.' I used to tease her and tell her that we needed to put that on the sign, *Bluejay Street Just Plain Old Baptist Church.* Olivia was never ordained—'at least not by human hands,' she would say—and she liked to point out that Spurgeon and Moody were never ordained either. I started to say I wish she could be at my ordination, but she *will* be there. She was there this morning. I could feel her presence. I'll always be thankful that God brought her into my life."

"And I'm thankful you told us about her," Dr. Corrie commented.

"Is Preacher Olivia with Jesus up in Heaven?" Asalee asked.

"Yes, Az, that's where she is."

"Neat! That's where Mama Stell is. I bet they know each other," Asalee stated matter-of-factly. It delighted her to think of Heather's friend and her friend being together. She knew Mama Stell would really like Preacher Olivia.

"Asalee's talking about my wife and Evelyn's mother," Wallace explained to Heather. "Estelle died about three months ago. When Asalee was little, she had a hard time saying 'Estelle,' so Estelle became 'Mama Stell' to her." Turning to Asalee, Wallace continued, "I guarantee you Preacher Olivia and Mama Stell know each other."

Evelyn was laughing, and Gordon asked her what was so funny. "I was just thinking about Mama and how strong willed she was," Evelyn answered. "She and Olivia would be a matched pair. Heather, I guarantee you both of them are in on this."

"Well, you know that line in Samuel Stone's hymn," Dr. Corrie observed, "Yet she on earth hath union with God the three in one, and blissful sweet communion with those whose rest is won..."

"We sang it this morning," Karen said.

7

allace was elated when he learned about all the people coming up from Tennessee for Heather's ordination. Before they left Gordon and Evelyn's, he asked Heather to write down a list of the people she was expecting, and he told her to get word to them not to make motel reservations. Wallace began making phone calls when he got home. Joan Ayers was the first one he called, and she helped him make some more calls. By Wednesday night, there were places for all of the Tennessee bunch. Carol signed up for a houseful—Heather's sister Laura and friends Chrissie and Susan—and then invited Heather down to spend the night as well. Joan and Russ Ayers volunteered to take Heather's grandmother. Matt and Sarah Beth Coggins said that David and April Simmons and their two boys could stay at their place. Barbara Halstead said that she and Ed would be glad for somebody to stay with them, so Joan signed them up for Bill and Wanda Holt. Wayne and June Ethridge signed up to host Lance and Betty Robinson since they had room to park the motor home at their farm. Marie Jernigan signed up for Jack and Ruth Harper. Linda Gail and Wes Trimble said they would take in John and Becky Tant. Wallace said he wanted Heather's parents to stay with him.

Mike went to the Baptist Book Store on Friday with to pick up a blank ordination certificate. He looked at the standard Broadman Press certificate used at his ordination in 1988 at Woodland Park, as well as several other options, but he was not satisfied with anything he found. Most of them were awash in a sea of masculine pronouns. None had room for the signatures of all the people they expected for the ordination council. Mike found the Bible Heather wanted, charged it to the church's book store account, and left it with instructions for it to be imprinted with Heather's name. The bookstore clerk, a young male seminary student, grimaced as he wrote down the imprinting instructions, *Rev. Heather Clarice Simmons*. Mike recognized him as one of those who had shouted fervent "amens" to Sturgill's recent chapel tirade against women preachers.

When Mike told Karen about the ordination certificate dilemma, she told him to go by the office supply store and get a couple of sheets of blank parchment, and to tell her what to put on the certificate. "That's why God made computers with desktop publishing programs," she explained. The next evening, Mike brought her the parchment and gave her the wording for the certificate. After supper, Karen sat down at her computer. Five minutes later, she handed Mike a first draft on plain computer paper. Even on the plain paper, it was beautiful, with Karen's carefully chosen type fonts duplicating the efforts of a master calligrapher.

Mike noted that Karen had made space for thirty signatures. "This'll be really nice when it's framed," he commented as she fed the parchment into the printer to produce the final version. "I saw Dr. Corrie today. He told me he'd take the certificate home with him after everybody signed it, said he'd bring it back on Sunday matted, framed, and ready for presentation. He had some cherry left over from building the dining room suite. He's already run the pieces on his shaper, cut them, and made the frame, said all he lacked was getting the glass cut. I thanked him for going to all that trouble. He said it was his pleasure, said he'd been telling himself for the last fifteen years that he'd eventually find some better use than firewood for that little bit of leftover cherry. He promised to make it pretty."

Sharon Chambers told Mike at church on Sunday that she would take care of the invitations to the ordination council, so Mike gave her the list of people to invite in addition to the deacons of Clear Springs. The list included Mary Kate Sessions, director of missions Jeff Dowridge, all the pastors in the association, minister of education Carolyn Williamson and minister of music John Hobgood from First Baptist in Ledford; Heather's father and the other four deacons coming up from Tennessee; three professors from Mid-Atlantic, Dr. Paul Kerns, Dr. Gordon Corrie, and Dr. Emory Leggs; and former Mid-Atlantic professor Rachel Minkins. Sharon said she would have the invitations done on church letterhead and ready for Mike's signature Sunday morning. Asalee would get to lick envelopes and stamps again. Licking envelopes and stamps was a minor role in the scheme of things, but Asalee would be pleased to have at least that small part in ordaining Preacher Heather.

*   *   *   *   *   *   *   *   *   *   *   *

Even though she knew Rachel Minkins would not be able to come to her ordination, it had nonetheless been important to Heather to invite her. Heather had never been in one of her classes, and their lives had overlapped by only one semester, but she would never forget her.

Heather was one of four remaining women in the Master of Divinity program at Mid-Atlantic. Only a few years before, as recently as the mid-'80's, the seminary had attracted dozens of young women preparing for ministry vocations. When Heather began corresponding with seminaries during her sophomore year at Graves College, Mid-Atlantic, under president John Pershing Arnold, was a wonderfully supportive climate for a woman called to ministry. Close to thirty percent of the Master of Divinity students were women. Theology prof Rachel Minkins was one of five outstanding women teaching in the school of theology. Dorothy Grant-Wiggins taught Greek and Biblical backgrounds. Judith Sizemore taught Old Testament and Semitic languages. Hazel Grogan, professor of church history, met Heather when she came up to visit the campus. Dr. Grogan took her out to lunch and gave her a tour of the campus. Nancy Woods Gregerson taught homiletics and worship. Heather sat in on one of her classes and one of Dr. Sizemore's classes. That was in 1986.

Later that year, John Mark Sturgill, hand picked for his loyalty to the fundamentalist political machine and his opposition to women in ministry, had been inaugurated as the eighth president of Mid-Atlantic Seminary, following the sudden death of John Pershing Arnold. Sturgill immediately set out to change everything that had attracted Heather Simmons to Mid-Atlantic.

When Heather arrived on campus in the fall of 1988, all of the women professors except Dr. Minkins were gone, and the number of women theology students had dwindled. No new women theology students had enrolled since the semester Heather enrolled. Rachel Minkins, one of the more popular professors on campus, struggled valiantly to stay on out of loyalty to her students. In November 1988, Sturgill gave Dr. Minkins an ultimatum: resign effective at the end of the semester or face a heresy trial.

The heresy charges were trumped up, but it did not matter. If she had chosen to face a heresy trial, she would have been going up against a hostile trustee board whose members already had their minds made up. As far as Sturgill and the trustees were concerned, the very fact of a woman teaching theology to men was heresy in itself. Dr. Minkins quietly resigned.

Heather remembered that cold, gray Saturday morning, the day after the fall semester ended and Christmas break began. She had taken her last final on Friday morning. That afternoon, she got her car serviced, did a little Christmas shopping, and packed for the trip home. She was about to get on the road when she noticed the Ryder truck backed up to the side door of Leland Hall, the entrance closest to the faculty office suites.

Heather walked over and made her way back through the dim, narrow hallways that faculty and students alike called "the catacombs." The offices that opened off the catacombs were not known by the numbers on the doors or by the names of their present occupants. Instead, they were spoken of in hushed reverential tones as *Dr. Towers' Old Office* or *Dr. Burkhardt's Old Office*. Heather walked back to Dr. Merrifield's Old Office. The door was open, the light was on, and boxes of books were stacked out in the hallway. There she found Dr. Minkins, dressed in a grungy sweatshirt, faded jeans, and an old pair of jogging shoes. She had no makeup on, and her hair was tied back in a pony tail. She was pulling the last of her books off the shelves and boxing them up. As she went through this ritual closing of a chapter in her life, the occasional tear trickled down her face, only to be wiped away with the sleeve of her sweatshirt. Heather hesitated a moment before saying, "Dr. Minkins, it looks like you could use some help."

"Oh, Hi, Heather. I thought I was the only one in the building. Yes, I suppose I could use some help if you're volunteering. I'm moving my books and everything else of mine out of here over to my apartment for the time being. I'll finish a lot faster if you help me. Just promise me one thing."

"What's that?"

"Promise you'll never call me 'Dr. Minkins' again. My name is Rachel."

"Rachel it is," Heather replied as they embraced.

Rachel said she had picked up the rental truck the night before, and she had arrived on campus about 6:00 that morning to pack up her office. Heather told Rachel she would stay until the job was finished. By 9:30, the truck was loaded, and Rachel asked Heather if she had eaten breakfast. Heather said she had not, that she was planning to hit a drive-through and get a bite on her way out of town. Rachel suggested the breakfast bar at Shoney's, her treat. They enjoyed a leisurely breakfast and still managed to get all the boxes of books and personal effects crammed into Rachel's apartment before noon. Heather drove Rachel's car and followed her to the truck rental place to return the truck, and Rachel then took Heather back to campus. They sat in the car talking for a while, and Heather said she needed to get on the road to west Tennessee. The two women embraced, and Rachel said, "Before you go, I want to pray for you."

"And I'd like to pray for you," Heather replied. She would always cherish the memory of that prayer time with Rachel Minkins. It was the last time she had seen her. Since then, Heather knew what Paul meant when he wrote to Timothy of *the gift that is in you through the laying on of my hands.* Even though Rachel wouldn't be able to come to her ordination, Heather knew she would draw strength from Rachel's powerful blessing for the rest of her life.

* * * * * * * * * * * *

Mike wished they had put *R.S.V.P.* on the invitations to the ordination council. Thinking about who might come had become the default mode for his mind—whenever he was not dwelling on any of the other things commanding his attention, he would catch himself thinking about that. They had invited all the pastors in the Sanders County Association, even Billy Fite. Mike hoped Brother Billy would register his objection to Heather's ordination by staying home. While Brother Billy didn't need any help to make a complete fool of himself, Mike was sure Heather would be pleased to assist him. She would handle him as skillfully as Claude Bradley had two years ago. Mike was impressed with Claude and hoped that he would come. He knew Dr. Corrie planned to be there. Heather said that she had talked to Dr. Leggs and learned that he and Paul Kerns planned to ride down together. Mike saw Greg Nash in the student lounge on Thursday, and Greg said he would be there.

It had been difficult to work out a time they could get together, but Mike and Karen had Heather over for dinner one night so they could plan the order of service for her ordination. Heather had only three special requests. She showed Mike and Karen the brief but moving letter she had received that day from Rachel Minkins and said that she would like for Carol Richardson to read it at the ordination service. Mike read the letter, commented that it would make a powerful charge to the candidate, and suggested they use it that way. Heather liked the idea. She told Mike and Karen that she was working on a brief tribute to Olivia Harris that she wanted to include in the service, and she said she would like to present it herself. Heather's one other request was that her grandmother have the ordination prayer.

It was especially important to Heather that Granny Becker offer the ordination prayer. "Granny knows God," she explained succinctly as she picked up the thread of the story she was telling at the Corries', about the time when she was sixteen, when she attempted to publicly acknowledge her call to preach, and Dr. Hathaway and the evangelist came to her home to talk with her.

"They made me feel like I'd done something horribly wrong. Of course, to their way of thinking, I guess I did. I felt humiliated, confused, angry, hurt, and I don't know what else. It's hard to give a name to some of what I felt. After they left, I cried a long time, cried so hard I threw up. I felt weaker and sicker than I ever felt with the flu. I couldn't eat any supper. I left the rest of my family eating supper and walked over to Granny Becker's. She lives about a quarter-mile from my parents. It was Thursday, and the revival was still going on. I told Mom and Dad to go without me, and they didn't make an issue of it. The walk over to Granny's did me good, and I felt better by the time I got there. When I got to her house, she met me at the door and told me Mother called to tell her I was on my way over there. She said, "Sounds like you need to talk about what's on your mind, and that's more important than either one of us going to church tonight." We sat in the swing on her back porch. I tried to tell her how I felt after Dr. Hathaway and the evangelist came to talk to me, but all I could do was cry. She pulled me close and held me, swung us gently in the swing. We must've sat there like that for an hour, Granny just holding me and swinging us in the swing. Then she began to talk to me. She said she wasn't impressed with the evangelist either, and she didn't think we were missing a whole lot not going to church that night. She told me, just because a preacher said something, it didn't make it so, and she told me to read my own Bible, do my own thinking and praying, and to listen to what God says to me, even if it's different from what the preacher says. Just because those two preachers came to the house, she said, it didn't mean God sent them. Granny went in the house to get her Bible. She came back, sat down in the swing, and read Jeremiah 23:21 to me, *I have not sent these prophets, yet they ran; I have not spoken to them, yet they prophesied.* She said, the way she looked at it, if God wants to call a woman to preach, that's God's grace and God's business.

Then, she hugged me tight and started praying for me. Granny helped me so much, and I'm thrilled she's planning to come. I definitely want her to have the ordination prayer."

"And I can see why. She sounds like a really special lady," Karen commented. "I can't wait to meet her."

"She's on Cloud Nine about coming up here I talked to her the night before last, and she said she felt better than she's felt in years, so the excitement must be good for her."

"Well, there's something to be said for that," Mike observed. "I've sure seen a big difference in Wallace since we started planning your ordination. He's so excited about Clear Springs getting to do your ordination. First time I've seen him really happy since Estelle died."

* * * * * * * * * * * *

On the Sunday they had dinner with the Corries, Mike mentioned that his parents and sister were coming up for graduation on Friday and staying over until Monday to be there for their last Sunday at Clear Springs and to help get ready for the movers. Dr. Corrie said they would be welcome to use their guest house. Evelyn asked Mike for the phone number of his parents, and she called that evening to invite them.

* * * * * * * * * * * *

The time since the inauguration of John Mark Sturgill had been the most turbulent in the history of Mid-Atlantic Seminary. In less than four years, there had been a turnover of more than sixty percent in the faculty of the school of theology. A few, such as legendary theology prof Henry Davidson Bell, evangelism prof Kenneth Conley, and church historian Robert Lee Whitaker, were in a position to retire any time they wanted. Unable to work with

Sturgill without compromising their most deeply held convictions, the three patriarchs retired at the end of the spring semester in 1988. John Pershing Arnold had put together one of the finest theological faculties ever assembled in a Baptist seminary, but that superb faculty was scattered to the four winds as faculty members too young to retire read the handwriting on the wall and took teaching positions or pastorates elsewhere. Mike's graduating class was the smallest since 1958. Many students, alarmed at the ultra-conservative direction in which Sturgill was taking the school and the new breed of men (no women, of course) being hired for teaching positions, dropped out or transferred to other seminaries. Many gravitated to other denominations in the process. Mike and Heather had pursued their theological education on a battlefield. The abrupt change in the seminary's direction, the high turnover of faculty and students, along with the forced resignation of Dr. Minkins, put Mid-Atlantic on thin ice with the accrediting agencies.

Mike scanned the list of people slated to receive the Master of Divinity degree. Angela Leahy and Tammy McGinnis were graduating with him. That would leave Heather Simmons and Melissa Nesbitt as the only women Master of Divinity students. They would pursue their last year of studies under an administration, under a majority of professors, and alongside many students who could see no conceivable reason for a woman to pursue theological education. Sturgill and his hand-picked faculty were not far removed from the ancient rabbi who wrote *"It is better for a scroll of the Law to be burned than for it to be taught to a woman."*

In one more year, Heather and Melissa would be gone from campus. The rumor mill had it that the trustees planned to close the school of theology to women as soon as they were gone. They had already closed it to anyone who had ever been divorced. In one more year, Paul Kerns, Gordon Corrie, and Emory Leggs would be retired, and Sturgill's much-touted transformation of Mid-Atlantic would be complete. Corrie had once planned, since his health was good, to teach until he was seventy. That had changed, just as Mike had changed his plans to pursue a Ph. D. in New Testament with Paul Kerns. Neither of them could stop Sturgill and his new faculty from leading Mid-Atlantic boldly backward into the Nineteenth Century.

*   *   *   *   *   *   *   *   *   *   *   *

Friday, May 25, 1990 dawned a beautiful spring day on the campus of Mid-Atlantic Seminary. Graduation exercises were scheduled for 10:00 AM. The previous Friday night had been Mike's last shift at the motel, and Wednesday had been Karen's last day to work. Mike took his last final and turned in his last paper on Tuesday. Grady, Julia, and Amanda had arrived about noon the previous day, settled into the Corries' guest house, and they had all attended the graduation banquet at the Sheraton Riverton Plaza. Mike and Karen took a bit of perverse pleasure in having their faded blue Ford Fairmount wagon parked by a valet more accustomed to Lincolns, Mercedes, and BMW's. Mike was awake at 5:00 on the morning of graduation. He was dressed and ready to go out the door at 7:00 when Karen and Asalee got up.

"Couldn't sleep," Mike explained as Karen peered sleepily into the living room. "The coffee's ready. You look like you could use a cup. I woke up and couldn't go back to sleep, so I got on up, ate some toast and a bowl of cereal, took a shower, and got dressed. I want to walk over to the seminary. I'll see you and Asalee over there."

Karen understood Mike's need to be alone. She said she would bring the bag with his cap and gown. It was a little less than a mile from the Seminary Courts apartments to the campus. He started walking about 7:30, reflecting along the way on his three years at the seminary and the cataclysmic changes in the institution during that time. For some, the changes were cause for celebration, while others viewed them with profound sorrow. All agreed that the changes had been massive and far-reaching.

*   *   *   *   *   *   *   *   *   *   *   *

Jimmy Ray Burkette, newly-installed dean of the school of theology, brought the commencement address. The essence of it was that the seminary, after fifty years in the stranglehold of liberalism, had been rescued, purged of Bible-doubting professors, and returned to the vision of its founders by the current trustees and the Sturgill administration. Mike wondered how Kerns, Corrie, and Leggs felt, since the fifty-year span Burkette painted as a dark period in the seminary's history encompassed their entire teaching careers. Burkette implied that most of the pastors who came out of Mid-Atlantic during those years were at best a bunch of ineffective dolts who couldn't grow a church, and at worst a bunch of infidels out to undermine the faith of good Baptists. Burkette didn't know Dan Jordan, Mid-Atlantic class of '76, at Talmadge Street in Denham, or Becky Summerville, class of '80, campus minister at Rullman College. Mike doubted that Burkette even knew Leggs, Kerns, and Corrie all that well. To Burkette and the Sturgill administration, those Mike regarded as the seminary's best and brightest were liabilities in the new order. Mike felt a sense of embarrassment that his wife, who had worked so hard to get him through seminary, his parents, who had just started going to church together, and his daughter had to sit through Burkette's tasteless and inappropriate remarks.

Burkette eventually finished, and Mike breathed a sigh of relief when the powerful notes of the chapel organ began playing the majestic tune of *God of Grace and God of Glory*. He wondered whether those who planned the graduation ceremony knew enough church history to appreciate the magnitude of their gaffe. The hymn text was written by Harry Emerson Fosdick, who epitomized the kind of liberalism of which Burkette had just boasted of purging the seminary.

There was no time for snickering over that monumental gaffe. The awarding of diplomas had begun. Mike stood with his graduating class and prepared to go up and receive his hard-earned degree. He was near the end of the line, between Barry Wagner and Jack Wiggins. Though he had completed four years of college and three years of seminary and would soon hold a Master of Divinity degree in his hands, Mike was under no illusion that he had mastered Divinity. It struck him as absurd that anyone finite and mortal should be declared a "Master of Divinity."

Dean Burkette was calling out the names of the graduates, "..Eric Daniel Turner, David Wayne Underwood, Barry Jefferson Wagner, Michael Grady Westover..." Mike braced himself and walked across the stage. Asalee stood up in the pew for a better view. Mike reminded himself that this would be the only time in his life he would ever need to speak to or shake hands with John Mark Sturgill and Jimmy Ray Burkette.

⋆   ⋆   ⋆   ⋆   ⋆   ⋆   ⋆   ⋆   ⋆   ⋆   ⋆

Graduation ceremonies were concluded by 11:30, but it was after 1:00 when Mike and his family got away from campus. There were so many classmates Mike wanted to introduce to his parents and sister, and he wanted to speak to the ones who came up from Clear Springs. Asalee had latched onto Aunt Mandy and Papa Wallace and taken them on a quick tour of the basement of Stearns Hall where she had gone to day care. When the crowd thinned out, Grady mentioned that his breakfast was starting to wear off. "Let's go find something to eat, my treat," he said as he tossed Mike the keys to his Lincoln Town Car. Grady liked big heavy cars. He always said he wanted Julia to have the extra protection around her if she were to be in an accident, and he said he didn't like his big frame folded up on a long trip. "You'n Karen leave your car here," Grady directed. "We'll pick it up after awhile. We'n all get in mine. You drive, Son, since you know your way around here and I don't. Find the best spread of food in town."

"Does seafood sound good to everybody?" Mike asked as he circled Leland Hall and pulled out onto Morgan Avenue. "Heibler's down on River Street is the best in town. Great seafood and plenty of it, they bake all their own bread…"

"And don't forget the desserts," Karen added. "We go there a couple of times a year, birthdays and anniversaries."

There were no dissenting votes, and Mike headed the big Lincoln toward Heibler's. "So, how was the trip up here?" Mike asked.

"Good," Grady responded, "'cept for that stretch of I-40 from Knoxville to where you pick up 81. Some construction, really had it backed up. I could've walked that stretch in less time than it took to drive it. Aside from that, it was a pretty good trip."

"It sure was nice of the Corries to invite us to stay in their guest house," Julia added. We've really enjoyed getting to know them. They're really good people."

"You'd think we were family," Amanda added. "The guest house is really nice, and they can't seem to do enough for us. Mrs. Corrie fixed a wonderful dinner for us last night."

"I'm not surprised," Mike noted. "She's Wallace and Estelle's daughter."

"Speaking of Dr. Corrie," Grady spoke slowly and thoughtfully, "I didn't much appreciate that guy that was the main speaker at graduation today. He made it sound like him and his bunch was the first ones in fifty years that believed the Bible. Now you know me. I don't know much about the Bible, though I've been reading it more here lately. I've heard you talk about Dr. Corrie, Dr. Kerns, and Dr. Leggs. I talked a long time with Dr. Corrie last night, looked over that Chevy pickup he restored, saw his woodworking shop. You introduced me to Dr. Kerns and Dr. Leggs today. I think I'd learn a lot if I spent some time with those men. I know you learned a lot from them, Son, and I don't 'preciate one bit what that clown said today. He was goin' on and on about how they got shed of a lot of professors they used to have. All I can say is, if they're talkin' about gettin' shed of people like Dr. Corrie, Dr. Kerns, and Dr. Leggs, they're a bunch of damn fools."

"Grady..." Julia interrupted, "Watch your tongue! Your grand-daughter's in the car."

"I *am* watching my tongue, and I know Asalee's in the car. I'll never let her hear me call a man a damn fool unless he is one. Like I said, I didn't appreciate that damn fool Burkette one bit."

* * * * * * * * * * * *

Russ Ayers called about 11:00 Saturday morning to say that the Tennessee bunch had arrived, and he told Mike to load up his family and come on down because he had the grill fired up and there was plenty of food. He said that Heather had spent the night with Carol, so she was already there. Karen told Mike that sounded good to her, since her kitchen was packed up, and she was about to send him to Krystal for a sack of hamburgers. Asalee responded enthusiastically when Mike said Russ told him to bring her bicycle and Wallace the Dog. Mike packed a change of clothes so he could freshen up at Russ and Joan's before going to the ordi-nation council. He tied Asalee's bike on top of the station wagon with bungee cords while she fixed Wallace's old beach towel on the back seat. Karen got the camera so they could take a picture of Wallace the Dog with Wallace the Deacon Chairman.

* * * * * * * * * * * *

Mike rode in Russ Ayers' van with him and the other deacons from Clear Springs who had been at the cookout. Heather rode with her father in his van, along with the other four deacons from Tennessee. They pulled into the parking lot at Clear Springs about 5:40, twenty minutes early for the ordination council, and noted about ten cars already there. Mike recognized Mary Kate Sessions' Buick Roadmaster, parked next to Joe Norris' truck. Joe had promised to come early and have the building unlocked and the air conditioning on. Joe was helping Mary Kate get her father out of the car as Russ pulled his van up alongside them. Mike recognized a couple of the other cars there. The old red Toyota Corolla belonged to Greg Nash, the student pastor at Bolton's Chapel. The gray Taurus belonged to Dr. Leggs, and Mike remembered that Dr. Kerns planned to ride down with him. The beautifully restored red and white '65 Chevy pickup that Mike had often lusted after belonged to Dr. Corrie.

Once inside the building, Mike noted that Joe had the chairs arranged in a big circle in the fellowship hall, and he had a large cooler full of ice and assorted cans of soft drinks in the kitchen. He was pleased to see Claude Bradley talking with Dr. Corrie, and he was even more pleased not to see Billy Fite. While a solemn purpose had brought them together, it was a congenial group. Wallace was working the crowd, welcoming each of the guests to Clear Springs. Mike really didn't want to bring the many lively conversations to a close and call the meeting to order. Mike looked over at Heather, who seemed poised, confident, and comfortable even though some of those who came up from Tennessee were teasing her about being on the hot seat.

Mike called the council to order and asked each one present to introduce themselves and tell which church they came from. Dr. Kerns agreed to serve as clerk of the council, and Mike asked Mary Kate Sessions to open the meeting with prayer. He then asked Heather to begin by telling the group about her Christian experience and call to ministry. Heather was very much at ease fielding that question. She related the story she told over dinner at the Corries' and told about the cold rebuff she got at age sixteen when she tried to publicly acknowledge her calling. She told how God had confirmed her calling through the support she received from some in the church at McMillan, her special relationship with her grandmother Becker, and how God brought Olivia Harris and Rachel Minkins into her life.

Heather's testimony seemed to answer the questions of everyone on the council. Mike went around the room and gave everyone an opportunity to ask questions or simply offer a word of affirmation and encouragement. Carol Richardson observed that all of her questions were answered before she got there, since her two daughters had grilled Heather more thoroughly than any ordination council could.

John Tant spoke slowly and thoughtfully. "All of my questions were answered before I left Tennessee. Heather, I want you to know there's never been any doubt in my mind that the Lord called you to preach and to be a pastor. It floored me when I found out about the brush-off Brother Coggins got from our pastor. Heather, Becky and I came up here because we've known you all your life, and we realized that God had his hand on you for something special when you were a little girl. When you were seven years old, Becky was teaching you in Sunday School, and you told her that you were going to be a preacher when you grew up. She told me about it on the way home, and she said, 'she was serious, John, and I believe her.' I remember that night during the revival when you were in high school. The preacher had the strangest look on his face, white as a sheet, told us you'd come up to rededicate your life, couldn't rush you back to your seat fast enough, and you left church crying that night. Becky and I knew why you went forward. When you were in college, we slipped off one Sunday and went to hear you preach at that little church in Pendleton where you were filling in. First time I ever heard a woman preach, and you're still the only woman preacher I ever heard, but you brought a good message, and that was before you went to seminary. But there's another reason I came up here. I'm chairman of deacons at First Baptist Church in McMillan, Tennessee, and I want to say I'm ashamed of what our pastor did, the way he treated Brother Coggins, and the way he didn't even present the call for ordination to the deacons so we could make a recommendation to the church..." There were "Amens" from Heather's father and the other deacons from McMillan. "I came to apologize to you, Brother Wallace, to you, Heather, and to Clear Springs Baptist Church. Kevin Stone does not speak for everybody in First Baptist Church of McMillan, Tennessee. I appreciate Clear Springs Baptist Church from the bottom of my heart. If I lived around here, this is the church I'd join. Brother Mike, I thank God for you and the good work you did here. All of us appreciate the warm reception from the people here and your gracious hospitality. I pray the Lord's continued blessing on this church. This church is going to do well under Heather's ministry."

"Thank you for those kind words, Brother John," Wallace responded. "We appreciate all of you making the effort to come up here."

"Does anybody else have a question for Heather or anything else you want to say?" Mike asked the group.

Claude Bradley spoke up. "Sister Heather, tonight's the first time I ever met you. I came because Brother Mike sent me an invitation, just like he sent to all the pastors in the association. I came because I believe the churches in the association ought to help each other when they can. It's obvious to me, meeting you for the first time, hearing your testimony and your answers to the questions you were asked, that the Lord's been at work in your life. No doubt in my mind God called you to preach. Hearing the testimony of these people who've known you all your life, I couldn't help but think of what God said to Jeremiah over in Jeremiah 1:5, *Before I formed thee in the belly I knew thee, before thou camest out of the womb I sanctified thee, and I ordained thee a prophet unto the nations.* Now I'm just a country preacher, got a high school education, never been to college or seminary. I wish I had more education, but I know the Lord. I've been in the ministry thirty-two years, and I can tell when God's working. Sister Heather, God ordained you a long time ago, before you were born, just like He did Jeremiah. All we can do is recognize what God's done and give you our blessing. Brother Mike, I'd like to make the motion that this council present a favorable report to the church, recommending that they proceed with the ordination of this good minister of the Gospel."

Roy Simmons seconded Claude's motion, Mike called for a vote, and the council was unanimous. Roy was the first of twenty-eight who lined up to sign the certificate and the flyleaf of the ordination Bible. Heather looked at the two remaining spaces on the certificate and thought of Olivia Harris and Rachel Minkins.

* * * * * * * * * * * *

Wallace said the Sunday worship attendance was the largest he could remember. The weather was ideal for dinner on the grounds, which was fortunate, because there were far too many people to squeeze into the fellowship hall. The people of Clear

Springs put on a fabulous spread of food, and it was not a bit too much. Still more people arrived in time for the ordination service at 3:00. Wallace said the only times he had seen that many at Clear Springs was when they hosted the annual meeting of the association.

After Wallace presented the Bible and the beautifully-framed ordination certificate, Mike announced, "Heather's grandmother, Mrs. Gladys Becker, asked me if she might say something before we're dismissed, on behalf of all of those who are here from First Baptist Church in McMillan, Tennessee. Mrs. Becker..."

Granny Becker walked up to the pulpit with slow, measured step, steadying herself with her cane. "On behalf of all of us from McMillan," she said, "I want to thank you for the hospitality you've shown us this weekend." Despite her frail appearance, her voice was strong, clear, and confident, like the voice of her grand-daughter. "We've never had family treat us any better, and we'll always remember you and love you. I'm an old woman, eighty-two years old. The doctors tell me I've got enough wrong with me to kill two or three people, but, praise the Lord, I feel good today! If I felt any better, I'd float on up to glory. Gettin' to help ordain my granddaughter's been the best blessing I ever had." She paused momentarily, her voice choking with emotion. "I'm like old Simeon was when he saw the Christ Child. If the Lord wants to take me home right now, I'm ready to depart in peace. But I didn't get up here just to tell you what a happy old woman I am." Granny Becker cut a glance over to John Tant, seated on the second pew, behind Heather and her parents. "John," she chuckled, "I still can't believe y'all elected me spokesperson for all of us from McMillan." Turning her eyes back to the congregation, she continued, "I rode up here in the van with my daughter and son-in-law and their family. We got to talkin' about the way the pastor of First Baptist in McMillan did Brother Coggins when he called about ordainin' Heather, tellin' 'im no woman'd be ordained at his church while he was pastor, didn't even talk to the deacons or present it to the church. It's not just that. It's all this tom-foolery about the pastor bein' the ruler of the church, and men havin' to be in charge of everything, and the church not bein' a democracy, an' puttin' down any kind of ministry by women. I've been a member of First Baptist seventy-three years, since I was nine years old. Preacher F. T. Carlton baptized me in 1917. I've never belonged to any other church—at least I hadn't 'til early yesterday morning." A hush fell over the congregation. Heather's jaw dropped as a look of utter amazement registered on her face. She had heard nothing about this talking to the Tennessee bunch yesterday, and her lifelong friends had not breathed a word about it at Carol's the night before. Granny Becker continued, "We pulled into the rest area on I-40 just beyond Crossville, Tennessee yesterday morning, and Brother Lance pulled in beside us with the motor home. We got to talkin' with the ones in the motor home. All the way from McMillan, they'd been talkin' about the same thing we were talkin' about. We got together right there in that rest area and had a good long prayer meetin'. We all believe the Lord's leadin' us the same way, and we'd be scared not to follow. We left home as eighteen members of First Baptist Church. We'll be going back as eighteen charter members of Providence Baptist Church. Y'all pray for us, 'cause none of us has ever helped start a church before. Most of us've never belonged to any church other'n First Baptist. We were all talkin' as we ate dinner, about how we feel more at home here than we've felt at First Baptist in a long time. You've shown us the kind of church we want to be. This mornin' was the first time I ever saw a woman serve the Lord's Supper, and it sure felt good. We want to be a church that believes God calls men and women the same for every way there is of servin' the Lord. A lot of us have responsibilities in the church we came from, and we're not going to walk away from that. We're gonna meet for prayer and worship on Saturday nights for now an' keep goin' to First Baptist 'til the end of the church year. Come the first Sunday in October, we'll have our first Sunday morning worship service. Heather's daddy owns the Ford place in McMillan. He's gonna move the cars out of the showroom, and that's where we'll have services 'til we can do better. Providence Baptist Church has a big favor to ask of Clear Springs. We need to borrow your pastor one Sunday." Mrs. Becker motioned for Heather to come and stand beside her. "Heather, Honey," she asked as she put her arm around her granddaughter, "we want you to preach at the first Sunday morning service of Providence Baptist Church."

Wallace stepped up and said, "Sister Becker, I reckon this church has always believed in helpin' a sister church whenever we could." Turning to Heather, he added, "Preacher, you plan on goin' down to Tennessee that first Sunday in October."

Heather was overcome with emotion as she embraced her grandmother and Wallace. Karen handed her some Kleenex, and she recovered her composure enough to say, "I accept your invitation." Laughing through her tears, she added, "I'm probably the first person to split a Baptist church from five hundred miles away, and I know Providence is the first church in Baptist history to be organized in an interstate highway rest area!"

It was almost 5:00 when the congregation joined hands to sing *Blest Be the Tie That Binds*. It was after six when Mike, Karen, and Asalee exchanged hugs with the last of the lingering crowd and headed home to spend their last night at 1703-A Armstrong Circle.

8

The movers arrived at 7:00 sharp. By 10:30, they were loaded and ready to roll. Grady helped Mike strap the suit-cases with their essential overnight things onto the luggage rack atop the station wagon. Asalee fixed Wallace's old beach towel behind the back seat so he could stretch out and go to sleep on the trip. The movers said they would stop for the night around Atlanta and get into Harrington about mid-morning the next day. Mike and Karen planned to swap out driving and run the trip straight through. Carl and Joyce Baxter had invited them to spend the night and have breakfast before meeting the movers. This was their first time to be moved by professionals. Mike particularly enjoyed not having to wrestle with Karen's piano.

After the movers drove away, Mike made sure the lights were off and the back door was bolted. He locked the front door, pulled it shut for the last time, and drove to the seminary campus. Karen, Asalee, and Wallace the Dog waited in the car and Mike's parents and sister waited in the Lincoln while Mike went to the housing office in to turn in the keys. Karen suggested the drive-through at McDonald's on the way out of town. As Mike headed the car onto the interstate, he set the trip odometer to measure their progress. Once on the interstate, he was quickly reminded of the other reason his father liked big cars with big engines. Grady honked his horn and pulled out to pass them. He, Julia, and Mandy waved as they went by. Mike watched the Lincoln grow smaller and smaller in the distance until it disappeared over the horizon.

Karen had the seat reclined a little, a pillow behind her head, and her shoes off. Her ankles had swollen more with this pregnancy than with the last one, that or she had forgotten how much they swelled when she was pregnant with Asalee. She never missed an opportunity to take off her shoes and elevate her feet. The discomforts notwithstanding, she was pleased to be pregnant again. She and Mike wanted another child, but they had waited because of his seminary studies. When the home pregnancy test was positive in January, Karen told Mike this baby would be his graduation present.

Asalee was holding a big paper cup while Wallace ate the ice out of it, to the amusement of people in passing cars. Mike was driving with his left hand. With his right hand, he held hands with Karen. She guided his hand to where he could feel the life growing inside her. "The baby's been moving a lot today," she commented. "Strong little kid. 'Course, Asalee was a wiggleworm, too."

"Daddy…" Asalee stretched the word out like a piece of taffy, her voice registering a note of mild irritation. "Was I a wiggleworm when I was inside Mommy?"

"You're *still* a wiggleworm, Azzie. You wiggled and stretched and kicked just like the new baby."

"But I was glad you moved around a lot," Karen picked up the thread. "That's one of the ways we knew you were strong and healthy. We'd have worried if you'd been too still. It didn't feel too good when you decided to kick really hard, but I liked feeling you move around, and I like to feel the new baby moving. Someday you'll be all grown up and have babies, and you'll know what I'm talking about." Asalee was relieved of the opprobrium she felt at being called a wiggleworm, once she understood it to be a good thing.

"Are you feeling OK, Hon?" Mike asked Karen.

"I'm OK, just catching a little rest while I can. The last few days have been unreal. I didn't realize how tired I was 'til I stopped to catch my breath. Feels good to take off my shoes and lean the seat back. Let me know when you want me to drive a while."

"You just rest. I'm fine for now. Amazing how well I've adjusted to sleeping like a normal person since I quit the night job. I don't mind driving, especially since I'm not driving a big truck and I didn't have to move furniture. It's nice to be moved by professionals."

"Yeah. Those guys are good. We had most of the packing done, but I was still impressed with how quickly they got loaded up and ready to roll."

"I'm glad I didn't have to wrestle that piano of yours. It's beautiful, but it's a pain to move. The cabinet on that thing must be rosewood veneer over lead."

"That was my great-grandmother's piano," Karen replied sternly.

"And the cabinet of your great-grandmother's piano is rosewood veneer over lead," Mike retorted. "The movers were gruntin' and cussin' under their breath. There's a reason that piano sat in the same spot for seventy years. Rob and I like to have killed ourselves movin' it out of Ma Kemp's house and gettin' it onto my truck, and then gettin' it off the truck and into the apartment in Denham. Like I said, I'm glad you got it, just thankful I'm not the one moving it. It's all right with me, once we get it in the house at Harrington, if it stays in the same spot for the next seventy years, until I'm dead and gone, and then somebody else can worry about how to move it."

"You think we'll be at Harrington a long time?" Karen asked, her voice taking on a more serious tone.

"I hope so. I hate moving. But, to tell you the truth, I don't think I'll make a career out of this church." Mike could speak a little more candidly now that Asalee was asleep in the back seat.

"You remember when we were at Harrington for the trial sermon, how they had all the pictures of the former pastors on display? I jotted down the names, dates, and how long they were there. The longest tenure was a guy named John Leland Walters, twenty-two years. Harry Reynolds, the guy who just left, was there sixteen. He had the second longest tenure. The average is about seven years. I'm going with the intention of staying. It seems like a nice community, good place for our kids to grow up. I don't intend to uproot you and the kids every time somebody gets their feathers ruffled. I like what Brother Woodrow says about that, about tellin' some guy, "You can move your membership for the price of a stamp; it'd cost me a couple thousand dollars to move my furniture and get another place to live."

"Yeah, only one thing. That was at his previous church, when he pastored up around Cullman. Brother Woodrow's the one who ended up moving. Unless the guy he said that to is dead, he's probably causing grief for the pastor who's there now."

"I know one thing. We're not even moved in yet, and already I'd pay to move the membership of Franklin A. Brinkley, Chairman of the Board of Deacons of Harrington Baptist Church."

"I'd chip in a quarter to move Geneva Millican's membership to where she could be somebody else's pain in the butt," Karen added. "We could move Roland on the same stamp."

"And don't forget the lovely lady who rules the roost in the nursery. Another stamp for her." "Yes, her too by all means. So, you think we could clear up the worst of the problems with seventy-five cents' worth of stamps?"

"Well, just a couple of problems with that. They'd go on to be a royal pain somewhere else, and others would step up to take their places and act just like them or worse. Harrington's got the potential to be a good church, but it's also got the potential to be a widow-maker. I'm hoping for the best, but I'd be lying if I didn't admit there are some things about it that scare me. The only church I know how to pastor is Clear Springs, and I know I can't pastor Harrington the same way I pastored Clear Springs. For one thing, I won't have Wallace at my right hand…"

"Yes, I do wish we could take Wallace with us. Wallace has been the stabilizing influence in the church. If Clear Springs depended on pastors to hold things together, they'd be in sad shape."

"They sure would. That leads me to something I've been thinking about. Wallace is eighty-six, and he's in great shape for his age, but that can't last forever. I wonder who's going to be the stabilizing influence when Wallace is gone. I have my ideas, but tell me what you think."

"Well," Karen replied thoughtfully, "of the deacons who're active, Joe's the next oldest. He's a good guy, but he's not assertive enough to do what Wallace has done, and I don't think he's as perceptive as Wallace. Joe'd let some people run over him. He's as tenderhearted as he can be, good deacon, but he'd be a disaster as chairman. Russ or Wayne could do it, with Russ being the better of the two, but I don't think it's going to be on the basis of age, and I don't think it's going to be any of the men. Are you thinking what I'm thinking?"

"Carol?"

"Mmmhmm. Wallace sees Carol's strengths, and he has tremendous respect for her, though she and Linda are the youngest deacons."

"I know he does. I've noticed this past year with Carol being secretary of the deacons, Wallace has been leaning on her a lot, calling on her to do things he would've done not too long ago, like presenting the statement from the deacons following my resignation. As for Wallace telling Carol to do it because she's good with words, well, granted, her grammar's a little more polished, but Wallace can be eloquent when the situation calls for it. He's never been afraid to get up in front of people and talk to them, never had any trouble getting his ideas across. I don't see him slipping on that. What he did, getting Carol to present the statement from the deacons, was intentional. He'll be the one to appoint and anoint his successor, and that was his way of saying Carol's his choice. Elijah hasn't passed his mantle down to Elisha, but he's letting her try it on."

"I think you're right. Wallace isn't giving up just yet. I thought for a while after Estelle died that he was going to grieve himself to death. Then he started volunteering at the hospital, and that helped him. He saw his leadership was needed through the change of pastors. Ordaining Heather boosted his spirits. And him going and trading for that new truck, not talking to his kids before he did it, was a good sign, his way of saying, 'Y'all don't dig my grave just yet.'"

"Funny thing," Mike mused, "Wallace doesn't crave power in the least. He encourages people like Carol to develop their gifts. He'll listen to anybody in the church. When the Richardson girls told him they wanted to talk to him about calling Heather, he sat down with them after church and asked them, 'Tell me why you think Preacher Simmons'd make us a good pastor,' and he listened just as respectfully as he would with any adult in the church. Carol said he and the girls talked about a half hour, and then he told them, 'Well, Meg and Jess, I think you're right. I'm in favor of calling her.' Wallace has the kind of power Franklin A. Brinkley, Chairman of the Board of Deacons of Harrington Baptist Church, only dreams about."

As they approached Knoxville, Karen suggested that it might be a good place to get off and look for a place to eat lunch. Remembering the cardinal rule of southern barbeque—the worse the building looks, the better the barbeque is, Mike found a good barbeque place. There was a shady place to park the car, so they were able to leave Wallace the Dog in the car while they took advantage of the screened-in room full of picnic tables with red and white checkered oilcloth tablecloths. Karen and Asalee walked around and stretched their legs while Mike got a big cup of crushed ice to put in Wallace's water dish before they went in to order their food.

*   *   *   *   *   *   *   *   *   *   *   *

Karen drove from Knoxville to the rest area at Calhoun, Georgia. After a rest room—cold Coca-Cola—leg stretching—dog walking break, Mike took over driving again for the last leg of the trip. Asalee was soon absorbed in a coloring book, and Mike picked up the conversation where they had left off several hours before. "You think we're making a good move, going to Harrington?"

"That's kind of like asking me if I want to have a baby. "It's pretty far along in the process to ask that question."

"Yeah, I know. What I mean is, it's pretty hard to know going in if we're doing the right thing or making a bad mistake. Some of what I'm feeling is normal cold feet. I prayed about it a lot, you did too, we both did, but it's like Thielicke says, 'God really can be silent.' I know I'm called to be a pastor, but I can't say with absolute certainty that Harrington's *the* place God wants us to be. We prayed for a call to a full-time pastorate when I graduated, and this is the only opportunity that presented itself…"

"Well, I haven't heard any voices from Heaven, either. I agree with what you said in one of your sermons here while back at Clear Springs, that there's a lot of freedom for us to make choices within the will of God, and God often lets us choose among several options. I think you're right. There's not just one person you can marry or one church you can pastor and be within the will of God. You make your choice, commit to it, and go with it. We've prayed, looked at our options, and made the best decision we could. We're both uneasy about some things, but neither one of us is dragging the other into it. It'll be a harder church to pastor, but that doesn't mean that it's not God's will for us to be there."

* * * * * * * * * * * *

It was dusky dark when Mike took the exit off I-85 south of Atlanta for the two-lane that would take them the last twelve miles of the trip into Harrington. He thought he would remember how to get to the Baxters' home, but he asked Carl to give him the directions again over the phone to be safe. He pulled the scribbled directions from his shirt pocket and handed them to Karen so she could navigate.

* * * * * * * * * * * *

"Mike Hon…" Karen said, a note of consternation in her voice, "I love you, but I can't read your writing when you scribble things. Maybe if I'd followed in Daddy's footsteps and gone to pharmacy school…"

"I think it says *'right on Freeman Valley Road, cross bridge, first driveway on right.'* More than once, Mike had found it necessary to call Karen from the grocery store because he couldn't decipher his own scribbled handwriting on the grocery list. After they crossed the little bridge on Freeman Valley Road, he recognized the large brick mailbox with the sign on top that read *Carl W. Baxter—Baxter Custom Homes—1070 Freeman Valley Road*, and he turned up the long winding driveway to the Baxters' elegant country home, about a quarter-mile off the main road.

Asalee, half-asleep on the back seat, rubbed her eyes, stretched, yawned, and roused Wallace enough to fasten his leash onto his collar. In her most grown-up voice, she impressed upon Wallace the fact that they were at their destination, that they had been asleep most of the trip, and that it was time to wake up.

The spacious three-car garage at the Baxters' home was occupied by Carl's Ford F-350 dually pickup, the maroon Crown Victoria, and Samantha's white Camaro. The driveway in front of the garage and the walkways around the house were well-lighted with flood-lights that switched on automatically when a car came up the drive-way. Carl liked the rustic, old-fashioned look as evidenced by the big front porch with rocking chairs and two porch swings, the wide plank floors, and the exposed beams, but he also appreciated subtle touches of modern technology such as state-of-the-art climate control, lighting, and security systems.

While Asalee walked Wallace in the grass at the edge of the driveway, Carl helped Mike untie the luggage from the rack on top of the car and bring it in, while Karen brought Wallace's old beach towel and his food and water dishes from the back of the car. Asalee brought Wallace in, and he and the Baxters' dog Bullet sniffed each other. The two dogs judged each other to be harmless and decided to live at peace with each other. "We've been waiting for you. Have y'all had supper?" Joyce Baxter asked as she hugged the Westovers and welcomed them to her home. "I fixed a big pot of vegetable soup and some cornbread. Figured you wouldn't want anything real heavy this late."

"Thanks, Joyce, that sounds great," Karen responded. "We didn't stop again for supper because we didn't want to run ourselves any later getting here."

"So, how was the trip down here, Preacher?" Carl asked.

"Good. We got on the road about 10:00. My parents and my sister came up for graduation and stayed over for our last day at Clear Springs. The movers got there early this morning. We were pretty well packed up and cleaned up, so they were loaded and ready to roll by 9:30. We saw Mom and Dad off, turned in the keys to the apartment, and got on the road. Stopped for dinner in Knoxville, found us some seriously good barbeque. All things considered, we made good time. The movers said they were going to stop somewhere down below Atlanta for the night, get an early start, and meet us at the house around mid-morning. Karen's folks are coming up tomorrow to help us get unpacked."

"Well, I guess y'all will get to see them pretty often, being this close by. Williston's not too awful far from here. Being close to the state line like we are, we've built a fair number of houses over in Alabama. Built a big'un, mansion, for a lawyer over't Roanoke last year. The man had the money to spend, and I was glad to help him spend it. I made better'n a third of what I made all year on that one job. It's over on Route 22, between Roanoke and Wadley, biggest house in Randolph County, sits up on a hill, real pretty place, way back off the road. I guess that's the way y'all'd go to Williston, it's the closest way. If you go that way, you'll pass right by it. It took us a little over an hour, 'bout an hour and fifteen minutes to go from here to Williston when the pulpit committee came over there to hear you."

"Glad your parents are coming over," Joyce added. "I look forward to meeting them. Some of us women are bringing lunch and supper over tomorrow so you won't have to try to cook before you get all the way unpacked and have a chance to go buy groceries."

* * * * * * * * * * * *

Carl had left the keys to the parsonage with Joyce. After a good country breakfast, Mike and Karen thanked Joyce for the hospitality and got ready to go on over to meet the movers. Joyce suggested letting Asalee and Wallace stay with her, and she would bring them over when she came at lunchtime. Asalee had taken a liking to Joyce, so she was fine with that, and Wallace the Dog was not awake enough to express an opinion about anything. Samantha Baxter had finished all of her classes on Friday, and she was awaiting high school graduation on Thursday night, so she and Bullet were sleeping in as well.

It was about five minutes before 8:00 when Mike and Karen pulled into the driveway of 722 Alabama Avenue, one block off Peyton Street, around the corner from Harrington Baptist Church. They were the first ones to arrive. Mike unlocked the door and followed Karen into the empty house. Half of the windows were stuck shut with fresh paint, but Mike managed to get a few of them open. Karen discovered the switch for the attic fan and turned it on. The smells of fresh paint and carpet dye were about to make her sick, so she breathed a sigh of relief at the rush of fresh air.

The house was a modest, comfortable three bedroom home that appeared to have been built in the mid-to-late '50's. Karen liked the large eat-in kitchen with ample cabinet space and all-new appliances. The large living room and dining room combination looked absolutely cavernous without furniture. Karen thought about what Geneva Millican said the Sunday Mike preached the trial sermon, how she had praised Earline Reynolds who was "always entertaining at the parsonage." Clearly, this room was designed as a second fellowship hall for the church.

Mike and Karen walked back through the rest of the house. There was a small hallway in the center of the house, off the living and dining room. The one bathroom and two of the three bedrooms were accessible from the hall; the third bedroom was accessible from the kitchen or by going through the middle bedroom. As they opened the bedroom doors, Mike and Karen noted that the plush new carpet extended only as far as the hallway. The master bedroom was done in the same dirt-brown commercial carpet as the hallways of the educational building at the church. The other two bedrooms were done in the same awful seventies-vintage gold carpet as the church auditorium. In the bedroom off the kitchen, several scraps had been pieced together, and the seams were plainly visible. More carpet is manufactured in Georgia than in the other forty-nine states combined, and outlets sell top-quality carpet at bargain prices, but the trustees had only seen fit to put new carpet in the part of the house that would be seen by those who were entertained at the parsonage. The bedroom carpets were twenty years old, and these rooms had received carpet only because there were scraps left over from carpeting the church.

Karen and Mike had forgotten how much voices echo in an empty house. Walking through the house, they felt some of the same emotions they felt seven years earlier at the motel in Gatlinburg when they were alone together for the first time as a married couple. In the room that would be their bedroom, the room with the dirt-brown commercial carpet, they embraced, and their lips met in a long, passionate kiss.

"Geneva Millican would be absolutely appalled if she saw us," Karen said with mock sternness when they came up for air.

"Which is why I'm thankful she can't see us," Mike replied as he ran his hands over Karen's breasts. They were still caressing and kissing when they heard someone at the door. They disentangled themselves from each other's embrace, and Mike went to the front door. Through the large picture window, he saw the blue Olds Cutlass belonging to Karen's parents in the driveway. He and Karen felt like teenagers having their amorous play interrupted by the sudden arrival of her parents. Karen was emerging from the hallway into the living room, and she and Mike both had sheepish looks on their faces as Mike opened the door and welcomed Harold and Margaret Owen into the empty house.

"Hi, Dad! Hi, Mom! Didn't expect you this early," Karen said. "We just got here ourselves, just been walking around in the house, getting windows open and the attic fan on to try to pull some of the paint smell and the smell of the new carpet out so we don't get overcome."

"We left home about 5:00 on account of losing an hour at the state line," Harold explained. "Great little place down at Roanoke that's real reasonable, serves up the best country breakfast you'll find anywhere. We stopped and ate there on the way over."

"Just what your father needs," Margaret stage-whispered to Karen. "Not quite two years down the road from having five bypasses, and he's working on stopping himself up again."

"Now Mama," Harold protested, "it took me fifty-eight years to get stopped up the first time, so I figure it'll take me another fifty-eight years to get that stopped up again. I don't go eating like I did this morning all the time. This morning was a special treat, and I'll burn it off helping these kids get moved in."

Margaret gave up nagging her husband about his dietary habits, at least in a direct way, as she asked Mike, "How are Wayne and June Ethridge doing?"

"Great. They were at church Sunday, usually there every Sunday. Ol' Wayne looks good, says he feels good, still working hard, no sign of slowing down."

"That's good," Margaret said. "I never will forget them. We got a card from them at Christmas." Karen would never forget them, either. In September of 1988, a month after Mike was called to Clear Springs, Karen got the call from her brother Rob saying that their father had suffered a bad heart attack and that he would be transferred to University Hospital in Birmingham as soon as they got him stabilized. It was a Wednesday, and Mike called Wallace to ask him to cover prayer meeting because he would be at the airport getting Karen on the first available flight into Birmingham. They didn't have enough money for all of them to fly down, and Karen told Mike that, at least until they found out more, it would be best for him to stay and take care of Asalee and go on to work and classes. When Mike and Asalee got back from taking Karen to the airport, there were two messages on the voice mail. The first message was Karen's brother, saying that his father was scheduled for coronary bypass surgery Friday morning. The second message was June Ethridge, calling to say that she and Wayne were packed and ready to leave for Birmingham as soon as Mike called to let them know which hospital Harold was in. Wayne answered the phone when Mike returned the call. Wayne said that he had undergone a triple bypass after a heart attack in 1985—"like to have left this ol' world," as he put it. Wayne and June got on the road about 9:30 that night, took turns at the wheel, and drove straight through to Birmingham, arriving mid-morning on Thursday, in time to visit and pray with Harold before his surgery. They stayed with Karen and the family until Harold was out of surgery and in the recovery room. The next morning, they came back to the hospital to be sure Harold was still doing well before they started home. By that spring, Harold had made a good recovery, and he and Margaret came up to see Mike, Karen, and Asalee and visit Clear Springs. Harold and Margaret had treated Wayne and June to a dinner theater production of *Fiddler on the Roof* in Riverton, and they spent one night with Wayne and June before returning home to Alabama.

Mike took his father-in-law through the house, ending the tour with the enclosed garage, the best part of the house as far as Mike was concerned. Since there were no chairs in the house, Karen and her mother sat on the front steps, talking about the progress of Karen's pregnancy, the anticipated birth of the baby, what they were going to name the baby, and what they were going to call the baby. For the children of southern parents, those two questions— what to name the baby and what to call the baby—are often unrelated and have very different answers. Karen's favorite aunt was named Evelyn Elizabeth Kemp according to the family Bible and the birth certificate, but everyone called her Earline. Uncle Joe Westover, Mike's great-uncle, was actually Robert Edgar, but Mike always knew him as Uncle Joe.

Mike and Harold opened the garage door and came around to the front of the house where Karen and Margaret were. As they did, an old yellow Datsun pickup pulled up into the driveway. Harsh metallic scraping sounds indicated that the truck was way overdue for a brake job, but it came to a stop about a foot from the rear bumper of Harold and Margaret's car. The man who got out looked to be about seventy, but he was still active and vigorous. His old yellow truck, with its ladder rack and a big toolbox behind the cab, was obviously a work truck.

"Royce Green," the man introduced himself as he thrust out his hand to Mike. "Met you the Sunday you preached the trial sermon, but I know you haven't had a chance to learn all the names in the church yet." Mike reintroduced Karen and introduced her parents to Royce. Royce continued, "Just came over to take a look at the new carpet they put in the front of the house. The guys just put it in yesterday afternoon. We tried our best to get that old carpet to look decent, but it was too far gone. That carpet was brand new when the Reynolds moved into this house in 1974. Anyway, we put new carpet, top of the line stuff, in the front of the house. We figure y'all will be entertaining a lot, so we wanted to make it look nice."

Mike and Karen resisted the urge to ask whether the shabby carpet in the bedrooms would be all right since the people they entertained at the parsonage would never see it. Royce went inside to inspect the work of the carpet installers. As he did, they heard the sound of air brakes as the moving van made the tight turn from Peyton Street and pulled up in front of 722 Alabama Avenue.

* * * * * * * * * * *

While the movers were unloading furniture and placing it in the house under the watchful eyes of Karen and her mother, Mike and his father-in-law took the Oldsmobile and headed to a hardware store Mike had spotted nearby on Martin Luther King Boulevard, which most people still call Monument Avenue, to purchase the letters to spell *Westover* on the mailbox. Mike had decided early in their married life that he would leave placement of furniture and hanging of pictures entirely up to Karen. Like the psalmist, he resolved not to involve himself in great matters or in things too high for himself. Wherever Karen chose to put things was fine with him. He was just pleased to have somebody else doing the grunt work, especially with the piano.

"Sure is nice to have you kids close by," Harold commented as he headed the car back toward the house from the hardware store. "Especially since y'all are about to have another baby. I can't wait to see Asalee. Haven't seen her since Christmas. Lil' girl's growing like a weed, and seeing her a couple times a year doesn't cut it. Rob's and Bill's kids are right there in Williston and I see them all the time. It'll be nice to see y'all more often, and Margaret's planning to take a week off and come up here to help out when the baby's born."

"That's what Karen was telling me after the last time she and her mother talked. She sure was a big help when Asalee was born, since neither one of us had taken care of a baby before. Karen had a good pregnancy, good delivery, no problems the first time around. So far, she's doing fine with this one. The only drawback to this move has been having to change obstetricians halfway through her pregnancy. She got a recommendation for an obstetrician from one of the women in the church here who is pregnant. Karen called her office and got an appointment for Tuesday of next week, and the doctor in Riverton's already faxed all of Karen's records down here."

"Do y'all know if it's going to be a boy or a girl?"

"It's another girl. Asalee's excited about the new baby, and that's helped her deal with the move. She's fascinated with her mom's pregnancy, likes to put her hands on Karen and feel the baby moving. Karen took her along when she went for her last checkup with the obstetrician in Riverton. He let Asalee listen to the baby's heart, and she came home all excited talking about that. She's taken to putting one of her stuffed animals under her shirt and pretending to be pregnant. Az has been a spoiled only child for six years, so I know she's bound to feel some jealousy when the baby's born. We're trying to involve her as much as we can in getting ready for the baby, and I think she'll play the big sister part to the hilt."

"Well, Rob and Bill sure enjoyed being the big brothers when Karen was little. Rob and Bill are fourteen months apart, but there's five years between Bill and Karen. The boys were always real protective of her. All I can say is, it's a good thing that you treat Karen right and you're faithful to her. Otherwise, those two boys'd come after you."

"I'd also have to deal with my father if I didn't treat her right. First time I took Karen up to Denham, Dad took me aside and said, "Son, I think this'n's a keeper. You picked yourself a good 'un. Better marry 'er fast before she changes her mind.""

"Margaret and I think Karen picked a good'n, too," Harold commented. "We've been AWOL long enough. They'll be sending a search party out for us if we don't get on back to the house."

＊　＊　＊　＊　＊　＊　＊　＊　＊　＊　＊

When Harold and Mike returned to the house, there were several more cars parked in the driveway, and Mike recognized the maroon Crown Victoria belonging to the Baxters. As they got out of the car, Asalee came running outside with Wallace the Dog in hot pursuit. Harold bent down, and Asalee lunged into his arms. Wallace had his front paws as far up on Harold as they would reach, barking excitedly as though he had just chased a cat up a tree. With Wallace barking after him and Mike following a few steps behind, Harold carried his granddaughter up the steps and into the house. Someone had set up one of the folding tables from the church fellowship hall, and the table was adorned with an abundant spread of food—a large tray of cold cuts and cheeses, several different kinds of bread, a couple of big bowls of potato salad, an assortment of desserts, a picnic cooler full of ice, and a half dozen two-liter soft drinks. The movers were well along in their work, with only boxes remaining on the truck to be unloaded. The day was starting to turn hot, and it was not too difficult for Karen and Margaret to persuade the movers to take a break and help themselves to the ample lunch the women from the church had brought in.

Harold started fixing himself a plate, and Mike was about to, when Karen called him aside into their bedroom and closed the door. Mike could tell by her countenance that she was quite upset about something. "What's wrong?" he asked, having no idea what had just transpired.

Mike had rarely seen Karen this angry. Her lower lip was trembling, she was on the verge of crying, and her voice sounded shaky as she began, "It's—it's that woman, Hilda Mae Snyder. The one who runs the nursery and doesn't want anybody messing with it. She lives right across the street from us, and she has nothing better to do than watch our every move. Right after you and Daddy left, she came over to bring the dessert she fixed. She came a half hour before the rest of them, just waltzed right in without knocking or announcing herself or anything. She's been driving me crazy following me all over the house. She's inspected every piece of furniture we own to see if it's decent enough to be in Harrington's parsonage. She's made snide remarks about us having a dog in the house and how unsanitary she thinks that is. The icing on the cake was when she stuck a key into the front door to see if it still fit, and it did, since the trustees didn't change the locks. She said she'd always had a key to the parsonage so she could keep an eye on things when the pastor was gone. Mike, go ahead and eat, and then you and Daddy go right back down to that hardware store and get some new locks. I'm not sleeping in this house one night with that woman having keys to our house." Karen was livid as she added, "Mike, I'm going to be sent up the river for murder before it's over. I'm ready to kill that woman with my bare hands."

9

ike's responsibilities as pastor of Harrington Baptist
Church did not begin until Sunday June 3. Interim pastor Bob McKnight was scheduled to conclude his ministry with the Wednesday night prayer meeting on May 30. Mike
planned to spend Wednesday getting settled into his office and
organizing his books. Eric Latham had called to say that he would
stop by around 4:00 to go over the music and the order of service
for Sunday.

All of Mike and Karen's furniture and belongings were in the
house and unpacked. Harold and Margaret had worked until 6:00
the evening before unpacking boxes, hanging pictures, and putting up curtains. Mike and Karen realized that they were going to
have to invest in some furniture. Their old sofa and chair that was
decent enough for the apartment at the seminary suddenly looked
shabby in the cavernous living and dining room at Harrington.
The sofa and chairs would be all right to put back in the den,
which currently was empty except for Karen's desk and computer.
Karen's piano looked nice in the living room. The dining room
end of the big front room was bereft of furniture. Mike and Karen
possessed only a kitchen table and chairs; a dining room suite was
one of the purchases they had postponed since they didn't have
room for one in the apartment at the seminary.

Harold insisted on paying for the new locks when he and Mike went back to the hardware store. They came home with three locks keyed alike for the exterior doors. With the new locks installed, Mike and Karen had the only keys, so the house was safe from the prying eyes of That Woman. Karen could not bring herself to speak of their neighbor across the street as "Hilda Mae" or "Mrs. Snyder." She assured Mike that, while it might be out of character for her to do so, she could call Hilda Mae Snyder much worse things than That Woman.

Wednesday morning came cool and rainy, so Karen, Asalee, and Wallace decided it was a great morning to sleep in. Mike went to the church about 7:00 to start unpacking books and organizing his office. Helen Walters, the part-time church secretary, did not come in until 9:00, so Mike had the place to himself. The office was sparsely furnished—a metal desk, a four-drawer file cabinet, a reasonably comfortable low-backed swivel chair, one wall of built-in bookcases, two oak framed chairs upholstered in a burnt orange fabric, and a black rotary-dial telephone. The chairs looked like the kind one often sees in a waiting room. Mike guessed that they came secondhand from the waiting room of Lee Walters' dental office. The movers had stacked all of the boxes marked "church office" in the middle of the floor.

Mike's first act as pastor of Harrington Baptist Church was to turn his desk around ninety degrees and push it up against the wall. Dan Jordan had his office at Talmadge Street in Denham arranged that way, and he told Mike the reason. Dan said that talking across a desk is intimidating to the person on the other side, making him feel like a kid who has been sent to the principal's office. Mike resolved to never talk to anyone across a desk and, as soon as possible, to come up with something better than those burnt-orange waiting room chairs. He did not want anyone who came to his office to sit in the same chair in which he once sat while awaiting a root canal.

The phone rang a few minutes after 8:00. Mike caught it on the first ring and tried to sound professional on this, his first official telephone call as pastor of Harrington Baptist Church. "Good morning. Harrington Baptist Church. This is Pastor Mike Westover."

"Lighten up, Preacher. This is Ted down at the *Harrington Courier*, published once a week whether anything happens or not." Mike recognized the voice of Ted Coleman, the youngest deacon and a member of the hiring squad. "I called your house, and Karen said I'd find you at the church."

"Trying to get my books unpacked and organized. Karen's tired from the move, so she and Asalee decided this cool rainy morning would be great for sleeping in. I'm a morning person, been over here since 7:00."

"Could you come down to my office at the paper this morning about 11:00? Paper comes out on Friday, and I want to put you on the front page. If you can come in, I'll get a good picture of you, give you a nice writeup, and take you out to lunch."

"Sounds good to me, Ted. See you at 11:00." As he hung up the phone, Mike heard the opening of the door at the end of the hall, the rattle of keys, and the sound of footsteps coming down the hall toward his office. "Good morning," he called out to whoever it was.

"Is that you, Pastor?" a woman's voice responded. As Mike came out of his study into the hall, he saw church secretary Helen Walters fumbling with her keys and opening the secretary's office.

"It's me." As soon as the words were out of his mouth, Mike knew they were grammatically incorrect, and that the correct form would have been "It is I," but he had never heard anyone in real life use the correct form. He hoped that his secretary would not be one whose mission in life was to sit in judgement on his grammar. "You must be Helen Walters. I met you the Sunday of the trial sermon. It's going to take me a while to learn the cast of characters, get names and faces matched up."

"Well, you've got one right. I'm Helen Walters. I've been the church secretary for thirty-two years, since the days of manual typewriters, wax stencils, hand-cranked mimeographs, rotary phones, four-digit phone numbers, and three-cent stamps. Just call me Helen like everybody else does."

"OK, Helen. Since you've been on the job longer than I've been alive, feel free to call me Mike like everybody else does. By the way, I remember looking at the pictures of the former pastors and seeing one by the name of Walters. Any kin?"

"My husband's grandfather, John Leland Walters. He was the one who baptized me in 1939 when I was ten years old. You can do the arithmetic, so you know how old I am. He was a legend, served this church twenty-two years, longest tenure in the history of the church, died in the pulpit, fell over dead from a heart attack one Sunday night. His son, my father-in-law, was John Leland Walters, Junior, and my husband is John Leland Walters III. Most people call him Lee or Doc, either of which suits him fine. Lee's father was a general practitioner, practiced forty-five years in Harrington until he died in '72. Lee's going to be just like his father and grandfather. He started practicing here in '51, took over the practice from old Dr. Gladney when he retired. I've been after Lee to retire, but I fully expect him to die with his hands in somebody's mouth. Our daughter Leslie, we just had the one child, is an oral surgeon. We were hoping she'd come into practice with her dad and eventually take over, but she's married to a dentist, and they're in practice together in Atlanta, up at Buckhead. I think they'll stay there, can't say I blame them. They'll make more there than they'd ever make down here in Harrington."

"I can relate to that at least a little," Mike commented. "My father's an automotive machinist, rebuilds engines. It's a second generation family business. I worked with him part-time all through high school, college, and the three years I taught school in

Denham before I went to seminary. Dad was hoping I'd come into the business with him. I could do it, do it well, make good money. Dad's made a good living at it, gets a lot of business from people restoring antique cars. He's good on the old stuff. I'm glad I know how to do the work in case I ever need to fall back on it to make a living, but my heart's not in it. Anyway, I've been over here getting my books unpacked and setting up my study. I want to settle in and start to work."

"I look forward to you getting started. We've been without a pastor eight months, since Brother Reynolds left. Brother McKnight's been a good interim, nice man and a good preacher, but it's time we called a pastor."

"I met him the Sunday I preached the trial sermon. I only got to talk briefly with him. Everybody seems to like him, at least everybody on the committee speaks well of him."

"Susan Whitmire especially," Helen replied coolly.

"Oh? Why is that?"

"You haven't caught on? Susan and Brother McKnight have become a hot item here lately."

"First I've heard about it. If there's anything between them, she's certainly been discreet about it, never mentioned it in our conversations with the committee. She told us her husband's dead, that's all."

"Poor old Jim Whitmire," Helen sighed. "Sick with cancer about a year and a half, fought it like nobody I ever saw, only fifty-five when he died. Fine man, vice president of the Bank of Mintz County, very active in the church, served as a deacon. He's only been dead a little over a year, and Susan's going after Brother McKnight like some love-sick teenager. Disgusting, if you ask me. His wife's been dead a good long while, five or six years. They started seeing each other in January, before Jim was dead a whole year. And he's seventy-one years old. Now Preacher, don't you think that's too big an age difference?" Before Mike could open his mouth to speak or engage his brain to formulate an answer, Helen reiterated, "And I think that was absolutely disgraceful, her not waiting 'til Jim's body was good and cold."

Whenever anyone used that "Preacher, don't you think…" formula, it was a matter of principle for Mike to express a divergent opinion. "Well," Mike began as he gathered his thoughts, "I think it's their business. Brother McKnight's a young-looking seventy-one, I wouldn't have guessed him to be that old. He's not ready for the nursing home just yet. Susan appears to have plenty of life left in her, too. Both good people as far as I can tell, both love the Lord. If they love each other, that's great. They haven't asked for my advice, but if they do, I'll tell them to go for it."

Helen Walters' stern look over the top of her reading glasses told Mike that he had not given her the answer she wanted. "Well, I don't think it looks good," she reiterated icily.

"Like I said, they haven't asked for my advice. Anyway, I need to get over to the house and put a suit on. Ted Coleman called this morning, wants me to come by so he can get a picture of me and do a writeup for the paper. I'm going to be the lead story on the front page of the *Harrington Courier*."

"Ah yes, Ted Coleman," Helen commented with the same coolness with which she had spoken of Susan's romantic involvement, "one of the new people who've come into the church. Been here seven or eight years. Mr. Homer Bazemore was editor of the *Courier* for forty-odd years. He sold the paper and retired back around '82 or '83. Nobody in the family, certainly not that no-good son of theirs, wanted to take over. Mr. and Mrs. Bazemore are good people, Methodists. Poor old Mr. Bazemore's in the nursing home up at Carrollton now, real bad with Alzheimer's, doesn't recognize anybody, not even his wife. Ted bought the paper when Mr. Bazemore retired. Ted's not from here. He's from over't Macon."

As he got in the car, Mike pondered his first hour of working with Helen Walters. If Ted and Brenda were still new people after seven or eight years, he wondered how long it would take him and his family to gain full acceptance. Arriving home, he found Karen and Asalee still in their nightgowns, cozied up in front of the television watching *Sesame Street.*

"Hi, Hon," Karen called out from the living room as Mike came in the kitchen door. I thought you were going to work at the church all morning. Surprised to see you home so early."

Asalee stretched up for a hug from Mike. With her full weight hanging from his neck, Mike replied, "That's what I planned to do, but Ted Coleman called this morning..."

"Yeah, I know. He called here first, woke me up. I told him he'd find you at the church."

"He wants me to come in about 11:00. Ted runs the weekly paper here. Wants to take my picture and write a front page story about us. Paper comes out on Friday, and he thinks it might help bring a few more in for our first Sunday. I need to put on a suit to have my picture made. Ted's taking me out to lunch afterwards."

"That's good, because you'd probably be making a sandwich if you ate here. Kitchen's closed and cook's off duty. We're all laying low. Wallace hasn't moved since you brought him back in from doing his business early this morning." About the time she uttered those words, a very groggy Wallace, who had been asleep on the floor beside Asalee's bed, came stretching and walking stiffly into the living room. He had awakened sufficiently to realize that Asalee was no longer in bed. As he emerged from the darkness of the bedroom, the look on his face said that he really didn't mean to be up just yet, and he would resume his slumber as soon as he found Asalee. Seeing her curled up on the sofa next to Karen, he went through his ancient canine ritual of circling three or four times before collapsing in a pile at Karen's feet and picking up where he left off.

Mike put on a white shirt, always a safe bet, along with the dark-gray pinstripe suit that he had worn the previous Sunday at Clear Springs. He still had the tie Karen selected hanging with it, so he did not need to trouble her to match up a tie for him. He was already wearing gray socks. The combination would do fine for a black-and-white photo. He put on his newest pair of black Florsheim dress shoes, and he was good to go.

Ted had asked Mike on the phone if he knew his way around well enough to find the courthouse. Mike assured him that he did, and Ted told him that the *Courier* office was on the square facing the east end of the courthouse. Mike was twenty minutes early when he found a parking place on the square, so he took time to read the historical markers in front of the court-house. He learned an interesting bit of trivia, that the county was originally Ferguson County, and that the name was changed in 1868 to honor the memory of Captain Cicero Mintz, a Ferguson County native who died leading his company in a heroic charge against a Union gun battery at Gettysburg.

Many of the commercial buildings on the square looked to be of comparable vintage to the courthouse. Mike noted three that had dates carved on a piece of marble cemented into the brick-work near the top of the storefront. "Gowin Bros. 1898" was the inscription on the building that housed Harry's Barber Shop and Bishop's Walgreen Agency Drugs. Only the year, 1902, was inscribed in the center of the cornice on a vacant building that had last been a furniture store. The third building Mike saw with a date stone on it was his destination, a red-brick building with old-fashioned arch-top windows on the second floor and a brown canvas awning over the sidewalk. The sign in the window, painted many years ago in gold leaf lettering, read *The Harrington Courier* and, beneath those words in smaller letters, *Serving Harrington and Mintz County Since 1889.* The rectangular marble stone just below the cornice read "Courier Building, 1895."

Mike had the feeling of stepping through a time warp as he opened the screen door and stepped into the office of the *Harrington Courier*. The old building was in a remarkable state of preservation, having been in continuous use by the newspaper for which it was originally built. The floors were well-oiled heart pine, and the counter separating the lobby from the office area was quarter-sawn oak in a dark golden-brown finish that matched the wainscoting. Slow-turning ceiling fans suspended on long shafts dared any insect to fly beneath them. White milk-glass globe lights hung from the high pressed tin ceiling, which was painted bright aluminum to improve the lighting. Two women sat in ergonomic office chairs, working at modern computer terminals perched atop century-old oak desks. As Mike came up to the counter, the older woman, a pleasant, grandmotherly sort, got up from her desk and said, "Yes, sir. How may I help you?"

"I'm Mike Westover, pastor of Harrington Baptist Church, here for an 11:00 appointment with Mr. Coleman."

Before she could say anything, a voice from the back of the building called out, "Mr. Coleman retired and moved to Florida five years ago. I'm Ted. Come on back, Preacher." Ted proceeded to introduce Mike to the two women working in the office. Madeline Naylor, the woman who had greeted him, was the office manager. "Madeline came with the building when I bought the place, best part of the deal, couldn't run this place without her," Ted quipped. The younger woman, Mike learned, was a member of Harrington Baptist Church. Vicky Blevins, who appeared to be in her late twenties, told him that she was Susan Whitmire's daughter and that her husband Bruce was Rudy and Bobbie Blevins' son.

Ted directed Mike back to the photography studio he had set up in the room next to his office. After shooting a half-dozen proofs, he let Mike choose the one he liked best. "We'll run this one in Friday's paper," Ted explained, "and then we'll keep it on file. I'm trying to build a photo file of all the prominent people in town..."

"So I'm one of the prominent people?"

"In this town, pastor of Harrington Baptist Church is as prominent as you can get. I keep file photos of all the pastors, everybody in city or county government, business owners, school administrators, coaches and athletes, doctors, lawyers, judges, town characters, people over a hundred, and anybody else I have a chance to get in front of the camera. That way, if you up and die on us, I've already got a photo I can run with the obituary without troubling your family."

"I hope you don't need it for my obituary. I just got here."

"Me too," Ted laughed. "I'll have more occasions to use your picture. One of the things our paper can do that the big daily papers can't very well do is cover news of the local churches. People don't read the *Courier* to find out what's happening in the Persian Gulf or even what's happening in Atlanta except as it affects Harrington and Mintz County. If they want that, they can read *The Atlanta Constitution*. People read the *Courier* to find out what's happening in Harrington and Mintz County. I try to do good coverage of church news. Same thing with sports. We cover the Little League, church leagues, and local sports as well as the Atlanta paper covers the Braves and the Falcons. I've had people get upset with me, though. Some folks complained that I was printing more news from the black churches than I was from the white churches. I told them it was because they were sending me more news, and if the other churches'd send me their news, I'd print it, too. Take the two biggest black churches, Zion A. M. E. and Greater New Hope Baptist. I can count on at least one good story a month from each of those churches, a well-written article, some good pictures with captions, or both. They send me good stuff, and I use it. Especially Zion A. M. E. There's a young guy over there, Derek Elliott, just finished his junior year of high school. Lot of interest in journalism. He's the official reporter for Zion A. M. E. Everything he feeds me is well-written, factually correct, grammatically correct, and neatly typed. Good photographer, too. So I called him to see if he wanted to do some freelance work. He's covered a city council meeting and a couple of county commission meetings, and I'm going to have him doing a lot of local sports this summer. He wants to study journalism at the University of Georgia, and I'm going to do all I can to help him get a scholarship."

"Sounds like he has a lot of potential. I look forward to meeting him."

"And you will. Now let's get everything together for the article about you so I can give the notes to Vicky before we go to lunch. She's good at taking my rough notes and turning them into a finished story. We put the paper to bed on Wednesday afternoon and go to press early Thursday morning. Most of this is right from your resume. Let's see, native of Denham, Georgia, did a B. S. in Education at Rullman College. Master of Divinity from Mid-Atlantic Baptist Theological Seminary?" Ted asked.

"Right," Mike confirmed.

"Tell me a little about your wife..."

"Karen's maiden name was Owen, from Williston, Alabama. We met at Rullman College. She's a computer science major, worked with an advertizing agency in Riverton while I was in seminary. We've been married seven years, one daughter Asalee, six years old, expecting our second child in September. Karen's a good musician, sings and plays the piano beautifully. Very organized person, good Bible teacher. We're partners in ministry, she's as good with people in crisis as any pastor I know." With a laugh, Mike added, "She makes me look a lot better than I really am."

"I was impressed with her when we talked over Sunday dinner the day you preached for the committee. And your little girl is a delight."

"Thanks, Ted. Asalee'll be starting first grade when school opens. Seems only yesterday she was a baby. They grow up fast."

"Tell me about it. My oldest is fourteen, thinks she's grown and knows it all. Your time's coming, Preacher. Wait'll she's a teenager." Quickly returning to his interview questions, Ted continued, "So tell me about the church you served in Virginia..."

"Clear Springs Baptist Church near Ledford, Virginia. Historic old church, dates back to 1846. Since 1882, all their pastors have been seminary students. Only about 75 active members, but a very healthy, vibrant congregation. I'll always thank the Lord that I was able to start my ministry there. Very progressive church, first in the Sanders County Association to ordain women deacons, and the church just called a very gifted young woman, Heather Simmons, as pastor. I'm thankful for what I learned in seminary, but I'm just as thankful for what the church taught me. I'm confident that Clear Springs will continue to do well, and Heather will have a good ministry there, just as I did."

"And your observations about Harrington so far?"

"I'm still learning my way around, and it'll take a while to learn all the names in the church, but Karen and I look forward to a long, fruitful ministry here. Harrington is going to be a good place to bring up our children. The church has a rich history and a promising future. Excellent facilities, good lay leadership, friendly congregation. I plan to be very involved in the community, and I look forward to meeting the other pastors in Harrington and Mintz County."

"OK, Preacher, let me give these notes to Vicky so she can turn them into a nice writeup. The rest of the paper's ready to go to press, and that's all we lack having the front page finished. Let's go find us some good groceries." After giving Vicky the interview notes and the photo, he turned to his office manager and said, "Madeline, go ahead and set up a complimentary subscription for Preacher Westover, 722 Alabama Avenue, same as it was for Preacher Reynolds."

The rain had stopped about 10:30, the clouds had dissipated, and the day was turning hot and muggy. Ted turned the air conditioning on full blast before he backed the car out of the angle parking space in front of the *Courier* building. As he headed north on Church Street and then turned right onto Court Street, he began narrating, "Four main streets in old downtown Harrington that make the square around the courthouse. Court Street's on the north side, Tennessee Avenue's on the south side. Church Street's on the east side, that's the street that runs in front of the *Courier* office, and Commerce Street's on the west side. Court and Tennessee run east and west, Church and Commerce run north and south. We just turned off Church Street onto Court Street, and we're going to turn back to the right onto Depot Street. Best food in town, the Lonesome Whistle Cafe. Used to be the Central of Georgia depot. Brantley Jacobs bought the building from Norfolk Southern, spent a fortune fixing it up. He was in the restaurant business in Atlanta for years and did well. He didn't want to all the way retire, just slow down a little, move to a smaller town and a slower pace. Brantley's a nice guy. His wife has a gift shop in what used to be the passenger waiting rooms, sells a lot of locally made quilts, arts and crafts, and such on consignment. Brantley has the restaurant in what used to be the freight room. Nice atmosphere, lots of railroad artifacts, old photos of Harrington and Mintz County people and places. The food's always good, and they don't skimp on the portions." As Ted parked the car, he continued his commentary on the best eating place in town. "Brantley and Betty did a nice job fixing the place up. One thing you'll have to get used to down here, like a lot of small towns, everything's closed on Wednesday. All the stores close, bank's closed. The Lonesome Whistle's open, so we'll see a lot of business people enjoying a leisurely lunch on their day off. The Courier office, the grocery store, the drug store, and the Lonesome Whistle are about all that's open on Wednesday."

"That's just like Denham where I grew up."

"Well, it was a big adjustment for me coming from Macon. Brantley closes on Sunday and Monday. Says he knows he'd do a lot of business if he opened on Sunday, but he doesn't care. Doesn't have a thing to do with religion. Brantley's the town agnostic, wife's a lapsed Catholic. Brantley said he'd worked seven days a week for thirty years and he was tired of it, said that was why he moved down here. Says he makes a decent living working five days a week. Not a church going man, but he hates to keep anybody who wants to go from going. Being closed on Sunday, he's not keeping any of his employees from going to church. If you want to go out on Sunday or Monday, there's the Old West Steak House, the Pizza Hut, or McDonald's, all of them over on Martin Luther King Boulevard, which most people still call Monument Avenue."

*   *   *   *   *   *   *   *   *   *   *   *

Mike and Ted were a little ahead of the noon rush. "Two for non-smoking, Ted?" Brantley asked. As Ted nodded affirmatively, Brantley continued, "And your guest is?"

"Mike Westover, just moved in yesterday, new pastor at Harrington Baptist Church."

"Welcome to Harrington, Reverend. I hope you enjoy eating with us today, and I hope you'll be in Harrington a long time and that you and your family will eat with us often."

"I'm sure I'll enjoy it," Mike replied. "I'm very impressed with all the work you've done on the old depot, love the atmosphere, and Ted tells me the food's wonderful."

"This is a unique building, built in 1897, not many like it left. We take a lot of pride in it, take pride in serving good food and keeping our prices reasonable so folks can afford to eat with us. I'm fifty-seven years old. Restaurant business is all I've done my whole life. I enjoy working with the public, talking with the regulars who come in here. We like it here, town's been good to us. We have a lot of people come from out of town on Friday and Saturday nights, but even then most of our crowd is local people."

"Well, if the local crowd's here all the time, you must be doing a good job."

"Thanks, Reverend, and I hope you enjoy it. Missy will be your server. She'll be with you in just a moment." Brantley excused himself, leaving Ted and Mike to ponder the many enticing offerings on the menu.

* * * * * * * * * * * *

The Lonesome Whistle had been all that Ted promised, and Mike resolved to take Karen and Asalee there. Ted paid the check and left a good tip for the pleasant young woman who had been their server.

"Thanks for lunch, Ted. You picked a great place. I'll have to bring Karen and Asalee here," Mike commented as they walked toward the car.

"Glad you liked it, Preacher. Brantley's built a good business, generated a lot of good will when he fixed up the old depot. Got it on the National Register of Historic Places, had a big ribbon-cutting ceremony. Mr. Blake Dayton, last agent at the depot, ninety-eight years old, came and cut the ribbon. Good thing they had the ribbon cutting when they did. Mr. Dayton died in his sleep two days later. Anyway, Preacher, I told 'em I'd be out of the office until about two o'clock. It's 12:40 now. You got time for me to show you around a little?"

"Sure, Ted. I'm free until 4:00 when I need to meet Eric to go over the music for Sunday. Brother McKnight's doing prayer meeting tonight, so give me the grand tour." As Ted pulled away from the depot, Mike continued, "By the way, when I left the church this morning, I told Helen where I was going, and she acted kinda cool all of a sudden, referred to you as 'one of the new people,' said you'd been here seven or eight years. She said, 'Ted's not from around here, you know. He moved here from Macon.' Like that was on a different planet."

"Oh yes," Ted laughed. "Sounds like something Helen'd say in one of her more pleasant moments. She's not overly fond of me."

"I got that impression. How long do you have to be here before you're not 'one of the new people' anymore? You'd think seven or eight years is long enough to establish yourself anywhere."

"Preacher, as long as you're the first generation of your family in this town and, I'm sorry to say, in the church, you'll be one of the new people. Pastor Reynolds used to say that Harrington Baptist Church receives members by birth and marriage. He had to be careful where and to whom he said it, but it's the truth. Brenda's from Macon too, so we'll probably be new people if we're still here when we're eighty. We almost went under the first two years after I bought the paper from the Bazemores. A lot of people didn't renew their subscriptions, some of the businesses quit advertizing in the paper. They didn't like somebody who wasn't from here running the paper, and I made changes that some people didn't like."

"Such as?"

"About three months after I took over the paper, Zion A. M. E., one of the black churches I was telling you about, called a new pastor, Reverend Jennings, the one who's there now. I called and invited him to come by and get his picture made for the paper, interviewed him, did a nice front-page article like I'm doing for you, and took him to lunch afterward. Some people didn't like me doing that. Until I took over, the paper had never carried an obituary, engagement announcement, or wedding writeup pertaining to blacks. I called the pastors of the black churches, and I called the funeral director at Carter Funeral Home in Hansonville, that's the funeral home most of the blacks in Harrington use. I told them the paper was under new management and the old ways were changing. They believed me when they saw the frontpage writeup about Reverend Jennings. If it hadn't been for new subscribers we picked up in the black community and the fact that there was no other paper to carry the legal notices, we would've gone under. Most of the ones who quit taking the paper or quit advertizing came around when they saw we were here to stay."

Ted followed Depot Street north to Court Street and turned right as he continued his monologue. "Right here on your right is Webster Funeral Home. Leonard and Bill Webster, father and son. About two thirds of your funerals'll be with Webster. Old Harrington establishment." Ted made a right turn and headed south on Baker Street. "Now this is Baker Street Church of God on the right. Strong, active congregation, runs about 175 in worship, young pastor about your age, Jeremy Griffin's been here about a year, seems to be doing well."

"And the street we're crossing now is…" Mike asked.

"Tennessee Avenue. If you turn right and go down two blocks you'll be back to the court-house square. Now let's take a right on Carolina Avenue. Remember you've got six state streets; Tennessee, Carolina, Alabama, Virginia, Florida, and Georgia, all run east and west. OK, this is McDowell Funeral Home on your left, been here about twenty years. Two-thirds of your funerals'll be with Webster; the rest'll be with McDowell. Now if we were to turn right up here at Church Street and go north two blocks, we'd be back on the square on the side where the *Courier* office is, but we're going to go south for now." As he put on his left turn signal, Ted continued his commentary, "This is Harrington United Methodist Church. Some of them didn't like it when the conference sent them a woman pastor last year, but most of them have gotten over it. Eleanor Flint Basden. Sharp lady. Husband Ben's principal at Harrington Middle School. Eleanor was a nurse, made a mid-life career change, went to seminary after her kids were grown. She was born and raised in Harrington, whole family used to be members of our church. When she came to terms with her calling to be a minister, she and Ben just quietly left and went over to the Methodist church because they knew Methodists were more open to women in ministry. While she was in seminary, they assigned her to Reid's Chapel, little church over in the east end of the county. She finished seminary last spring. At conference time, when they played musical chairs, she got moved uptown to Harrington Methodist. She's won their respect, and ol' Ben's been her biggest fan, supported her all the way. She preached at the Easter sunrise service this year, brought as good an Easter message as I've ever heard anywhere. Now we're crossing Alabama Avenue, the street you live on, and you see the two churches up ahead facing each other. The one on your left is Harrington Presbyterian, and the one on the right is..." Ted said as he turned into the parking lot, put the car in park, and shut off the engine, "Greater New Hope Progressive Missionary Baptist Church."

"Sounds like the name of a black church."

"It is. I'm going to fill you in on some history you need to know, because we've got people still nursing grudges over it. This is our old building, built in 1888. Our present building was built in 1963, and this building was put up for sale. The county was looking at it for a courthouse annex, but a more suitable building became available, so that fell through. Greater New Hope came up with the money and bought it cash on the barrelhead. Now historically the black section of town's been on the other side of Salyers Creek, south of Virginia Avenue and east of Baker Street. When they bought this building, it was the first time blacks had ever owned property on this side of town."

Mike and Ted got out of the car, and Mike admired the magnificent old edifice surrounded by ancient oak trees that two men could not reach around. The massive stone walls looked to be a foot thick, and the windows were real leaded stained glass. With its steep slate roof and high bell tower, it had infinitely more aesthetic appeal than the thinly-disguised prefab steel structure with faux-Colonial columns that Harrington Baptist Church now called home. The old building was beautifully maintained, and the grounds were immaculate. Mike walked over to read the inscription on the cornerstone. Bracketed between a cross and the compass-and-square symbol of Freemasonry, the inscription read:

Harrington Baptist Church
Organized August 20, A. D. 1887
Cornerstone Laid October 1, A. D. 1888, A. L. 5888
Rev. John C. Beckett, Pastor
"Except the Lord build the house, they labor in vain that build it." Psalm 127:1

"Can I help you, sir?" Mike was startled by the voice of the small, thin, elderly black man.

His khaiki pants and shirt were old and stained, and his shirt was soaked with perspiration. A baseball cap with a *Cat Diesel Power* logo shielded his eyes from the midday sun. Mike had almost stumbled over the old man who was on his knees pulling up weeds around the foundation and shrubbery.

Extending his hand to shake hands, Mike answered, "I'm Mike Westover, new pastor at Harrington Baptist Church. Just admiring this beautiful old church, so well-kept."

"Pleased to meet you, Reverend," the old man said as he wiped his right hand on his pants leg before taking Mike's extended hand. "Sorry my hands are dirty and I'm all hot and sweaty. My name's Prince Hammondtree."

"Pleased to meet you, Mr. Hammondtree. No way to do what you're doing without getting dirty and working up a sweat. You're doing a good job, got the grounds looking nice."

"As it ought to be at the house of the Lord, Reverend. I usually do this early of a morning, come over here about 6:30 or 7:00 before it gets so hot, but I got rained out of doing it early." Just then the older man spotted Ted standing over by the car and called out to him, "Deacon Coleman! Lord it's good to see you again!" As he put his arm around Ted, he told him, "Sure did 'preciate that nice writeup you gave us about the church's seventy-fifth anniversary. That sure would'n'a happened when old man Bazemore had the paper!"

"Well, from my acquaintaince with him and some of the stories I've heard, I expect you're right. It's nice to be able to print some good news now and then. Besides," Ted added with a laugh, "y'all pulled my fat out of the fire. If it hadn't been for black folks who started taking the paper and the legal notices, I wouldn't've made it those first two years."

"Yessir, folks're kinda skittish about change, they don't like it," Mr. Hammondtree observed. "But that don't mean it's not good for 'em. The changes you made needed to be made. I seen the way it was before and I see the way it is now, and it's a lot better since you took over."

"Have you been in Harrington all your life, Mr. Hammondtree?" Mike inquired.

"All seventy-two years, except for the time I was in the Army in World War II. Born down yonder on Pelfrey Street, four houses down from where I live now, March 4, 1918. Joined this church when I was twelve years old, 1930. Reverend Mooney, Cephas Mooney, the one that started this church, baptized me. Old man was born back'n slavery times, past eighty years old when he baptized me in Salyers Creek just below the Baker Street bridge. I was the last'n he baptized 'fore he died. I was ordained a deacon under Reverend Stewart the year we bought this building."

"Ted told me that this was originally the building of Harrington Baptist Church," Mike commented. "So you were here when Greater New Hope acquired this building."

"Yessir, I was, Reverend. Reverend Seals, Reverend Franklin Seals, was pastor where you are now. Fine man, fine a man of God as I ever knowed. We wouldn't a' had this building if it had'n a' been for him. The Lord meant for us to have this building, no doubt about it. Our old building down yonder on the corner of Florida Avenue and Carver Street's where Miracle Temple Church of God in Christ, Bishop Driver, is now. We was bustin' out at the seams. Harrington Baptist had the same problem. They wanted to build more Sunday School rooms and couldn't do it without giving up their parking lot. So they went'n bought land over on the other side of town'n built that big building where y'all are now, went in debt up to their eyeballs. They had to sell this building and get the money to pay down their mortgage, or they'd a' been payin' 'til Jesus comes again. Your church was stuck with a big note that was killin' 'em and a buildin' they couldn't sell no way no how. Reverend Stewart, Reverend Arthur Stewart, he's with the Lord now, was our pastor. He said he kept prayin' about our need for a bigger building, said the Lord kept remindin' 'im this building was for sale. He kept tellin' the Lord ain't no colored folks ever owned property on this side'a town. The Lord said He knowed that, but they's a first time for everything. So Reverend Stewart went to see Reverend Seals. Reverend Seals told him the church had the building listed with Mr. Walter Holliday's real estate company for $60,000, but he said the church was in a tight to sell it and get what they could to pay down their note. Reverend Seals told Reverend Stewart to get his trustees together, go see Mr. Holliday, make an offer, put a contract on it, and go from there. Miracle Temple was a new church just getting started, but they scraped and scrounged and come up with $15,000 to offer us for our old building. Trustees agreed, and church voted to sell it to 'em for that, on the condition we was able to buy this building. So we had that $15,000. That very week, old Mother Tatum passed, 96 years old. Come to find out, she had a $10,000 life insurance policy she'd taken out, paid up years ago, with the church as beneficiary. That gave us $25,000. Our people give like nothin' I ever seen in my life, some of us mortgaged our houses, went into our savings, sold jewelry, cashed in insurance policies, brought in all the money on one special Building Fund Sunday. Three different deacons counted it, I was one of 'em. We collected $25,211.18 on top of the $25,000 we had." Unlocking the massive wooden doors of the sanctuary and ushering Mike and Ted into the cool semi-darkness of the old stone edifice, Deacon Hammondtree motioned to one of the heavy, dark-finished oak pews. "Now Reverend, Deacon Coleman done heard this, but I expect you'd best sit down for this part of the story. 'Sides, it's too hot to be standing out there in the sun. Like I said, three deacons, myself included, counted that money, and all three of us come up with the same amount, $25,211.18. Ol' Deacon Pete Hardy, he's with the Lord now, talk to 'im when you get to Heaven, he'll tell you the same thing I'm tellin' you. He's the one that took the money home with him, put in under the mattress he slept on, said he'd never seen that much money at one time, he was scared to death havin' that much cash in his house. Monday morning, he took it straight to the bank soon's it open, stood there and watched 'em open the bag and count the money. The teller counts

it an' says, 'Uncle Pete, y'all made a mistake countin' this money.'
Deacon Hardy knowed we had'n done no such thing, that we
counted it right. Deacon Hardy said he might not have but a
fourth grade education, but he could count and add good as anybody. He thought she was tryin' to short us and say it was less'n
what we counted. So he ask her, 'How much of a mistake?' and
she says 'exactly $5,000 in your favor. I come up with
$30,211.18.' So she counted it again, got the same thing. Two
more tellers come over and counted, got the same thing. Directly
ol' man Stoney Nelson, Stonewall Jackson Nelson, president of
the bank, comes over and counts it hisself, and he come up with
the same amount. That $25,211.18 was every penny we could
scrape together. Ol' Deacon Hardy, rest his soul, poor as Job's
turkey, he sure didn't have no extra $5,000 to kick in. That money
was in a locked bank deposit bag from the time we counted 'til the
time that bank teller counted it. We called Reverend Stewart an'
told him what happened. He said wad'n no doubt in his mind it
was a miracle, said if the Lord could multiply the loaves and fishes
to feed five thousand people, He could put an extra $5,000 in that
money bag. I know the Lord worked a miracle. To this day, if you
wanna hear some shoutin' in this ol' church, see some of us gray-
heads get happy, all you got to do is start singing *My father is rich
in houses and lands, He holdeth the wealth of the world in His
hands, Of rubies and diamonds, of silver and gold, His coffers are
full, He has riches untold...* Well, Reverend Stewart called the
deacons and trustees together, told us we'd best take that $5,000
miracle as a sign God means for us to have that building. We went
up to Mr. Holliday's real estate office and told 'im we wanted to
put a cash contract on that building for $55,211.18, not a penny
more or a penny less." With a boisterous laugh, he added, "Lord,
let me tell you, Reverend, I didn't know a white man could turn so
many different colors! Ol' man Holliday look like his body and

soul was gonna part company. He hem-hawed around, first time he ever had a stuttering problem, he says, 'N-n-now y'all know no c-c-coloreds has ever bought property on this side of town, and that building was a white church for seventy-five years, and hit's right across the street from another white church.' Reverend Stewart told 'im we knowed exactly which building it was, and where it was, and what the history of it was. Reverend Stewart said the Lord was also aware of all of that, but He meant for us to have that building. Ol' man Holliday asks us how come the odd amount, why not just make it an even $55,000, or $55,200, and we told 'im that was the exact amount the Lord gave us, and that was what we wanted to offer. We didn't want some old widow who couldn't give but a dollar or two or some child who gave a nickel or a dime or some pennies to not have their part in buyin' that building. He seen we wad'n gonna back down, so he says, 'let me go call our pastor an' see what he thinks.' Hit wad'n five minutes 'fore Reverend Seals walked through that door! He introduced hisself, shook hands with all of us. Then he turn to ol' man Holliday'n says, 'Walter, these gentlemen've brought a legitimate offer on behalf of their church. Write out a contract for the amount they're prepared to offer. We'll have a called meeting of the trustees at 7:00 tonight. Trustees'll make a recommendation to the church, church'll vote on whether to accept or reject the offer.' Reverend Seals stood right there over his shoulder'n watched 'im fill out the contract, my brother Lennox signed it as chairman of the trustees. Harrington Baptist voted by a margin of eight votes to sell us this building. We went to the bank, got a certified check for $55,211.18, took it to ol' man Holliday's office. Reverend Seals met us over there, and the two of them an' Reverend Stewart and my brother Lennox walked over to the courthouse to record the deed. Wad'n none of 'em thinkin' 'bout there'd be a $12 fee for recording the deed. Reverend Seals said, 'Walter, I got six dollars on me. How 'bout I pay six dollars and you pay six dollars.'"

"That's an amazing story," Mike commented.

"Yes 'tis, Reverend. But I guess you know Reverend Seals got run off from the church where you are now. Some people's gonna answer for what they done to that man of God. Some of 'em was already down on 'im cause he wouldn't have nothin' to do with that White Citizens Council that ol' man Bazemore an' ol' man Holliday was headin' up. Reverend Seals refused to come and pray over their meetin's, told 'em there wadn't any words he could say that'd bring God in on it. He told 'em from the pulpit, looked straight at ol' man Holliday an' said, 'Now if y'all want to have just a plain Citizens' Council, bring black and white folks together, pray together, eat a meal together, and talk about how to solve some problems, I'll come and pray over that, and I'll be glad to be a part of it. But don't ask me to be a part of your White Citizens Council, and don't ask me to pray over it.' Well, ol' man Holliday wrote down what he said, and ol' man Bazemore put it on the front page of the paper."

"So what happened then?"

"Folks in this town dragged that poor man and his family through hell backwards. Polices started followin' him an' his wife around every time they got in the car. Neither one of 'em had ever had a speedin' ticket, all of a sudden the two of 'em got seven speeding tickets in five days' time. John Birch Society was big around here back then, and some a' them Birch nuts started the rumor that Reverend Seals was a communist. Reverend Seals and his wife had two fine children. Kids at school shunned 'em, called 'em names, wouldn't have nothin' to do with 'em. I was the janitor at Harrington Elementary, so I seen how they treated the little boy. Nicest lil' boy you ever saw, always address me as 'Mr. Hammondtree,' 'stead'a callin' me by my first name like most'a the children did. I went to the principal when I saw a kid bounce a rock off'n his head, knocked 'im out cold and he bled like a stuck pig. I was the first one to 'im, an' I had the little boy's blood all over me when I told the principal that I seen it happen and I seen who done it, but he said the police and courts wouldn't take the word of some colored janitor, especially considerin' the girl I saw throw the rock was from a right prominent family in this town. Mr. Burton didn't even call the police, an' I guess it was just as well 'cause they wouldn't a' done nothin' nohow. Folks in the church started sayin' it didn't look good for the pastor's children to be gettin' in so much trouble at school, and a lot of 'em started holding back their offerings or designatin' all they gave for the building fund, wouldn't pay his salary, tried to starve 'em out. Mrs. Seals had worked at the bank the whole time they'd been in Harrington, all of a sudden they told 'er they didn't need 'er anymore, didn't give 'er no reason but it didn't take no Mr. Einstein to figure it out. Our church, Zion A. M. E. and Miracle Temple took up special offerings to help Reverend Seals and his family, and we all took groceries to his house. Reverend Seals got threatenin' phone calls, obscene calls, all hours of the day an' night. One night somebody drove by and shot a high-powered rifle through the living room window. Reverend Seals' daughter was playin' the piano, bullet hit 'er in the back'a her neck, right at the base of her skull, killed 'er instantly. Polices come'n made a report, you know how that goes, crime never was solved 'cause they didn't try too hard, still ain't nobody been charged with killin' the young lady."

"Did anybody see anything, Deacon Hammondtree? Any witnesses?" Ted asked.

The old man gathered his thoughts and spoke slowly. "Yes, they was one good witness. Reverend Garnett, pastor at Baker Street Church of God was comin' home from a meetin' at his church. Reverend Garnett said he'd just crossed Peyton Street when he saw a pink and white '58 Pontiac slow down real slow in front of Reverend Seals' house. He seen somebody in the back seat pullin' a rifle back in the car and he heard the shot, and then the car took off like it was fired out of a cannon. Reverend Garnett swerved in front of 'em try'n to cut 'em off, but whoever it was just run up on the sidewalk, clipped Reverend Garnett, spun 'im around in the road'n kept goin'. Reverend Garnett tried to get the tag number of the car, but he said it look like a gunny sack was tied over the tag. He seen the bullet hole in the picture window and the girl slumped over the piano, and he stopped to see what he could do to help. He was the one that called the polices and the ambulance and called ol' Doc Walters. Doc Walters pronounced the girl dead right there in the living room. Poor girl never knowed what hit 'er, slumped over that piano with her head half blowed off'n blood all over the place."

All three men had tears running down their faces. Neither Mike nor Ted ever knew Franklin Seals, but they were both husbands and fathers who deeply loved their wives and children. Like Franklin Seals, they were purveyors of sometimes-unpalatable truth. That was enough of a connection.

"Reverend Seals and his wife asked Reverend Stewart and Reverend Garnett to conduct their daughter's funeral," Mr. Hammondtree continued the story. "Now some of the folks in Harrington Baptist did'n think it'd be a good idea to have a colored preacher in their pulpit, so we had the young lady's funeral right here at Greater New Hope. Reverend'n Mrs. Seals said it'd be a great comfort to 'em if they could bury their daughter in the colored cemetery down at the end of Pelfrey Street, so that's where we buried her. I holp dig the grave. Dr. King heard about it on the news the night the girl was killed. Him'n Mrs. King drove all the way down from Atlanta to pay their respects, did'n nobody know they's comin' 'til they walked into the funeral parlor. My wife'n I invited 'em to stay the night in our home. They did, an' Dr. King spoke a few words at the funeral the next day. Hit wad'n long after that, the deacons called Reverend Seals in'n told 'im that, while they certainly felt sorry for him 'bout his daughter's death, they felt like he'd caused enough trouble in the church and community, an' they felt like it'd be best if he'd resign for the good of the church. Brother Otis Garvey had a big truck, so him'n my brother Lennox moved Reverend Seals down to Mississippi where he had family. 'Bout six months later, Reverend Seals had a heart attack and died, young man, wad'n but forty-one years old. They brought 'im back here an' buried 'im next to his daughter. I holp dig his grave, too." With a rag he pulled from his hip pocket, Mr. Hammondtree dabbed at the tears trickling down his face before concluding, "So, you might say they's really two murders. They's still people walkin' round this town got blood on their hands, an' they's people in your church knows 'zackly who killed the young lady, they just ain't sayin'."

IO

Asalee, the fifth generation to play upon the yellowed ivories, was fascinated with her mother's old rosewood piano. She loved the rich, resonant tones that she had been hearing since she was in the womb. Because of the lifelong exposure to her mother's playing and singing, she had a better sense of pitch than most children her age. She could sing on pitch, and she had started picking out simple melodies by ear. Rather than discourage her, Karen made a game out of it. She would sing a few bars of a simple melody, have Asalee sing it back to her, then challenge her to pick it out on the piano. Asalee enjoyed the game, blissfully unaware that she was being educated. All Mike could think about, as he lay awake watching Karen sleep, was Karen, Asalee, or both sitting at the piano, their backs to the picture window, just like Debbie was when the single shot from a 30.06 ended her life.

Mike reminded himself that the killing of Debbie Seals occurred twenty-six years ago. Many things had changed since then. The people at Harrington Presbyterian were long since accustomed to a black congregation being across the street from them, and relations between the two congregations were cordial. The Mintz County public schools had been integrated since 1966, and the old Florida Avenue Colored School, which once housed all twelve grades, had been completely renovated as the new Harrington Middle School. In 1968, the county floated a bond issue and built a new elementary school and a new high school, complete with a modern stadium. A whole generation of black and white children had gone to school together. The segregation academy started by the big independent Baptist church on the Hansonville Highway dwindled to a handful of students before going under financially in 1985, almost taking the church down with it. The wife of the pastor at Zion A.M.E. and the wife of the editor of the *Harrington Courier* were professional colleagues at Harrington Elementary School, and the two couples were friends who sometimes went out socially. A black high school student did freelance reporting for the local paper. Blacks worked at the courthouse and in local businesses. Some owned houses north of Salyers Creek. Old man Walter Holliday died in the early 1970's, and his granddaughter Cheryl Groves now owned her grandfather's real estate company, which she renamed Red Carpet Realty. While Mike and Ted were talking with Prince Hammondtree, a police car passed by. The officer waved and kept going. Mr. Hammondtree said the officer was his nephew and a trustee of Greater New Hope. George Lewis, a member at Miracle Temple Church of God in Christ, represented Ward 3 on the city council. Natasha Ware, a member of Zion A.M.E., operated a florist shop on the square and served on the Board of Education. Much had changed since racist hysteria led to the killing of Debbie Seals and the firing of Franklin Seals as pastor of Harrington Baptist Church.

In one way, Mike felt foolish for wanting the piano away from the window, and he thought it was unnecessary to tell Karen about the killing of Debbie Seals. She might go years and never hear about it. Ted was in town seven years before he heard about it. It was extremely unlikely that such a terrorist act would take place in Harrington in 1990. Most whites had come a long way in their racial attitudes. Many of those who were involved with the Klan or the White Citizens Council were dead. Most of those remaining were old, embarrassed by their actions years ago, or both.

On the other hand, a cold-blooded killing occured, and no one had ever been charged with the crime. If the men involved in the killing were in their twenties at the time, they would now be in their forties or fifties. Most likely, some or all of them were still around, and they needed to be held accountable. They were probably leading decent respectable lives. For all Mike knew, some of the men in that pink and white Pontiac on the night of February 10, 1964 could be in his congregation. When he preached on Sunday, he might well be looking into the faces of people who knew who killed Debbie Seals, who decided long ago that it was best to let sleeping dogs lie. He had to tell Karen about the killing. She would eventually find out, and it would be better if she heard it first from him.

Mike pondered how a group of deacons could call for a pastor's resignation only a week after his daughter was slain. During choir rehearsal Wednesday night, Mike kept Asalee with him in the church library, where he found an old church directory listing the active deacons for the 1963-64 church year. Some of them, he noted, were still around. Jack Miller, Lee Walters and Royce Green were still active. Roland Millican and Rudy Blevins were no longer active deacons, but they were still very much a part of the church. They gave Franklin Seals a week to remove his books and personal effects from the church office, thirty days to vacate the parsonage, and thirty days' severance pay. The Sunday after his forced resignation, Seals preached at Greater New Hope. The next day, he and Mrs. Seals withdrew their son from Harrington Elementary School, and Otis Garvey and Lennox Hammondtree moved the family to Mississippi.

Sleep came fitfully and sporadically for Mike that night. He had the clock radio set for 6:00, but he woke up at 5:40, shut off the alarm, and got up. After putting on a pot of coffee, he shaved, showered, and got dressed. He toasted a couple of Pop Tarts to go with the coffee. He didn't want them, but the acid in the coffee would give him an upset stomach if he didn't eat something.

The door to Asalee's room was open. She was sound asleep, so still and peaceful that the rise and fall of her chest as she breathed was barely perceptible. Asalee had grown considerably since she first began sleeping in her antique iron bed, but she still looked small and delicate, all thirty-eight pounds of her lying there. All Mike could think of as he looked at Asalee's tiny frame lying in bed was what Prince Hammondtree said about how small Debbie Seals looked as she lay in her casket. Mike tiptoed into Asalee's room, bent over, and kissed her lightly on the forehead. Then he walked into the room where Karen was still sleeping. She roused enough to ask what time it was when he sat down on the bed, and she asked him to reset the clock for 8:00. He gave her a hug and a kiss and told her that he would be back at lunch time so they could go open their accounts at the Bank of Mintz County before it closed at 2:00.

It was 6:50 when Mike backed out of the driveway and headed east on Alabama Avenue. He turned right at Church Street and saw Mr. Hammondtree out already, sweeping the sidewalks around Greater New Hope Progressive Missionary Baptist Church. He waved, but the old gentleman did not see him. He drove across the Salyers Creek bridge and came to the stop sign where Church Street ends at the intersection with Virginia Avenue. He turned left and headed east on Virginia Avenue, remembering that Ted said the historically black section of town was south of Virginia Avenue and east of Baker Street. Mr. Hammondtree told him that he would find the cemetery at the south end of Pelfrey Street. There was a four-way stop at Virginia Avenue and Baker Street. Just after crossing Baker Street, Mike saw a spacious red brick church on his right, a stately English Gothic structure with a steep slate roof, pointed-arch windows and doors, and two matching towers. Between the twin front doors was the sign that read *Zion African Methodist Episcopal Church*. Another time, Mike would stop and admire the lovely old church, but on this morning he kept driving until, just beyond the church, he saw the sign for Pelfrey Street. He made the right turn and drove through two blocks of neat, well-kept single family homes. There was another four-way stop at Georgia Avenue and then a few more houses on either side of the street before it ended in a cul-de-sac at the entrance to the cemetery. The narrow road that wound through the cemetery had been paved at one time, but the pavement was broken, pot-holed, and patched in many places. Otherwise the grounds were well-kept, shaded by several big oaks, a towering rifle-barrel straight yellow poplar, and a couple of shag-bark hickories. Some of the plots were enclosed by masonry walls or low wrought-iron fences. Mike parked the car and got out. He had no idea where to look, but it was barely 7:00, and no one would know or care if he didn't get to the church before 9:00. The grass was still wet with dew as Mike walked slowly among the graves. Seeing *Hammondtree* on a marker, he walked over for a closer look, pausing to read *Lennox B. Hammondtree, January 11, 1903—July 3, 1988* and *Eula Clark Hammondtree, November 7, 1906—December 30, 1989*. There were a couple more markers with names he recognized from his conversation with Prince Hammondtree.

Perhaps it was a voice or just a thought passing through his mind, and he did not know the source of it, but in any case it was clear, *Just down the hill a little piece on your left, just beyond that hickory tree.* Not more than twenty feet beyond the hickory tree,

Mike looked down and saw two simple rectangular granite markers, flush with the ground, each at the head of a grave covered in crushed marble and outlined with bricks set in the ground at a forty-five degree angle. Hot tears ran unchecked down his face as he read *Deborah Jean Seals, December 20, 1949—February 10, 1964* and *Rev. Franklin B. Seals, July 17, 1923—August 26, 1964*. A third marker, at the head of an unused grave space, read *Jane Carden Seals, September 23, 1926*. Although the family had no relatives close by, someone had lovingly kept up the graves.

Mike was startled to see that it was 8:35 when he looked at his watch. He did not realize that he had lingered so long. He had been crying, thinking, and praying, mostly praying, praying the kind of prayer for which there can be no words, the kind of prayer in which the Spirit makes intercession with groanings that cannot be uttered.

* * * * * * * * * * * *

Helen Walters' car was already in the church parking lot when Mike got there at 8:50. Mike checked the glove box and found the small travel-size pack of Kleenex that Karen always kept there. He dabbed the last trace of tears from his face and hoped Helen would not be able to tell he had been crying.

"Good morning, Pastor. How're you this morning?" Helen called out cheerfully.

"Pretty good, I guess. Allergies acting up a little," Mike offered as an explanation for any redness that might remain. "Took a couple of Sudafed before I left home, so I should be OK. How about you?"

"Fine. You just missed your friend Ted Coleman. He dropped this off for you." Helen handed Mike a large brown envelope with the *Harrington Courier* address printed in the upper left corner and the scribbled words *For Bro. Mike from Ted C.* in the address area. Mike almost ripped it open while he was standing in Helen's office, but he caught himself. He retreated to the privacy of his study, took out his pocket knife, and opened it. The envelope contained a stack of photocopied excerpts from old newspapers bundled together with a large paper clip, topped with a note scrawled on a page from a scratch pad,

Bro. Mike—

After our conversation with Mr. Hammondtree, I decided to see what I could find in the archives. I copied these for you.

Ted

Pulling off the paper clip and Ted's note, Mike found himself looking at the obituary for Debbie Seals from the February 14, 1964 issue of the *Courier*.

DEBORAH JEAN SEALS

Deborah Jean Seals, 14, of 722 Alabama Avenue, died suddenly at her home on February 10. Miss Seals, an eighth grader at Harrington Junior High School, was born December 20, 1949 in Riverton, Virginia, the daughter of Rev. Franklin B. Seals and Jane Carden Seals. She was a member of Harrington Baptist Church. In addition to her parents, she is survived by one brother, Michael Seals of Harrington; grandparents, Mr. and Mrs. George W. Seals and Mr. and Mrs. Stanley J. Carden; great-grandmother, Mrs. Verna Grayson, all of Langley, Mississippi, and numerous aunts, uncles, and cousins. Funeral services were held on Wednesday February 12 at Greater New Hope Progressive Missionary Baptist Church with Rev. Cleon Garnett, Rev. Arthur Stewart, and Rev. Martin Luther King, Jr. officiating. Special music was presented by Miss Seals' piano teacher, Dr. Emile Broussard. Pallbearers were Clarence Bishop, Gowin Bishop, Ben Basden, Prince Hammondtree, Lennox Hammondtree, and Riley Hammondtree. Interment was in Pelfrey Street Colored Cemetery with Webster Funeral Home in charge of arrangements.

The next page was the headline story from the same issue of the *Courier*:

BULLET KILLS LOCAL GIRL

Harrington Police report that a 14 year old Harrington girl died Monday at 8:05 PM when a bullet fired from a high-powered rifle passed through the living room window of her home and struck her in the back of the neck as she was playing the piano. The dead girl was identified as Deborah Jean Seals of 722 Alabama Avenue, daughter of Rev. and Mrs. Franklin B. Seals. Rev. Seals, pastor of Harrington Baptist Church, has been the subject of considerable controversy stemming from his integrationist views and his role in the purchase of the old Harrington Baptist Church building by a negro church. Miss Seals was pronounced dead at the scene by Mintz County Coroner Dr. J. L. Walters. Dr. Walters stated that the girl died instantly from a single 30.06 bullet that struck her in the back of her neck at the base of her skull. Police Chief Bud Lowery stated that police believe the shot was fired from a passing car. Rev. Cleon Garnett, pastor of Baker Street Church of God, stated that he was returning from a meeting at his church when he saw a pink and white 1958 Pontiac Catalina slow down in front of the Baptist parsonage. He told police that he saw someone draw what appeared to be a rifle back into the car and he heard a shot before the car sped away. Garnett said that he attempted to block the path of the Pontiac, but the Pontiac ran up on the curb, clipped the front of his 1961 Ford Falcon, spun it around in the road, and kept going. Garnett told police that he was unable to get a tag number or to identify any of the four White males he saw in the car. Harrington Police are continuing their investigation. Anyone with information is asked to call the Harrington Police Department, telephone 7026.

The newspaper photos did not reproduce well, and Mike was just as glad that they did not. One showed a grim-faced Chief Lowery pointing to the half-dollar size hole in the picture window of the house that Mike and his family now occupied. The other photo, the kind that one expects to see in one of the crime tabloids rather than a small-town weekly, showed the piano Debbie Seals was playing when she was killed. Even in the photocopy of the grainy newspaper photo, Mike could see blood splattered all over the keyboard and the music book from which she had been playing. The photo confirmed that Karen's piano was in precisely the same place.

On the same front page, another headline screamed **NEGRO AGITATOR IN TOWN FOR SEALS FUNERAL.** Mike put that page aside without reading the two paragraphs of text under the headline and continued leafing through the newspaper articles. One, dated October 18, 1963, was a vitriolic editorial denouncing Seals for his opposition to the White Citizens Council and his advocacy of a dialogue involving citizens of both races. The editorial maintained that Seals, a native of Mississippi who received his seminary training in Virginia, should certainly understand and accept the southern way of life. It called for him to stay out of politics, keep his liberal views to himself, and stick to preaching the Gospel.

Putting that page aside, Mike turned to a copy of the November 22, 1963 front page. The day President Kennedy was killed, Mike noted, although he was not old enough to remember that event. In all fairness to the *Courier*, the content of the paper would have been put to bed on Wednesday afternoon the 20th, and the paper would have been printed the next morning. Yet, it still struck Mike as bizarre that, on the day that the president of the United States was murdered, the headline of the *Courier* would be **NEGRO CHURCH BUYS OLD HARRINGTON BAPTIST BUILDING.** A virulent editorial in that issue decried "the purchase of this splendid old edifice by a negro church unlikely to appreciate its rich history and unique architectural features," predicted that the building, one of the most frequently-photographed and painted churches in the state, would soon be a "decrepit ruin," and warned that "the movement of negroes to a previously all-White section of our town establishes a dangerous precedent. We predict that this purchase will be a tragic mistake for the negro church, since few negroes have any desire to come to a white section of town in order to go to church."

The next article was from the February 28, 1964 issue, its bold headline, **REV. SEALS RESIGNS HARRINGTON BAPTIST,** ludicrously out of proportion to the brief paragraph of text:

Rev. Franklin B. Seals, controversial integrationist pastor of Harrington Baptist Church since 1959, resigned last Sunday at the request of the Board of Deacons, according to chairman of deacons Roland Millican. Mr. Millican told the *Courier* that Rev. Seals will not be returning to the pulpit of Harrington Baptist Church, and that Rev. Norman Lancaster, Associational Missionary for the Mintz County Baptist Association, is scheduled to preach this Sunday.

The final page that Ted copied for Mike was Franklin Seals' obituary from the September 4 issue:

FRANKLIN B. SEALS

Mr. Franklin B. Seals, 41, of Langley, Mississippi, a former Baptist minister who served Harrington Baptist Church from 1959 until February of this year, died suddenly on August 26 in Langley, Mississippi of an apparent heart attack. Born July 17, 1923 in Langley, Mississippi, the son of George W. Seals and Hattie Mae Galloway Seals, he was a graduate of Mid-Atlantic Baptist Theological Seminary. Before coming to Harrington, he served churches in Virginia, Mississippi, and Alabama. At the time of his death, he was a truck driver for Magnolia State Poultry Company. Survivors include his wife, Jane Carden Seals, to whom he was married June 19, 1947, his parents, and one son, Michael Seals, all of Langley, Mississippi; two brothers, and three sisters. He was preceded in death by his daughter, Deborah Jean Seals, on February 10, 1964. Funeral services were held in Mississippi on August 28. Following graveside services conducted by Rev. Arthur Stewart and Rev. Cleon Garnett, interment was in the Pelfrey Street Colored Cemetery in Harrington on August 29. Webster Funeral Home was in charge of local arrangements.

Mike noted the conspicuous absence of any editorial comment about the killing of Debbie Seals. It seemed to him, even considering the tensions existing at the time, that all reasonable people would agree that shooting into an occupied house and killing an innocent child was going too far, but even a very tame editorial response calling the killing "regrettable" or "unfortunate" was not to be found. The *Harrington Courier*, under editor Homer Bazemore, was not able to report the killing of Debbie Seals without taking a cheap shot at her father's "integrationist views." Mike stuffed the papers back into the envelope. It was information that might ultimately be useful, but it made him sick. He put the envelope aside to concentrate on preparing two sermons for Sunday.

* * * * * * * * * * * *

Karen was expecting Mike to come by for her and Asalee about noon. He had told her about the wonderful lunch he enjoyed with Ted at the Lonesome Whistle, and he promised to take her and Asalee there after they opened their bank accounts. They had been in Harrington three days, and he had not yet led his first service as pastor of Harrington Baptist Church. Already, Mike noticed how good it felt to walk out of the drab hallway of the educational building into the bright sunlight. Maybe, he reasoned, it was just the perfect weather on this last day of May that affected him that way.

Karen and Asalee were ready when he got home. Mike headed the car out to Martin Luther King Boulevard, which most people still call Monument Avenue, to the Bank of Mintz County. Marletta Brumbelow, the bank employee who helped Mike and Karen open their account, was courteous and efficient. It was a slow day, and no one was ahead of them. The whole affair took less than twenty minutes, and much of that time was spent in amiable conversation. Marletta appeared to be close to Mike and Karen's age. Her desk was adorned with photos of her husband and two sons. One of her boys appeared to be about Asalee's age, and the other one looked to be three or four. Mike and Karen learned that Marletta's father was Henry Conway, pastor of Greater New Hope Progressive Missionary Baptist Church. Her husband was a mechanic at Groves Chevrolet, and their older son would be starting first grade at Harrington Elementary in the fall.

Mike pondered the fact that, at the same bank that fired Jane Seals to tighten the screws on her husband because of his "integrationist views," they had just had their accounts set up by a young black woman who was climbing the professional ladder at the bank. They had chatted with her about their children starting first grade together. Perhaps they would be in the same class-room. Telling Karen about the killing of Debbie Seals could wait, at least it could wait until after lunch.

Lonesome Whistle owner Brantley Jacobs recognized Mike and greeted him by name. Brantley's affable manner and good recall of names contributed to the success of the Lonesome Whistle as much as the unique decor, good food, and generous portions. Betty Jacobs was equally pleasant. Missy, the one who had served Mike and Ted the day before, was their server. After she took their orders, Karen and Asalee browsed in the gift shop while waiting for their food. They were halfway through their meal when a deep, resonant voice called out Mike's name. Bob McKnight would have been a natural to do the voice of God in a script that called for God to speak audibly from Heaven. If one failed to see him and did not know the origin of the voice, he might look heavenward and say, "Yes, Lord." Brother McKnight and Susan Whitmire were together, and both of them waved across the room to Mike, Karen, and Asalee. After they ordered their food, Susan and Brother McKnight walked over to the Westovers' table. Susan was euphoric, and Brother McKnight had his arm gently around her shoulder. "We have lunch together every Thursday, been doing that for the last couple of months. Guess you've heard the gossip," Bob chuckled.

"I was told that y'all were seeing each other," Mike replied.

"And I can guess who told you," Susan added as she stood next to Bob with her left hand coyly hidden behind her back. "I've got something to show you," she said as she brought her hand around to show the Westovers a diamond solitaire engagement ring.

"Wow, cool!" Asalee observed.

"Congratulations, and it's a beautiful ring," Karen commented.

"I gave Susan the ring last night," Bob explained. "We thought it best to wait until I concluded the interim at Harrington. I never thought I'd marry again after Lillian died, but the Lord brought Susan into my life rather unexpectedly."

"And I certainly wasn't looking so soon after Jim died last year," Susan added. "We both had good marriages the first time, and being widowed was devastating for both of us. We've come to love each other very much, and we'd like to get married at the church on August 18. That's a Saturday, at 4:00 in the afternoon."

"And of course we want you to do the ceremony, Brother Mike," Bob added.

"I'd be honored. The date's good as far as I know. I'll confirm the date and call you."

"I've got two weeks vacation starting that weekend," Susan explained.

"And I'm on permanent vacation," Bob quipped. "By the way, the church was very generous with me last night at the appreciation dinner, so I told Brantley to bring me your check, too. Enjoy your lunch, and help yourself to dessert. It's our treat."

* * * * * * * * * * * *

Karen needed the car to go grocery shopping that afternoon, so she drove when they left the Lonesome Whistle and dropped Mike off at the church. Mike had discovered the well-worn footpath through the woods behind the house that came out behind the church, a distance of less than a hundred yards, so there was no need for him to drive to the church except at night or in bad weather.

Opening the bank accounts and having lunch with Karen and Asalee temporarily diverted Mike's mind from the contents of the big brown envelope on his desk. He was engrossed in sermon preparation when the phone rang a little before 6:00. It was Asalee, calling to tell him that supper was ready. "Mom's not in a good mood," she whispered. "She wants you to look at the front door, and she's gonna kill that woman across the street. She means it, Daddy."

Mike closed up his office and quickly traversed the trail through the woods to the house. A furious Karen showed him the remains of a key broken off in the front door. He barely dissuaded her from calling the police to report an attempted break-in. After supper, he got a pair of needle-nosed pliers and extricated the broken key. "I got it out," Mike announced triumphantly.

"So what are you going to do with it?" Karen shot back.

"Throw it away, I guess. It's no good."

"Buzz! Wrong answer! Give it to me."

Mike obediently placed the broken key in Karen's outstretched hand, and she proceeded with all deliberate speed toward Hilda Mae Snyder's house.

"I told you, Daddy, she means it," Asalee said. "Mom's gonna kill That Woman."

"You stay here, Az. Sit right here on the front steps where we can see you until we get back." Mike caught up with Karen as she was about to cross the street. He knew better than to try to deter her from her mission of confronting Hilda Mae Snyder.

"Why, come in, Pastor, Mrs. Westover. How nice of you to come over to visit!" Hilda Mae chimed sweetly as she held the storm door open.

"We didn't come to visit," Karen shot back. "We came to return something that belongs to you." Karen handed her the broken-off key that Mike had extricated from the lock. "I'm sure you have the other piece of it in your purse."

"B-but-but...but I-I..." Hilda Mae stammered, "I've always had a key to the parsonage so I could keep check on things when the pastor was gone."

"So you could snoop, you mean!" Karen retorted. "You scared the daylights out of me walking in on me Tuesday, and you drove me crazy following me all over the house. Today Asalee and I leave just long enough to go the grocery store, and I come back, try to put my key in the door, and your key's broken off in the lock!"

"Karen's father and I changed the locks," Mike added. "Your key no longer fits, and we are not planning to give you a key."

"I was ready to call the police and report an attempted break-in," Karen continued. "Mike talked me out of it this time. Next time he won't be able to."

"Well, I-I d-didn't mean any harm..." Hilda Mae whined.

"Let's make a deal," Karen replied firmly. "You don't mess with our house, and I won't mess with the nursery, which you seem to think you own, and I won't have to call the police on you."

"She means it, Hilda," Mike stated flatly.

Without further pleasantries, Karen spun around and headed home. Mike caught up with her before she crossed the street. After Karen disappeared into the house, Asalee looked up at Mike and solemnly inquired, "Daddy, did Mom kill That Woman?"

* * * * * * * * * * * *

Karen felt considerably better after the confrontation with That Woman. By the time they put Asalee to bed at 9:00, she was able to see the humor in the situation. She and Mike got ready for bed and then snuggled up on the sofa to watch television. For an hour or more, they watched TV together, enjoying the closeness with each other.

"We need to move the piano somewhere else, away from that picture window," Mike said as he broke the silence.

"Why? That looks like the obvious place for it to me. It looks good there. Why do you want to move it?"

"Something happened a long time ago, 1964, and I don't think there is much likelihood that it could happen now, but I still think we ought to move the piano to be safe."

"What happened in 1964? Mike, you're not making any sense."

"Karen, there was someone killed sitting at a piano that was in exactly the same place your piano is. Somebody drove by and shot a high-powered rifle through the window, bullet hit the girl in the back of the neck at the base of her skull. I laid awake last night, thinking about you playing the piano with your back to that picture window, and how much Asalee likes to pick out tunes on the piano and sit on the bench with you when you're playing. All I could think about was you and Asalee sitting on the piano bench with your backs to that window, and how much I love both of you and don't want to see anything happen to either one of you."

"Who was the girl who was killed?"

"Debbie Seals. Fourteen years old, daughter of Franklin Seals, pastor at Harrington back then. Somebody shot into the house to terrorize them, trying to run them out of town. The bullet hit her while she was playing the piano, killed her instantly."

"That's horrible. Did they ever catch whoever it was who killed her?"

"No, they never really tried to. They're scot-free, probably good solid citizens now. I may get to preach to some of 'em Sunday."

"Why would somebody go to that extreme to run a pastor off?"

"When Harrington built the building they have now," Mike explained, "they needed to sell their old building, across the street from the Presbyterian Church on Church Street, one of the prettiest old churches I ever saw. A black church, Greater New Hope Baptist, came up with the money and bought it, first time blacks had ever owned property north of Salyers Creek. The church voted by an eight-vote margin to sell it to them. They didn't want to do it, but they would've gone under financially if they hadn't.

Seals was in favor of selling it to them. Some of them were already down on him because he wouldn't have any part of the White Citizens Council they had back then. He offended some powerful people, and they were determined to do what it took to run him off. The deacons called for Frank Seals' resignation the week after his daughter's death."

"That's about as low as you can get. Any of those deacons still around?"

"Lee Walters and Royce Green are still active deacons. Rudy Blevins and Roland Millican are still in the church. Roland was chairman at the time. Preacher Seals had a heart attack and died six months after they ran him off, just forty-one years old. He and his daughter are buried in the black cemetery down at the end of Pelfrey Street."

"Where did you find this out?"

"When Ted gave me the grand tour of Harrington yesterday. We stopped by Greater New Hope, Harrington's old building. Nicest old gentleman, his name's Prince Hammondtree, was pulling up weeds and picking up trash. He's retired, wife died last year, so he lives by himself. He comes over every day to take care of the church building and grounds. Ted and I talked better'n two hours with him. I want you to meet him."

"And I want to meet him. Let's fix dinner and invite him over one night. Is Monday night OK with you?"

"Fine as far as I know. I'll see if I can catch up with him tomorrow morning and invite him. Back to what I was saying about the piano..."

"Yeah, I'd feel better if we got it away from the window. That gives me the creeps."

"I'll have to get some help. No way those little casters will roll on this carpet. Ted brought me a bunch of newspaper articles out of the Harrington paper about the stuff that went on back then. Scary stuff."

"I want to see it. Bring it home tomorrow. Why didn't the committee tell us this stuff?"

"Well, Hon, it was a long time ago. Ted was on the committee, and he found out about it the same time I did. I guess it's one of those things that comes under the 'we don't talk about that' rule."

11

Bruce and Vicky Blevins worked with the youth fellowship on Friday nights. Mike went over and spent some time with the group, sat in on their Bible study time, and played some volleyball with them. After the youth fellowship dismissed, he casually mentioned the need to move the piano. Bruce knew the whereabouts of a piano dolly in the choir room. He and Vicky stopped by the parsonage, followed by another car containing two members of the Harrington High School wrestling team, Jeffrey Hanna and Evan Noland and their girlfriends Jodie Freeman and Kristin Kinney. Bruce, Mike, Jeffrey, and Evan made short work of moving the piano while Asalee introduced Vicky, Jodie, and Kristin to Wallace the Dog and her entire entourage of dolls and stuffed animals.

"Saw your Mom's engagement announcement in the paper today…," Mike commented to Vicky.

"We ran into them when we ate lunch at the Lonesome Whistle yesterday," Karen added.

"They make a nice couple, seem very happy together."

"Well, I hope Mom's not making a mistake," Vicky replied. "She's an adult, and I can't tell her what to do, but eighteen years is a big age difference if you ask me, and it's so soon after Daddy died. She and Daddy had a very good marriage for twenty-nine years, and she was wonderful to him the whole time he was sick. She kept her promise of 'til death do us part,' so I suppose she's got a right to be happy. Nothing against Brother McKnight—it's just hard for me to see my mother with another man. I guess I'll get used to it."

"Both of my parents are living and together, so are Mike's, so I can't say I know how you feel." Karen responded, "I can see where it would be hard. But, like you said, your mom did all she could for your dad while he was living, and there's nothing else she can do for him now. It's not a denial of her love for your dad for her to love Brother McKnight now. They told us that neither one of them was looking to get into a romantic relationship. They feel like the Lord brought them together."

"And maybe He did. It's just hard right now. I've accepted it, but I'm not jumping up and down with excitement. I'll be nice to him as long as he's good to my mother. That's the best I can do right now."

"Well, Vicky, the best you can do is the best you can do. You're being honest about how you feel. You've decided to be kind to them. That's progress. It's easier to control our actions than it is to control our feelings, but our feelings usually fall in line with the way we act. God only holds us responsible for our behavior, not our feelings."

"I guess you're right. Brother McKnight's over at Mom's house now helping babysit our kids. Our kids think he hung the moon and the stars."

"Well, Preacher," Bruce opined, "I hope you're here a long time. That piano is a bear to move."

"Tell me about it," Mike concurred. "That piano belonged to Karen's great-grandmother, and she willed it to Karen. Karen's brother and I like to have ruined our insides moving it from Ma

Kemp's house to our apartment in Denham. I was sore for a week. Thanks, guys. There was no way those little casters were gonna roll on this carpet."

*   *   *   *   *   *   *   *   *   *   *   *

"Any interesting mail today?" Mike asked Karen after the piano movers left. "I saw the paper, but I didn't look at anything else."

"Got a card from Carol Richardson. She and the kids are planning to spend the week of July 4 on the beach at Panama City. Carol's college roommate lives about ten miles from there. She's been after her ever since the divorce to come down and spend a week with her. Carol went back to her oncologist Monday. Everything looks good, and he released her back to Mary Kate. They're taking the trip to celebrate, and they're coming by to see us and visit our church on the way down there."

"Great. It'll be good to see them, catch up on everybody at Clear Springs. First Sunday in July'll be communion. Since Carol's a deacon, I'll ask her to help serve."

"That'd be good, only I don't know how some of the people here will react to a woman serving communion. They've never had women deacons, and most of them've never seen a woman serve communion."

"It'll be a change for 'em, that's for sure. I like what Mr. Hammondtree says, 'Folks're kinda skittish about change. They don't like it. But that don't mean it's not good for 'em.'"

"Why do I get the feeling I'm going to hear that quote in a sermon before long?"

*   *   *   *   *   *   *   *   *   *   *   *

The 11:00 news had just come on when Mike and Karen were startled by the sound of a siren close by. Karen pulled back the drapes and looked out the window in time to see the Mintz County EMS ambulance stop in front of 723 Alabama Avenue. "It's an ambulance, Mike," she observed as Mike joined her at the window. "It's at That Woman's house. I did it."

"Did what?"

"Killed her, Mike. I think I killed That Woman, confronting her the way I did about the key."

"Karen, Hon, if she got worked up enough over that to have a heart attack, it's her own fault." As the paramedics unloaded a gurney and two duffel bags full of medical equipment from the ambulance and rushed to Hilda Mae's front door, Mike added, "It's her fault she needed confronting in the first place. I'll walk over there and see what's going on."

The rotating emergency beacons cast an eerie red glow over everything in the vicinity, and the powerful floodlights on the side of the ambulance lit up Hilda Mae's front yard as bright as day. After about ten minutes, the paramedics rolled the gurney bearing Hilda Mae out to the ambulance, and Mike followed carrying the duffel bags full of medical equipment. One of the paramedics climbed into the back of the ambulance with That Woman, and Mike handed her the bags. Her partner got in the cab, turned off the emergency lights, and drove slowly away. Karen had a sinking feeling that Hilda Mae was dead and that she had in fact killed her. She was relieved when Mike returned to report that Hilda Mae was fine. "They're taking her to the emergency room to check her out. One of the EMT's said she's a regular customer. Every time something upsets her, she calls 911 and says she's having shortness of breath and chest pains. To hear her tell it, she's got the worst heart this side of Oak Hill cemetery. You would've loved this. One of the EMT's had her stethoscope, trying to listen to Hilda Mae's heart, and Hilda Mae's running her mouth a mile a minute. The paramedic tells her, 'Mrs. Snyder, for somebody who can't breathe, you sure do talk a lot.' I had to swallow my tongue to keep from laughing."

"So you think this was staged for our benefit?"

"Definitely, and we can look forward to encore performances."

"I'll try harder next time."

"Try harder to do what?"

"Kill That Woman," Karen answered resolutely.

* * * * * * * * * * * *

Sunday June 3 dawned a clear, beautiful day. Mike was up, dressed for church, and drinking his second cup of coffee when Karen and Asalee got up. He had stayed in his study at the church until about 10:00 putting the finishing touches on his sermon for the morning service. It was as ready as it was going to get, but he had gotten up early to mentally preach through it a couple of times.

At 119, the Sunday School attendance was a little above average. The front-page feature in the *Courier* brought in a few more people, and church members who seldom attend will come to check out a new pastor. The worship attendance was about 150. Organist Jean Brinkley played well, but she was overshadowed by Jenny Latham's artistry at the piano. The congregation sang enthusiastically, and the choir's anthem, though not a difficult piece, was nicely done. Eric had worked with them on intonation, rhythms, and dynamics, and the attention to detail was apparent. Karen sang in the choir as she was accustomed to doing at Clear Springs. Asalee had connected with Ted and Brenda Coleman's seven-year-old Molly, so she was more than happy to sit with Molly and her older sister. The service proceeded smoothly and on schedule. Franklin A. Brinkley, Chairman of the Board of Deacons of Harrington Baptist Church (Karen wondered if all of that was on his birth certificate and driver's license), though pompous and arrogant, had at least done a good job organizing the deacons to serve the Lord's Supper in an orderly, efficient manner. Mike pronounced the benediction precisely at noon, and hiring squad chairman Carl Baxter rushed Mike, Karen, and Asalee to the head of the line in the fellowship hall.

The gathering in the fellowship hall was pleasant enough. Mike and Karen finished eating quickly so they could circulate among the people, speak to as many as possible, and start to work on learning the cast of characters. When he did the welcome and announcements, Mike reminded the church that whereas they had only three new names to learn, four counting Wallace the Dog, he and Karen had about two hundred. Two tables were laden with housewarming gifts. Virgil Blackmon, director of missions for the Mintz County Baptist Association, had been present for the morning service, and he stayed for dinner. Mike and Virgil chatted briefly before the service, and Mike asked him to assist at the communion table. Carl Baxter hated talking in front of people, so he quickly drafted Virgil to emcee the dinner.

It was about 2:00 when Mike, Karen, and Asalee bade farewell to the last of the crowd at the dinner. Several people helped carry the housewarming gifts to the car. Karen was pleased to see all the new bath towel sets, and Asalee was glad to get a few more stuffed animals out of the deal. Carl and Joyce even remembered Wallace with a large rawhide bone.

The deacons meeting was scheduled for 4:30, with the evening service to follow at 6:00. Once they got home and brought all the things in from the car, Mike changed out of his suit into an old pair of jeans and relaxed in the recliner until time for the deacons meeting. He had no sooner kicked back in the recliner than he was sound asleep. Karen woke him up about 3:45. He freshened up, put on his suit, and walked the shortcut through the woods to the church, arriving fifteen minutes early, just as David Groves pulled into the parking lot. Ted Coleman was in the car with him.

Mike unlocked the side door of the educational building and turned on the lights. "Hey, Preacher," David said as he gave Mike a pat on the shoulder, "Good message this morning. So many people talking to you at the dinner, I didn't get a chance to tell you."

"Thanks, David. Which room do we use for the deacons meeting?"

"We always meet in this first big room where the older men's Sunday School class meets," Ted answered. "Doc Walters' class." It occurred to Mike that the meeting place was symbolic of the power struggle going on in Harrington Baptist Church. The four older deacons had the home court advantage, meeting in the same room in which their Sunday School class met. Every time they attended a deacons meeting, Ted Coleman, David Groves, and Jerry McWhorter were encroaching on the sacrosanct space of Frank Brinkley, Jack Miller, Doc Walters, and Royce Green. Mike, being newly arrived and nine years younger than the youngest deacon, was even more of an interloper.

Frank Brinkley was the last to arrive, walking in precisely at 4:30. His entrance was such that Mike halfway expected someone to call out "All rise!" The man's face could not have been more expressionless had he been dead and embalmed. No one attempted to exchange pleasantries with this inexorable, humorless man. Brinkley, who looked to be in his early sixties, was dressed in a dark, crisply-pressed three-piece tailored suit, a starched white shirt, and a silk tie with a subdued pattern of dark diagonal stripes, looking like either a funeral director or a lawyer dressed for court. He was the only man other than Mike who was wearing a suit, and Mike's decent off-the-rack suit looked cheap and tawdry compared to Frank Brinkley's costly threads. Mike did not have the temerity to do it himself, but he knew Wallace Coggins would not hesitate to let a few pounds of air out of Franklin A. Brinkley, Chairman of the Board of Deacons of Harrington Baptist Church. Wallace would compliment Frank on the expensive suit and then tell him that Gresham Brothers Funeral Home has just the right casket to go with it.

Frank set a slim, pricey-looking leather briefcase on the table, opened it, took out a file folder of papers, and announced in a droning voice, "The June 1990 meeting of the Board of Deacons of Harrington Baptist Church will now come to order." After calling upon Jack Miller to open the meeting with prayer, he continued, "Deacon Lee Walters will present the minutes of our last meeting."

It took Lee no more than three minutes to summarize a deacons meeting that lasted an hour and a half. The essence of his report was that the deacons met on May 6 and that Royce Green opened the meeting with prayer. The deacons had rehashed the work of the finance committee and the maintenance committee before hearing David Groves' report from the pastor search committee. David told them that Mike had accepted the church's call, and that Mike and his family would move into the parsonage on May 29 and begin pastoral duties on June 3. Frank Brinkley had griped about the "highly irregular" way the church had gone about calling a pastor. For Frank, that meant that he, as Chairman of the Board of Deacons, had not automatically been asked to chair the pastor search committee.

After Lee read the minutes, Frank called for old business, and David Groves mentioned the obvious fact that Mike was present in the meeting. He reported on the appreciation dinner for interim pastor Bob McKnight, and indicated that the work of the pastor search committee was now complete. Royce Green, who was also a trustee and chairman of the maintenance committee, reported that the painting of the parsonage was complete and that the new carpet in the living room, dining room, and hallway had been installed. Jack Miller, who chaired the finance committee in addition to serving as a deacon, reported on how much money had been spent on the renovation of the parsonage, expenses of the pastor search committee, and moving expenses for Mike's family.

Frank then called for new business. When no one else had anything to bring up, he turned a steely glare toward Mike and said, "I have something to bring up. I've said all I'm going to say about the highly irregular manner in which our new pastor was called, but..."

"Thank the Lord!" Ted Coleman interjected. "I'm tired of hearing it, Frank. You've never shown me where we did anything contrary to Scripture or the constitution and bylaws. The church has called Brother Mike Westover as pastor. It's settled, Frank. Get used to it and get over it! Let's all support our pastor and work with him, and let's move on."

Frank was only momentarily nonplussed by the fact that one of the new people would be so insolent as to confront him in such a way. He made no response at all. It was as though someone had stopped and then restarted a tape recording. Frank gathered his thoughts and continued, "as I was saying, it has come to my attention as chairman of the board of deacons that our new pastor and his wife, who have been on the field less than a week, have already managed to deeply offend a faithful long-time member of this church..."

"Brother Frank!" Mike interrupted. Mike startled himself by the quickness with which he responded to Frank Brinkley. He refused to let this pompous, overbearing man intimidate him. "If you have a problem with something I said or did, you need to talk to me privately, and if you have a problem with something Karen said or did, you need to talk with her before you bring it up in a deacons meeting."

"The pastor's right, Frank," Jerry McWhorter added. "It's not fair to jump the pastor about something when you've only got one side of it and the pastor may not even know what you're talking about."

"Oh, he knows exactly what I'm talking about," Frank retorted. "Hilda Mae Snyder, my wife's mother, called me in tears over the nasty run-in she had with Mr. and Mrs. Westover right on her own front steps Thursday evening. Mrs. Westover used very abusive language with her and threatened to call the police on her. My mother-in-law was so upset that she ended up having a spell with her heart, had to be rushed to the hospital..."

"Like she does every time she gets herself worked up about something," Doc Walters interjected. "If her heart was half as bad as she lets on, she would've been dead twenty years ago. That woman'll outlive all of us." Mike made a mental note of the family connection, that Hilda Mae was Frank's mother-in-law. He expected Lee to side with Frank on most things, but it was good to know that he had little patience with Frank's mother-in-law. "Let's at least hear what the pastor has to say, Frank."

Mike recited the events of Thursday evening and what led up to the encounter, beginning with Tuesday, when Mike and Harold changed the locks after Hilda Mae walked in on Karen unannounced and brazenly tested her key to be sure it still fit. He told the deacons about Karen returning from the grocery store to find the key broken off in the lock. He acknowledged that they were both angry when they confronted her, but he assured them that Karen had not used abusive language. Mike stood his ground, telling Frank that he and Karen expected to be secure from prowlers, and that yes, Karen did warn Hilda Mae that she would call the police if it happened again.

"I'm with the pastor on this one, Frank," Jack Miller responded. "I don't think any of us want people walking in on us or snooping when we're gone. I didn't vote in favor of calling you, Brother Mike, but Hilda Mae's been a pain in the ass, excuse my language, to every pastor we've had for the last thirty years. I don't know how she got a key to the parsonage. Let me know what you spent on the new locks, Preacher, and I'll see to it that you get reimbursed."

Seeing that two of his regular allies were supporting Mike and that no help appeared to be forthcoming from Royce Green,

Frank backed down. His face thawed a bit, and he said, "Well, Pastor, she can be difficult sometimes. Just try to be patient with her, handle her with kid gloves, try not to upset her, and tell your wife to do the same."

Mike was emboldened by the unexpected support of Lee Walters and Jack Miller, and he knew that Ted, David, and Jerry were with him. "Brother Frank, Karen and I made it very clear to Mrs. Snyder that if she tried to force her way into our house again, we would let the police deal with her. I assure you, I'll be courteous to her, and I won't do anything on purpose to upset her. I can't be responsible for her getting herself worked up. Now, Brother Frank, don't you ever jump me in a deacons meeting before you speak to me privately and before you get your facts straight. If you have anything to say to Karen, you need to speak directly to her. I do expect you to be courteous and respectful to her, just as I'll be whenever I speak to your wife."

The stone face of Frank Brinkley softened a little more, and he averted his eyes as he meekly muttered, "Of course, Pastor." Mike was pleased that he had won some grudging respect from this man, but he still did not like him, and he was sure this would not be the last time that he would have to deal with Frank's bullying tactics. Frank mumbled, "That's all I have gentlemen. If no one else has anything to bring up, we'll be adjourned. Brother Ted, dismiss us in a word of prayer."

Ted artfully wove the apostle Paul's words about *speaking the truth in love* into his closing prayer, and the deacons meeting was concluded at 5:40, twenty minutes before time for the evening service to begin. On his way to the auditorium, Mike spoke cheerfully to Frank, "Hey, Brother, that's a sharp-looking suit you got on."

"Thanks, Pastor." Frank proceeded to brag to Mike about the fine work of the Vietnamese tailor up at Buckhead who custom-made all of his suits.

"I bet Webster Funeral Home's got just the right casket to go with it," Mike added, knowing that Wallace would be proud of him.

* * * * * * * * * * * *

The evening worship attendance was about half of the morning attendance. Most of the older adults only came to the morning service. Mike noticed about a half dozen high school age young people who had been at the Friday night youth fellowship who were not present at the morning service. The evening service was refreshingly informal. Jenny Latham accompanied the congregation on the piano when they sang *Footsteps of Jesus* and *Victory in Jesus*. Eric had his guitar, and he accompanied the singing of a medley of praise choruses. A quartet composed of Eric and Jenny Latham and David and Cheryl Groves did some impressive *a capella* harmonizing on *I'll Fly Away, Jesus Hold My Hand,* and *Children of the Heavenly King* before time for Mike to preach.

Mike had gotten a good introduction to southern gospel singing at Luckett's Creek. He liked it better than Karen did. The final selection the quartet sang was from *The Sacred Harp*. It was well over two hundred years old but new to Mike. The haunting melody and simple words lodged permanently in his brain. For weeks and months afterward, as he walked the trail through the woods from the parsonage to the church, he often caught himself singing,

Children of the Heavenly King, as ye journey sweetly sing.

Sing your Savior's matchless praise, glorious in His works and ways.

We are trav'ling home to God in the path the saints have trod,
They are happy now, and we soon their blessedness shall see.

* * * * * * * * * * * *

The front door was already open, and Mike greeted Prince Hammondtree as he came up the steps. "Good to see you, Deacon Hammondtree. Come on in." Mike took Mr. Hammondtree's derby hat and sat it on top of the piano. "I'd like you to meet my wife Karen and our daughter Asalee." As he greeted Karen and Asalee, Wallace the Dog came up, sniffed of him, and decided to make him welcome. As Mr. Hammondtree reached down to pet Wallace, Mike continued the introductions, "and this is Wallace. Asalee named him after the deacon chairman at our last church."

"I'm sure he felt honored," Mr. Hammondtree laughed.

"As a matter of fact, he did. Wallace the Deacon Chairman carries a picture of Wallace the Dog in his billfold, shows it off to everybody. He says having that dog named after him was the greatest honor he ever received. It brought tears to his eyes to know Asalee thought that much of him." As he directed Mr. Hammondtree to the kitchen, Mike continued, "Hope you don't mind eating at the kitchen table. We'd never lived in anything but small apartments until we moved into this house, so we haven't bought a dining room suite yet."

"Don't think nothin' about that, Reverend. I didn't come to see your furniture, I come to see you. I'm thankful to be with good people who love the Lord. 'Sides," he added with a laugh, "looks like y'all need to furnish a nursery 'fore you worry too much about a dining room suite."

"I'm six months along," Karen said, "so I guess that will have to come first. I'm due around the first of September. We've still got Asalee's baby bed, cradle, and changing table stored with Mike's parents over at Denham, just a matter of getting over there to get it between now and the time we need it. We're looking forward to a little sister for Asalee." After they were all seated at the table and Mike returned thanks for the food, Karen continued, "Do you have children, Mr. Hammondtree?"

"Got five of 'em, Mrs. Westover. Mildred's the oldest. She's fifty, teaches up at the high school, math teacher. Girl always was a whiz at numbers, just like her mama. My wife could add and subtract numbers in her head faster'n you could write 'em down, Mildred's the same way. Junior's forty-four, 'lectrician, lives down't Columbus. Riley's forty-two, lineman for Georgia Power, lives here in Harrington. Phoebe's thirty-seven, or will be next week, married Reverend Troy Dennison, he teaches school and pastors Thankful Baptist Church over't Hansonville. She works for Family and Children's Services, works with Mrs. Whitmire, one of the ladies in your church."

"Oh, yes, Susan Whitmire," Mike commented. "She was on the pastor search committee."

"And then Martin's my youngest," Mr. Hammondtree continued. "He's thirty-three, works for the post office, mail carrier. All of 'em turned out good. 'Course, they had a good mama who had a lot to do with it. Ophelia'n I was married fifty-one years when she died last year, had a heart attack and died September 14. I was twenty an' she was seventeen when we married. Nice lady, pretty woman, treated me good, sure was a good momma to our children. Wish you could'a knowed her."

"I do too," Karen responded sympathetically. "You must miss her a lot."

"That I do. I know how to cook'n keep house, do for myself in that way, always did try to help 'er out in that respect stead'a 'spectin' her to do it all the way some men do. I like to cook and bake, always did, and I did more of it after I retired. I can cook as good a meal as Ophelia could, but I don't have nobody to sit down'n enjoy it with me. So, much as I'm enjoyin' this good food, I'm enjoyin' more'n anything not eatin' by myself."

"We're glad you're here to enjoy it with us," Mike replied. "I've enjoyed getting to know you, and I wanted Karen and Asalee to have the pleasure. I told them that amazing story about the miracle and how Greater New Hope was able to buy our church's old building…"

"Amazing it was," Mr. Hammondtree responded thoughtfully, "and it happened just the way I told you, Reverend. No doubt about it bein' a miracle."

"It's a beautiful old building," Karen added. "Asalee and I rode by it Friday when I took her down to see where she'll be going to school."

"Harrington Elementary's where I worked for thirty-eight years, from the time I got out of the service in '45 'til I retired in '83. Started when Harrington Elementary was in the old building where the Board of Education and senior citizens' center is now, moved to the new building with 'em in 1966, which was the first year white an' colored folks went to school together. So I know all about your new school, Miss Asalee. One of my nieces teaches third grade over there. Her name's Mrs. Hobbs. She might be your teacher when you get to the third grade. Asalee, you gonna want to stay in school, study'n get yourself a good education. If I'd had the chance to go to school more, I'd'a sure done it. When I was growin' up, school for colored folks did'n go no farther'n eighth grade. Ophelia'n I seen to it that all our children went to school. They all finished high school." With a laugh, he added, "My boy Junior got it in 'is head one time he was gonna drop outta school soon's he turned sixteen'n go to work at Porter Mayfield's service station. I asked 'im where he planned on livin'. He said he was gonna keep livin' at home, an' I told 'im not if he wad'n goin' to school. Rest of our kids must'a got the message, 'cause none of the rest of 'em ever talked any of that foolishness 'bout droppin' outta school. Junior finished high school an' went to trade school, makes good money as a 'lectrician. All of 'em got some college or trade school. Both my girls got their masters' degrees. I can tell you're a smart little girl, so I expect you to do good in school. You'll be goin' to school where I used to work."

"Cool," Asalee responded. Karen and Mike had joked about that being the adjective of the month.

It disturbed Asalee to hear that black children once had to go to separate schools where they didn't have enough books and the books they had were old ones that the white schools didn't want anymore. Asalee said she didn't think that was fair, and Mr. Hammondtree said colored folks didn't think it was, either. He told her that a lot of good people, white and colored, worked hard to change it. Asalee told Mr. Hammondtree that she had learned about Dr. King in kindergarten, and she was in awe when he told her that Dr. and Mrs. King spent the night in his home one time. He didn't tell her that they were in Harrington for Debbie Seals' funeral, because it was getting close to her bedtime. He did tell her about the way a lot of children shunned Michael Seals because his daddy helped Greater New Hope buy Harrington Baptist's old building, and how Michael used to sit and talk with him at recess when the other children wouldn't play with him. "Michael's all grown up now," Mr. Hammondtree explained. "He's a doctor. Him'n his wife and children come to see me every now and then." With a distinct note of pride, he added, "His oldest little boy's named after me." Mr. Hammondtree showed Asalee a picture of Michael Seals' family, along with pictures of his grandchildren and great-grandchildren.

Mike and Karen's conversation with Mr. Hammondtree continued long after they put Asalee to bed. Mike got out the envelope of newspaper articles that Ted had copied for him and showed it to Mr. Hammondtree. Tears glistened in the older man's eyes as he said, "Law, yes, I remember. Rev'ren and Mrs. Seals sure was good people, and they had two of the sweetest children. Debbie, the one that was killed, was in third grade when they come to

Harrington, so I knowed both children. It was the saddest thing I ever seen, the night that girl was killed. Polices never tried to find out who done it, that or they knowed who did it'n covered for 'em. Reverend Garnett took Reverend and Mrs. Seals and their little boy down to his house. Ophelia and I come and cleaned up the blood from where the girl was shot. Mrs. Seals said she never wanted to see that piano again, so me'n my brother Lennox hauled it away for 'em. The Sunday after Reverend Seals resigned at y'all's church, he come'n preached for us at Greater New Hope. That was the last time he ever preached. His son told me it was the last time his daddy ever set foot in church, said 'is daddy took to drinkin' right heavy after that. I ain't sayin' it was right for 'im to do that, but I can't say what I mighta done if somebody'd killed one a' my children. I don't believe the Lord held it against 'im for a minute. I still say he's one a' the finest men of God I ever knowed, and what happened after his daughter got killed did'n change my mind about that. The Bible says *if we believe not, yet He abideth faithful: He cannot deny Himself.* The Lord knowed Reverend Seals couldn't take no more, that's how come He took 'im on home. Rev'ren, Mrs. Westover, they's people in your church knows 'zactly who killed the Seals girl. They just ain't sayin'."

12

"Mike, Honey. They're here! Can you turn loose of what you're doing and come on home?" Karen asked excitedly over the phone. Mike's day had started with an early morning trip to Tanner Medical Center in Carrollton where Bobbie Blevins was having surgery. After he got back from Carrollton, he spent the rest of the day working in the office. He needed to stick close to home because they were expecting Carol Richardson and her kids in time for supper. Mike's predecessor had left behind a nice gas grill complete with a full bottle of LP gas. It was a perfect evening for grilling hamburgers and hot dogs, and Karen had decreed that he would be in charge of the grill. Mike was about to call it a day anyway, so he locked up his office and hurried home by way of the path through the woods.

As Mike came within sight of the house, Little Bill Richardson came running toward him yelling "Brother Mike! Brother Mike!" When he got close enough, Little Bill leaped into his arms. He was a chunky little fellow, handsome and robust, built like his grandfather Russ Ayers. Mike braced himself and grunted from the impact when he caught Little Bill's full weight in mid-air and tossed him up on his shoulder like a fifty-pound sack of potatoes. Bill Richardson had remarried almost immediately after divorcing

Carol. He already had two children with his new wife, and he seemed to have no time for the children of his first marriage, so Mike became a father figure to Little Bill during their time at Clear Springs.

When he arrived at the house carrying Little Bill, Mike saw Russ Ayers' van in the driveway. Carol and the girls were unloading suitcases and sleeping bags. After setting Little Bill down, he exchanged hugs with Carol, Meg, and Jessica and helped them carry their things into the house.

"Great to see y'all. How was the trip?"

"Good," Carol replied. "Dad told me to take his van and he'd use my car while we were gone. It's got more room than my car, and the air conditioning works. Karen gave us good directions, so we drove right to your door, no problems. Little Bill's more excited about seeing you than he is about the beach. From the time I told the kids we were making this trip, all he's talked about is going to see Brother Mike."

"You're looking good, Carol," Karen commented as Carol staked her claim on the recliner.

"How are you feeling?"

"A little tired from driving, but not as bad as I thought I'd be. I told you in the letter that I took my last radiation treatment and the oncologist thinks we got the cancer in time and everything looks good. He turned me back over to Mary Kate. As for making the trip, Mary Kate told me to use common sense and rest when I get tired. I feel pretty good, just about back to normal, better since I finished the treatments. The kids've been great all through this cancer ordeal, and I wanted to reward them as much as anything. Besides, we hadn't had a real vacation since before Bill and I divorced, so it was time. How're you enjoying the new church?"

"It's OK," Karen responded.

"You don't sound real enthusiastic."

"I don't know. It's a lot different from Clear Springs. Some wonderful people, church has a lot of potential. We like the community and most of the people, with some notable exceptions— remind me to tell you about That Woman across the street. It's going to be a more difficult church for Mike, and they expect more of a pastor's wife than Clear Springs does. Part of that's because it's a bigger church. Part of it's being full-time and living just around the corner instead of thirty miles away. We've got some power struggles going on, and the church has some dirty little secrets they don't talk about. It's a church that's been hard on pastors in years past."

While Bill Junior stuck close to Mike, Megan and Jessica went with Asalee and Wallace the Dog to burn off some energy out in the back yard. Karen and Carol were left to continue the conversation in air-conditioned comfort. "Looks like you'll be a lot more comfortable once you have that baby," Carol commented. "and you look like you'd go into labor if you sneezed."

"Supposed to be two more months. We might try for a third child somewhere down the road, but I want to plan for cooler weather next time. I don't want to be this big in the hottest part of the summer again."

"Tell me about it," Carol laughed. "Megan's birthday is August 31. The year she was born was the hottest, muggiest summer I ever remember. We were living in a house in Ledford with no air conditioning, just a couple of fans that didn't do anything but move hot air around. Meg was a big baby, nine pounds two ounces, and I was as big as the side of a barn carrying her. I thought I'd die of heat prostration before that girl was born!"

"Thank God for air conditioning! Doctor says everything looks good. The sonogram shows we're going to have another girl. I like my new obstetrician better than the one I had in Riverton, and she's way ahead of the one I had with Asalee. How's everybody at Clear Springs?"

"Most of us're doing pretty well. Maude Sessions had another stroke two weeks ago, and she's not doing well. Poor ol' Arthur's crippled up so bad with rheumatoid arthritis, he's not able to take care of her. Mary Kate stays with them at night, and they've got somebody there in the daytime along with the home health care nurses coming in, but it looks to me like they're going to have to give up and put them in the nursing home. Mary Kate can't do what she's doing and keep up her practice."

"I hate to hear that, but it doesn't surprise me. She wasn't doing all that well when we left. How's the church doing?"

"Great. I tell you, Heather's doing a super job. No doubt in my mind the Lord brought her to us. People've really accepted her. Meg and Jess love her to death. She hasn't missed a Sunday having somebody take her home for dinner. We had a new family join the church last Sunday..."

"Who?" Karen asked eagerly.

"Bensons. They visited the first time on your last Sunday, the day we ordained Heather. Arlene Benson, teaches at Clear Springs Elementary with Sarah Beth Coggins. Arlene's a single parent, situation like mine, husband left her for another woman, decided all of a sudden after they had two children that he didn't want to be married any more. She's got two boys, ten and thirteen. They came by letter from Central Avenue in Ledford. Pastor over there told her if she didn't have her own career and if she'd been more submissive to her husband, she might still be married. Well, that was the last straw! Arlene's got a lot of spunk and she knows her Bible! She told him if her exhusband'd loved her the way Christ loved the church, and if he hadn't thought he was God's gift to women, they might still be married. She walked out of that church and never went back. The pastor at Central Avenue's good buddies with Billy Fite, real gung-ho on this 'men have to be in charge just because they're men' foolishness. I don't know what gets into some of these preachers, Karen, but I like Mary Kate's theory."

"What's that?"

"Testosterone poisoning. Anyway, Arlene got to where she felt beat up on every time she went to church, and she decided it wasn't healthy for her boys to be exposed to that mess. What the preacher said, blaming her for the divorce, was the icing on the cake, so she stopped going to church for a good while. Sarah Beth kept after her to come to Clear Springs, told her she wouldn't hear that mess at Clear Springs. They came the day we ordained Heather, been coming ever since. She and the boys really like Heather, and it turns out that Patrick, the older boy, already knew Nathan Trimble from school. Both of Arlene's boys have really connected with Wes Trimble. By the way, Heather's going to do her first baptism in the creek the fifteenth of this month."

"Who's being baptized?"

"Brian Benson, Arlene's younger boy. He joined the church on profession of faith when his mom and brother came by transfer of letter. And there's one more. You'll never guess who the other one is. Ed Halstead."

"You're kidding!"

"I'm not kidding. We've been praying for him ever since he and Barb got married. When Heather met with the deacons to talk about her becoming our pastor, Wayne asked Heather what she'd do, little as she is, if some big ol' boy like Ed got saved and wanted to be baptized. Linda was sitting next to Wayne. She turned to him and said, 'Daddy, right there's the reason we let big strong men like you be deacons, too.' Ed's been in church with Barbara and the kids every Sunday here lately. He made his profession of faith last Sunday. When Heather presented him to the church, she looked over at Wayne with a big grin and said 'Brother Wayne, you're gonna help me baptize this one.' Then, she turned to the congregation, with ol' Ed standing beside her, towering over her, and said, 'now right here's the reason we let big strong men like Brother Wayne be deacons, too.'"

"That's wonderful! I can't wait for Mike to hear that."

"Oh yes," Carol continued. "There's so much to tell you. I can't believe how much has happened since y'all left. Somebody who used to come to Clear Springs before your time has come back. You remember Ed Halstead's brother, Lester."

"The one who stirred up the stink at the association over you and Linda being ordained? You're not telling me he's back, are you, with y'all having a woman pastor?"

"Oh, no, not Lester!" Carol laughed. "The church wouldn't let that turkey come back, but Lester's soon-to-be ex-wife Wanda's been at Clear Springs the last three Sundays. She stayed with Lester 'til the kids were grown. The day after their youngest boy joined the Marines, she packed up her clothes and left while Lester was at work. You know how Wes Trimble's always buying cars that need a little work, fixing them up in his spare time, and selling them. Wes found her a little Nissan Sentra, put it in good shape, and sold it to her for what he had tied up in it. She's got a job at WalMart until she finds something that pays better, and she helps take care of Maude and Arthur when she's not at her other job. That's been good for her, Maude and Arthur bragging on her, thanking her every time she does anything for them, telling people how sweet and kind she is. She needed to hear some kind words after being married to Lester Halstead twenty-seven years. That's longer than the sentence for most felonies. Ed thinks he might be able to help her get on over there where he works. Lester never would let Wanda have a job outside the home. Forty-five years old, and she'd never seen her name on a paycheck before! Lester controlled all the money, gave her an allowance like you would a child. Wanda's closest family's way out in Texas, what little family she's got. Lester married her while he was stationed at Fort Hood, married her a week after she graduated from high school. Wanda told me that Ed said he didn't blame her one bit for leaving his brother, said he'd hate to have to live under the same roof with him, told her he didn't see how she stood it as long as she did. Ed and Barbara told her she was welcome to stay with them until she could get on her feet. The church is treating her like she never left, since she never wanted to leave in the first place. She was miserable listening to Billy Fite every Sunday. Wanda moved her membership back to Clear Springs the first Sunday she was there. She told Heather she wanted to say something to the church, and she said, 'I've always loved this church. I never wanted to leave, and it feels good to be back. I want to move my membership back here because my heart never left.' Wallace, bless his heart, said 'Movewereceive'er, and if True Gospel won't grant her letter, I move we go ahead and receive her on statement of her Christian experience. We've known her longer than Billy Fite has.' I said 'Brother Wallace, that's the most skillfully worded motion I ever heard, and I second it.'"

"Speaking of Wallace, how's he doing?"

"He's got to have cataract surgery on one of his eyes next week. Otherwise, he's going strong. He's like a kid with a new toy ever since he bought that truck. He's talking about, as soon as he gets over the cataract surgery, taking a trip and seeing some of our former pastors. He wants to see you and Mike and Asalee, he wants to see your new baby when it's born, and, of course, he wants to see the dog that was named after him. Brother Steve Kane, the one who baptized me, is pastoring a church in North Carolina. He's one of the ones Wallace wants to see. And then he plans to be in McMillan, Tennessee when Heather preaches at the first service of the new church. Wallace said that's why he bought that new truck, so he could make the trip he wants to make, said he was afraid to trust his old car on a long trip. He still volunteers at the hospital. The Ledford paper had a nice writeup about him a couple of weeks ago, even printed a picture of him when he was nineteen years old back in 1923, standing beside the first engine he worked on. Everybody at Clear Springs bought up extra copies of the paper that week. I meant to bring you one and forgot it. I'll mail you a copy."

"Excuse me! Sorry to interrupt the conversation," Mike interjected. "The charcoal's just right. Let's get hamburgers and hotdogs on the grill."

* * * * * * * * * * * *

Asalee and Little Bill fizzled about 10:00, but Carol and her daughters talked with Mike and Karen until after 2:00 in the morning. Every time the conversation seemed to be winding down, somebody would say something that would start a new thread, and they all lost track of the time. Megan told Mike and Karen what she had told Heather the previous Sunday, that she believed God was calling her to be a preacher. "Preacher Heather told me it's a good thing I'm at Clear Springs, because there aren't many churches that encourage girls who want to be preachers." As Mike and Karen hugged Megan, they all had tears running down their faces, and Mike added, "I'm proud to be the one who baptized you, Meg, and I think you'll make a fine preacher. You've got a good pastor and a good church to encourage you. I'll pray for you and do all I can to help you."

* * * * * * * * * * * *

Mike caught up with Franklin A. Brinkley, Chairman of the Board of Deacons of Harrington Baptist Church, as he came in for Sunday School. "Brother Frank, if you don't mind, I'd like to have a deacon from my former church who is visiting with us assist me at the communion table."

"Of course, Pastor, that's fine with me. Tell him to go right ahead." Mike did not question the assumption underlying Frank's choice of pronouns.

The worship attendance was barely over a hundred, but that was to be expected with the Fourth of July holiday. Mike announced that there would be no evening service and that the deacons meeting would be postponed until the following Sunday because of the holiday. It was the church's custom to have only the morning service and to postpone afternoon meetings on the Sunday closest to the Fourth, and Mike was glad. He could relax with Carol's family and not have to rush back for a deacons meeting and an evening service. If some people got upset about a woman helping with the communion service, they would have a week to get over it.

The four deacons taking up the offering and serving communion were Jack Miller, Ted Coleman, Jerry McWhorter and Royce Green, two old guard and two new people. Karen was in the choir. Asalee, along with Molly Coleman, was sitting with Carol and her family, two pews from the front.

Jack, Ted, Jerry, and Royce all assumed that Franklin A. Brinkley, Chairman of the Board of Deacons of Harrington Baptist Church, would come up to assist Mike at the communion table and serve the deacons who were serving the congregation. That was his usual practice, and he had not told them otherwise.

During the welcome and announcement time, Mike welcomed all who were visiting and added, "We're delighted to have some dear friends from my former pastorate with us today, Carol Richardson, her two daughters Megan and Jessica, and her son Bill." Mike noted the look of utter confusion on Frank Brinkley's face. Frank concluded that Carol's husband must be in the restroom or something and that he would come in later, but he was confused as to why Mike didn't mention him, since he was a deacon and would be assisting Mike at the communion table in a few minutes. As Mike concluded his sermon, he could see that Frank was growing more perplexed by the minute, waiting for Carol's husband to show up. Frank finally got up from his seat, tiptoed to the front pew, and sat down next to Royce Green, thinking that something had caused a change in plans and that Carol's husband would not be there after all. His face turned ashen when Mike said, "I've asked Deacon Carol Richardson from Clear Springs Baptist Church to assist me at the Lord's table today." When the other deacons got up to serve the congregation, Frank was left sitting on the front pew looking bewildered. After the congregation was served, the deacons took their seats on the front pews. Ted and Jerry were on the pew to the left of the aisle, and Mike served them. Jack, Royce, and Frank were seated on the other side of the aisle, where they were served by Carol.

When he got home, Frank found the letter from the deacons at Clear Springs to the deacons at Harrington. He had folded it and stuck it in his big heavy Bible between Revelation and Concordance, where it might well have remained for somebody else to find long after he was dead and buried. He had only skimmed over it, and he had not shown it to the other deacons. It was the first time Frank had bothered to look at the signatures. He read and re-read the second signature, *Carol Ann Ayers Richardson.* It was very legible, written in a small, precise hand that looked like the engraving on a wedding invitation. The last signature, *Linda Gail Ethridge Trimble,* was written in bold strokes reminiscent of John Hancock.

⁂   ⁂   ⁂   ⁂   ⁂   ⁂   ⁂   ⁂   ⁂   ⁂   ⁂   ⁂

Mike and Karen had a folding card table, and Mike stopped at the WalMart in Carrollton on his way back from his hospital visit

Friday and picked up four stackable plastic chairs to help with the logistics of serving meals while Carol and her family were visiting. Asalee felt very grown-up sitting with Megan and Jessica at their own table in the dining room.

They all gathered in the kitchen, and Carol offered the prayer of thanksgiving for the food before they fixed their plates. Mike had just put the first bite of meat loaf in his mouth when the phone rang.

"Preacher, this is Brenda Coleman," the voice on the other end gushed breathlessly. "I'm sorry to call when you're probably just sitting down to dinner, but I didn't get a chance to speak to you at church and I couldn't wait to tell you how much I enjoyed the service this morning and how much it meant to me for the woman from your former church to help with communion. I did get to talk with her. She's a delightful person."

"Thanks, Brenda. Carol was ordained while we were at Clear Springs, and she's one of the best deacons you'll find anywhere. She's in the same profession you're in, teaches high school biology."

"And she's a deacon just like me," Brenda added. "Brother Mike, Ted and I both were ordained at the church we came from in Macon. The hardest thing about moving to Harrington was giving up my deacon ministry. Our pastor in Macon was very helpful and affirming, so I really enjoyed being a deacon. When we joined here, Brother Reynolds told us he wasn't against women deacons, but he didn't think the church was ready to deal with that issue. He felt like it'd be best not to say anything to the church about me being ordained. You would've thought it was some dark, shameful secret, like we were talking about me having a criminal record or something. I'm sure he meant well, trying to keep down controversy in the church. But it's sad if we have to keep secrets and have a long list of things we can't talk about in order to keep peace in the church. My experience of serving as a deacon will always be an important part of my Christian experience. It's bad when you have to deny a part of God's work in your life to join a Baptist church."

"And that's really what you had to do, isn't it?"

"It really is. Our church in Macon was the only church I belonged to before we came to Harrington. We'd had women deacons since I was in high school, back in the early 70's. My aunt Charlotte Raines was the first woman ordained there, and my mother's a deacon. I was so used to seeing women serve communion, I was miserable here on communion Sundays, seeing only men serving. I tried every way I could to deal with it. I volunteered to help in the nursery on Sundays we had communion, but that didn't last long. I realized I'd soon be facing murder charges if I spent another Sunday cooped up in a small room with Hilda Mae Snyder. I'm sure that woman means well, but...oh, well, I'm not going to go there. Then, I decided to stay home on communion Sundays, but I only did that once, and I didn't feel right doing it. So, for most of the last seven years, I've just felt miserable and cried inside when we had the Lord's Supper. I tried every way I know to get around it and get over it, but I feel like a second-class member of the church when I see only men serving the Lord's Supper. The Lord's Supper stands for something I believe with all my heart, but sometimes I wonder whether I should partake of it feeling the way I feel. It meant more to me today than it has in a long time."

"Well, Brenda, I really appreciate you telling me that. I didn't ask Carol in order to make a point about women deacons. I asked her for the same reason I asked Karen's father when they were at Clear Springs on communion Sunday. But, I won't be surprised if this helps get us started talking about the subject. I was surprised nobody said anything about it to me at church this morning."

"And they may not," Brenda cautioned. "The ones who have something to carp about go running to Franklin A. Brinkley,

Chairman of the Board of Deacons of Harrington Baptist Church, or one of the older deacons. This church is not noted for direct, honest communication. If they don't like something you say or do, they won't come to you. They'll go running to one of the older deacons, who'll jump you about it in the deacons meeting, telling you about all these people who've been calling and complaining to them, but they'll say they can't tell you who called them, so you don't have any way to respond to the person who expressed the concern. It may be one or two chronic complainers, or it may be Frank, Royce, Doc, or Jack posing as the spokesman for some invisible multitude because they don't have the guts to just say 'this is what I think.' By the time it gets to you it sounds like the whole church is up in arms and ready to turn into a lynch mob. It drives Ted up the wall. Sometimes on Sunday nights after a deacons meeting, he's so wound up he keeps me awake half the night talking out his frustrations. It's usually that same mess about what 'they, several, some of 'em, a lot of 'em, or all of 'em'—Ted's term is 'the great vague they'—are supposed to be saying. Anyway, Brother Mike, I didn't mean to get off on that tangent. Let me let you get back to your dinner..."

Bill Junior had finished eating and gone out to play with Wallace by the time Mike got back to the table. Just as he sat down to resume eating, the phone rang again. He started to get up and answer it, but Karen stopped him. "Let the voice mail get it. You can call whoever it is after we eat. That's why God created voice mail. So who was on the phone?"

"Brenda Coleman."

"Oh yes," Carol interjected, "I remember speaking to her after the service. Woman about my age, long dark-brown hair, wire-rim glasses. She came up to me, tears streaming down her face, hugged me, and told me how much the communion service meant to her. She thought it was wonderful that I'm an ordained deacon. I told her that our pastor is a young woman seminary student, and she said, 'Wow! Really! Praise the Lord!' and she hugged me so tight I thought my eyes were going to pop out of my head."

"Brenda's one of my favorite people here," Karen added. "Very exuberant personality. I'd like to see her at work in the classroom. She teaches fourth grade. Just being around her, you can tell she'd be good at it. Teaches the same age group in Sunday School, too. The little girl, Molly, who was sticking close to Asalee at church, is Ted and Brenda's youngest. Brenda's husband Ted is the editor of our local paper. Good guy, he's been a big help to Mike. Anyway, what'd Brenda have on her mind, Honey?"

"Just calling to say how much she appreciated the service this morning, and how much it meant to her to see a woman helping with the communion service. And I just learned something about Brenda we didn't know."

"What's that?"

"She's an ordained deacon. She and Ted were ordained at the church they came from in Macon. When they joined here, Harry Reynolds, my predecessor, told her he thought it was best not to tell the church she was an ordained deacon, told her he wasn't personally opposed to women deacons but he didn't think the church was ready for that. She's been miserable on communion Sundays the whole seven years they've been here, said she feels like a second-class member of the church when she sees only men serving communion. She talked about how serving as a deacon was an important part of her Christian experience, and she said 'It's bad when you have to deny a part of God's work in your life to join a Baptist church.'"

"I couldn't do it," Carol stated flatly. "I couldn't be a member of a church that says I'm limited in the ways I can serve the Lord because I'm a woman or because I'm divorced. And then there's what Meg told you, how she feels like God's calling her to preach.

I try to spend ten or fifteen minutes one-on-one with each of my kids before they settle down for the night. The night Meg told me that, it blew me away. I just held her close, and we talked, cried, and prayed a long time after the other two were asleep. I know Meg won't be thirteen 'til the end of next month. I don't know if she'll still feel like God's calling her to preach when she's older. I knew I was going to be a teacher when I was a lot younger than Meg. From the time Maude Sessions taught me in the first grade, I never wanted to be anything but a teacher. Heather said she knew she was going to be a preacher as far back as she could remember. Megan's always been a very spiritual girl. I'm not bragging on her just because she's mine. She's head-over-heels in love with the Bible, very sensitive and compassionate, sharp mind, very articulate for a thirteen year old. I won't be surprised if she's locked in to what she's supposed to do in life. I couldn't take her to a church that tried to tell her God doesn't call women to preach. At Clear Springs, she gets to hear a woman preach, and preach well— Heather's a powerful preacher to be so young. Meg knows it's a possibility for her, and she's got a good role model."

"So what would you do if you didn't have a church like Clear Springs?" Mike asked.

"I guess I'd have to start one. You know, it's a funny thing. My kids've fully accepted Heather being our pastor, and they're used to Linda and me being deacons. When I was Megan's age, it never occurred to me that a woman could be a deacon, let alone a pastor. The first time I ever saw a woman serve communion was the first time Linda and I did it. The first time I saw a woman do a baptism, I was the woman! I'll never forget the Sunday Jess made her profession of faith. You presented her to the church, and then you looked over at me and said, 'Carol, you're going to baptize this one!' I never thought about a woman being a deacon until Mary Kate called and told me the church in Canfield wanted her to be a deacon and she asked me what I thought about it. Maude and Arthur asked Daddy to take them over there for Mary Kate's ordination, and it ended up with Clear Springs calling off services and the whole church going. The next thing I knew, Clear Springs asked me, a divorced woman, to be a deacon! When Mary Kate did the charge to the candidates at mine and Linda's ordination, it was the first time I'd ever seen a woman speak from the pulpit. Heather's the only woman I ever heard preach a sermon. I never thought about a woman doing that before she came along. Before my eyes were opened, I accepted the way it was. Now, I couldn't go back to the way it used to be. It's like what Paul says in Galatians about going back under the law after experiencing grace. You can accept the old way 'til the Lord shows you better, then you can't go back. I went around the world to answer your question. If I lived in a community where there was no church that accepted people of all races and believed that men and women were equally capable of serving the Lord, I'd have to find some more people who believe the way I do and start a church. I'd never take my daughters to a church that imposed limits on how they could serve the Lord."

* * * * * * * * * * * *

As he and Karen were getting into bed, Mike remembered to pick up the phone and check the voice mail. There were two messages from Eric Latham. The first one was the call Mike almost answered at lunchtime. Eric was calling to tell Mike and Karen that Jenny was in labor. The second call must have come while they were showing Carol's family around Harrington. Eric had called with the news that he and Jenny had a new baby boy, and that all was well.

13

Mike usually hated leaving messages on answering machines, but he made an exception for the answering machine of Franklin A. Brinkley, Chairman of the Board of Deacons of Harrington Baptist Church. He was relieved to get a recording when he called Tuesday night to tell Frank that he and his family would be spending the Fourth of July with his family up at Denham. He left a message with the phone number where he could be reached if an emergency arose. In case Frank didn't get the message until after the fact, he also called the Colemans and left word with Brenda. One old guard deacon and one new people deacon. Actually, two new people deacons, but the church didn't know that Brenda was a deacon, too.

Mike and Karen had been looking forward to the Fourth. It had not taken them long to realize that the only way he could take a full day off with his family would be to go out of town. Grady and Julia had called Sunday night to make sure they were still planning to come up. Asalee was eager to see her grandparents and her Aunt Mandy. Grady said the new swimming pool was open, the freezer was full of choice steaks, and the grill would be hot. Mike and Karen promised to be there.

As soon as Mike stopped the car in his parents' driveway, Asalee sprang from the car and hit the ground running, squealing

"Grandmommy! Granddaddy! Mandy!" as Mike's parents and sister emerged from the house to greet them. Wallace the Dog was hot on her heels. Karen, being seven months pregnant, moved a little more slowly. Mike remained behind with her as she gingerly pulled herself up out of the car, and the two of them walked toward the house at a more leisurely pace. Asalee wore her bathing suit on the way over, and she and Mandy were in the pool by the time Mike and Karen traversed the distance from the car to the house.

"Come on in the house, kids," Grady Westover called out. "Mandy's done been swimming this morning. Her'n Asalee went straight to the pool. How y'all been?"

"Pretty good," Mike responded. "Been looking forward to getting over here. We've been needing to come up for air, do some swimming, eat some steaks, and look over what you've got going in the shop. If we were at home, somebody'd think of a reason they needed to call me and I'd think of something I needed to be doing."

"Sounds like our pastor. People run him ragged. On top of that, his wife's a preacher, too. Him an' his wife'n kids're comin' out here if somebody don't call and shanghai one of 'em with somethin' that can't wait til' tomorrow. Nice folks, all their family's out'n Missouri someplace, so we invited 'em to hide out here, spend the Fourth with us, an' I told 'em to come swim in our pool anytime they want to." With a laugh, Grady added, "I suggested they park their car over back of the shop so nobody'd see it and track 'em down that way."

"Look forward to meeting them."

"Yeah, I tell you, Son, I used to think a preacher had the easiest job in town. I've changed my mind since you got to be a preacher and I started goin' to church pretty reg'lar. I sure couldn't do a preacher's job. Too many people want to be your boss, and there's never a stoppin' place."

"Looks like our second grandbaby's really growing," Julia commented as she patted Karen's belly and gave her a hug. "How're you feeling?"

"OK. I tire our pretty easily, but my obstetrician says everything looks good. She did an ultrasound, and it looks like we're having another little girl."

"Y'all settled on a name yet?" Grady asked.

"Deborah Estelle. The first name, Deborah, has a long story behind it—we'll tell you some other time. Estelle's after Estelle Coggins at Clear Springs."

"Pretty name," Grady commented. "One a' my grandmothers was named Deborah. Deborah Jane Burnham, married Ira Justice. She died when Mike was a year old. We got a picture of 'er holdin' Mike when he was a baby."

"That's a pretty name," Julia agreed, "and we'll spoil Deborah Estelle just like we did Asalee Nicole. Grady's got your baby bed and changing table and all that stuff down out of the attic. You won't have room for it all in your car, so Mandy's gonna follow you home in the truck and come back tomorrow."

"That'll give Mike and me some time to ourselves," Karen laughed, "because we all know where Asalee'll ride, and Wallace'll go with Asalee."

Grady proceeded to get the grill ready while Mike went in the house to change into his swim trunks. Karen and Julia were relaxing in lounge chairs by the pool when they heard a car pull up in the driveway. "Oh, good, they're here. Our pastor and his family," Julia said as she recognized the car. "Grady, Hon," she called out loudly enough for her husband to hear her, "the Perkins' are here." Turning back to her daughter-in-law, she muttered, "I don't know what I'm going to do if your father-in-law doesn't swallow his pride and start wearing his hearing aid. Only time he puts it in is when he goes to church."

Mike thought it significant that Grady did not see the need to get himself fitted for a hearing aid until he started going to church. Before that, he insisted that the problem was not with his hearing but with everybody else mumbling. At one time, Grady would not have been that interested in hearing what a preacher had to say. Mike had just emerged from the house when his father launched into the introductions. "Hey, Mike, want you to meet our pastor Terry Perkins, his wife Christa, twin daughters Lindsey and Courtney, and son Todd."

"'Pleased to meet y'all," Mike said as he shook hands with Terry and Christa. "I'm Mike. That's my wife Karen, the pregnant one over by the pool with my mother, and that's our daughter Asalee in the pool with Mandy."

"Been looking forward to meeting you, Mike," Terry responded. "Your dad's been telling me about you, said you were pastoring a Baptist church over at Harrington. How long you been there?"

"About six weeks. Served a little country church close to Ledford, Virginia while I was at Mid-Atlantic Seminary."

"Ah, yes, Mid-Atlantic," Christa commented. "I almost went there. My name is Christa, and I am a recovering Southern Baptist. I was youth minister at a Southern Baptist church in Missouri while I was in college, lock-ins with seventh and eighth graders, car washes with high school kids, Ridgecrest, the whole nine yards. Been there, done that, got the t-shirt. I saw the handwriting on the wall, joined the Methodist church, went to Candler, never looked back. That's where Terry and I met, so it worked out for the best." Then, apologetically, she added, "Of course, I don't know what your feelings are about women preachers…"

"Well, a lot of women are sweet and pretty," Mike mugged facetiously. "I believe women have souls and they can be saved and go to heaven when they die. Some of y'all can cook a great meatloaf, and Lord knows we men couldn't reproduce by ourselves. Still, you women were first in the Edenic fall, more easily deceived and all of that, so y'all really shouldn't be serving in leadership roles entailing ordination. Gotta preserve the divinely-ordained order of submission, you know." Christa had a sense of humor, and Mike was not able to keep a straight face through the whole routine. "No, seriously, I'm just in favor of excellence in ministry, and some excellent ministers happen to be women. Like Heather Simmons who followed me at Clear Springs."

"Your student pastorate called a woman after you left?" Christa asked incredulously.

"They did. Heather just finished her second year at Mid-Atlantic. Good preacher, you'd be impressed with her. She filled in for me when I preached for the committee from Harrington and again when I preached the trial sermon. I didn't know how the church would respond, but it was love at first sight. They never even looked at anybody else. When Heather's home church refused to ordain her, it was no big deal. Clear Springs hadn't ordained a preacher since 1874, so they decided it was high time they ordained another one. They did it up right. That ordination was the grandest celebration I've ever seen."

"That's one thing I miss about being Baptist, the freedom a local church has to do whatever it believes to be right, that and immersion baptism," Christa commented. "Clear Springs didn't need anybody's permission to ordain Heather. A Baptist church can do anything it believes the Lord is leading it to do, provided they've got the integrity to do it and they're willing to live with the repercussions."

"And Clear Springs has the integrity and the willingness. I'd only been there about a month when the church ordained its first two women deacons, and one of them was divorced. One of the pastors in the association stirred up a big stink at the annual meeting, tried to get us thrown out. My chairman of deacons, Wallace Coggins, eighty-six years old, great guy, wish you knew him, said 'Well, this church is 144 years old, been in the Sanders County Association the whole time, always supported the association right well for a small church, but if they want to throw us out on account of us ordainin' Carol and Linda, let 'em do it. I'd rather get kicked out than have the association start telling us who we can ordain. If we let 'em tell us who we can ordain as deacons, the next thing you know they'll be tellin' us who we can call as pastor.'"

"Whoa! Talk about being prophetic!"

"Yeah, more than he realized at the time. Nobody was thinking about a woman pastor at the time. Anyway, talking about Heather, she's one of the last two women M. Div. students at Mid-Atlantic. No women left in the Ph. D. or D. Min. programs. The school of theology's going to be closed to women after this year, as though they were besieged by women beating the doors down to get in. They've already closed it to men who've been divorced."

"That's tragic. It was an incredibly good place a few years ago. When I was considering Mid-Atlantic in the early 80's, there were women all over the place, and I came so close to going there, glad I didn't. But that's wonderful about Clear Springs calling Heather. Sounds like a remarkable church."

"It is. I'll always be thankful I got to start my ministry there. They were good to us, very gracious and forgiving. But you're right about the seminary. When Sturgill forced Dr. Minkins out, the Riverton paper ran an editorial saying Mid-Atlantic is becoming famous for who *used* to teach there."

"Tell me about it. When I visited the campus, all the women professors were still there, you mentioned Rachel Minkins, then there was Dorothy Grant-Wiggins, Judith Sizemore, Hazel Grogan, Nancy Woods Gregerson, all of them were still there. It was wonderful back then, but I knew it wasn't going to last. I heard Dr. Gregerson in chapel one time when she visited our college campus. She was one of the best preachers I've ever heard, I'd put her in the league with Fred Craddock and George Buttrick. The ones who got to do homiletics with her were very fortunate."

"Never got to hear her. "I had Dr. Leggs for homiletics, he was good, but you're not the first one I've heard rate Gregerson that highly. When I got there, Rachel Minkins was the only woman left on faculty. I don't know how she stuck it out as long as she did. I had my first year theology courses with her, and I'm glad I did. She's teaching somewhere up in British Columbia now."

"Y'all go ahead'n swim," Grady interjected. "I just got the grill started, got to wait for the charcoal to get just right before we put the steaks on. Julia's got potatoes in the oven, and I fixed two crock pots full of baked beans, my recipe, early this mornin'. If you want something to drink, there's a little bit of everything iced down in that big washtub over there. Help yourself, there's plenty. There's some Nugrape in there for Asalee. I always get Nugrape when Asalee's coming 'cause I know that's what she likes."

"Thanks, Grady," Terry responded. "We've been looking forward to being out here today, really appreciate you inviting us, and I'm dying of curiosity to know what it is you said you were going to ask me after we eat."

"And you'll find out after we eat, Preacher. How you like your steak cooked?" Grady proceeded to poll everyone to find out how they liked their steaks, pronounced the charcoal to be just right, and began placing thick T-bone steaks from the picnic cooler onto the grill along with hot dogs and hamburgers for the children. Seeing that Wallace the Dog was eyeing his every move, Grady turned to him and said, "Wallace ol' boy, this is gonna be the happiest day of your life when you get hold'a all these bones."

The little inflatable donuts around Asalee's upper arms made her unsinkable, and she quickly made friends with the Perkins twins and their younger brother, all of them good swimmers. Christa and Mandy became *de facto* lifeguards. Julia and Karen continued to sun themselves at poolside. After a couple of dives and laps around the pool, Mike and Terry relaxed in the shallow end and continued their conversation. "So how long've you been in Denham?" Mike asked.

"Two years, same for Christa and her two-church charge. It's a challenging church, District Superintendent says it's a church that wonders why so many of its former pastors left the ministry. It's got its headaches like any church, but overall I think we're having a good ministry. I'm hoping the conference will leave us there a couple more years. The church has suffered from too much pastoral turnover. Christa feels the same way about both of hers. There's a new subdivision going up halfway between Christa's two churches, and each of her churches has gained two families from the new subdivision. As for Denham Methodist, I can't explain it any other way except to say the Lord's working. The church had been declining slowly for the past ten or fifteen years. All of a sudden, we've started to see some growth. We're not back to the size the church was at its peak, but we're on the way back up. We're reaching folks like your parents who've lived around here all their lives, people with teenagers and grown kids who haven't been a part of any church in their adult lives. I never cease to be amazed by it."

"Great! I hope they let you stay put. Harrington Baptist has declined from its peak in the late 50's and early 60's. We run about 135 to 140 in morning worship, compared to about 225 when the church was at its peak. Harrington has a reputation as a widow-maker, it's been hard on some pastors in the past. My predecessor was there for sixteen years, but I get the impression they rode him pretty hard toward the last. So, no way of telling how long we'll be there. It's a lot different from my student pastorate. You couldn't find two churches more different."

The conversations in and around the pool were cut short by the booming voice of Grady Westover announcing, "The steaks're lookin' about right. Julia, Mandy, y'all be seein' 'bout the baked potatoes an' baked beans. Mike, make yourself useful stead'a ornamental—be roundin' up butter'n sour cream, steak sauce'n such outta the Frigidaire. Then let's all gather 'round'n let Preacher Terry say grace."

*   *   *   *   *   *   *   *   *   *   *   *

"Brother, you sure know how to cook a steak," Terry commented as he finished eating. "Everything's delicious. So nice of y'all to invite us out here today."

"Our pleasure, Preacher. Now, I said I was gonna ask you something soon's we got done eatin'." Julia did not know what Grady had in mind, but she sensed that it was something momentous. Her expectancy was contagious. Even Asalee was listening as her grandfather continued, "I been readin' over in the Book of Acts about ol' Philip baptizin' that guy from Ethiopia. The guy shows Philip some water'n asks 'im what stood in the way of 'im bein' baptized. Ol' Philip asked 'im if he believed Jesus is the Son of God, an' he asked 'im if he wanted to be baptized with all 'is heart. Well, I believe in Jesus, believe He's the son of God'n that He died on the cross to save me. If He cared enough about me to do that, I want to start livin' for Him, an' I reckon that starts with bein' baptized. Mike, Terry, right there's the water. Let's do it."

Mike, Karen, Julia, and Mandy had tears running down their faces. They and all the others were speechless as Grady continued, "Now, Brother Terry, I don't know if you ever put one all the way under water the way the Baptists do it. If you hadn't, you're fixin' to. I want one a' y'all on each side of me, an' I want y'all to baptize me the way Baptists do it, under the water. I want to be baptized like a Baptist, but I want to join the Methodist church."

Terry, somewhat taken aback, managed to reply, "That's not a problem, Grady."

Mike, equally nonplused, asked, "You want to do it right here right now, Daddy?"

"That's what I said, Son. I did'n tell your mama, but I had this in mind when we had the pool put in. I enjoy goin' for a swim ever' evenin', and y'all are always welcome to swim in it, but this pool was put here for any church that needs a baptizin' place, an' I want to be the first one baptized in it."

Mandy and Julia raced to get the camcorder and a camera while the others gathered at poolside for a good view. Mike heard the camcorder humming and the camera clicking as he, Terry, and Grady climbed down the ladder into the water. Grady faced the family and friends gathered beside the pool, with Mike on his right and Terry on his left. Mike reached out his right forearm as he gently coached his father on how the baptism would be done. "OK, Daddy, put your hands on my forearm. That's good. Now the last words I'll say before we put you under the water will be 'buried with Him in baptism.'" Mike began the familiar baptismal formula, "In obedience to our Lord and Savior Jesus Christ, following the example Jesus gave us when He was baptized by John in the Jordan River, and upon your profession of faith in Him, I baptize you my brother in Christ, Grady Charles Westover, in the name of the Father, the Son, and the Holy Spirit. Buried with Him in baptism..." As he spoke those words, he and the Methodist preacher baptized Grady the way Baptists do it, under the water. With even greater clarity than the camera or the camcorder, Mike's mind recorded the joyful look on his father's face as he and Terry brought him up from the water. Mike concluded the baptismal formula, "Raised to walk in the newness of life in Christ Jesus," and his father reached out and embraced him for the first time Mike could remember. Mike had never doubted his father's love, but Grady never was an emotionally demonstrative man. Nothing but the grace of God could turn Grady Westover into a weeper or a hugger, and he had been turned into both.

As he was released from his father's embrace, Mike heard a splashing sound and turned to see his sister in the pool, walking toward him with tears streaming down her face. She had handed her camera to Karen and climbed down into the pool. The Spirit must have spoken to Terry, telling him to step aside. Mike met Mandy in a shallower part of the pool. They exchanged no words, but they did not need to. Mike looked over at his father and said, "Daddy, come here. There's nothing in the Bible that says you have to be a preacher or a deacon to help with baptism."

After Mike and Grady baptized Mandy, they were all sitting around the pool silently pondering what had transpired. Even the children sensed that it was a holy moment, and they were quiet. Karen broke the silence. "We're used to having communion when we baptize. Mike, I guess NuGrape soda's the closest thing we've got to grape juice, and there's probably some saltines or some kind of crackers in the house."

"Would Ritz crackers be OK?" Julia asked. "That's the only kind we have."

"Ritz crackers and NuGrape soda will do just fine," Christa answered authoritatively.

"Preacher Christa," Grady interjected, "since Mike and Terry did the baptizin', how 'bout you leadin' the communion service."

"I'd be delighted to, Grady. Karen and Julia, if you'll prepare the elements, get a plate with some Ritz crackers, open a can of NuGrape and pour it into cups for us. Grady and Mandy, you can serve the congregation..."

*   *   *   *   *   *   *   *   *   *   *   *

It was after 8:00 when Mike and Karen started the two-and-a-half hour trip back to Harrington. Mandy was behind them in Mike's old yellow pickup, bringing the nursery furniture, Asalee, and Wallace the Dog. Mike knew he had to go back to the routine of pastoring Harrington Baptist Church—get two sermons ready for Sunday, prepare for the deacons meeting Sunday afternoon, two or more committee meetings a week for the rest of the summer, help with last-minute preparations for Vacation Bible School, and get everything squared away for the middle school girls to go to Camp Pinnacle. August would bring deacon nominations and Susan Whitmire's wedding. As he and Karen talked about the unforeseen events of the day, Mike was not ready to think about any of those things. He simply relished being a minister of the gospel. Neither Mount Rushmore-face Franklin A. Brinkley, Chairman of the Board of Deacons of Harrington Baptist Church, Geneva and Roland Millican, nor That Woman, not even all of them put together, could take that or the joyful experiences of the day away from him. Mike found himself thinking of the second stanza of *Higher Ground:*

My heart has no desire to stay
Where doubts arise and fears dismay
Though some may dwell where these abound,
My prayer, my aim is higher ground.

* * * * * * * * * * * *

At the end of the week, Brenda Coleman was still the only one who had called to register an opinion about Carol helping with communion. Mike decided not to worry any more about it. He concluded that those who did not like it had decided not to make an issue of it since she was just visiting for one Sunday.

On Sunday morning, Mike told the church about the baptismal service in his parents' swimming pool and the communion service with two Methodist preachers, Ritz crackers and NuGrape soda. As he did, he read facial expressions that ranged all the way from Brenda Coleman's radiant countenance, laughter, and tears of joy, to the stone face of Franklin A. Brinkley, Chairman of the Board of Deacons of Harrington Baptist Church, to the mortified look on Geneva Millican's face when he told about using Ritz crackers and NuGrape soda for communion.

Mike and his family were invited home for Sunday dinner with the McWhorters. Elaine and Jerry asked Mike to tell them more about the Fourth of July baptismal service, and that conversation provided a natural opening for ten year old Cassie to say that she had almost responded to the invitation that morning. Cassie said she would like to be baptized, and Mike talked with her after dinner about the meaning of baptism, making sure that she understood the commitment that she would be making. Jerry reminded his daughter that they would be attending the evening service and suggested that she could respond to the invitation then. They all wished that the visit could last longer, but Mike had to get back to the church by 3:00 for three solid hours of meetings before the evening service. The deacons meeting was at 4:30. Then, Mike had learned that morning that two members of the church council would be unavailable during the week and that they would have to meet on Sunday afternoon as well, so Mike reluctantly agreed to schedule that meeting at 3:00, before the deacons meeting.

The council had to finalize the calendar for the new church year that would begin in October, and Mike hoped they would be able to finish it that afternoon. Like the finance and nominating committees, the church council had to have its recommendations ready for the September deacons meeting. After review by the deacons, the recommendations would be presented to the church in the September business meeting in order for everything to be in place for the beginning of the church year on October 1.

The requirement of running everything by the deacons made little actual difference in the work of the committees, but it drove Mike up the wall. Because of the Labor Day holiday, the September deacons meeting would not take place until the second Sunday, so it only made three days' difference in when the committee recommendations were due. Mike had thoroughly studied the constitution and bylaws, and he arrived at the same conclusion as Carl Baxter, Ted Coleman, and David Groves. There was nothing that required all committees to report to the deacons. On paper, it appeared that the committees reported directly to the congregation, but it was a long-established tradition that everything had to be run by the deacons before it could be presented to the church. Mike guessed that, eons ago, the deacons simply demanded that it be so, no one challenged them, and the committees meekly complied and established the precedent for future generations.

As chairman of the hiring squad, Carl Baxter had been the first to break the unwritten rule. Franklin A. Brinkley, Chairman of the Board of Deacons of Harrington Baptist Church, took that as a personal affront. It did not look as though Frank was inclined to forgive Carl anytime soon. In the six weeks that Mike had been pastor of Harrington Baptist Church, Frank had not spoken to Carl. Frank answered Carl's greetings with an icy glare and refused to speak to him or shake hands with him. Ted Coleman and David Groves told Frank to get over it and make peace with Carl, but their efforts seemed to deepen Frank's resolve to carry the grudge to his grave.

Clearly, there were two competing models of what deacons should be and do. Ted and David saw their role as helping the pastor with pastoral care, crisis ministry, evangelism, and visitation of prospective members. Frank Brinkley, Jack Miller, Lee Walters, and Royce Green wanted the deacons to be a governing board that supervised the pastor and managed the business affairs of the church. Jerry McWhorter was malleable enough to be pressed into either mold. Had it not been for second-guessing the work of committees and relaying gripes to the pastor, Frank, Jack, Lee, and Royce would not have known what to do in a deacons meeting. They would have been able to manage just fine with no more than two or three meetings a year. After all, there is only so much that can be said about the logistics of taking the offering and serving communion.

*   *   *   *   *   *   *   *   *   *   *   *

"Young man, you made me out to be a fool last Sunday, and I don't appreciate it one bit!" Frank Brinkley erupted at Mike in the deacons meeting.

Before Mike could open his mouth to defend himself, David sprang to his feet, grabbed the Chairman of the Board by the collar of his crisp white oxford cloth shirt, hoisted him to his feet, and shoved him against the wall. David was nose to nose with Frank, shouting in his face like a Marine Corps drill instructor. His fist was drawn back and his voice trembled with rage as he bellowed, "Don't *ever* let me hear you address the pastor of this church like that again! If you ever speak to our pastor like that again, your teeth'll be in your stomach and it'll take every man in this room to pull me off'a you!" With that, he shoved Frank roughly back down into his chair.

"Frank, you owe our pastor an apology," Jerry stated firmly. "You're way out of line. Brother Mike and his family had dinner with us after church today, and my daughter Cassie talked to him about making her profession of faith and being baptized. Brother Mike was so kind and patient talking to her, answering her questions, making sure she understood things. We're fortunate to have the pastor we've got, and I'm not just saying that because my wife was on the committee. He's doing a good job, and I don't have a problem with anything he's done so far. If you've got a problem with something the pastor said or did, you've got every right to tell him, but you don't have a right to be disrespectful."

Frank could see that David, Ted, and Jerry were sticking together and that Jack, Lee, and Royce were sitting there like bumps on a log rather than rushing to his defense. He backed down. "Sorry, pastor, I guess I was a little out of line, but you did make me look foolish having that woman help with communion."

"Her name is Carol, Carol Richardson. I told you ahead of time I was going to ask her, and you said, 'Sure pastor, go ahead, no problem.'"

"You told me that you were going to ask a deacon from your former church…"

"And I did," Mike explained. "Carol's a deacon, one of two women who serve as deacons at Clear Springs. She was ordained under my ministry."

"Well, when you said a deacon from your former church, I assumed you meant a man. When you recognized the woman and her children, I just assumed her husband was here somewhere and that he was the deacon who was going to help with communion. How was I to know your former church had women deacons?"

"I can't be responsible for your assumptions," Mike stated firmly. "And for what it's worth, Carol doesn't have a husband. She's divorced. Anyway, you should've known that Clear Springs has women deacons. The deacons of Clear Springs sent a letter commending me to the deacons of this church. If you'd read it, you would've seen the signatures of Carol Richardson and Linda Trimble. Most people named Carol or Linda are women."

"We never saw a letter from the deacons of Clear Springs," Ted Coleman interjected. "Do you have the letter, Frank?"

"Oh, that letter. Sure, I got it. I just never thought much about it."

"Well, Frank," David Groves responded, "the pastor said it was addressed to the deacons of this church. That's all of us, Frank, not just you. I want to know what it says."

"Here it is, if you think it's all that important," Frank muttered as he pulled the letter out from between the pages of his Bible and thrust it into David's hand.

After reading it aloud, David reiterated, "This is definitely addressed to all of us, and it certainly speaks well of our pastor. The pastor's right, Frank. If you'd read it, you would've seen the signatures. I think the whole church should see it. By common consent, Frank, I'm going to post it on the bulletin board where everybody can read it. I'm sure no one objects."

"Just one thing, Pastor," Royce Green spoke up. "I don't see that any harm was done by the woman helping serve communion the one time she was here, but don't get the idea that you're gonna be ordainin' divorced people, women, or divorced women in this church. Not while I'm living and serving as a deacon."

"Speaking of deacons," Frank said, "Deacon nominations come up in August. The bylaws say that we're supposed to publish a list in the August newsletter of all ordained deacons holding membership in this church who have not served actively within the past year along with a list of all male resident members over 21 years of age who are married and who have never been divorced. Jack and Jerry are rotating off the active deacon board, so we'll ask the people to vote for two people from those lists."

"Helen's already got the lists ready on the computer," Lee added.

* * * * * * * * * * * *

Mike arrived at the office about 7:30 Monday morning, logged onto the computer in Helen's office, and clicked on "list files." He found the file for the August newsletter and opened it. There was the list of all but one of the ordained deacons belonging to Harrington Baptist Church. As Franklin A. Brinkley, Chairman of the Board of Deacons of Harrington Baptist Church, had pointed out, the bylaws were very clear, *all ordained deacons holding membership in Harrington Baptist Church*. Mike typed in *Brenda Coleman*, placing her name alphabetically after Rudy Blevins. Before he had time to think too much about it and perhaps change his mind, he saved the change to the file and exited Helen's computer.

14

Mike scheduled Cassie McWhorter's baptism for the morning service on August 5 to coincide with communion, which the church always observed on the first Sunday of the month. Dan Jordan at Talmadge Street always observed communion when he baptized, and Mike liked the idea. Clear Springs readily embraced the practice, although Myrtle Norris and Joan Ayers had at first been reluctant to take the church's white linen tablecloths and century-old silver communion service down to the creekbank. Mike was able to prevail upon them only because they each had two grandchildren being baptized that day. After that, he never heard any objection from anyone. They had often used the hood of Joe Norris' truck for a communion table when they baptized in the creek. Myrtle always made Joe wash the truck the day before a baptismal service so she and Joan would have a clean surface upon which to spread the white linen cloths. With an indoor baptistry, there were no logistical barriers to combining the two services. The baptistry at Harrington was not as spacious as Mike would have liked, but there was enough room to have a deacon assist with baptism. Jerry was delighted when Mike asked him to help baptize his daughter. He said the only time he could remember a deacon helping with baptism was the time Harry Reynolds baptized Euless Redden, a six-foot-six mountain of a man. Reynolds, being of average build and afflicted with chronic back problems, asked David Groves to help with that one.

The week after Cassie's profession of faith, ninety-three year old Mrs. Addie Jane Aldridge, the oldest member of the church, had outpatient cataract surgery. She was in good spirits when Mike visited her at home the next day. A retired teacher, she was remarkably healthy and active for her age, and anyone trying to guess her age would have supposed her to be no more than eighty. Articulate and witty with a treasure trove of wonderful stories, she was one of the most delightful conversationalists Mike had ever met. He sat spellbound as she told about her conversion in a brush arbor meeting in 1908 and her subsequent baptism in the icy waters of Salyers Creek. Since Cassie was close to the age Mrs. Aldridge was when she was baptized, Mike knew that Cassie would enjoy hearing the story, and he thought it would be good for the church to hear it while she was still around to tell it. It would be better than any sermon he could preach that Sunday. "Mrs. Aldridge," Mike asked, "could I ask a big favor of you?"

"I don't know, Pastor. It depends on what it is. Being ninety-three years old, there are many things I'd like to do that I'm no longer able to do."

"But there are still many things you can do quite well, such as telling the story you just told me about your conversion in the brush arbor meeting and your baptism in Salyers Creek in 1908. You're the only one who can tell that story. The Sunday that I baptize Cassie, I'd like for you to tell the whole church what you just told me. It would be very encouraging to Cassie."

"Oh, pastor! You want me to come up to the pulpit? I don't know what our church would think about a woman speaking from the pulpit."

"Well, Mrs. Aldridge, your age and the fact that you're the oldest member of the church confers some privileges upon you. You're so respected that nobody would have the audacity to say anything negative about you speaking in church."

Mrs. Aldridge paused a moment before she spoke. "Do you really think so, Pastor?"

"Yes, I do, Mrs. Aldridge."

"Then I shall do it. Cassie is such a sweet child, so polite and well-mannered. If you think that an old woman telling her story will encourage her, I shall be pleased to give my testimony."

"Thank you. It'll be encouraging not only to Cassie but to the whole church. I look forward to hearing it again."

As Mike was leaving, Mrs. Aldridge walked with him to the door. Despite her diminutive size, her voice had the authoritative tone of a veteran classroom teacher as she stretched to her full 4' 10" height and said, "Bend over, Pastor, so I can give you a hug." As Mike complied with the order, Mrs. Aldridge's face broke into a playful smile. Her unbandaged eye looked more like Asalee's or Cassie's than an old woman's. It belonged to the eleven-year-old girl baptized in Salyers Creek in 1908. It was eleven-year-old Addie Jane Peyton who added in a half-whisper, "You know, Pastor, I never did believe in that foolishness about women keeping silent."

* * * * * * * * * * * *

After two months in Harrington, Mike still had not met any of the other pastors in the Mintz County Baptist Association, and he had only met Director of Missions Virgil Blackmon once. The associational pastors conference did not meet during the summer, and even that forum would not afford him the opportunity to meet all of them, since many churches in the association were served by part-time pastors who worked at other jobs during the day.

He had met some other pastors in Harrington and surrounding Mintz County. In the latter part of June, he received a letter from Eleanor Flint Basden, pastor of Harrington United Methodist Church. As president of the Mintz County Ministerial Association, she had written to invite him to the next meeting at Zion A. M. E. Mike was pleased to discover that the ministerial association was interracial as well as interdenominational, and that it did not stop meeting during the summer. He welcomed the prospect of being part of such a group. Attending the meeting had afforded him the opportunity to see the inside of Zion A. M. E.'s stately edifice. Arriving early for the meeting, he was greeted by Zion A. M. E. pastor Andrew Jennings, who took great pride in showing him the elegant 1912 sanctuary. Mike was disappointed that none of the other pastors in the Mintz County Baptist Association came to the meeting, but he nonetheless found a congenial group of colleagues. The summer meetings were without formal agenda, so Mike had the opportunity to talk more at length with his colleagues and get names, faces, and churches matched up. The members of the group shared prayer concerns and prayed for each other, after which they enjoyed a delicious lunch prepared by the women of Zion A.M. E. Mike found himself seated across the table from Henry Conway and Eleanor Flint Basden, who was described by Conway as "the woman who changed my mind about women preachers."

Mike had looked forward to meeting Eleanor ever since Ted Coleman told him about her. A pleasant, attractive woman whose auburn hair was intermingled with gray, she appeared to be about fifty. Mike continued the conversation with her as they walked to their cars after the meeting adjourned. "So, how long were you at Harrington Baptist?" he inquired.

"All of my life, until we left in '85. Lawrence Carson baptized me when I was nine. My parents, Jesse and Martha Flint, were active in Harrington Baptist until they died. Dad died in '81, Mom died last year. Mom wanted me to conduct her funeral at Harrington Baptist, some people weren't too thrilled over that, but I did. My husband grew up in Harrington Baptist, too. Ben's father died when Ben and I were in high school. He was the ordinary for Mintz County, what they call a probate judge now. Ben's mother, Lola Mae Basden, still comes to your church."

"I think I remember meeting her. We've got a pretty good contingent of older women. 'Little old lady with gray hair and glasses' describes a fourth of the church, so I'm still learning names and faces."

"You will be for a while," Eleanor laughed. "I was born and raised in Harrington, and I'm still working on names and faces at my church. Anyway, as I was telling you, Ben and I grew up together, went to school and church together, only boy I ever dated. We were married in 1963 at Harrington Baptist, first wedding in the new building. Franklin Seals did our wedding."

"So you knew Franklin Seals, the one whose daughter was killed?"

"Yes, how did you know about that? That's one of the things they don't talk about at Harrington Baptist."

"An old black gentleman by the name of Prince Hammondtree told me. Ted Coleman introduced me to him."

"I've known Mr. Hammondtree since I started first grade in 1947. He was the janitor at Harrington Elementary when I was a little girl, still worked there when my children were in school. He knew every child by name, always kind and pleasant to all of the children. He's a good man, as good as they come. Knows everybody in Harrington and knows their family back a couple of generations. You can count on what he tells you being right. I ride my bicycle to the church office in good weather, and I usually get out early when Ben leaves to go to the school. I go past Greater New Hope, and Mr. Hammondtree's always out there early, keeping the place spruced up. When his garden's coming in, he'll have a sack of vegetables waiting for me. Such a nice man, he can say 'good morning' to you and make you feel better the rest of the day. Anyway, you asked if I knew Franklin Seals. I knew him well. He came to Harrington in January 1959, my senior year in high school. My father was chairman of the pulpit committee. Ben and I got very close to Frank and Jane and their children. I felt the first stirrings of my call to the ministry while he was here, though I kept it to myself for years. Brother Seals was the kind of pastor I want to be. The campaign to run him off got started in earnest in the latter part of '63, right after Ben and I married. I'm sorry to say my parents and Ben's mother were among the ringleaders. So was Uncle Royce."

"Royce Green? He's your uncle?"

"Oh yes, I should warn you. I'm kin to a bunch of people in your church, so you may find out more than you want to know. My mother was Royce's sister. Joyce Baxter, Carl's wife, is my sister. Billy Ray Flint, don't know if you've met him, he doesn't go to church much, but his wife is there most Sundays. He's my brother, manages the parts department at the Chevrolet place. My father owned Flint Furniture Company on the Tennessee Avenue side of the square, served on the city council and one term as mayor. Daddy had musical talent running out his ears, Joyce's girls take after him in that respect. He was into gospel music in a big way, good bass singer. He could get down there on that *hasten glad and free* line in the chorus of *I Am Resolved* and those walking bass parts in *I Surrender All.* He played the piano by ear, used to lead singing at church, sold pianos and sheet music at the furniture store."

Eleanor paused, torn between the urge to laugh at the absurdity of what she was about to say and the urge to cry from the pain underlying the absurdity. "It's a funny thing. My brother gets roaring drunk nearly every weekend and cheats on his wife like crazy. He comes by it honestly. Daddy'd come home every night and start drinking after supper, drink until he fell asleep, every night except Wednesday, he'd stay sober for prayer meeting and choir practice. He thought he was God's gift to women, worst skirt chaser this town ever saw, but he was a deacon in the church. I became the black sheep of the family when Ben and I stood against our families and supported Brother Seals. Ben's mother hasn't forgiven me yet. It didn't endear us to either of our families when we joined the Methodists. Mother and I made peace after Daddy died. We were actually very close the last two years she lived. She and Joyce reconciled toward the last. She was a different person when she got used to not being under Daddy's thumb. Mother could be every bit as funny as Carol Burnette. I never saw that side of her while Daddy was living. Joyce and I are close now, closer since Ben and I joined the Methodist church. That gave us a common bond, in that we'd both made a major decision that Mother and Daddy disapproved of. You see, Mother and Daddy were against Joyce and Carl getting married because Carl had been divorced."

"I didn't know that."

"Yeah. His first marriage lasted less than a year. I always liked Carl. I've known him since elementary school. He and Ben were buddies all through school, still hunt and fish together. Ben and I double-dated in high school with Carl and the girl he married the first time. They got married a couple of months before he was drafted and sent to Vietnam. She started running around on him while he was in boot camp, got pregnant and had a child by another man while he was overseas. Carl was devastated, it like to have killed him. Ben and I were happy for both of them when Carl and Joyce got interested in each other."

"That tells me a lot I didn't know, like why Carl's never been asked to be a deacon."

"And probably never will be," Eleanor added.

"Ted Coleman told me that you and Ben used to be in our church, but nobody told me that you and Joyce are sisters."

"We are, and I'm glad to say we're very close, now that we've both stood up to Mother and Daddy. Supporting Brother Seals and, later on, becoming a Methodist and following through on my call to ministry were my ways of standing up to them. Marrying Carl was Joyce's way. We have lunch together once a week and talk about everything. Joyce still carries a lot of guilt about all that went down with Brother Seals. She felt in her heart the same way Ben and I did, but she felt like she couldn't stand against our parents. I reminded her that she was just nineteen years old then and that she was still living under Mother and Daddy's roof. It was easier for me because I was four years older and married to Ben. I'm not sure I could've stood against them without Ben's support, and Ben doesn't think he could've stood against his mother without my support. Ben's mother's never forgiven him. Dysfunctional families wrote the book on loyalty. The whole business of putting on the front of being a normal family, covering up for Daddy's drinking, abusive behavior, and womanizing, it was all part of the same package. Mom almost felt guilty, felt like she was betraying Daddy, when she made peace with me after he died. Ben and I have stayed in touch with Jane Seals over the years, so I gave Joyce the address and suggested that she write to her and tell her how she felt, how she wishes she had stood with them years ago. She got the sweetest letter back from her. After Mother died, Joyce told me that Mother had asked her for Mrs. Seals address and phone number. About a week before she died, knowing she didn't have much time left, Mother called her. Joyce said they talked almost an hour, and Mother was a lot more at peace after that. I guess Mr. Hammondtree told you Brother Seals had a heart attack and died a few months after the church ran him off. He and Debbie are buried in the black cemetery down at the end of Pelfrey Street."

"I know. Mr. Hammondtree told me. I went down there early one morning and found the graves. I was pleased to see that somebody's kept the lot up."

"Joyce and I did that. We took Carl's truck, went and got a load of crushed marble and some bricks, worked all day one Saturday leveling up the markers and cleaning them, fixing the crushed marble over the graves and outlining them with the bricks. That was back last summer, the day before Fathers Day. When it was finished, we took some pictures to send to Mrs. Seals, talked about our memories of Brother Seals and Debbie, read some Scripture, prayed, and cried together. It was good for me, and it helped Joyce find some peace."

"So tell me what you remember about Debbie. My wife and I are expecting our second child in about six more weeks. We have a six year old daughter, and we know that this one's going to be another girl. We've decided to name her Deborah Estelle. Deborah is after Debbie Seals, and Estelle is after a really sweet older lady in my student pastorate who died right around the time our baby was conceived."

"That's a pretty name. Debbie was a lovely girl, and I'm not just saying that because of the tragic way she died. She was little for her age, her daddy always called her Peanut. She was fourteen, but she didn't look more than eleven or twelve when she died, small and delicate. Debbie took after her mother with real pretty olive complexion, dark eyes, and straight black hair. She was quiet and introspective, though she had a sophisticated sense of humor that sailed right over the heads of a lot of people. She was like her father in that respect. She was a good student, very focused, wrote poetry, but above all she loved to play the piano. When things got so bad and kids would shun her or say hurtful things to her, that's the way she dealt with it, she'd come home and play the piano, and she could play so beautifully! The more people hurt her and her family, the more beautifully she played. She could play some very difficult classical pieces, play them well. By the time she was twelve, she was too advanced for any of the piano teachers in Harrington. Brother Seals used to take her to Carrollton every week for piano lessons with one of the music professors at West Georgia College. Debbie gave piano lessons to younger children to earn her spending money. She had about six or seven students. One of them is now the music teacher at Harrington Elementary and our pianist at the Methodist church. Sometimes I close my eyes when Cindy's playing a prelude or an offertory, and it's like I'm listening to Debbie again. Debbie liked to play in church. Some of the people appreciated the music she played, but some of them got their noses out of joint and said the music she played was too high church. You know how it is when a church is gearing up to run a preacher off, they look for stuff to nitpick about, and they don't stop with him. They dissect his wife and children, too. Some of them gave Brother Seals grief over the classical music Debbie played in church, so she stopped playing in church. The Christmas Eve service in 1963 was the last time she played in church, other than playing for a funeral the Saturday before she was killed."

"And I understand that it wasn't long after she was killed that the deacons called for Brother Seals' resignation?"

"The very next week. Some of them—my father and Uncle Royce included—even used his daughter's death against him. Brother Seals had gotten to be good friends with the pastor at Greater New Hope when they bought our old building, so he and Mrs. Seals asked him to have a part in Debbie's funeral. Some people got all upset about that, so they had the funeral at Greater New

Hope. Debbie's murder made the 11:00 news the night she was killed. Dr. Martin Luther King and his wife heard it, and they came to the funeral home to pay their respects and express their sympathy to the family. Somebody started the rumor that Brother Seals brought Dr. King in to try to start protest marches and demonstrations. Nothing could've been further from the truth. The first time Brother Seals met Dr. King was at the funeral home when Debbie was lying in state. Ben and I were standing near the door, where the stand was with the guest book, when they came in. I knew who they were from seeing him on the news on TV. After they signed the guest book, Dr. King turned to Ben, introduced himself and his wife to us, and asked us to introduce them to the Seals family. Dr. and Mrs. King didn't say a whole lot, but they were so kind and compassionate. They had tears running down their faces as they stood over Debbie's casket. They embraced Brother Seals and his wife and wept with them, and I'll never forget seeing Dr. King get down on his knees to talk to the Seals' little boy Michael. Mr. Hammondtree invited Dr. and Mrs. King to spend the night with him and his family. They accepted the invitation, and Mrs. Seals asked Dr. King to say a few words at the funeral. He said he'd be honored to do so. That's how it all came about. It was shameful how little support the Seals family got from Harrington Baptist Church. Only a handful of people from Harrington Baptist came to the funeral, but I'll never forget one who came."

"Who was that?"

"Mrs. Addie Jane Aldridge. She had been Debbie's fourth grade teacher. I told you Debbie played for a funeral the Saturday before she was killed. The funeral was for Mrs. Aldridge's husband, Chester. The Aldridges were very supportive of Brother Seals. Mr. Aldridge died suddenly with a heart attack the week before Debbie was killed. He was so upset and angry over the way the church was treating Brother Seals, that's probably what brought it on. The Aldridges loved to hear Debbie play. Debbie was so hurt by all the criticism that she said she would never play in church again, but she played at Mr. Aldridge's funeral and played the best I ever heard her play. She was killed two days later. Less than a week after burying her husband, Mrs. Aldridge came to Debbie's funeral and read two poems that Debbie wrote."

"That must've been terribly hard for her. It sounds like she's a very courageous lady."

"Miss Addie's a sweetheart, though she can be tough as a pit bull when she needs to be. I have so much respect for her. She retired about 1960, a good while before the schools were integrated. Back then, the only school for blacks was in the building where Harrington Middle School is now. They had all twelve grades under one roof, and it was terribly overcrowded. Miss Addie decided to go down there and see what she could do to help. She discovered there were only two first grade teachers, and they each had more than forty children. Miss Addie volunteered to take some out of each class and make a third class. There was no vacant classroom for her to use, so Zion A.M.E. made space available, and she taught first grade there for two years without being paid a cent. The Atlanta paper picked up on what she was doing, did a nice feature article about her, which shamed the school board into hiring more teachers for the black school and setting up some portable classrooms to relieve the overcrowding. Miss Addie kept volunteering, tutoring children who needed extra help. It made her furious that there were never enough textbooks or library books, and that what they had was worn out or outdated, books the white schools had discarded. She kept going to the school board meetings to plead for books for the black children, and she wasn't getting anywhere. Roland Millican was chairman of the school board, and he was the most tight-fisted of all of them when it came to doing anything for the black children. Miss Addie told Roland she was going to run against him if he didn't change his ways. He thought she was bluffing. Anybody who'd ever had her for a teacher could have told him that Miss Addie doesn't bluff. When it came time for the Democratic primary in 1962, Miss Addie ran against Roland and bumped him off the school board. It was a close race, but she beat him. Florida Avenue Colored School started the 1963-64 school year with all new textbooks, a new media center, and a new library. Miss Addie served on the school board and continued to do volunteer tutoring until she was in her eighties. When she was elected to her second term, they chose her as chairperson. She led the Mintz County Board of Education through desegregation."

∗ ∗ ∗ ∗ ∗ ∗ ∗ ∗ ∗ ∗ ∗ ∗

As Mike drove back to his office from the ministerial association meeting, he thought about the diminutive ninety-three year old woman he had visited the day before and the things he had learned about her from Eleanor Flint Basden. He wondered whether the man whose campaign slogan had been *Keep Mintz County Schools Segregated* still bore a grudge against his old political nemesis whose campaign cards called attention to her forty-five years of teaching experience in Mintz County. He thought about the young girl he and Jerry would be baptizing Sunday morning and breathed a prayer for her, that the consequences of her baptism would be as far-reaching as the consequences of a baptismal service that took place long ago in Salyers Creek.

The image came to Mike's mind of the ripple effect that is created when an object breaks the surface of the water. As he waited for the light to change at Alabama Avenue and Church Street, he quickly jotted down the thought on a piece of scratch paper, *What is the ripple effect of your baptism?* That thought would find its way into a sermon another time. This Sunday, Miss Addie's testimony and Cassie's baptism would be the sermon.

15

As she took her seat in the sanctuary before the service began, Cassie McWhorter felt a little awkward in the white baptismal robe she was wearing over her orange and yellow floral-print swimsuit. Her feet almost but not quite touched the floor when she sat all the way back in the pew. The tile floor under the pews felt very cold to bare feet. The auditorium was carpeted in that awful gold color that was popular back in the seventies, when her parents were in high school, except for the part under the pews, which was covered in the same yucky-brown dirt color tile as Grandma McWhorter's kitchen.

Cassie was not afraid of being put under the water. Learning to swim had come easily for her, and she was like a dolphin in the swimming pool. Ever since she and her family went to Sea World last summer, Cassie had known what she wanted to be when she grew up. She would be a dolphin trainer at Sea World while she was in college, and then she would be a marine biologist so she could work with dolphins. Actually, she thought it would be way cool to *be* a dolphin, except for having to eat raw fish. She had tried sushi one time and didn't like it. The only way Cassie McWhorter ate fish was battered and fried, like they fix it at Captain D's, with gobs of tartar sauce. Actually being a dolphin was not one of the career paths open to her, so she didn't have to worry about eating raw fish, but she wanted to get as close to those graceful, playful, intelligent creatures as she could. Being a marine biologist sounded so awesomely cool that she had made a point to learn how to spell it, and she had often practiced writing *Cassie E. McWhorter, Marine Biologist.*

Cassie was, however, more than a little bit nervous about being up there in front of the whole church in the baptistry. It was total embarrassment, not total immersion, that she feared, since it is a well-known fact that embarrassment is the leading cause of death among ten-year-old girls. She could just see the obituary in the *Harrington Courier:*

LOCAL GIRL DIES OF EMBARRASSMENT

Cassie Elise McWhorter, age 10, of 863 Court Street in Harrington, daughter of Mr. and Mrs. Jerry McWhorter, died Sunday August 5 from total and complete embarrassment when she fell down the steps and did a belly flop into the baptistry at Harrington Baptist Church, causing water to splash out and drench all the old men on the back row of the choir, including but not limited to Franklin A. Brinkley, Chairman of the Board of Deacons of Harrington Baptist Church. Although she was not injured by the fall, the resulting embarrassment proved to be fatal. Her bratty 7 year old brother Anthony, who is among the survivors, still thinks it was the funniest thing he ever saw. Had she not been embarrassed to death, Cassie would have been a fifth grader at Harrington Elementary School this fall.

Although she liked Brother Mike, Cassie was glad that her dad would be in the baptistry with her. At the moment, she was sitting on the second pew, behind the deacons, between her mother and Miss Addie. Cassie had always liked Miss Addie. She couldn't stand Geneva Millican, who wore way too much funny-smelling perfume, acted crabby toward all the children, called her by her sister's name half the time and talked down to her like she was three years old. *Puh-leeze! Excuse me while I barf!* Unlike Geneva Millican, Miss Addie knew the name of every child in Harrington Baptist Church, and she never talked down to them. She always spoke to Cassie and called her by name. Cassie felt very grown-up when Miss Addie talked with her. Although Miss Addie was not given to using such expressions as *way cool* or *awesomely cool*, and she used the term *cool* only in reference to temperature, Miss Addie had expressed her approval of Cassie's plans to become a marine biologist.

Cassie's jaw dropped when Miss Addie gave her the tiny, very old-looking velvet-covered jewelry box and a note written with a fountain pen in quaint, old-fashioned Spencerian script on expensive vellum stationery. Before she opened the note, she looked in awe at her name on the envelope, *Miss Cassie Elise McWhorter,* written in Miss Addie's elegant hand. She had never seen her name written so beautifully. Cassie had always hated her middle name, but she even thought *Elise* was pretty the way Miss Addie wrote it. Cassie's mother had taught her that it was good manners to open the card or note before opening the present. With great care, she opened the envelope and read the note from Miss Addie:

August 5, 1990

Dear Cassie,

On the day of your baptism, I want to give you something that I have cherished since I was eleven years old. I am now ninety-three, and I know that I will soon go to be with the Lord whom I have known and loved since I was a child. Although I taught more than a thousand children, Mr. Aldridge and I were never able to have any children of our own. It would make me very happy for you to have this gold necklace with the gold cross pendant. My parents gave it to me the day I was baptized in 1908. As you wear it, may the cross always remind you of Jesus' love for you and for the whole world.

I pray that your life will be as blessed as mine has been. May you always love and serve our Lord Jesus Christ.

Sincerely,

Mrs. Addie Jane Peyton Aldridge

Enclosed with the note was a small, sepia-tone photograph, mounted on embossed cream-colored card stock, of a girl about Cassie's age dressed in clothes like people wore long ago. Even before she turned it over to read the old-timey writing on the back, Cassie recognized her. The girls reached across eight decades to embrace like two little old southern ladies, and Cassie kissed Addie on the cheek. Carefully opening the old velvet-covered jewelry box, Cassie took out the necklace that must have cost a lot of money, even in 1908. She tried to open the clasp, but her hands were trembling too much and she had too many tears in her eyes to see what she was doing. Elaine whispered to her that she might want to wait until after she got baptized to put on the necklace, but Cassie told her no. She promised to take it off before she went in the water and put it back on as soon as she dried off and got dressed. Remembering how impatient she had been at age ten, Elaine opened the clasp and fastened the beautiful old necklace around her daughter's neck. A smile came to Miss Addie's face as she recalled "forgetting" to take the necklace off before she went in the water. If the water in Salyers Creek didn't hurt it, Miss Addie reasoned, the water in the baptistry wouldn't hurt it either. Miss Addie resolved to tell that story in Cassie's defense if the need arose. The need would not arise because Elaine, like Miss Addie's mother in 1908, had decided not to make an issue of it.

As Jenny began playing the prelude, Cassie leaned back against her mother, and Miss Addie caressed her right hand in her hands. Cassie only knew that the music was beautiful and soothing, and that her anxiety was beginning to dissipate. Jenny was only a couple of measures into John Field's *Nocturne No. 5 in B Flat Major* when Miss Addie recognized the melody. She often cranked up the Victrola and put on her favorite record, a scratchy 78 of Rubenstein playing that piece. She and Mr. Aldridge had amassed a collection of classical recordings that included the works of many great composers, but the piano compositions of Field and Chopin were the ones they played most often. Jenny chose the piece without knowing the significance it held for Miss Addie, who had asked Debbie Seals to play Field's *Nocturne* at Mr. Aldridge's funeral. It was one of Debbie's favorites, and she had played it so gracefully. Jenny played it well, too, but Miss Addie closed her eyes and listened to Debbie play it again.

* * * * * * * * * * * *

Miss Addie carried a cane, but the only times it touched down were to steady her when she first got up, when she went up or down steps, and when she had to negotiate uneven ground. At other times, it was hooked over her arm with the end swinging freely in mid-air. The doctor had prevailed upon her to start using it after her knee replacement surgery, but most of the time she regarded the thing as an unnecessary encumbrance that was some-times useful for thumping the floor when she was being emphatic about something. Mike took her hand as she stepped up onto the pulpit platform and again as she stepped up onto the little ply-wood box, about two feet square and six inches high, that Carl Baxter built the day before to put behind the pulpit so Miss Addie would be visible to the congregation. The offer of Mike's hand was the kind of simple courtesy she spent forty-five years drilling into her students, so she did appreciate it, but she could have made it up to the pulpit on her own just fine. She was as excited about giving her testimony as Cassie was about being baptized.

"Good morning, boys and girls," Miss Addie began. Amid laughter from the congregation, she continued, "I'm used to saying that when I get up in front of a group of people. At ninety-three, I suppose I have a perfect right to address all of you as 'boys and girls.' I taught at least half of you at school, at church, or both. Hold up your hand if you were ever one of my students." Miss Addie beamed as she saw dozens of hands go up. Her distance vision was still good enough to see the smile on the face of seventy-nine year old retired teacher Lunell Bishop, who was Lunell Freeman before she married. In 1917, six-year-old Lunell Freeman had been a first grader at the one-room school in Freeman Valley when twenty-year-old Miss Addie Jane Peyton began her teaching career, and she was an important influence in Lunell's decision to become a teacher. Miss Addie taught all of Lunell's children. When Roland Millican thought Miss Addie was bluffing about running for his seat on the school board, Lunell tried her best to warn him that Miss Addie doesn't bluff. He wouldn't listen, so she let him find out the hard way. Lunell voted for Miss Addie, even though her husband voted for Roland. When Miss Addie ran for reelection, Clarence voted for her, too. He and Lunell were strong supporters of Brother Seals. Clarence said he wouldn't vote for Roland for dog catcher after the way he treated Brother Seals, and he told him so to his face. That, and Clarence said he'd just never pictured a woman holding public office, but he had to admit, once she was in there, Miss Addie did a good job, better than Roland had ever done. When it came time for the 1966 Democratic primary, one of Miss Addie's campaign posters went up in the window of Bishop's Walgreen Agency Drug Store.

Miss Addie was in her element, handling the congregation as skillfully as she once handled classrooms full of children. Her dry wit and pleasant smile were strategic weapons for disarming the opposition. "Last week when I was getting over my cataract surgery," she began, "our pastor came by to see me. He told me Cassie was going to be baptized this morning, and he asked me to tell you about my baptism eighty-two years ago. I told him I would be delighted to do so. I remember it very clearly. It doesn't seem that long ago, because my life, which may seem very long to you, doesn't seem long at all to me. I don't know how I got to be this old! I still do a double-take when I look in the mirror and see an old woman looking back at me, and I have to stop and think how old I am. I distinctly remember being no older than Cassie! I brought Cassie a photograph of me at that age to prove that I was once ten years old. I remember the dress I was wearing when that picture was made. My mother made it for me. It was a very pretty burgundy color, trimmed in cream-colored embroidery, and I still think it was the prettiest dress I ever owned. I was close to Cassie's age when my uncle, Preacher Tim Nestor, baptized me on the first Sunday in September 1908. I turned eleven on July 26, 1908, six weeks before I was baptized. Cassie will be eleven on October 2. If you want to see the place where I was baptized, go out Bailey's Mill Road and look to your left as you cross the bridge. Bailey's Mill is gone, but the dam is still there, and you can see the foundation of the mill in the winter when the kudzu dies down. When I was a girl, the mill was still running. I used to go there in the wagon with my father to have our corn ground into meal. There was an old covered bridge over Salyers Creek at Bailey's Mill. The piers of the old bridge are still there. Right under the bridge, just below the dam, is where Uncle Tim baptized me. I was one of about two dozen he baptized that day."

Even the stone face of Franklin A. Brinkley, Chairman of the Board of Deacons of Harrington Baptist Church, seemed to soften a little as Miss Addie continued, "Just like Cassie, I grew up in a Christian home. Our family lived in the Peyton's Crossroads community, about seven miles out from town. We farmed forty acres, and we raised chickens and hogs. All of us worked on the farm, and my father, John David Peyton, also worked as a telegraph operator for the railroad. He was a deacon at Peyton's Chapel Baptist Church. Now, Peyton's Chapel has a full-time pastor and services every Sunday. When I was a little girl, it was half-time. We'd have thirty-five or forty on a good Sunday. Uncle Tim Nestor, Mother's brother, was our pastor all through my childhood years. He made his living as a blacksmith, because the churches couldn't pay him enough to live on, and I think he got the inspiration for some of his sermons on Hell looking at the fire in his forge! Uncle Tim preached at Peyton's Chapel on the first and third Sundays of the month and at Freeman Valley on the second and fourth Sundays. Uncle Phil, his oldest brother, was the second pastor of this church. My mother, Sarah Elizabeth Nestor Peyton, came from a family of preachers. Bartholomew Lang, the fourth pastor of this church, married Mother's youngest sister, Aunt Nellie. Uncle John Beckett, the first pastor of this church, was Grandmother Nestor's brother. I was about eight or nine when he died, but I remember him. He had the most spectacular handlebar mustache I ever saw! Even though I didn't grow up in this church—I moved my membership here in 1922 when I married my husband and took a teaching position in town—I've known every pastor who ever served Harrington Baptist Church. I grew up surrounded by preachers. Two of my brothers, Lawrence and Will Peyton, became preachers. Mother just might've been a preacher, too, except that people back then hadn't entertained the thought that a woman could be a preacher. She knew how to use her Bible to talk to people about the Lord and help them in times of trouble. Mother was one of the last of the old-time midwives, and many a baby girl was named Sarah in her honor. She often helped out where there was sickness, and I've known of people who were dying to ask for her instead of a preacher. I had a very happy childhood as the youngest child of parents who loved me and taught me about the Lord from infancy. Those good influences pointed me toward faith in Christ, but they didn't make me a Christian. I had to make a choice. I knew about Jesus and His love for me, but I had to make up my mind how I was going to respond to Him. I had to call upon the Lord, ask Him to forgive my sins, and ask Jesus to come into my heart and be the Lord of my life. It was during the annual revival, the third week of August, what we called 'laying by' time on the farm. We had services every day for a week, three services a day, morning, afternoon, and evening. It was too hot and muggy to have services in the church building, and more people came than usually came to church, so we couldn't have gotten them all in the building anyway. The men in the community built a brush arbor every year at revival time, or 'protracted meeting' as we called it back then. Some of you don't know what a brush arbor is, so I'd better explain it. The men would clear off a place, cut some poles from pine saplings and lash them together into a framework that they would overlay with tree branches to make an open pavilion. We'd gather under the brush arbor, and a half a dozen preachers would take it time about preaching. Uncle Phil and Uncle Tim did some of the preaching, as did Uncle Bart Lang. Another one I remember was Preacher Joshua Brinkley, Frank's great-grandfather. He was an old man, at least I thought he was old at the time. He was probably in his seventies. I remember him because he had only one arm. He told us all about losing his right arm at the Battle of Chickamauga, but Daddy always said, the way he heard it, Preacher Brinkley only got a finger shot off at Chickamauga, and that he lost the rest of his arm in a sawmill accident right after the war. On the afternoon I went forward, Preacher E. L. B. Hamilton, Elijah Hamilton, the third pastor of this church, was preaching. I'd been under conviction and miserable all week. Thursday afternoon, when the invitation was given, I couldn't wait any longer. I was so afraid I'd do something wrong, end up looking foolish, and die of embarrassment..."

Cassie was already absorbed in Miss Addie's story. When Miss Addie spoke of the fear she faced in 1908, Cassie felt a powerful, timeless bond with eleven-year-old Addie Jane Peyton. She was amazed to learn that, even in 1908, total embarrassment was the leading cause of death for pre-teen girls. She was greatly encouraged by the story of how Miss Addie stared death in the face and lived to tell about it.

"I had to put that fear aside and obey God," Miss Addie concluded. "And, that's what Cassie did, too. Cassie," Miss Addie said as she turned her attention from the congregation to the one little girl being baptized, "that's what you'll need to keep doing the rest of your life. You'll have to make many decisions that come down to whether you'll obey God or give in to your fears. I acquired a reputation over the years for knocking down hornet nests. Most of them needed to be knocked down. I've been known to be plainspoken. Mother used to say that plain talk is easily understood, so I speak the truth in love with both barrels and then decide whether I need to reload. When I retired, I was still in good health and able to do a day's work. If I'd tried to sit at home and be old, they would've had to cart me off to Milledgeville, especially if I'd ever started watching game shows and soap operas. I loved teaching, and I was too healthy to sit around practicing to be dead. The Lord put it on my heart to go down to Florida Avenue Colored School and see what I could do to help. I knew they didn't have enough teachers, or enough of anything else for that matter. I had some reservations about going down there. I had to deal with the same question I faced under that brush arbor in 1908, the question of whether I would obey God or give in to my fears. There's a stanza of *Just As I Am* that says:

Just as I am, tho' tossed about, with many a conflict, many a doubt;

Fightings within and fears without, O Lamb of God, I come!

I had all those conflicts, doubts, fightings, and fears when I went down there and asked the principal, Mr. Robinette, what I could do to help. He told me he had only two first grade teachers. One had forty-four children in her class, and the other one had forty-five. I told him to take fifteen out of each class and give them to me. I taught first grade there for two years without being paid a cent. I had to teach my class at Zion A.M.E. Church because there wasn't room for us at the school. Some people didn't think a white woman ought to be teaching black children. I didn't care what they thought because God told me to do it. I loved those children. They knew it, and they loved me. Teaching them was no different from teaching any other children, except for not having enough books and supplies, which led to me running for the school board. By serving on the school board, I could help see to it that black children got the same educational opportunities as white children. Those children were as intelligent as any white children I ever taught, and they could learn anything white children could learn, but they were being shortchanged because they didn't have the books and supplies they needed. They were packed like sardines in an overcrowded school with too few teachers. Over fifty years ago, the Lord showed me that segregation was nothing but a stronghold of the devil. I started praying back then for an end to it. The Lord gave me the privilege of leading the school board through desegregation!"

Lest anyone think that she was incredibly brave, Miss Addie went on to explain, "Every time I made a decision about obeying God, I had to face my fears. When I was eleven, I was afraid of being embarrassed to death. When I was teaching my first graders at Zion A.M.E., the Ku Klux Klan burned a cross in front of my house one night, and my husband and I were afraid we might be burned out of our home, assaulted, or even killed. I discovered that all fear feels about the same. The fear of being burned out, assaulted, or killed at sixty-four feels just like the fear of being embarrassed to death at eleven. When I was sixty-five, the Lord made it plain to me that I needed to run for the school board. I was afraid I'd lose with about two percent of the vote, that eleven-year-old fear of being embarrassed to death. I felt just like when I was sitting in that brush-arbor meeting, deciding whether to obey God or give in to my fears. Now, you may think I've rambled a long way from the subject on which our pastor asked me to speak, but I really haven't. All through my life when I've dealt with that question of whether to give in to my fears or obey God, I've remembered that first Sunday in September 1908. I was wearing a plain white cotton dress and the necklace my parents gave me that morning, the gold necklace with the gold cross pendant that I gave to Cassie this morning. Daddy was standing in the water, taking the hands of the baptismal candidates as they stepped down into the water. I wasn't afraid of the water. I was a powerful swimmer, as good as either of my brothers. I used to swing out over that creek on a vine, let go, and plunge into that icy water. I knew the creek bottom like the back of my hand, but the day I was baptized, my heart was beating so hard I was sure everybody could hear it, and I was glad Daddy was there to take my hand. I remember the pebbles, worn smooth by the water, under my bare feet as I waded out to where Uncle Tim was standing, where the water was chest-deep on me. I remember that cold water swirling around my whole body when he put me under. For a moment, I thought I was dying, but I wasn't afraid. I remember drying my face on the towel draped around Daddy's shoulders, and how he hugged me right there in the water in front of everybody and took my hand to help me back to the creekbank. I remember all of that when I'm faced with a decision of whether to obey God. I remember, and I know what I need to do. Cassie, when you come to the hard decisions in life, remember your baptism. Close your eyes and feel the water, and you'll know what you need to do. Once you know what you need to do, do it and leave the consequences to God. Once, as a young woman, I heard the famous preacher Harry Ironside. I remember him saying, 'It's up to us to see that we do right, and it's up to God to see that we come out right.' Cassie, *Trust in the Lord with all your heart, and lean not unto your own understanding. In all your ways acknowledge Him, and He will direct your paths.*"

Mike took Miss Addie's hand as she stepped down from the box that Carl built and again as she stepped down from the pulpit platform. Mike was glad he had not planned to preach that morning. His best sermonic effort would have been inept stammering compared to Miss Addie. As Jenny played the introduction, Eric invited the congregation to stand and sing *Shall We Gather at the River.* Eric once protested that the song had absolutely nothing to do with baptism, and that the river referred to in the song was the heavenly river that flows by the throne of God. The only connection to baptism, he pointed out, was that the song mentions a river, and baptisms sometimes take place in rivers—a very tenuous connection, he argued, when there are more appropriate songs in the hymnal. Former pastor Harry Reynolds told him that he had pointed out the same thing early in his ministry at Harrington. He had been told that the church was accustomed to singing that song when they had baptism, and they didn't want to end the tradition. The same thing applied to *On Jordan's Stormy Banks I Stand,* which also has nothing to do with baptism, which the church also expects to sing at every baptismal service. Brother Harry told Eric to live with it, because some things aren't worth getting killed over. That, Brother Harry maintained, was the secret of his long tenure, learning to choose his battles carefully. As church traditions go, Harry said, singing *Shall We Gather at the River* and *On Jordan's Stormy Banks I Stand* at baptismal services is pretty benign. Eric still didn't like it, but he had made peace with it.

On the first stanza of *Shall We Gather at the River*, the choir members came down and took their places in the congregation. Cassie breathed a sigh of relief, knowing that if she should accidentally stumble and do a belly flop into the baptistry, at least she would not splatter Franklin A. Brinkley, Chairman of the Board of Deacons of Harrington Baptist Church and the other old men on the back row of the choir. She saw Brother Mike leave the pulpit platform and head back into the educational building. That was her cue. She paused for a quick hug and kiss from Miss Addie before going with her parents. Cassie knew just how Miss Addie felt as she stood on the creekbank in 1908. She and her parents made their way through the catacombs and up to the second floor hallway, where she watched her father go with Brother Mike into the men's dressing room. She and her mother went into the women's dressing room, where her cousin, Kristin Kinney was waiting to assist them. Cassie could hear the congregation singing. They were on the last refrain of *Shall We Gather at the River*, and she would soon be joining her father and Brother Mike in the baptistry.

Cassie sat on the top step and put her feet in the warm water as Jerry and Mike came down into the baptistry. As the congregation finished the final chorus of the hymn, Mike opened the curtains and spoke to the congregation. "I'm not planning to preach today. I knew, when I asked Mrs. Aldridge to tell us about her baptism, that we were going to hear a powerful message. Another reason I'm not preaching today is because Cassie McWhorter is going to preach to us. Baptism is an acted-out sermon. Cassie, through her baptism, will preach to us about death, burial, and resurrection. Paul tells us, *if we are united with Him in the likeness of His death, we will also be united with Him in the likeness of His resurrection.* Baptism reminds us of the death, burial, and resurrection of Christ. It reminds us that every believer is dead to sin and raised to walk in the newness of life in Christ. It reminds us of the promise of the resurrection for all who have hoped in Christ. All of that is proclaimed through the dramatic sermon we call baptism. Preacher Cassie, come preach your sermon!"

Jerry took his daughter's hand as she stepped carefully down into the baptistry. Cassie felt considerably relieved when she felt both feet planted firmly on the bottom. She faced the congregation, with her father on her right and Mike on her left. Elaine went without hosiery that morning so she could stand knee-deep in the water with the camcorder to get a close-up of Cassie's baptism.

"Cassie Elise McWhorter," Mike asked, "do you believe that Jesus is the Son of God, do you trust Him as your savior, and do you intend to follow Him as long as you live?"

Cassie surprised herself with the strength of her voice as she said, "Yes, I do."

Jerry and Mike each had a hand on Cassie's back. Jerry held a white handkerchief in his right hand, and Cassie's hands grasped his forearm. His voice was breaking with emotion and hot tears streamed down his face as he said, "In obedience to the command of our Lord Jesus Christ, and upon your profession of faith in Him, I baptize you my sister in Christ and my child in the faith, Cassie Elise McWhorter, in the name of the Father, the Son, and the Holy Spirit."

"Buried with Him in baptism," Mike added as Jerry covered Cassie's nose and mouth with the handkerchief. Jerry and Mike put Cassie under the water, and it was just like Miss Addie described, except the water was warm. Cassie felt the water swirl all around her body, and she really did think she was dying, but she felt incredibly calm and free of fear. She was a bit startled to hear Mike say "Raised to walk in the newness of life in Christ Jesus," and to discover that she was, in fact, alive.

16

Old Preacher Joshua Brinkley died in 1919, five years before Franklin A. Brinkley, Chairman of the Board of Deacons of Harrington Baptist Church, was born, but Frank grew up hearing the legends about the colorful one-armed preacher. Josh Brinkley's well-worn Bible, wire-rim glasses with tiny oval lenses, and big Elgin pocket watch were among Frank's most cherished possessions. According to family legend, Josh Brinkley was a war hero who often boasted of his exploits. To hear him tell it, his heroism was equal to that of Captain Cicero Mintz, the fallen hero of Gettysburg for whom the county was named, the only difference being that Captain Mintz, who did not live to boast of his valor, had his statue on the courthouse lawn and the county named in his memory. If he had lost his life instead of his arm, Josh Brinkley maintained, there would have been considerable debate about renaming the county, and it could well have been named Brinkley County. He seemed to resent the fact that he never received the acclaim he deserved, but he realized, if he had received it, he would have been dead and unable to enjoy it. In later years, he came to regard being alive and able to give a firsthand account of his exploits as an adequate consolation prize. Moreover, he said, if he had died in combat, albeit gallantly, he would have been unprepared to meet his Maker, and he was thankful that he lived until he could make his calling and election sure. He said he lost his arm the same way as most one-armed Confederate veterans, having it shot off while he was reaching up to reload his .50 caliber muzzle loader under heavy enemy fire. In later years, after time had thinned the ranks of Mintz County men who had been in the war with him, he often moved congregations to tears telling of his dramatic conversion as he lay wounded and near death on a pew in a little church that had been pressed into service as a field hospital at Chickamauga. Preacher Brinkley claimed to have been a wild young reprobate who drank, gambled, cursed, caroused, and chased women before he was saved. According to his recounting of his conversion, he had lost a great amount of blood from his wounds. As he drifted in and out of consciousness, awaiting his turn on the communion table that had become an improvised operating table, where a surgeon would mercifully finish the work of a New Hampshire sharpshooter, the Lord appeared to him and gave him one last opportunity to repent. Preacher Brinkley said he promised the Lord, if He would spare his life, the whiskey administered to him at the field hospital would be the last drink he would ever take, and he would live as a Christian and preach the gospel the rest of his days. The Lord apparently took him up on the deal, because Josh Brinkley lived to be eighty-seven and preached his last sermon three days before he died. In his last sermon, he once again moved the congregation to tears, telling how the Lord gave him the grace to forgive and pray for the salvation of the New Hampshire sharpshooter who shot his arm off. He concluded his final sermon by painting a moving word picture of a scene in Heaven. He would have a new body with two good arms, he would meet that New Hampshire sharpshooter, embrace him, and the two of them would rejoice in the Lord together for all eternity. When he gave the altar call, dozens of people came forward to pray and seek salvation. That was the version of the story that Franklin A. Brinkley, Chairman of the Board of Deacons of Harrington Baptist Church, grew up hearing. Frank had not known what to make of Miss Addie's assertion that Josh Brinkley only got a finger shot off at Chickamauga, and he lost his arm in a sawmill accident right after the war.

On the Sunday of Cassie's baptism, Miss Addie invited Mike, Karen, and Asalee home with her for dinner. Over dinner, Miss Addie explained that she didn't tell all of the story about how Preacher Brinkley lost his arm because she didn't want to embarrass Frank unnecessarily when doing so would not have been germane. Had it been germane, she said, she would not have hesitated. As Mike and Asalee helped clear the table and serve the banana pudding, Miss Addie finished the story about one-armed Preacher Brinkley. She said that her father got his information from his father, Elmer Peyton, who had been a first sergeant in the same unit with Private Joshua Brinkley. It was in camp before the battle began, not in the heat of battle at Chickamauga, that Private Brinkley got his finger shot off. Josh Brinkley was neither the first nor the last soldier to shoot off his trigger finger to get himself sent home with a medical discharge. As for the loss of the arm, Miss Addie said Preacher Brinkley's missing arm could have served as a very compelling illustration for a sermon on the dangers of running a sawmill while intoxicated.

According to Miss Addie's recollection, Preacher Brinkley always sounded downright nostalgic when he talked about life before his conversion. She said that her daddy once told him, if he missed his old life that badly, he ought to go back to it. There always was some question about whether he had ever completely, as the apostle Paul said, *put off the old man and his ways*. Preacher Brinkley was rarely without a flask of whiskey in his saddlebags, which he always claimed to be for medicinal purposes."Papa used to say," Miss Addie recalled, "despite Preacher Brinkley's healthy appearance, he required more medication than most people." She went on to say that Preacher Brinkley kept a black woman, Lizella Harbin, as a mistress and had several children by her. "There are quite a few black Brinkleys in Harrington and Mintz County, all of them descendants of old Preacher Brinkley and cousins to Frank, whether he claims them or not. That sort of thing happened much more often than people want to admit, so there are black people and white people with common ancestors much more recent than Adam and Eve. It's not just the Brinkleys. One man who was on the school board with me years ago made all kinds of dire predictions about what would happen when we put white and black children in the same schools. I knew he had kinfolk he didn't claim, so I spoke the truth in love with both barrels. I told him, 'Gene, think of that first day of school after we integrate as a big family reunion. Some of the children will be meeting their half-brothers, half-sisters, and cousins for the first time. It'll be the biggest family reunion this county's ever seen. We ought to have a gospel singing and dinner on the grounds!' Gene, bless his heart, turned so pale, I thought for a moment I'd killed him. That was what was so bad about segregation, the hypocrisy of it. The very ones preaching segregation the loudest were sleeping with black women. Some had mistresses, like Preacher Brinkley. Black women who worked for white families often had duties other than cooking, cleaning, and taking care of children. Sometimes, it was out-and-out rape, and the law wouldn't do a thing if a white man raped a black woman. I suppose I take after my father in that respect, having no tolerance for hypocrisy. Daddy had no patience with hypocrisy, which is why he had no confidence in Preacher Brinkley. He was a quiet, gentle soul with a wonderful wit about him, which he used to let the air out of people who were too full of themselves. I've been known to do that, too," Miss Addie admitted with an angelic smile. "Daddy took preachers with a grain of salt. He'd have us laughing until our sides hurt with his impressions of the preaching style and mannerisms of various preachers, including the ones kin to Mama. Mama would get onto him and say 'John David Peyton, you're going to be struck by lightning one fine day!', but she'd end up laughing in spite of herself when he did his impression of Preacher Brinkley. Once, when I was twelve or thirteen, I laughed so hard at Daddy's impression of Preacher Brinkley that I hyperventilated."

The conversation moved on to other subjects as they relaxed in the parlor after dinner. "Oh yes, Pastor, I meant to tell you," Miss Addie commented, "I was quite pleased to see Brenda Coleman's name on the list of ordained deacons who are members of the church and eligible to serve as active deacons. I never knew that she was an ordained deacon. When was she ordained?"

"She and Ted were ordained when they lived in Macon," Mike explained. "They served together at University Drive Baptist Church in Macon. When they came here, Brother Reynolds asked them not to say anything about her being ordained because he didn't think the church was ready to deal with that issue."

"Oh Good Lord!" Miss Addie exclaimed, her voice registering unmitigated disgust. "I'm so weary of that drivel about 'people aren't ready for this' or 'people aren't ready for that!' I had to contend with so much of that on the school board. I'd like to find a respite from such falderal at church! If Moses had waited until everybody was ready, the Israelites would still be in Egypt! The church is not ready to deal with that issue, my foot! We have a woman mayor, a black police chief, a black city councilman, and a black woman who also runs a business serving on the school board, all former students of mine who hug my neck every time they see me, and the sky has not fallen. Spare me this foolishness about the church not being ready for a woman deacon! Brenda's a fine young woman. She and Ted have been such a blessing to our church, and I've heard very good things about her as a teacher. She puts her whole heart into whatever she does. She'll make a fine deacon for our church. I shall certainly vote for her. Now that I'm ninety-three, I can't get out and campaign like I did when I was running against Roland for the school board, but I can still use a telephone. I shall certainly make some calls on her behalf."

If it had been anyone other than Miss Addie, Mike would have questioned the propriety of campaigning for deacon candidates. Any effort to dissuade her would be futile, and she would be discreet about it. Before Mike could gather his thoughts to say anything, Miss Addie was off on another subject. "Speaking of telephones, let me show you my new phone! It was a birthday present from my niece, and I am so pleased with it. Kathleen's so kind and thoughtful. I taught her, too. The arthritis in my fingers was making it hard for me to dial my old phone. This new phone Kathleen gave me has push buttons with great big numbers. The buttons are lighted so I can see them in the dark, I can see the big numbers without my glasses, and pressing the buttons is much easier than turning a dial. I'd never used a pushbutton phone until Kathleen gave me this one. Her husband came by and installed it for me, and I'm absolutely delighted with it. Anybody who wants my old phone can have it. I didn't realize how heavy the receiver was on that old thing until I picked up the one on my new phone. It's as light as a feather! Not only that, it's such a pretty bright blue color. When I got my old phone, there was no choice of colors. All telephones were black. I was satisfied with my old phone only because I'd never used any other kind. My old phone was the one that was installed in 1936 when we first subscribed to the telephone service. That's how it is with so many things. People are satisfied with what they have because it's all they've ever known. I used that old phone fifty-four years, but I wouldn't go back to it for a thousand dollars. I'm so glad Kathleen got this new phone for me and didn't fret over whether I was ready for it!"

*　*　*　*　*　*　*　*　*　*　*　*

Franklin A. Brinkley, Chairman of the Board of Deacons of Harrington Baptist Church, never mentioned what Miss Addie said concerning his great-grandfather, but Mike noticed that he seemed a little less stuffy, almost human, at the deacons meeting that afternoon. He actually bordered on being pleasant, something disturbingly out of character for him. Miss Addie had crossed the line between testifying and preaching, but Mike had been right in his bet that her advanced age and long years of membership in Harrington Baptist Church had earned her the right to preach whenever she felt like it. Nobody said anything negative in the deacons meeting about her sermon, and several, including Royce Green of all people, said they really enjoyed it. The appearance of Brenda's name on the list of ordained deacons was never mentioned. Mike fully expected either Frank or one of the other old guard deacons to say that a whole bunch of people had called them all upset about it. None of the old guard mentioned it, which led Mike to suspect that none of them had read the newsletter. Franklin A. Brinkley, Chairman of the Board of Deacons of Harrington Baptist Church, said that he was pleased with the orderly, efficient manner in which the offering had been taken and communion had been served that morning. The deacons, having run out of anything else to talk about, moved on to rehashing the work of the maintenance committee. They agreed that it was a good idea to get Bill Gentry to check out the furnace before cold weather. The most uneventful deacons meeting since Mike came to Harrington adjourned at 5:25, a full thirty-five minutes before time for the evening worship service.

Ted walked back to Mike's study with him, and Mike invited him in. "Sorry my desk is all cluttered up," Mike apologized. "Believe it or not, there's a system to it."

"And you're trying to figure out what it is. Lighten up, Preacher. You've seen my desk down at the *Courier*, so we're even. I was surprised that nobody mentioned Brenda's name being on the list. Nobody's called us at home about it either. Apparently nobody reads the newsletter except Brenda and me."

"And Miss Addie," Mike added. "Nothing slips past Miss Addie."

"Well, being in the journalism business, I'm glad somebody else in town reads besides the two of us and you and Karen. So what did Miss Addie have to say about it?"

"She thinks it's wonderful. I told her that Harry Reynolds asked Brenda not to say anything about being ordained because the church wasn't ready to deal with that issue. Miss Addie said the Israelites would still be in Egypt if Moses had waited until everybody was ready."

"She's right about that. Brother Harry was a good man, but his greatest fear was that he'd do something controversial, offend someone, and cause them to leave the church. The problem with that is, it gives a few negative people veto power over everything the church tries to do. We've got people who've held this church hostage for years by threatening to leave if the church does this or that. Most of 'em have no intention of leaving, but the church is afraid to call their bluff. Pacifying people like that has never been one of my priorities, but it seems to be the church's priority sometimes. Brenda feels the same way I do. I like what Miss Addie said about speaking the truth in love with both barrels and then deciding whether she needs to reload. That's Brenda to a tee. She's a sweet woman, but she won't roll over and play dead for anybody. I like that. That was one of the qualities that attracted me to her in the first place. That's why I was shocked when she went along with

Brother Harry's request not to let it be known that she was ordained. She regretted it as soon as she did it, and it bothers her to see only men taking the offering and serving communion. She was accustomed to seeing both men and women do that. When you let the woman deacon from your former church help with communion a couple of months ago, Brenda couldn't keep quiet anymore. It was a burden off her soul when she called you that afternoon. Speaking of not rolling over and playing dead," Ted changed the subject, "I admired the way Karen dealt with Hilda Mae. That was good. I couldn't believe she had a key to the parsonage and tried to come in and snoop while y'all were gone. It was time for somebody to stand up to her."

"Yeah, Karen did speak the truth in love with both barrels, didn't she?" Mike concurred. "I was right proud of her myself. Karen says that, when it comes to ulcers and high blood pressure, it's more blessed to give than to receive. Hilda Mae's left us alone ever since Karen convinced her that she'd call the police and press charges if it happened again. That, and she's afraid to come over because we have a vicious dog."

"You're talking about Wallace?" Ted cackled. "When I stopped by your house, ol' Wallace opened one eye, took a dim view of me, and went back to sleep. Never moved again the whole time I was there."

"Yeah, that vicious dog. Hilda Mae's the only person in Harrington that he's ever showed his teeth to. He doesn't even bark at the mailman or the UPS guy."

"Sounds like ol' Wallace is a good judge of character. Maybe we ought to include him in the deacon selection process, let him sniff all the candidates, disqualify anybody he growls at." "Good idea," Mike agreed. "I'm sure he'd approve of Brenda, especially if she pets him."

"You think Brenda'll get many votes?"

"Ted," Mike cautioned, "y'all need to plan on her being elected."

"What makes you say that?"

"Miss Addie. She just appointed herself Brenda's campaign manager. Ask ol' Roland whether Miss Addie knows how to run a campaign. She's not able to campaign as vigorously as she did when she was running against Roland for the school board, but she can still dial a telephone. Her niece just gave her a new push-button phone with large buttons and great big numbers, and she's quite enamored with it. You saw the hands of all Miss Addie's former students this morning. If she only calls her former students, that'll be enough to throw the election."

* * * * * * * * * * * *

Susan Whitmire invited Mike and Karen over on Tuesday night to finalize the wedding plans over dinner with her and Brother McKnight. Asalee was also invited, but she had a previous engagement. It was Molly Coleman's eighth birthday, so Ted and Brenda let her invite Asalee to spend the night. It was a significant growing up milestone for Asalee, her first time to spend the night with anyone other than family. The two invitations coincided perfectly, and it was an opportunity for Karen and Mike to enjoy adult company and a respite from child care.

Karen especially had been looking forward to seeing Susan's house. About two years before Jim took sick, he and Susan had purchased the old Holliday homeplace up on Court Street and restored it to its Victorian grandeur. In the 1920's, the old house was one of many Victorian "painted ladies" to have its gay colors smothered under layers of white lead-based uniformity. Miss Addie told Susan and Jim that, when she was a young girl, the Holliday house was a pretty pale robin's egg blue trimmed in a darker shade of blue, but not quite as dark as a navy blue. Jim and

Susan worked for days with paint scrapers, cutting through thick
slathered-on layers of white paint to uncover the original colors so
they could have paint custom-mixed to match the colors that had
been applied when the house was new in 1884. They found some
photographs of the house made around the turn of the century,
and Miss Addie and old Doc Lindsey told them what they could
recall about the way the house was landscaped years ago. Jim and
Susan had just about finished the landscaping when Jim's pancre-
atic cancer showed up. When Jim became too weak to help her
any more, Susan, along with their daughters and sons-in-law, kept
planting flowers and shrubs. They hired a man with a backhoe to
rip up the concrete sidewalks so Johnny Grant, a masonry contractor who had been a friend of Jim's from high school days,
could recreate the original brick walkways. Until four days before
he died, Jim would drag himself out of bed and sit on the porch,
watching the progress while apologizing to Susan and the girls for
not being able to help them. When Jim died, Johnny lacked about
a half day's work having the walkways finished. Jim wanted his
body lie in state at home, so Johnny and his helper set up flood-
lights and worked into the night to have the walkways ready in
time for the viewing. Susan was more sentimental about her house
than Brother McKnight was about his, and selling his house was
more advantageous for them financially, so there was a Red Carpet
Realty sign in front of his house on Bailey's Mill Road. Bob told
Susan that, as a boy growing up in the cotton mill village, he had
always wondered what it would be like to live in one of those elegant
old houses up on Court Street. At seventy-one, he finally had the
chance to find out, and he was not going to pass it up.

Susan's wedding was going to be fairly simple as church
weddings go, but it would be the most elaborate one that Mike
had done. He was a little nervous about it, and, at home, he sometimes referred to it facetiously as "the royal wedding of Prince Bob

and Lady Susan." Mike had performed a grand total of three weddings. Two were small, simple affairs at Clear Springs, and he had done an outdoor wedding for his cousin Laura Westover up at Moccasin Creek State Park the previous summer. Bob put Mike more at ease about the wedding when he said, "Brother Mike, I've been in the ministry so long, when I first started out, all we had was the Old Testament. As many of 'em as I've done, these big weddings make me nervous as a cat, but I want to do our wedding up right, because I'm marrying a fine woman. I'm sure you can handle it."

"Thanks for the vote of confidence," Mike responded. "You and Susan seem to be really good for each other, so I'm pleased to be doing the wedding for you."

"I do wish that some people in the church could accept our relationship and be happy about it," Susan mused, "but if they can't, they'll just have to get over it. We are very much in love with each other, and we're going to be married no matter what some mean-spirited people have to say about it. We've been the subject of some nasty gossip, but we haven't done anything to be ashamed of. We've never spent the night together or gone to bed together, and we won't until we are married."

"Not that we haven't been tempted," Bob smiled as he gave Susan a hug. "Susan's a very attractive woman with a sweet spirit. The desire is very strong."

"And it's mutual," Susan added. "We're both looking forward to our wedding night. I feel sorry for people who think that people our ages shouldn't have such desires. I'm too old to bear children, but I'm not too old to enjoy life."

"Besides," Bob laughed, "I've been around a long time, but I don't feel all that old, and our relationship has made both of us feel younger. However much time we have left in this world, we want to spend it together. We're both in good health. Neither of us feels any compulsion to start acting old just yet. I think the ones who are wagging their tongues about us are just jealous.

Turning to Mike, Susan said, "I'll miss being at Harrington every Sunday, but I'll be going with Bob wherever he's preaching."

"And that's perfectly understandable," Karen commented, "I'd make the same decision if I were in your place."

"I am taking next Sunday off from preaching, though," Bob added, "so I can move my membership to Harrington. We'll be in church with you at Harrington any time that I'm not off preaching somewhere. Knowing Harrington's history, you could use the support."

"Thanks," Mike replied. "I'll be glad to have you. Even though you'll be away a lot doing interim work and pulpit supply, I appreciate your support, and I look forward to having the benefit of your experience."

"So how much longer before you have that baby, Karen?" Susan asked. "It can't be much longer."

"Doctor says September 3, but I have a feeling it might come early."

"So have y'all decided on a name?"

"Deborah Estelle. We already know from the ultrasound that it's a girl. Deborah is after Debbie Seals, Franklin Seals' daughter, and Estelle is after Estelle Coggins, a delightful older woman in our church at Clear Springs who died just about the time our baby was conceived."

Susan was stunned, and all the color drained out of her face as she asked, "Who told you about Debbie Seals?"

17

Mother Eunice York was the first to hold Deborah Estelle Westover after her birth in the choir room adjacent to the auditorium of Greater New Hope Progressive Missionary Baptist Church. Henry Conway, the pastor at Greater New Hope, had talked to Mike at the ministerial association meeting in July and asked him to come and preach on the afternoon of August 19 and bring the choir from Harrington Baptist. As much as he welcomed the opportunity to preach there, Mike hesitated to accept an invitation so close to Karen's due date. After conferring with her, he called Pastor Conway and accepted. Karen said that, since the date was a full two weeks from her due date and since she had gone a week and a half beyond her due date with Asalee, she thought it would be safe to go ahead. At the wedding on Saturday and that morning at church, several women commented on how low Karen was carrying the baby, but Karen felt fine and had no indication she was about to go into labor. Her water broke while the choir was singing, just before Mike was to get up to preach, and the contractions came rapidly.

Mother York, who had lost count of how many babies she had delivered over the years, took charge of the situation. "Law, Child," she spoke soothingly, "birthin' babies be the most natural thing in the world, 'sides, you done had one, so this'n'll come easier. First'n's the hardest. They's no time to get you to the hospital, but don't you be worried. I had seven in ten years' time, 'cludin' one set a' twins, had 'em all at home, an' I been deliverin' babies since long time 'fore you's born, 'fore y'mama was born. I caught a many a baby when they wad'n money to send for no doctor or when the baby come faster'n the doctor could get there. You in good hands, Child." With both pregnancies, Karen's worst fear had been that she would go into labor and not be able to get to the hospital in time. When the very thing she feared most happened, she was surprised to find that she did not really feel afraid. Mother York seemed to know what she was doing, and her bed-side manner was most reassuring. Karen felt a calmness come over her soul when, having no alternative, she placed herself in the capable hands of Mother York.

Mike helped Tishina Robinette, a nurse who was a member of Greater New Hope, move chairs out of the way and get Karen down onto the floor of the choir room. Prince Hammondtree raced to his house and grabbed pillows, sheets, and a blanket. Mike held Karen's hand and mopped perspiration from her forehead while Tishina timed the contractions and stood by to help the woman who had delivered her thirty-four years before. Brenda Coleman and Marletta Brumbelow, the young woman who had helped Mike and Karen open their bank accounts, kept running back and forth from the choir room to the auditorium to keep the combined congregations posted on the progress. Someone suggested calling 911, and Mother York told them to go ahead, but that she could already see the top of the baby's head. Karen mustered every ounce of her strength to give one last push, and the practiced hands of Mother York received Deborah Estelle Westover at 4:12 PM.

It was not necessary for Brenda and Marletta to announce the birth. Deborah Estelle did that herself with a piercing cry that was clearly audible in the auditorium, announcing not only her birth but also the fact that she was starting life with a fine pair of lungs. She seemed exhilarated with the feel of the first air in her lungs and delighted with the discovery that she could really make a lot of noise when she wanted to. "Rev'ren, you'n Miz Westover been blessed wit' a fine lil' girl," Mother York declared. "She's a strong baby! Look at 'er, wigglin' like a fish outta water, eyes wide open lookin' at everything they is to see! Got no way to weigh 'er, but she's a good healthy size an' her color's good. What's 'er name gonna be?"

"Deborah Estelle," Mike replied.

"Miss Deborah, you a mighty pretty baby, an' such a pretty name, too," Mother York spoke tenderly. Deborah Estelle was still wet and slippery with amniotic fluid when Mother York kissed her on the forehead before moving aside to let the two Mintz County EMS paramedics who had just arrived cut the cord. After the paramedics checked Karen and Deborah Estelle and determined that all was well, Tishina and Mother York got the baby cleaned up and gave her to Karen to nurse. Deborah was about twenty minutes old when the paramedics rolled the gurney bearing mother and child down the center aisle of Greater New Hope Progressive Missionary Baptist Church, to the delight of the waiting congregation. One of the older children started singing *Jesus Loves the Little Children*, and the whole congregation joined in. Twelve year old Nikkia Brinkley had a cheap 110 camera in her purse with three exposures left on the roll of film. The paramedics paused for her to snap the first pictures of Deborah Estelle Westover before they loaded the gurney into the ambulance.

Conway assured Mike that he would invite him back to preach some other time when his wife was not giving birth. After placing Asalee in the care of Ted and Brenda Coleman, Mike paused to hug Mother York and Tishina. The choirs sang a while longer after Mike left, and the service concluded with Conway doing some impromptu sermonizing on Psalm 127:1, *Lo, children are an heritage of the Lord,* before calling on Deacon Prince Hammondtree to offer a prayer of thanksgiving for the safe arrival of Deborah Estelle Westover. As he drove toward the house to retrieve the things Karen had asked him to bring to the hospital, Mike thought about the sermon he had planned to preach. He felt sure that it would have been well-received if he had had the opportunity to preach it, but he knew the people at Greater New Hope enjoyed Deborah Estelle's birth more than they would have enjoyed hearing him preach.

Mike still wanted to preach at Greater New Hope, sometime when Karen was not giving birth, as Conway suggested. When he was teaching school in Denham before he went to seminary, Mike had visited Sweet Zion Missionary Baptist Church there one Sunday. One of his students, Marcus Dixon, was being licensed to preach, and he had gone to hear him deliver his first sermon. He remembered how the whole congregation got involved, and how easy it was to get caught up in the rhythm of call-and-response. Every time Marcus paused to catch his breath, someone in the congregation would call out, "Weeelllll...," "Come on, now...," "Talk to me...," "That's right...," "Preach it, brother..," or "All right...." Marcus did not know it at the time, but Mike was coming to terms with his own call to preach, and the service at Sweet Zion and Marcus Dixon's first sermon had been a catalyst in Mike's surrender to the call. About three months after Marcus preached his first sermon, he and his family came to Talmadge Street Baptist Church to hear Mike's first sermonic effort. Mike also remembered Mack Farrell, a black student who was one of his classmates at Mid-Atlantic. They had been in Dr. Leggs' homiletics class together. When it was Mack's turn to preach in class, he began by saying, "Now, I'm accustomed to having help when I preach, so do feel free to talk back to me." It was the liveliest class in Mike's time at Mid-Atlantic. He was accustomed to an occasional "Amen" from Wallace Coggins or Russ Ayers, but he had never experienced anything like the congregational involvement that is the norm in black churches. He was determined to take advantage of the first opportunity to preach with some help from the congregation of Greater New Hope.

On the way to the hospital, Karen learned that the two paramedics transporting her were the same ones who had responded to the call to That Woman's house a couple of months earlier. Karen told Sherry, the paramedic in the back of the ambulance with her, about finding That Woman's key broken off in the front door and how she had confronted her about it, which led to the 911 call. Sherry regaled Karen with some of her own war stories about That Woman, and it amused Karen to learn that the Mintz County EMS people long ago bestowed the same moniker on her. "At least, that's what we call her when we're on our best behavior," she clarified. "You're a preacher's wife, so I won't tell you some of the things we've called her. The way That Woman carries on, you'd think she was going to up and die any minute. She'll live to be a hundred out of pure spite. My heart'll quit before hers does."

By the time the ambulance backed up to the emergency entrance at Tanner Medical Center, Karen was beginning to see the humor in the circumstances of Deborah's birth. "Every preacher's kid can say she grew up in church," Karen commented to Sherry, "but this one can say she was born in church!"

* * * * * * * * * * * *

Growing up around his father's shop, Mike had the opportunity to assemble his first engine, a slant six Dodge, when he was barely thirteen, so it was inevitable that Grady Westover would come up with the wisecrack about his preacher son doing "ring and vow jobs." Mike thought back to the boyish delight he felt when that slant six started right up and ran smoothly with good oil pressure. That was the way he felt when the ring and vow job on Saturday was concluded. Everyone had their timing and their lines right. He had not gotten his tongue twisted up, as he had feared that he might. It was flawless from start to finish, running as smoothly as the first engine he built. Bob and Susan were elated. Methodist pastor Eleanor Flint Basden was in the audience, and she complimented Mike highly on the wedding ceremony when she spoke to him at the reception. After the reception, Bob's son and daughter-in-law drove the newlyweds to the Atlanta airport and put them on a plane to their honeymoon destination in Aruba. Vicky Blevins, Susan's daughter, had been at the service at Greater New Hope, so the newlyweds would learn about the new baby when they called Vicky that night.

Mike was glad Deborah Estelle had been born, but he was thankful that she did not make her appearance a day sooner. The wedding rehearsal Friday evening lasted an hour and a half because Susan wanted to be sure that nothing would happen that was not in the printed order of service, and there was no place in the order of service for anyone to have a baby. Everything went exactly as planned and rehearsed. On Sunday afternoon at Greater New Hope, they were not locked into a printed order of service, so Deborah Estelle's birth was not looked upon as a disruption. Mother York took charge in a reassuringly authoritative manner, the delivery was as flawless as the wedding, and the 911 call had been an afterthought. Greater New Hope received the birth of a child in lieu of a sermon as a delightful surprise from God. In one weekend, Mike had experienced opposite poles of planned liturgy and hang-loose-and-let-the-Spirit-lead spontaneity and delighted in both. As he conducted Bob and Susan's wedding and again as he comforted his wife in childbirth, he realized he was on holy ground.

At the hospital, Deborah Estelle tipped the scales at seven pounds and one ounce and measured twenty inches from head to toe. Both the pediatrician on call and Karen's obstetrician said that all was well, and to convey their compliments to Mother York and Tishina. As soon as he had that news, Mike found a pay phone and made the calls to his and Karen's families and a call to Wallace Coggins to get the word out at Clear Springs. He had just gotten off the phone when Ted and Brenda came in with Asalee and Molly in tow. Ted had his trusty 35mm Minolta hanging from a strap around his neck.

"We took the girls and fed them at Mickey D's, managed to convince them it would be a while before they got Karen and the baby settled in," Brenda explained.

"Well, congratulations, Preacher. Is everything OK?" Ted asked.

"Thanks, Ted. Everything's super, couldn't be better. The obstetrician's seen Karen, and the pediatrician's seen Deborah, everything looks good."

"As you can tell by the camera, Pastor, I'm here on official *Harrington Courier* business. Should've worn my Stetson with the press pass stuck in the hatband," Ted mugged as he took a small spiral-bound notebook from his inside coat pocket. "I'm here to see that the blessed event receives sufficient media coverage. We'll get a birth announcement with a picture of the baby in this week's *Courier.* Of course, as a professional courtesy, the *Courier* will grant permission to your hometown papers to print the same photo, just as long as they run a credit line under it that says 'Ted Coleman—*Harrington Courier*' in twenty-point type."

"Don't know about the paper in Williston, but I've known ol' Max Barnett at the *Maddox County News* all my life, and I'm sure he'd go along with that. The credit line, that is. I can't promise twenty-point type, unless it's a slow week and he's got a lot of space to fill."

The charge nurse on the maternity ward was from Harrington, and Ted and Brenda knew her, so Ted's press credentials were recognized long enough for him to go back to Karen's room with Mike to take some pictures while the baby was in the room. Asalee was eager to see her mother and her new sister, so the nurse said that, while she couldn't exactly grant permission for her to visit them, she could look the other way and not see her sneak in. Ted had a fresh roll of film in the Minolta, and he took about a dozen pictures before returning to the waiting room so Karen could nurse the baby. Karen was sore from the delivery, but she asked Mike to help her over to the recliner next to the bed. After helping her get situated, Mike picked Deborah up from the bassinet and brought her over to Karen. As Karen pulled back her robe and took Deborah to her breast, Asalee climbed over the side of the recliner and curled up beside her. As Deborah nursed, Asalee gently stroked her back with her fingertips. She was awestruck, and it was some time before she broke the silence to say, "Wow, this is so cool, Mom."

"Yes it is, Az," Karen agreed. "I think it's the coolest thing in the whole world. It seems like only yesterday you were this little and I was feeding you the same way."

"Was I as little as Deborah, Mom?"

"You were actually a little smaller. You weighed six pounds and thirteen ounces and you were nineteen inches long, so you were an inch shorter and four ounces lighter."

Harold and Margaret Owen, Karen's parents, arrived about 6:30, just as the Colemans were leaving. Mike's parents and sister got to the hospital about an hour later. The Westovers had a much longer distance to cover, but Grady once again demonstrated the merits of big cars with big engines. As soon as he got onto I-85, he did not let any grass grow under the Lincoln land yacht. Karen and Deborah were due to be discharged the next morning, and

Grady told Mike that he wanted him to use the Lincoln to take them home. After the grandparents and Aunt Mandy saw Karen and Deborah Estelle and expressed their opinions about who Deborah favored the most, Mike gave his father the keys to the Fairmount. Grady went out and got their luggage out of the Lincoln and put it in the Fairmount while Julia called around to find motel rooms near the hospital. After he brought the keys to the Lincoln back in to Mike, they all headed to the motel, and Asalee cheerfully went with her Aunt Mandy. Grady announced that he had spotted a Shoney's on the way in. He told Harold, Margaret, and Mike to show up there at 8:00 and he would treat them to the breakfast bar before time for Karen and Deborah to be discharged.

Mike gave Asalee her good night hug before she got in the car with Grady, Julia, and Mandy. On the way back to Karen's room, he walked by the nursery and looked in on Deborah, who was sleeping peacefully. Karen was exhausted, and Mike found her sound asleep when he returned to her bedside. He kissed her on the forehead before he kicked back in the recliner next to her bed. Mike was so tired that he thought he would be asleep within five minutes, but he was too wound up to sleep. He turned on the television, putting the speaker beside his head and turning the volume down low so as not to disturb Karen. He was still awake when it was time for the 11:00 news. After the news went off, he surfed the channels and settled on a *Barnaby Jones* rerun. Buddy Ebsen would always be Jed Clampett, no matter what other role he might be playing. As he watched the *Barnaby Jones* episode, Mike halfway expected Barnaby to suffer a Freudian slip and exclaim "Wheeee doggies!" The episode was one that he had seen a dozen times, and there was nothing more appealing on the TV. He killed the television and tried to go to sleep, but his mind would not settle. He kept turning over in his mind the way Susan reacted when they told her that they were going to name the baby after Debbie Seals. Karen mentioned it on the way home that night and they had talked about it late into the night that night and several times since. Perhaps Susan had not thought about what happened to Debbie in a long time, and she was merely surprised that Mike and Karen had heard of Debbie and knew about the circumstances of her death. Maybe it was nothing more than that, but Susan's reaction seemed too intense for that. Karen said on the way home from Susan's house that she thought Susan knew more than she was telling, and Mike told Karen that he was thinking the same thing.

*   *   *   *   *   *   *   *   *   *   *   *

Karen's mother had made arrangements to take a week off from work and stay with Mike and Karen to help out when the baby was born. Her presence was most helpful, especially since school was starting August 27 and they also needed to see about all the details of getting Asalee ready to start first grade. After bringing Karen and the baby home, Mike was dispatched to the store to pick up diapers, baby care items, and a few groceries. On the way, he swung by the church and saw Helen Walters' car in the parking lot. He went in and checked with her to see whether he had any messages. There was one message, she said, to call Virgil Blackmon.

"Anything urgent?"

"He said it wasn't an emergency, but it's important and he needs to talk to you."

Mike took the number and told Helen he would call Virgil from home. He then proceeded with his actual purpose for stopping by the church. He looked in the closet where the valves for filling and draining the baptistry were located and put his hands on the key to the church sign and the box of letters. He took the key and the box of letters out to the church sign on the front lawn. The *Welcome New Pastor Rev. Mike Westover* message had been up long enough for everyone in town to have had ample opportunity to see it. Mike opened the glass door of the sign and took down that message. He then selected the letters to spell out *Unto Us a Child is Born: Deborah Estelle Westover, August 19, 1990*. Then he locked the door of the sign, returned the key and the box of letters, and proceeded on to the store.

*   *   *   *   *   *   *   *   *   *   *   *

It was after supper before Mike thought about the note in his shirt pocket to call Virgil Blackmon. Mike had only met him once, on his first Sunday as pastor at Harrington, and he had not seen or heard anything else from him in the two and a half months that he had been there. He took out the note and dialed the number. "Brother Virgil? This is Mike Westover at Harrington. I had a message to call you."

"Hey, Brother Mike, thanks for getting back to me. I heard about the new baby. Congratulations, and I hope your wife and the baby are doing well."

"Thanks. Both of them are doing fine, brought 'em home around lunch time today. Karen's mother's here helping us out this week, and our six-year-old is playing the big sister role to the hilt. We've got another little girl, named her Deborah Estelle, seven pounds and one ounce, twenty inches, a good healthy size. She came faster than we expected, too fast to get Karen to the hospital. We had a fellowship with one of the black churches, Greater New Hope, Sunday afternoon. The pastor invited me to come and preach and our choir to sing. Karen's water broke and she went into labor right there at Greater New Hope, just about time for me to get up to preach. One of the women at Greater New Hope is a midwife. She took charge of the situation, and another member there who is a nurse helped her. They delivered the baby right there without any problems. It was hard on Karen delivering without any pain relief, but she did it, and it was quick and smooth. Karen's sore, but she's up and moving around."

"That's great. By the way, while I'm thinking about it, I sure did enjoy the piece in your newsletter about baptizing your father and your sister on the Fourth of July. Wish I could've been there. I know it was an unforgettable experience for the whole family."

"Yes, it was," Mike acknowledged. Mike did not doubt Virgil's sincerity in sharing the joy of the new baby and the recent baptisms, but he sensed that there was some further purpose in the call besides talking about the Westover family's recent blessings.

"Changing the subject, I hate to bring this up," Virgil began, "but I saw something in your newsletter that disturbs me a great deal."

"What's that?" Mike asked, although he was perfectly sure that he knew what it was.

"The list of people eligible to serve as deacons. Unless Brenda Coleman's a man with an unusual name, like that song Johnny Cash did about the boy named Sue, we've got a problem."

"Brenda's a woman. She's in her late thirties, teaches fourth grade at Harrington Elementary, husband Ted is editor of the *Harrington Courier* and an active deacon, Brenda teaches third and fourth grades in Sunday School. Delightful person, very genuine Christian, an asset to our church."

"I'm sure she is," Virgil responded coldly, "but if she's ordained and Harrington is thinking about letting her serve as a deacon, we've got a problem. Who ordained her and when?"

"Brenda and her husband were ordained at the same time, before they came to Harrington. University Drive Baptist Church in Macon ordained them, and they served together as deacons before they came to Harrington. When they moved to Harrington and joined the church here, Harry Reynolds asked them not to say anything about her being ordained, said the church wasn't ready to deal with that issue."

"And Harry Reynolds was right," Virgil shot back. "At least, I'm glad to hear she was ordained somewhere else. Son, this area's a lot different from over 'round Macon, or up in Virginia where you went to seminary. It's a pretty conservative vein of water that runs under this association, and that suits me just fine. I've been director of missions since 1979, pastored eleven years before that over't Fellowship where Larry Holland is now, served two terms as moderator before I became DOM, so I know the association pretty well. I can't help what some churches over't Macon or up in Virginia do, that dog won't hunt in Mintz County. You're fixin' to get yourself killed at Harrington and stir up a big stink in the association. My job's to keep down trouble in the association as much as I can, and that's your job as a pastor, to keep down trouble in your church. If you keep down trouble in your church, you make my job a whole lot easier, and you and I'll get along a whole lot better. This association's no more ready for women deacons than your church is."

Mike bristled at the tongue lashing and veiled threats, and he resented Virgil telling him how to do his job, so he had no desire to continue the conversation. He knew that the Biblical arguments against women deacons and ministers could not stand the light of sound exegesis. He knew that *the first* Baptist church, the Gainsborough, England congregation of John Smyth, had women deacons in 1609. Mike realized, however, that sound Biblical scholarship and insights from Baptist history would be wasted on this man who was concerned only with keeping the peace. It would be fruitless to debate the issue. Mike had more eternally significant things to do, like spending time with Asalee so she wouldn't feel neglected with the arrival of the new baby. Although he was much younger than Miss Addie, Mike had already decided he was too old to endure the argument that people just aren't ready for this or that. It was time to speak the truth in love with both barrels. "Brother Virgil," Mike said, "If Moses had waited until everybody was ready, the Israelites would still be in Egypt."

* * * * * * * * * * * *

Determined to work off some pounds, Mike picked up a yard sale bargain on a pretty decent old twenty-six inch heavyweight bicycle that was older than he was. The tires and tubes were dry rotted, but it was otherwise in good condition and not bad looking when he cleaned it up. He bought new tires and tubes, new handlebar grips, and a new seat, and still had less than forty dollars invested. The bike became his regular transportation to and from the church office. The realization that she was now The Big Sister inspired Asalee to ask Mike to take the training wheels off her bicycle. She was confident on two wheels, but Karen insisted that she start wearing a helmet and suggested that Mike get one as well. The trail through the woods to the church and the church parking lot provided a great place for them to ride without having to worry about traffic. Riding their bicycles together turned out to be something they both enjoyed, although it took some effort for Mike to learn not to run off and leave Asalee, since his wheels were half again the size of hers.

It was Margaret Owen's last day with them. She planned to drive back to Williston that night, since she had to be at work Monday morning. Karen's mother meant well, but she was starting to get on Mike's nerves. Karen was doing well with the baby, and Mike was ready for Margaret to go home so they could get their normal routine established again. Nonetheless, he had been appreciative of her help, and she had put on a wonderful Sunday dinner for them. After dinner, Mike suggested to Asalee that they get on their bikes and work off the big meal. Mike was turning many things over in his mind—the unpleasant conversation with Virgil Blackmon on Monday night, the more unpleasant call from Franklin A. Brinkley, Chairman of the Board of Deacons of Harrington Baptist Church Thursday night, the new family that had joined the church that morning, his sermon for the Sunday night service, and the deacons meeting following the service to count the ballots. Mike had been so angry at Frank Thursday night that he wanted to reach through the phone and choke him. Now that he'd had a couple of days to process it, he was beginning to see the humor in a deacon chairman finding out what was in his own church newsletter not by reading it himself, but by hearing about it from Virgil Blackmon.

18

Royce Green, bless his heart, had been right about one thing when he vowed that no woman would be a deacon at Harrington Baptist Church while he was living. He had stated that conviction adamantly in the July deacons meeting after Carol Richardson helped serve communion. He had asserted his position again, quite vociferously, on Sunday night when they counted the ballots. Brenda Coleman and Eric Latham emerged as the top nominees, tied with fifty-three votes each. Bill Gentry received forty-nine, Bruce Blevins forty-two, his father Rudy thirty-seven, and Roland Millican thirty. These six would be presented to the church on a secret ballot. The plans had been for two to be elected from the top six nominees to fill the two vacancies. Now, Mike assumed, they would be electing a third person to fill the remaining two years of Royce's term.

Royce might have lived to be wrong if he had fixed the brakes on his truck. Mike remembered how Royce's brakes were scraping metal-on-metal the day he and his family moved into the parsonage. Mike said something to Royce then about the dangerous condition of his brakes. He had even kidded him, saying that he was not in any hurry to conduct his first funeral at Harrington. Royce said he knew his truck needed a brake job, and he would get around to it eventually, but he didn't worry too much about it because he only drove the old truck around town doing odd jobs and maintaining his rental properties. He said he never drove it on the highway or got up much speed with it, since the engine was as far gone as the brakes.

It was a couple of minutes past 8:30 Monday morning when Mike learned about the accident. He had just gotten to the office after taking Asalee to Harrington Elementary for her first day of school. Church secretary Helen Walters had not yet arrived, and the phone was ringing when Mike walked in the door. It was That Woman, calling to say that she had heard about the accident on her police scanner. It had happened, she reported, about five minutes earlier at Peyton Street and Monument Avenue, and the description of one of the vehicles sounded like Royce's truck. The first officer on the scene reported that there was a fatality and that building materials were scattered all over the road. The other vehicle involved was a large ready-mix concrete truck. The pickup was upside down, crushed flat under the cement mixer. The officer who arrived first radioed for the fire department, an ambulance, and a wrecker large enough to lift the huge concrete truck. The dispatcher said she was sending the fire department and the ambulance, but the nearest wrecker of that capacity would have to come from Carrollton. "Preacher," That Woman concluded, "you'd better get up there and see if it's Royce. It's bound to be him."

Normally, Mike would have bristled at the thought of following a direct order from That Woman, but this time he grimly complied, pausing to make two quick phone calls, one to Ted at the paper and one to Karen, and to leave a note for Helen. By the time he hung up the phone and walked outside, he heard sirens. Knowing that the police would block Peyton Street to secure the accident scene, Mike decided to leave the car at the church and walk the three blocks up to the Phillips 66 on the corner of Peyton Street and Martin Luther King Boulevard, which most people still call Monument Avenue, to see what he could find out.

When Mike got within a block of the scene, he saw a Mintz County Sheriff's car with its emergency lights flashing pulled across Peyton Street. He recognized the deputy turning back traffic as Rodney Womack, who came to church with his wife Angela and their children when his work schedule permitted. "Hey Rod," Mike called out as he walked up to the patrol car, "what's going on up there?"

"Hey Preacher. It's a bad one. You can go on up there if you got a strong stomach. It's Royce Green, so you'll be doing the funeral. Witness gassing up his car at the Phillips 66 saw it happen. Said ol' Royce's brake lights come on, but he did'n even slow down, run right through the red light, smack dab in front of a big concrete truck. The concrete truck wad'n goin' more'n thirty miles an hour, but he was right at the intersection when Royce come sailin' through the light. It takes a lot to stop one a'them big boys even from thirty miles an hour, 'specially if he's got a full load. I know, I used to drive one. Guy drivin' the concrete truck said they hit 'fore he could get his foot on the brakes. Hit poor ol' Royce on the driver's side, rolled 'im over'n drug 'im upside down under the cement truck 'bout a hundred feet. They tried to back the cement truck off'a Royce's truck, but it's wedged under there so bad it just drags it, and they were afraid of turning the cement truck over if they kept trying. Fire department's dealin' with the gas spillin' outta Royce's truck, and they're tryin' to get eighteen yards of concrete unloaded while they're waitin' on the wrecker to come from Carrollton to pick up the cement truck."

A crowd had gathered by the time Mike got there, and he found the grisly scene pretty much as Rodney had described. Apparently, Royce had just come from Hutton Builders Supply down at the south end of Peyton Street. The lumber, plywood decking, and rolls of felt that had been on Royce's truck were scattered all over the road, along with bundles of shingles that had burst open upon impact.

Rodney Womack must have let Ted Coleman past the blockade on Peyton Street. Mike saw Ted's burgundy Caprice stop at the curb a couple hundred feet back from the intersection, and he went over to speak to him. "Hey, Ted, that was pretty quick."

"Got here quick as I could, Preacher. Is it Royce?"

"Yeah, it's him. I recognized what's left of his truck. Looks like he'd just come from Hutton's. His truck was loaded down with decking, felt, and shingles. Brakes were bad on his old truck, I know that. The day we moved into the parsonage, I heard 'em scraping metal-on-metal, almost rear-ended my father-in-law's car in our driveway. Looks like he finally blew a wheel cylinder and lost his brakes altogether. Guy getting gas at the Phillips 66 saw it happen, said Royce's brake lights came on but he kept rolling, ran the red light right square in front of the cement truck. Killed him instantly, no doubt about that."

"Ought to put bullheadedness as the cause of death on his death certificate," Ted commented as he and Mike walked over to the wreckage for Ted to take pictures. As Ted was taking the pictures, an unmarked metallic gray Crown Victoria, blue lights flashing on the dash and behind the grille, pulled up. The tall stocky-built man who got out of the car looked to be in his late thirties. He was wearing dress slacks, a pastel-blue shirt, and a conservative striped tie. He carried his service revolver in a shoulder holster, and his badge was attached to a leather holder that looped over his belt. "Pastor," Ted spoke up, "want you to meet our chief of police, Aaron Stewart. Aaron, this is our new pastor, Mike Westover."

"Pleased to meet you, Reverend. I hate for us to meet like this. I was hoping it'd be at church or over lunch or something. I've heard good things about you, sorry I couldn't be at church the Sunday afternoon your wife had the baby. The wife and baby doing OK?"

"Doing great, both of them. Mother York and Tishina Robinette handled the delivery just fine. Got us a pretty little girl, weighed seven pounds one ounce."

"Congratulations, glad they're doing well. Old Mother York's mighty good at that sort of thing. She delivered me and my twin sister. I was planning to go to church that day and be at the fellowship that afternoon, really looked forward to meeting you and hearing you preach, but I had an officer call in sick, so I had to work. I'm there when I can be. My grandfather was the pastor at Greater New Hope when we bought our building from your church. I was about thirteen years old at the time. I sure am sorry about poor ol' Royce. Can't say I'm surprised. I pulled him over one day last week because I heard his brakes scraping metal-on-metal, told him to get 'em fixed before he killed himself or somebody else, told him I didn't want to see that truck on the road again until the brakes were fixed. I went against my better judgement not giving him a ticket for defective equipment and having the thing towed. Guess that's what I should've done. Hindsight's always 20/20."

"Not your fault Royce didn't get the brakes fixed. He had a shop full of tools and knew how to do it himself. Wouldn't have taken him more than two hours to do the brakes all the way around. No telling how many close calls he had, said he knew the brakes were bad, but he just used the truck around town doing little jobs and keeping up his rental properties, never drove it out on the highway or got up any speed with it 'cause the engine was as worn out as the brakes."

"Yeah, suppose so, but I still feel bad about it. I'd appreciate it if you'd go with me to notify Royce's daughter. I ought to be used to doing things like that, but that's one part of this job I'll never get used to. I like to take a minister with me on death notifications whenever I can."

　*　*　*　*　*　*　*　*　*　*　*　*

While Chief Stewart conferred with the officers investigating the wreck, Mike used the pay phone at the Phillips 66 to call Karen at home and Helen at the church. He only had two quarters, so he asked Helen to call That Woman. Not even under these circumstances would he ask Karen to call her. As he was on the phone, the wrecker arrived from Carrollton. Bud Hutchison, who had been waiting with his rollback, hooked a cable to the flattened wreckage of Royce's truck and dragged it into the clear when the wrecker lifted the cement truck. The firemen went to work with power saws and the Jaws, tearing the wreckage apart to extricate Royce's body. Mike was relieved when Aaron Stewart motioned him over to his car. "We'd best leave these guys to handle things here and go on down to the Clerk of Court's office where Annette works," Stewart suggested. "I don't want her to hear it some other way before we get there. She's going to take it hard."

When Mike and Aaron walked into the clerk's office, Royce's daughter Annette Gresham was seated at her desk behind the counter. When she saw them come in together, open the gate at the end of the counter, and come toward her desk, all of the color drained out of her face and she began sobbing. Two other women who worked in the office rushed to her side, put their arms around her, and held her as she wept. "It's Daddy, isn't it?" Annette asked as Mike knelt in front of her.

"Yes, I'm sorry to say, it is."

"It was an accident," Aaron added. "It was instant. He didn't suffer. It happened at the light in front of the Phillips 66, Peyton Street and MLK Boulevard."

"It was the brakes on that stupid old truck of his, wasn't it?" Annette asked.

"That's what it looks like," Aaron replied. "Royce ran a red light right in front of a big ready-mix concrete truck. They hit before the truck driver could get his foot on the brakes. Witness saw it happen, said your dad's brake lights came on, but he kept right on rolling. Cement truck wasn't going fast, but he was at the intersection when Royce ran the light smack dab in front of him. Nothing the guy driving the cement truck could've done to avoid it. Based on what the witness told the officers, there won't be any charges against the truck driver. The law requires a blood alcohol test and drug test on all drivers involved in a fatal accident, and we don't have the results of that yet, but I don't think alcohol or drugs were involved. The DOT boys'll have to do their own investigation on account of the big truck being involved. I don't think they'll find anything. Harding Cement keeps their trucks in tip-top shape. Even if there was something wrong with the truck, it didn't cause the accident. The driver has a clean record. I'll reserve judgement until I see the toxicology report and the DOT investigation, but I doubt they'll tell us any more than we already know."

"Hardheaded old fool could've paid cash for any new truck he wanted and never missed the money," Annette said after she regained her composure. "Too tight and stubborn. That, or he could've taken one morning and fixed the brakes on that piece of junk. Did he kill anybody besides himself?"

"Your dad was by himself in his truck," Aaron answered. "They took the driver of the cement truck to the hospital to check him out. It jostled him around, jarred him. He was so torn up over it, I expect they'll give him something to sedate him as soon as they do the drug and alcohol test. He said it was the first accident he'd ever had, been driving a cement truck fourteen years."

"Well, thank the Lord Daddy didn't kill anybody else. Bad enough he had to go and get himself killed. I need to go over to the high school and tell Brad and Jeremy," Annette stated calmly. "They're going to take it hard. Both of them worked helping Daddy on Saturdays and when school was out. He was more like a father to them than their father ever was. My brother's stationed at McConnell Air Force Base out in Kansas. We need to get word to him. I don't know if they'll drive down here or if they'll be able to hook a military flight down to Dobbins."

"I'll help you make the calls to your brother and any other family," Mike offered, "and if they fly into Dobbins, I can arrange for somebody to pick them up."

"I'll drive you over to the high school to tell your boys and bring you back later to get your car," Aaron offered. Turning to one of the other women in the office, he continued, "Keisha, if you'd be so kind as to call over to the high school, let them know what's going on, it'd be a big help."

＊　＊　＊　＊　＊　＊　＊　＊　＊　＊　＊　＊

Captain Ray Green, his wife, and their children were able to make connections on a military flight from McConnell to Dobbins, so they got in about eleven o'clock that night, too late for Ray to be with Annette when she identified the body, but in time for him to go with her Tuesday morning to Webster Funeral Home to make the arrangements. David Groves picked them up at Dobbins and gave them the use of a car from his dealership while they were in town. Tuesday morning at the funeral home was Mike's first occasion to meet Ray. Annette and her two sons came to church sporadically, so Mike barely knew them. He would have preferred getting acquainted with Royce's extended family under less stressful circumstances than being thrust into the middle of their grief.

As he walked with them through their grief, Mike thought of something his pastoral care prof at Mid-Atlantic said about mixed feelings, that he had never had any other kind. That was underscored as he observed the grief of Royce's family. Their grief was mixed with a generous portion of anger. "If Daddy'd survived, I would've choked the living daylights out of him for driving that truck in that shape. It's not like he couldn't afford to do better," was the way Ray summed it up. Royce's death was totally preventable. A vigorous, active man in good health, he should have lived many more years. Certainly, his family had anticipated having him around a few more years. They were deeply saddened over his death, angry at him for getting himself killed unnecessarily, and they felt guilty for being angry at him when he was dead. At the funeral home, reminiscing with people who had known Royce over many years, they found themselves laughing at the legendary cheapness of a man who would spend a dollar to save a dime. Even though his cheapness led to his untimely demise, it was impossible not to laugh at the absurdity of it. He was on the board of directors of the Bank of Mintz County, but he acted like he didn't have two nickels to rub together. He had fought the trustees tooth and toenail over putting new carpet in the parsonage, insisting first on an all-out effort to clean and rejuvenate the trampled-down threadbare carpet that had been there since 1974. The shabby carpet in the bedrooms remained as a monument to the cheapness of Royce Green. He drove the rusty, rattletrap remains of a 1972 Datsun pickup with 300,000 miles on it when he could have paid cash for a plush, safe, dependable Cowboy Cadillac and never missed the money. His good car that he drove to church on Sunday was a 1976 Ford Torino in only slightly better shape than the truck. His clothing sizes had not changed in his entire adult life, so he still wore fashions of the sixties and seventies, seeing no reason to buy new clothes when his old ones were not completely worn out. Mike was surprised that the mortician was able to fix Royce up well enough to have an open casket. The family respected Royce's cheapness even in death, laying him out in the cheapest cloth-covered pine box, dressed in the ugly pale green leisure suit he wore to church the day before he was killed.

Royce had voted against calling Mike, and Mike had come to regard Royce mostly as a stump to be plowed around when it came to doing anything, especially anything that cost money. He tended to be an ally of the other three old guard deacons. Nonetheless, Mike found himself with mixed feelings about Royce's death. He never could bring himself to dislike Royce the way he disliked Franklin A. Brinkley, Chairman of the Board of Deacons of Harrington Baptist Church. Royce had supported Mike when the issue came up over That Woman's attempt to gain entry to the parsonage. He had made positive comments on a couple of Mike's sermons. He was a congenial, pleasant man most of the time. He shared Mike's interest in things mechanical. Mike admired the way that Royce had been more of a father than a grandfather to Annette's two boys. Royce's generosity toward Annette and her boys after she and Don divorced and his support of the church had been among the few exceptions to his legendary cheapness. Brad's and Jeremy's affection for him was deep and genuine. So was Mike's, to a degree that surprised Mike himself, as he became aware of the tears coursing down his cheeks on Tuesday afternoon when he was alone in his study preparing for Royce's funeral.

* * * * * * * * * * * *

Franklin A. Brinkley, Chairman of the Board of Deacons of Harrington Baptist Church, had been in the insurance business for thirty-five years, so he knew how to read fine print. His experience with understanding the precise language of insurance policies carried over into his meticulous approach to the constitution and bylaws of Harrington Baptist Church. It was what Frank said, not anything that Mike or one of the new people deacons said, that triggered Royce's tirade at the deacons meeting on Sunday evening.

Frank was as opposed to women deacons as Royce was, but he pointed out that there was nothing in the church's constitution and bylaws to prohibit a woman from serving as a deacon if the church elected her. The bylaws were clear enough on the point that only men could be ordained to deacon ministry at Harrington Baptist Church, so the church could not ordain a woman unless it first amended its bylaws, but nothing prohibited a woman ordained at another church from serving. Frank even admitted that Mike was right in listing Brenda among the ordained deacons holding membership in the church, since the bylaws governing the election of deacons stated very clearly, *a list of all ordained deacons holding membership in Harrington Baptist Church, with the exception of those currently serving as active deacons and those rotating off active duty who must remain on inactive status for one year before becoming eligible for re-election, shall be published in the July issue of the church newsletter.* After he got over his embarrassment about failing to read his own church's newsletter and learning about the presence of Brenda's name on the list from Virgil Blackmon, Frank admitted that Mike had done nothing but follow the bylaws to the letter. He said, if he had known Brenda was ordained, he would have felt obligated to put her name on the list himself.

Royce became furious at Frank's careful exegesis of the bylaws, and shouted "Ain't nothin' in there says we got to recognize her ordination!" With the painstaking precision of a Greek grammarian explaining the Granville Sharp rule on anarthrous nouns, Frank set Royce straight. He pointed out that Ted had been ordained by the same church that ordained Brenda, and the church had recognized Ted's ordination without question. David Groves had been ordained by a church in Atlanta before he moved to Harrington, and the church had recognized his ordination. Every pastor in the history of the church, Frank pointed out, had been ordained by some other church, and the church had never questioned their ordinations. Based on his study of the bylaws, Frank said, there was no provision for the church to refuse to recognize an ordination performed by another Baptist church. He likened it to the "full faith and credit" clause of the United States Constitution, which requires states to recognize the official acts of other states, so that a couple married in Alabama does not need to obtain a Georgia license and get married again if they move across the state line. Likewise, Frank argued, there is strong precedent for Baptist churches giving full faith and credit to the acts of other Baptist churches. Otherwise, he maintained, the church would have to rebaptize anyone who joined by transfer from another Baptist church. The church, he argued, could not recognize Ted's, David's, or, for that matter, the pastor's ordination and then arbitrarily refuse to recognize Brenda's. It was Franklin A. Brinkley, Chairman of the Board of Deacons of Harrington Baptist Church, not Mike Westover, who said that he didn't see how the church could recognize Brenda's baptism without recognizing her ordination at the hands of the same church that baptized her. Frank reiterated the point that he didn't like it one bit and that he was categorically opposed to women deacons, but he didn't see any way under the church's existing bylaws to keep her name off the ballot or keep her from serving if the church elected her. He pointed out that there was no way to complete the process of a bylaw change before time for the newly-elected deacons to take office.

The deacons met again just before the regular business meeting on the Wednesday night after Royce was killed to prepare a recommendation for filling his vacancy. Like many Baptist churches, Harrington had traditionally had seven active deacons because that is how many the Jerusalem church had according to the sixth chapter of Acts. The tradition became ensconced in the bylaws when the most recent revision was drawn up in 1957, so the church was obligated to secure someone to complete Royce's term. Franklin A. Brinkley, Chairman of the Board of Deacons of Harrington Baptist Church, expounded the relevant section of the bylaws in his inimitable way, and the deacons quickly agreed to recommend that the church elect three rather than two deacons from the top six nominees on September 16. The two with the largest number of votes would be elected to full three-year terms, and the one with the third-largest number of votes would be elected to serve the remaining two years of Royce's term. The church approved the recommendation without dissent.

On September 16, at the conclusion of the worship service, the deacons passed out the short stubby little pencils with no erasers, the kind you use to keep score on the golf course, along with ballots containing the names of the six top nominees. Mike recognized Franklin A. Brinkley, Chairman of the Board of Deacons of Harrington Baptist Church, to explain that each member of the church could vote for up to three of the six nominees. One hundred and eighteen ballots were collected, and the deacons gathered after the benediction in the older men's Sunday School room to tabulate the results. There were sixty-three votes for Eric Latham, sixty-one for Brenda Coleman, and fifty-nine for Bill Gentry.

As Mike pondered the outcome of the voting, he saw a tension between two competing understandings of what deacons should be and do. The strong votes for Eric and Brenda represented those who wanted the deacons to be lay ministers, and Eric and Brenda had been chosen for their spiritual qualifications. Bill, Mike suspected, had been chosen for his considerable knowledge of plumbing, electrical, heating, and air conditioning systems. Bill was a nice enough fellow, and he was unquestionably competent in his field, but one would have been hard pressed to find anyone with less knowledge of the scriptures, less of a clue about how to minister to a person in crisis, or less of an idea of where to start in explaining to anyone else how to become a follower of Jesus Christ. The most that could be said for Bill was that he was a member of the church, male, over twenty-one, married, never divorced, and fairly regular in attendance. The significant number of votes for him represented those who wanted the deacons to be a governing board that second-guessed the work of the finance and maintenance committees.

Since Eric and Bill were not yet ordained, Mike began making plans for their ordination on the first Sunday in October. It would have been a nice touch of irony, Mike thought, if Brenda had been elected to complete Royce's term, but he was glad to see her elected to a full term. He was likewise looking forward to having Eric as a deacon, and glad to see him elected for a full term. Bill was a man after Royce's own heart, a true kindred spirit to serve the remainder of Royce's term.

19

"DaddyDaddyDaddy!!!" Asalee squealed as Mike came in the kitchen door. "Guess who's coming to see us?" By the time she finished asking the question, she had shinnied up into her father's arms and locked her arms tightly around his neck. Before Mike could say that he didn't know, Asalee answered her own question. "Papa Wallace is coming, Daddy, Papa Wallace is coming! Mommy'n me just talked to him on the phone."

"Great, but you need to be a little quieter in the house with the new baby around." Playfully taking the tip of Asalee's nose between his thumb and index finger and giving it a little counterclockwise twist as though it were the volume knob on a radio, he added, "Turn the volume down, Azzie."

"Hi, Hon," Karen called out from the living room, "It's OK. Deb's awake, and she's used to Asalee making noise. I don't think she likes it too quiet. I played the piano about a half an hour this afternoon before Asalee came in from school. I had Deb in her carrier on the floor by the piano bench. She just lay there and listened to me playing, seemed to like it, just like Asalee did when she was a baby. Of course, I played a lot while I was pregnant, so I guess she's used to it. Besides, I want to keep her awake during the day so she'll be sleepy at night. I don't want her in the mood to play at two o'clock in the morning like she was the night before last."

"So when's Wallace coming?" Mike asked as he put a hand towel over his shoulder and picked up his month-old daughter.

"Well, you know he wants to be in McMillan, Tennessee when Heather preaches at the first service of the new church, so he's planning to be in church with us here the Sunday before that. Said he'd probably get here on Wednesday, be with us in prayer meeting that night, stay with us until Monday morning."

"Sorry I missed getting to talk to him. It'll do me good to see him, to be reminded that not all deacon chairmen are like Franklin A. Brinkley..."

"Chairman of the Board of Deacons of Harrington Baptist Church," Karen added in unison with Mike.

"Yeah, Ol' Wallace has been gearing up for the big trip ever since he bought that new truck. The last Sunday we were at Clear Springs, he told me he was fixing to get a cap put on the truck so he'd have a place to put all his luggage. Not many people eighty-six years old could drive a big trip like Wallace is taking. Glad he's able to do it. Hope I'm doing that well when I'm his age."

"You and me both. Wallace said he's done great since the cataract surgery, said his vision's good with his glasses, and he doesn't have any trouble driving. He went to Mary Kate for a check-up, just to make sure everything was in order before he set out on the trip. She said he's in great shape for his age, said she sees plenty of people much younger who're nowhere near as healthy. She told him to use common sense and rest when he got tired. He told her he'd take his time, stop to look at anything and everything that looked interesting. Wallace told me the last time he drove more than a hundred miles was back in '76 when he and Estelle went out to California and back to celebrate their fiftieth wedding anniversary, only time Estelle ever traveled outside

Virginia and North Carolina. He's not going to try to cover more than two hundred miles a day, and he's only going to drive in the daytime. He figures it's the last big trip he'll ever make, and he's got a long list of people and places he wants to see, mostly former pastors, old railroad buddies, and places connected with Southern Railway."

"It'll be good for him, and if he waits any longer, he might not be able to do it," Mike opined. "Of course, the two girls are gonna worry themselves sick from now until he gets back, especially Evelyn. At least Wallace broke her from nagging him to give up his place and move into their guest house. I was right proud of ol' Wallace that time. Evelyn and Ruth worry themselves to death 'cause they can't get him to act old. Now, the two boys, Matt and Ralph, are probably saying, 'Be careful and have a good time, Daddy. Call us if you have any problems.' I'm glad Wallace is stubborn enough not to let Evelyn and Ruth talk him out of it."

∗   ∗   ∗   ∗   ∗   ∗   ∗   ∗   ∗   ∗   ∗   ∗

It never would have happened while Royce Green was living, given his peculiar interpretation of I Corinthians 11:22 which made him categorically opposed to eating at church. Not only that, it involved spending a little money. Royce didn't like it when the church had covered dish dinners, and he refused to participate. Certainly, he was turning over in his grave if he knew that people were spending money to eat a catered meal at Harrington Baptist Church. Nonetheless, the idea of a catered dinner on Wednesday nights had been well received, and most of the people seemed indifferent to Royce's inability to lie peacefully in his grave. Mike approached Brantley Jacobs at the Lonesome Whistle about the catering, and he quoted the church a very reasonable price. The Lonesome Whistle's reputation for good food and generous portions helped sell the proposal. The idea had solid backing from the leaders of the children's and youth activities, as well as from music director Eric Latham. It surprised Mike when the three remaining old guard deacons offered only token resistance before going along with it. The demise of Royce had brought about a balance of power between the old guard and the new people. The deacons recommended that the church do the Wednesday night suppers on a break-even basis up to and including the night of the October business meeting, at which time the church would decide whether to continue. Brantley agreed to the trial period, and the first Wednesday night supper was served on the nineteenth, a week after the church voted to proceed. Close to sixty people came that evening, twice the number that had been participating in Wednesday night activities. Brantley put on a good spread of food that seemed to please everyone, and about seventy were signed up for dinner on the twenty-sixth. Mike added one more adult to his family's reservation, due to Wallace's anticipated arrival that afternoon.

*   *   *   *   *   *   *   *   *   *   *   *

After Deborah Estelle's birth, Karen had thought again about the way Clear Springs fixed the nursery at the back of the auditorium for the convenience of nursing mothers. She mentioned the idea to Jenny Latham, mother of a two-month-old, and Lori Pettit, also the mother of a new baby, who had joined the church a few weeks earlier. Their idea did not involve messing with the existing nursery and incurring the wrath of That Woman. Russ Ayers at Clear Springs used to say that you can dynamite a stump or just plow around it. Karen, Jenny, and Lori chose to plow around it. Deborah Estelle was a month old, and the promise Karen made to That Woman the day of the trial sermon, that she would never mess with the nursery, remained unbroken. Jenny and Lori likewise did not intend to mess with the nursery while That Woman was living. The three young women staked their claim on a room that was unused, so they were not uprooting anyone. It was one of the rooms at the back of the auditorium that could be closed off with a folding door to make an extra classroom or opened up to make overflow auditorium space. There were two such rooms, neither in use. The threesome conspired to meet on a Monday morning, and Mike's role was to see that the front door of the auditorium was left unlocked for them. Laden with essential baby supplies, cleaning supplies, and lugging their infants in their carriers, they converged on the scene around nine that morning. They gave the room a top to bottom cleaning and aired it out to get rid of the musty smell unique to unused space in church buildings. The cold dirt-brown asphalt tile that had been there since the building was built was clearly unsuitable for a nursery. Jenny had already measured the space and talked to Marty Freeland, who contracted all of the floor covering work on the houses her father built. When Jenny told him that it was for the church and told him what she had in mind, Marty said he had plenty of remnants on hand that would be sufficient to do that space and make it really nice. He agreed to donate the carpet and install it, since the whole job would take no more than an hour with the room empty. Marty showed Jenny the remnants he had that were big enough to do the room and told her to take her pick. She chose a luxurious, expensive plush burgundy cut-pile Stainmaster carpet. Marty promised that he and one of his helpers would run by the church around noon on the appointed day, put down the tack strips, and install the carpet with top quality padding. Jenny asked him to figure the going price for the job and told him that, since her mother was the church treasurer, she would see that he got a receipt for tax purposes. By two o'clock in the afternoon, the room was clean, fresh-smelling, newly carpeted, and furnished. Church secretary Helen Walters arrived before Karen, Jenny, and Lori got there, and she left after they left. Helen was back in the church office the whole time, completely oblivious to the work being done in the room at the back of the auditorium.

Brenda Coleman called Elaine McWhorter when she caught wind of the project. Joyce Baxter had already promised to buy a rocking chair for the room, and Brenda and Elaine said they would each buy one as well. Elaine and Brenda donated the changing tables, playpens, and baby beds they had used with their children. Karen, Jenny, and Lori chipped in to buy draperies for the one window and a decorative border to go around the top of the wall. The project was done in five hours, and it didn't cost the church a dime. Mothers with infants now had a choice. They could leave their little ones in the nursery back in the catacombs with That Woman, or they could care for their own babies, even nurse them, in the room at the back of the auditorium without having to miss the worship service.

Karen mentioned the project ahead of time to Miss Addie, who said she thought it was best to go ahead and do it. "If you girls try to go through regular channels," she advised, "your babies'll all be grown up with children of their own and I'll be dead and buried before you get permission. Just do it, then confess and ask for forgiveness when you're finished. That's what I always did. My husband was a deacon for thirty years, and that's the advice he always gave me."

"It was a shame the way Royce got himself killed, but his days were numbered anyway," Miss Addie remarked solemnly as she inspected the new nursery on Sunday. "If he'd lived a few more weeks, he would've died over this. He'd've had a fit of apoplexy at the very idea something could be done in this church without going through nine committees, being recommended by the deacons, and voted on by the church. The way he died was better in the long run. It was quicker, he didn't suffer like he would have over this, and you don't have to feel responsible for killing him."

Franklin A. Brinkley, Chairman of the Board of Deacons of Harrington Baptist Church, and Doc Walters were livid when they discovered the new nursery at the back of the auditorium. Miss Addie, Karen, Jenny, and Lori were all in the room when Frank and Doc happened to look through the open door and make the discovery. Karen and Lori had their babies in their arms, and Miss Addie was holding Eric and Jenny's two-month-old son.

"What the...?! Who authorized this? We've already got a nursery! My mother-in-law's been in charge of the nursery for forty years. We don't need this!" Frank bellowed.

"Frank, Frank, you'll upset the babies," Jenny spoke soothingly as she put an arm around his shoulders and smiled sweetly, "It's all right. Miss Addie knows God, and she got permission for us."

"And it didn't cost the church a cent," Lori added. "Everything was either donated or we paid for it ourselves. We wanted to be able to nurse our babies and tend to them without having to miss out on the worship service."

"That's all well and good," Doc spoke sternly, "but things have to go through proper channels. You young ladies can't go taking it upon yourselves to do things. This may be a good idea, but it should've been presented to the nursery committee, the financial arrangements should have been presented to the finance committee..."

"And then been subject to review by the board of deacons before being presented to the church for a vote," Franklin A. Brinkley, Chairman of the Board of Deacons of Harrington Baptist Church, added in his most intimidating tone. "The deacon board is responsible for reviewing everything before it's brought to the church."

"We wanted it done before our children were grown." The icy sternness of Karen's voice more than matched that of Doc Walters and Frank Brinkley.

Speaking as one having authority and not as the Scribes and Pharisees, Miss Addie added, "Frank, Doc, y'all look here. If Moses had waited for everything to go through proper channels, the Israelites would still be in Egypt. I told these girls it's easier to get forgiveness than permission. And, as Jenny pointed out, I do know God. I assure you, He has no objection."

* * * * * * * * * * * *

Despite being far from any rails he had ever run on, Wallace followed the map and Karen's directions and arrived at 722 Alabama Avenue about 4:30 Wednesday afternoon. Karen called Mike at the church to tell him Wallace was at the house. After holding Deborah Estelle and pronouncing her to be the prettiest baby he had seen in years, Wallace settled in the recliner in the living room until time to go over to the church. His canine namesake curled up at his feet. Asalee perched herself on the arm of the chair and proceeded to tell her Papa Wallace all about her exciting life as a first grader in Mrs. Elrod's class at Harrington Elementary School. Wallace would have needed only to close his eyes to be sound asleep, but he kept them open and listened to Asalee telling him about her best friend in first grade, Rosa Stewart, and how she thought Garrett Weeks had a crush on her, even though she was not sure that she liked him all that much. She explained that Garrett was sort of cute, but she didn't think she was ready to have a boyfriend. Wallace reminded her that she was still young and suggested that she take her time in matters of the heart.

The meal at church started at 6:00. Mike was already there, and Karen arrived about fifteen minutes early with Asalee, Deborah, and Wallace the Deacon Chairman. Asalee took charge of introducing Wallace to everyone at church as "my Papa Wallace," with either Wallace, Karen, or Mike supplying the additional information that his last name was Coggins and he was from Clear Springs. Wallace also told everyone with whom he talked that the Westovers' dog was named after him. He was perfectly comfortable striking up conversations with total strangers, so he proceeded to make himself at home at Harrington Baptist Church. When it was time for the dinner to begin, Mike recognized Wallace and called on him to say grace over the meal.

After dinner, the children went to their classes and the adults and high school age young people remained in the fellowship hall for prayer meeting. When Mike invited people to share prayer concerns, Wallace stood up. "Brother Mike," he began, "I'd like to y'all to join with our church, Clear Springs Baptist Church, in praying about a couple of things. First, pray for our pastor, Sister Heather Simmons. The Lord's blessed our little church with some mighty fine pastors over the years. I've known all of 'em since I joined the church in 1926. Brother Mike had a good ministry with us, and we miss him, but we've got another good one in Sister Heather. She's the first woman pastor our church's had and the first woman to pastor a church in the Sanders County Association. We love 'er, and she's doin' a fine job, powerful preacher, especially considerin' she's just twenty-four years old. Last spring when we called her, we asked her home church over't McMillan, Tennessee to ordain her. The pastor over't McMillan said no woman'd ever be ordained at his church while he's pastor, so we ordained 'er at Clear Springs. Eighteen people from the church in McMillan come up to Clear Springs for the ordination, and they believe the Lord's leading 'em to start a new church, one that believes that God calls men and women alike to preach the Gospel. About a dozen more've joined with 'em, includin' four that're 'waitin' baptism. A week from Sunday, they're havin' their first Sunday morning service, and they asked Sister Heather to come down'n preach, help 'em constitute the new church. I've never had a chance to help constitute a new church. Seein' how I'm eighty-six years old, I don't expect I'll get another chance. Sister Heather's daddy owns the Ford place in McMillan, and him'n his wife are part of the new church, so he's making his showroom available to the church on Sundays. Saturday night, we're gonna move the cars out of the showroom and set up folding chairs. Providence Baptist Church'll have Sunday services at the Ford place until they can get their own building. Lord willin', I'll be in McMillan for that service. Sunday afternoon at 2:00, we're goin' down to the creek for Sister Heather to baptize the ones that're 'waitin' baptism. Y'all pray for our pastor, pray for me as we're travelin', pray for this new church gettin' started. Pray for wisdom for 'em as they start lookin' for a pastor, that they'll be led to the kind of pastor your church has and the kind we have. Then I'd ask you to pray for the annual meeting of our association, the Sanders County Association up'n Virginia. Our church was established in 1844, been in the Sanders County Association all that time, but I expect we'll be voted out this year on 'count of us callin' a woman pastor. They come close to throwin' us out two years ago 'cause we ordained two fine women as deacons. The annual meetin's comin' up October 11. The ones wantin' to throw us out are sayin' they got the votes to do it this time, and I don't doubt it. Seems to me if some of our brethren'd fight the devil half as hard as they fight other Christians, we'd run the devil out of Sanders County, but I don't reckon everybody sees it the way I do. Lord willin', I'll be back up there for the annual meeting. We may get throwed out, but we're not gonna get rid of the fine pastor we've got just because some of 'em don't like us having a woman pastor. Pray for the Lord's will to be done, pray for peace and good sense to prevail, and pray that the Lord'll help us move on whatever the association does. The Lord's been blessing Clear Springs unlike anything I've ever seen, and the church's doing the best it's done in the sixty-four years I've been there. The devil's riled up about that, and, to tell you the truth, some people, 'specially some preachers, are jealous. Just pray that our people won't get discouraged if the association throws us out. Pray for our pastor to keep on doin' the good work she's doin', keep on preachin' the gospel like she's been doin'. Pray for the church to keep a'goin' in the direction it's headed." Wallace's voice broke with emotion at several points as he shared his prayer concern, and tears trickled down his leathery cheeks.

"I'm thrilled to hear all the good reports of what the Lord's doing at Clear Springs and at the new church getting started in McMillan, Tennessee," Mike responded. "My family and I will always have a place in our hearts for the church I served while I was a student at Mid-Atlantic Seminary. I'll always be thankful that I was able to begin my ministry there. Before we move on to other prayer concerns, let's have a time of prayer for the concerns Wallace shared with us—the new church, Providence Baptist Church in McMillan, Tennessee having its first Sunday morning service and being formally constituted as a church; the four people following the Lord in baptism; for Wallace and Heather as they're traveling; for the Sanders County Association as they have their annual meeting, and for Clear Springs as they continue to minister in Jesus' name. I'm going to ask Deacon Brenda Coleman to lead us in prayer..."

*   *   *   *   *   *   *   *   *   *   *   *

"So how was the trip?" Mike asked Wallace when they settled down in the living room after sending Asalee to bed for the night.

"Good. That new truck is the most comfortable thing I ever drove. I've been stopping to walk around and stretch my legs pretty often. For the most part, I stayed off the interstates and drove the two-lanes through all the little towns. You see more that way. Seems like every out of town trip I've made in the last twenty years has been to attend the funeral of somebody I worked with on the railroad. Won't be long 'fore the ones who're old enough to remember me and still able to get around'll be makin' a trip up to Clear Springs. I've been retired twenty-one years, don't seem like it, but I have, so the ones old enough to remember me have done got a good bit of seniority. Not but four of us old head Danville division engineers left who were regular board engineers on steam. Horace Whaley's eighty-four, I'm eighty-six, John Ed McCormick—"Wild Onion" we called him, sometime while I'm here I'll tell you how he got that name—Onion's ninety-one, and the oldest'n, Emmett Carroll's ninety-seven. I'm in the best shape of any of 'em, only one that's not in a nursing home. I been to see 'em all. Poor ol' Whaley's got that Alzheimer's Disease, seemed to enjoy havin' company, but he never did comprehend who I was. Onion lost a leg a few years back and he's nearly blind on accoun-t'a sugar diabetes. Wild Onion and Emmett both recognized me, seemed right glad to see me. Now let me tell you, ol' Carroll was a real engineer, the best on our division, I'd say he was one'a the best on the whole Southern system, or any railroad for that mat-ter. I fired for 'im when I was a young man, later on double-headed drag freights with 'im. They let me check 'im out'a the nursing home up't Lynchburg. I took 'im out'n rode 'im around, went down'n watched some trains go by. 'Fore I took 'im back, I fed 'im some good barbeque at a little place we used to eat at all the time when we's workin'. Lil' hole in the wall place, don't look like much, but they're open twenty-four hours, serving the best breakfast and the best barbeque in Lynchburg. Seems like half the people eatin' there any time you go in're Southern Railway crews, or Norfolk Southern it is now. It's still that way, though there wad'n none of 'em who'd been around long enough to know me or Emmett. Emmett retired in '58, eleven years 'fore I did. Well, you know me, I never met a stranger. There was this big long table, coupl'a crews layin' over, just come in to eat dinner. I went over'n introduced myself'n ol' Emmett. The fellows all said to pull up a chair an' join 'em. They wad'n a one of 'em boys over forty years old, I got grandkids older'n some of 'em. They's plumb in awe gettin' to talk railroadin' with two ol' geezers that worked on steam engines. Ol' Carroll told 'em the newest diesels he ever run was them ol' E8 covered wagons. Most'a them boys never saw an E8. They sure did'n know nothing about workin' on steam. Them boys insisted on buyin' our dinners. It seemed to do Emmett a lot of good. About the only family he's got is one sister who's in bad shape, not able to come see 'im, and some nieces and nephews who never come around."

"Sounds like it was good for both of you," Karen observed.

"It was. First time I'd seen Emmett in about ten years, probably be the last time I get to see him, at least the last time in this life."

"Who else have you had a chance to see?" Mike asked.

"Well, you've probably heard me speak of Isaiah Mathis a time or two. He's been dead a long time, but I got to see his grandson. Isaiah was my fireman when I first made regular board engineer, taught me more about runnin' an engine than any other man on the railroad, as fine a Christian gentleman as I've ever known. Estelle and I named our oldest boy after 'im. Matt's full name's Isaiah Mathis Coggins. If Isaiah'd been a white man, he'd'a been a road foreman 'stead'a slingin' coal for greenhorn engineers. Isaiah died in 1949, dropped dead with a heart attack firin' for a wet-behind-the-ears extra board engineer on one'a them ol' K class Consolidateds on a work train. Some'a the K's had stokers, but the one on that work train was hand-fired. Back when we used 'em in heavy freight service, before we got the Ms4's, we'd have two firemen on the ones that did'n have stokers. Firin' for a good engineer on them engines was hard work. If an engineer did'n know what he's doin', or if he had a mean streak, he could work a fireman to death, an' that's exactly what happened. Poor ol' Isaiah died on the deck of that engine, sixty-four years old, doin' a job that'd white-eye a twenty year old kid that wad'n in good shape. The boy runnin' the engine was a know-it-all who wad'n about to let some colored fireman teach 'im a few things. That was unfortunate, not only because he killed the best fireman on the division, but also because he might'a made a halfway decent engineer, possibly a decent human bein', if he'd had the humility to let ol' Isaiah give him some pointers. He was still the sorriest engineer on the division when I retired in '69. Did'n none of the crews like to work with 'im. That boy's nose is still cocked to one side on account'a him laughin' an' callin' me a nigger lover 'cause I broke down an' cried when I heard Isaiah was dead. Anyway, Isaiah's grandson, Isaiah the third, just retired, division road foreman of engines, like his granddaddy ought to've been, down't Knoxville. I spent the night with him'n his wife night 'fore last. Last time I saw 'im was at his granddaddy's funeral. I stopped for gas in Knoxville, an' I was gonna eat supper an' get a motel for the night. Saw a pay phone at the service station'n remembered Isaiah's grandson was in Knoxville the last I heard, so I looked up the number'n called 'im. He remembered me, said he remembered when he's 'bout six years old, ridin' the cab of the engine, sittin' in my lap, watchin' his granddaddy fire the engine. We were on the Canfield local with the 1102, same engine ol' Steve Broady got killed on when he come off White Oak Mountain too fast to make the trestle over Stillhouse Hollow. Isaiah's grandson said he remembered when we got out of Danville, remembered it like it was yesterday, how I got up from the engineer's seat'n told his granddaddy to give me the coal scoop an' take over runnin' the engine. Isaiah's grandson asked me where I was in Knoxville. I described the place to 'im, he said I wad'n more'n a mile from his house. Told me 'is wife was cookin' dinner'n gave me directions. They treated me like family. We stayed up past midnight lookin' at my old railroad pictures I brought with me. I had a real good one Estelle took in 1934, when I had hair on my head, of me'n ol' Isaiah standin' on the pilot of the 1102 at Coley's Station. I'd treasured that picture for years, reckon it was my favorite of all my railroad pictures, but I told Isaiah's grandson I wanted him to have it. Big ol' tears welled up in his eyes. He said it was the best picture he'd ever seen of his granddaddy, tickled 'im to death that the picture showed us standing on the pilot of the 1102, since he remembered ridin' that engine when he's a kid. He remembered so many tales he'd heard his grandaddy tell about our escapades, and he looks so much like his granddaddy, got ways just like 'im, it was almost as good as gettin' to see ol' Isaiah again, which I expect to do 'fore too many more years."

"Carol told us you were going to visit some of the former pastors of Clear Springs," Karen interjected.

"I've seen two of 'em so far, three now that I'm here. Plan to see Logan Clark on my way back from over't McMillan next week. Spent Saturday night and went to church on Sunday with Steve Kane up'n North Carolina. He was at Clear Springs back in the mid-sixties, baptized Carol, Linda, and Mary Kate, baptized three of my grandchildren. He's goin' on sixteen years where he is now, church just built a new sanctuary, seems to be doing real good. I sure am glad I got to see Dennis Palmer. He was at Clear Springs in the early '70's. Breaks my heart to see what he's been through. I wad'n brought up to go to church, had'n never been to church much 'fore I started courtin' Estelle, but I was taught to respect the man of God as far back as I can remember. Some folks brought up in the church never was taught that. Brother Dennis said he witnessed behavior in church business meetin's that would'n be tolerated in a decent bar. Some of these churches can be downright mean. I don't know all of what went wrong, I just listened to what he felt like telling me, but Brother Dennis was a fine pastor, good preacher, did a good job at Clear Springs, an' I had'n seen anything to make me think less of 'im. Far's I'm concerned, he's the same man he was when he was our pastor. Church he was at over near Raleigh ate 'im alive three years ago, an' he had'n been able to get a church since. On top of that, his wife left 'im about a year after the church chewed 'im up. I never knew her. Brother Dennis was still single when he was at Clear Springs, but I know you can't make somebody stay if they don't want to. That's what I told Carol Richardson when Bill left her. Brother Dennis is working at construction, out of the ministry, told me he had'n been to church in about a year. I stayed the night with 'im, slept on 'is couch. Livin' by hisself, he had'n been eatin' right, so I took 'im out to supper, an' we hit the breakfast bar at Shoney's the next mornin' as I was on my way out of town an' he was goin' to work. I talked to him about takin' off'n comin' up to see me, spend a week or two with me, when he can get some vacation time. I never seen a man look so tired. I don't mean just tired in body. Eatin' a good supper, soakin' in a tub of warm water, gettin' a good night's sleep'll restore a tired body. He needs to do that more'n he's been doin', but his soul's tired, too. I'm hopin' he'll take some time off, come up to Clear Springs for a week or two, rest his soul amongst people who care about 'im an' respect 'im as a man of God, people who'll still call 'im 'Preacher' an' do more'n just talk about grace. Brother Dennis broke down an' cried talkin' to me, tellin' me how much it meant to 'im for me to come see 'im'n how not one of the pastors in the association where he pastored six years had called on 'im for pulpit supply or invited 'im for a cup'a coffee or nothin'."

"I'm glad you were able to make contact with him, and it sounds like your visit was good for him," Mike commented. "I hope he takes you up on that offer to spend some time with you up at Clear Springs."

"I'm just an old man who's never belonged to any church other'n Clear Springs. It's hard for me to understand how some of these churches act, 'cause I'm used to how we do things at Clear Springs. Is this church here treatin' y'all right?"

"It's different," Mike responded thoughfully. "The expectations the church has of its pastor are naturally different when the pastor lives around the corner from the church and serves the church on a full-time basis. For instance, Wallace, you're perfectly comfortable visiting someone in the hospital and praying with them before they go into surgery, you can do that as well as most pastors, better than some, because the deacons at Clear Springs've always done a lot of the day-to-day pastoral ministry. They've had to, because the pastor was thirty miles away at the seminary and couldn't always take off work or classes."

"I've always been glad to help our pastors out like that. I've been blessed with mighty good health since I retired. Aside from a little hearing loss, don't know any old engineers that don't have some hearing loss, and bein' a little stiff when I first get up of a mornin', I'm in pretty good shape for a man eighty-six years old. If I'd'a ever sat down an' started actin' old, I would'n a' lasted no time. Gettin' to help our pastors from time to time's been the best thing about bein' retired. I'll do what I do long's I'm able, I'd do it if our pastor was full time'n livin' next door to the church. I don't care if the pastor is full-time, it's not right for the church to sit down'n expect the pastor to do everything. I can see where a full-time church would be different in a lot of ways, and I know there's no two churches alike, but you never did answer my question. Is the church treatin' you'n your family right?"

"Well, this church has chewed up some preachers, but so far they're treating us well. The salary package is OK for the size of the church, and we've got some fine people working with us. You met some of them tonight. We've got some who are a pain in the butt, like the woman who runs the nursery and lives across the street from us, we lovingly refer to her as That Woman. Then there's Franklin A. Brinkley, Chairman of the Board of Deacons of Harrington Baptist Church..."

"I met 'im tonight. Seems like an arrogant so-and-so. I'd say he missed 'is callin', ought to've been a general superintendent on the railroad. When he told me he was chairman of the board of deacons, I told 'im we wad'n big enough to have a board at Clear Springs, we just have deacons, an' the deacons're more concerned with tryin' to help our pastor than we are with tryin' to run the church."

"We do have two competing ideas about what deacons are supposed to do. Frank and a couple more, Jack Miller and Doc Walters, want to be a board that runs the church. All they want to do is be my boss, second-guess the work of the committees, keep a tight reign on everything, and make it hard on anybody who wants to do anything creative or different. We had another one like that, Royce Green, who died a few weeks ago, got killed in a car wreck. We've got three younger deacons who see it the way you do. With deacon rotation and filling Royce's unexpired term, we'll have a slight majority, four to three, who see their role as primarily one of ministry. The guys who see it as a position of power will be in the minority. If we can manage to elect somebody other than Frank as chairman next month, that'll be real progress."

"Speaking of electin' a deacon chairman," Wallace injected, "I decided to step down as chairman the end of this month. I'll still serve as a deacon long's I'm able, but it's time for somebody else to be chairman. I told 'em at the August deacons meeting that they'd need to be thinking about a new chairman. This month, we elected Carol chairman starting the first of October. She's got a lot more education that I do, an' she's a mighty good deacon. I've been a deacon since 1938, and she's one of the best I ever worked with. She'll make a good chairman, and the change'll be easier than if I put it off 'till I die at the throttle."

"You were a very good chairman," Karen commented. "A lot better than the one we've got, but there's a lot of wisdom in what you did, stepping aside so you can give your full support to Carol and help her get off to a good start, help the church get used to her being chairman. She'll do well. We just elected the first woman deacon in the history of this church. Her husband's already a deacon, one of the good ones."

"Is she the one who led the prayer time tonight?" Wallace asked.

"Right. Brenda Coleman. She and Ted were both ordained at the church they belonged to in Macon before they moved here. We didn't know she was a deacon until Carol and her kids came down in July and Mike had Carol help with the communion service."

"Yeah," Mike added, "when Ted and Brenda joined here, my predecessor asked them not to say anything about Brenda being ordained because he didn't think the church was ready to deal with that."

"Oh Good Lord!" Wallace exclaimed. "I get so fed up with that foolishness about people not being ready for this or that."

"You and Miss Addie," Karen interjected. "Miss Addie Jane Aldridge, retired teacher, ninety-three years old, she's the most progressive-thinking person in this church. I'll introduce you to her Sunday. Miss Addie says if Moses had waited until everybody was ready, the Israelites would still be in Egypt."

"She's got that right. So how'd you get 'em to go for a woman deacon?"

"Well," Mike began, "Brenda called me on Sunday afternoon after Carol helped serve communion to tell me how much the service had meant to her, and she told me that she was also an ordained deacon. It's a funny thing. The bylaws of this church only allow for men to be ordained, but there's nothing to prohibit a woman ordained at another church from serving. As part of the deacon election process, we're required to publish in the newsletter a list of all the ordained deacons who are members of the church, along with a list of all the men who are eligible to be ordained…"

"So," Wallace surmised, "you put her on the list, and the church elected her. If she had'n already been ordained, you couldn't've ordained 'er, but since somebody else ordained 'er, there's nothin' to keep 'er from servin'?"

"Exactly."

"Well, as your oldest daughter would say, that's cool." Then, with his voice taking a more serious tone, Wallace asked, "Think you'll get any flack in the association on account of having a woman deacon?"

"I expect we might. I know our director of missions is not real happy with me. Sounds like Clear Springs is taking some heat because of calling Heather."

"We are. We'll probably get turned out of the association this time. Ol' Billy Fite over't True Gospel's leadin' the charge, as you might expect. I look for 'em to go after First Baptist in Ledford while they're at it. They ordained some women deacons and ordained the woman who's minister of education over there after we ordained Carol and Linda at Clear Springs. Would'n surprise me if they went after Bolton's Chapel, too."

"Why's that? What'd ol' Greg Nash do to get on the wrong side of Brother Billy?"

"Invited our pastor to preach a revival back in August."

"I'm proud of him."

"And, as usual, ol' Lester Halstead's eggin' Billy Fite on. I guess Carol told you that Wanda left Lester soon's their last child left home, moved her membership back to Clear Springs, told us if it'd been up to her she never would've left. He's sore 'cause 'is wife got tired a' bein' treated worse'n a dog and left 'im, and he's got to lash out at somebody. We called for Wanda's letter when she come back to Clear Springs. Sister Heather got a red hot letter from Brother Billy sayin' Wanda wad'n entitled to a letter in good standin' cause she walked out on her husband an' said in any case his church would'n grant a letter to a church with a woman pastor an' women deacons. Sister Heather asked the deacons what we thought the church oughta do. Linda suggested she make a paper airplane outta Brother Billy's letter'n sail it into the trash can. The church ignored Brother Billy's letter'n took Wanda back on statement. We've known 'er longer'n Brother Billy has an' we always thought well of 'er. I expect Brother Billy'll bring it up at the association that we took one'a his members on statement after his church refused to grant a letter."

"Sounds like ol' Billy Fite. I always thought that turkey's last name suited him."

"Had'n never thought about that, but you got a point. One more big change we're gettin' ready to make at Clear Springs..."

"What's that?" Karen asked.

"Lord's been blessin' our church, we're seein' some growth. The Rollins' farm just down the road from the church has been sold, big subdivision goin' in there. We need a full-time pastor. Sister Heather graduates this spring, an' there's not much else place for her to go if she wants to be a pastor. The way the seminary's goin', they're attractin' a different breed of preachers, we're not gonna be able to count on findin' good student pastors any more. We voted to put Sister Heather on the field full-time soon's she graduates. Now, I want to live in the house Estelle and I shared 'til the Lord calls me home, but that's not gonna be too awful far away. I've told you how Estelle comes to see me in my dreams, an' I talked to her'n told 'er what I had in mind. I think she'd be right pleased with what I did. I went'n deeded mine'n Estelle's house over to the church on the condition I can live in it 'til I die. Soon's the Lord calls me home, Clear Springs has got a pretty good ol' house a quarter mile from the church for a parsonage. If I'm still around when Sister Heather graduates and goes full-time, we'll help 'er get an apartment in Ledford. Soon as the Lord takes me home, she can move into mine'n Estelle's house. Been a lot of love and happiness in that ol' house, an' I gave it to the church with the prayer that it always would be that way."

20

Over supper Friday night, Wallace kept his promise to tell how engineer John Ed McCormick acquired the nickname of "Wild Onion." Wild Onion, Wallace said, was noted for his love of fast women, fast engines, and good whiskey. That, and he was famous all along the line from Lynchburg to Danville for his artistry with the whistle cord on a steam engine. One could have started a fight in the call room over who was the best engineer on the division, but all agreed that Onion was the most accomplished whistle-cord virtuoso. He could sign his name with the whistle cord, quilling a four-note Nathan chime whistle so pretty it would bring tears to your eyes. It was back during World War II, Wallace related, when Southern Railway contracted to train locomotive engineers for the Army. "My nephew Forrest Coggins was Onion's fireman at the time, he's the one that told me all about this. They gave ol' Onion a twenty-two year old private first class who'd worked a coupla' months around the Illinois Central roundhouse in Paducah 'fore he's drafted, told 'im to teach the kid how to run an engine. Onion wad'n real happy with that assignment, but he mellowed when he found out the boy's father was a machinist in the Illinois Central back shops. It turned out the kid already knew a good bit about the workings of a steam engine, and he was a fast learner. Onion grudgingly took a liking to him'n proceeded to impart his considerable wisdom about railroad operations in general and running a steam engine in particular. Onion told ol' man Henry Butler, our road foreman, 'Cap, I hate to admit it, but they's more'n journal packin' 'tween that boy's ears. I got hopes for 'im.' Coming from Wild Onion, that was quite a compliment. Toward the end of the boy's training, he said something to Onion about how pretty the whistles sounded on them ol' Ms4's, that low, mournful sound, wish you kids could've heard 'em. The boy said he'd give anything to be able to quill one'a them four-note Nathans the way Onion could. Ol' Wild Onion fell headlong for the flattery, told the boy to show up for the next day's run with a fifth of Jack Daniels, and he'd teach him to be a Southern Railway whistle cord virtuoso. The kid showed up the next day with a fifth of Jack Daniels, and Onion kept his word as they rolled south out of Lynchburg on a redball freight with the 4835. Onion was tickled to death to get that engine, 'cause it had the sweetest whistle of any Ms4 on our division. By the time they got to Ledford, the kid was fully in charge of the engine and Onion was gettin' into the Jack Daniels. Forrest had a good hot fire, and the boy runnin' the engine had 'is cutoff set just right. Ol' Onion just settled down'n enjoyed the ride. The whip-crackin' of that Ms4's exhaust was music to his ears. He gave the kid a few quick pointers on how to quill a whistle. Wad'n long 'fore the boy had the hang of it. He blew the long-long-short-long, long-long-short-loonnnggg as they approached the Church Street crossing in Ledford, bein' real careful to hold the final note 'til the pilot of the engine's on the crossing, just like the rule book says. He did some fancy quilling on the approach signal for the Ledford depot, made a smooth stop, spotted the tender under the spout of the water tank like he'd been doin' it forty years. After they took water, they proceeded to that long siding south of Ledford. They had to wait for two northbound trains to meet them before they proceeded to Danville, so they had some time to kill. Forrest got off the engine and checked the lubricators. The kid stayed on the engine to keep an eye on the pressure gauge and sight glass. Ol' McCormick got to thinkin' somebody might smell the alcohol on his breath when they got to Danville. He spotted some wild onions growing near the siding, pulled up a mess of 'em. He munched them wild onions the rest of the way to Danville, hopin' they'd be strong enough to cover the smell of Jack Daniels. When they got to Danville'n cut off from the train, ol' man Butler, the road foreman, mounted the engine. That engine'd just been overhauled, and he wanted to know how it ran. Onion kept on braggin' about how good the engine steamed'n how good 'er stack talk sounded. Ol' man Butler knowed it wad'n natural for John Ed McCormick to be in that good'a mood, no matter how good the engine ran, just wad'n his nature, so he got close enough to get a whiff of his breath. Ol' Butler just looked at 'im, shook his head, and told 'im, 'John Ed, if it's all the same to you, I'd rather smell good whiskey than wild onions.' Ol' McCormick's been stuck with the nickname of Wild Onion ever since. He had a sense of humor about it, though. The rest of the time we had steam engines, before he started out on a run, he'd tie a wild onion to the number plate under the headlight."

＊　＊　＊　＊　＊　＊　＊　＊　＊　＊　＊　＊

After supper, when Asalee was out in the back yard with Wallace the Dog, Wallace asked Mike to be more specific about what he had said Wednesday night about Harrington chewing up some pastors. Mike told him about the events leading up to the forced resignation of Franklin Seals a week after his daughter was killed. After Asalee was in bed for the night, Mike brought out the big brown envelope of articles from the *Harrington Courier*. Wallace put on his bifocals, spread the articles out in chronological order, and read them all. Karen told him that Deborah Estelle's first name was after Debbie Seals, and Mike told him that Debbie's funeral was at Greater New Hope because some of the people at Harrington Baptist objected to a black minister having part in the service.

Wallace said that he wanted to see the graves of Debbie and Franklin Seals, and Mike promised to take him the next morning after breakfast. "There's some people in this town, prob'ly in your church, who know more'n they're tellin'," Wallace opined. "It's a strange feelin' to be talkin' 'bout this, sittin' in the room where the poor girl died. Can't imagine anything that'd be harder than buryin' one'a your children. I thank the Lord I never had to do that. I remember when Kimberly Ethridge and Jimmy Echols got killed the first year y'all were at Clear Springs. That was the hardest thing our church ever went through, havin' to bury two of our young people. Of course, you know Kimberly was Estelle's great-niece, but it felt like they's closer kin than that. I felt like I'd lost two of my grandkids. I'd known 'em since they's babies. Mark and Teresa, Jim and Becky, they're still havin' a hard time, expect they always will. I see 'em walkin' out'n the cemetery ever' Sunday between Sunday School an' preachin'. Seems like havin' one shot'n killed on purpose'd be worse'n havin' one killed in an accident. Tommy Ayers, bless 'is heart, did'n have no business drivin' drunk, but he did'n kill on purpose. Tommy's a tenderhearted boy, tore 'im up when he sobered up enough to understand he'd killed two kids he'd known since they's babies. Now whoever it was that fired the shot that killed the Seals girl, maybe they wad'n aimin' to kill, but it looks like they did'n care if they did. They's willin' to do whatever it took to run Brother Seals out a' town. I never did know Brother Seals an' 'is wife, but my heart goes out to 'em. I see in his obituary that he went to Mid-Atlantic Seminary. As soon's I get home, I'll call my son-in-law, see if he remembers 'im. Gordon was a student there in the late forties, right after the war, an' he started teachin' in '51, so they prob'ly met somewhere along the way. Ol' Gordon's got a good recall on names. He amazes me, recalls somethin' about ever'body he ever taught. He's amazed at how I recall just about ever'body I ever worked with on the railroad. It sounds like the Seals girl was a fine young lady. She sure did'n deserve to die like she did. Even if Brother Seals'd been livin' in open sin an' needin' to step down as pastor, which I don't think he was, there ought to'a been a little compassion for the man'n 'is wife right after they buried their daughter. I don't see how men that're s'posed to be Christians'n spiritual leaders in the church could be party to such goin's on. Most men that had'n never heard of Jesus would'a had more decency than that. By law, I suppose they wad'n but one killin', but far's God's concerned, they was two. This church killed Brother Seals as sure as if they put a gun to 'is head'n pulled the trigger. The ones that run Brother Seals off've got as much blood on their hands as whoever it was that shot 'is daughter. Any of 'em still around?"

"Most of 'em," Mike replied. "There was one, Chester Aldridge, Miss Addie's husband, who wouldn't knuckle under. He had a heart attack and died a few days before Debbie was killed. Three of them are dead. The other four are still around. Jack Miller and Doc Walters are active deacons. Jack rotates off the end of this month, and Doc has another year. We did have another one serving actively when we came here. Royce Green got killed in an accident a few weeks ago. Rudy Blevins and Roland Millican are not active deacons, but they're still in the church. Back in August when we did deacon nominations, Rudy and Roland got a fair number of votes, though I'm thankful to say not enough to elect them. Rudy was on the pulpit committee, so was Jack Miller's wife Freida."

"Did I meet any of them Wednesday night?"

"I'm trying to think who all was there," Karen answered. "I know Jack and Rudy were there. Honey, do you remember whether Doc Walters was there?"

"He was. He was squirming when Wallace asked us to pray for Heather, Clear Springs, the new church, and the situation in the Sanders County Association, like he didn't know if we ought to pray for a church with a woman preacher or not. He gave me a dirty look when I called on *Deacon* Brenda Coleman to lead the prayer time. You probably met him, and I know you met Jack and Rudy. Jack's run a body shop here in Harrington for years. Rudy coached football at Harrington High School before he moved up to principal. Rudy's been retired four or five years. Both of them, Jack and Rudy, are friendly, outgoing guys, wouldn't let a visitor leave the church without speaking to them. Roland wasn't there. He doesn't come on Wednesday nights unless it's business meeting. He has to come'n question everything in the treasurer's report and the minutes of the last business meeting. I can't say I've found much to like about Roland. He has no mind or convictions of his own. His wife's a domineering woman, got ol' Roland trained to jump when she says 'jump.' I started to say, 'poor ol' Roland,' but Karen brought up a good point about that, said he picked her out, so not to feel too sorry for him. Roland's so cowed down to her, all he needs is a dog collar and a leash."

"That's somethin' I never did like to see," Wallace commented, "a man cowed down to 'is wife or a woman cowed down to 'er husband, either one. Don't know which is worse, 'bout the same, I guess. That's why Lester Halstead never was asked to be a deacon when he was at Clear Springs, the way he treated 'is wife and children. I don't blame Wanda for leavin' 'im, don't see how she stood it long as she did. Wanda's got 'er shortcomin's like the rest of us, I 'spose, but she's a better woman than Lester ever gave 'er credit for bein', got a lot more sense than Lester ever give 'er credit for. Ol' Lester was a fool, not treatin' 'er better'n he did. He'd'a made things better for 'isself if he had. We sure are blessed to have Wanda back at Clear Springs, and she seems glad to be back. I'd known 'er twenty-five years, did'n even know she could play the guitar. She's good at it. Since she left Lester'n come back to Clear Springs, she's been playin' 'er guitar'n singin' with the children at church. It seems to be good for her, an' the kids love 'er to death. All the kids brighten up when she's around, you'll see a dozen kids tryin' to hug 'er 'fore she can get both feet through the door. Anyway, talkin' about men bein' cowed down to their wives, or women cowed down to their husbands, that's somethin' I always hated to see. I'm not sayin' Estelle'n I did ever'thing right, but we had a mighty good marriage for nigh on sixty-four years, and they's nobody but the Good Lord knows how much I miss 'er. Estelle'n I respected each other'n trusted each other, never was any reason for me not to trust her or for her not to trust me, always gave each other credit for havin' good sense. Wad'n neither one of us boss over the other'n, and wad'n neither one of us afraid a' the other'n. I don't know how come anybody'd marry somebody they did'n respect an' trust, or why anybody'd marry somebody they did'n think had good sense. I know some people do, but it never made any sense to me."

"Me either," Mike concurred. "Anyway, Jack and Rudy are as nice a fellows as you'd ever want to meet. Ol' Royce Green, the one that got killed here while back, was the same way. Doc's not as friendly and outgoing as Jack and Rudy, but he's decent and human most of the time. By all accounts, he's a good dentist, and his patients like him. Jack, Rudy, and Doc're not stuffy and arrogant like Franklin A. Brinkley, Chairman of the Board of Deacons of Harrington Baptist Church. Frank was ordained in '68, so he wasn't a deacon at the time everything went down with Franklin Seals."

"Yeah," Karen concurred, "it'd be easier to understand if the people who did the meanness seemed like mean, hateful people, but for the most part they don't. At least Jack, Rudy, and Doc don't seem like that kind of people, and Royce didn't either. Now, I think Geneva Millican would have no problem at all being that mean and heartless, and Roland's trained to follow orders. The rest of them, though, wouldn't be that mean individually, but get them together...well, you can see for yourself what went down."

"Let me tell you about the kind of meanness nice people can do," Wallace began. "I was about seven or eight years old, so it would've been 1911 or 1912." The tone of his voice, the distant look in his eyes, and the tears glistening on his lower eyelids indicated that he was reliving a terrifying memory that was seared into the very tissues of his brain. "I was just a little fellow, but I remember like it was last night. There was a lynchin' close to where we lived, about a mile from the Southern Railway yard in Riverton. Some white woman said a colored man raped 'er. I don't know if she was tellin' the truth, but the one the Ku Klux rounded up sure did'n do it. Daddy was out on a run when they lynched the young man, did'n find out about it 'til he come in from 'is run the next mornin' about sunup. The one they lynched wad'n more'n eighteen or nineteen years old, worked for the railroad at the coal chute in Riverton yard. Daddy said if he'd been arrested 'n tried in reg'lar court, he'd'a gone'n testified he saw 'im at work at the time the woman was 'sposed to been raped. Daddy's fireman could'a testified too, so could 'is conductor, cause they all talked to 'im when they stopped at the coal chute. The young man couldn'a raped a woman on the other side'a town at the same time he was coalin' up the tender of Daddy's engine. Nobody tried to get at the truth, an' nobody got a chance to testify in the young man's defense. Now, if you could'a got some a' them idiots off by themselves, if you could'a got twelve of 'em cooled down, sobered up'n impaneled on a jury, you might'a convinced 'em the young man was innocent, what with three sober, reliable white men testifyin' they saw 'im at work on the other side'a town at the time the woman's s'posed to've been raped. The law did'n do nothin', did'n show up 'til it was all over 'cept for cuttin' the boy down, and of course they did'n arrest nobody. Most of 'em that carried out the lynchin' was solid family men, nice as anybody you'd want to meet 'n talk to, a lot of 'em was in church the next Sunday, some of 'em leaders in the church. I don't understand it any better now that I'm eighty-six than I did when I's seven or eight, but I know seemin'ly decent people, even Christian people, can get caught up'n a frenzy'n, take leave of all sense an' reason, do all kinds of evil, then go right back to bein' nice people like nothin' ever happened. They wad'n much difference 'tween the way that young man got lynched and the way Brother Seals got run off from this church."

"From what I've been able to piece together, I think you're right," Mike concurred. "The church went in hock up to their eyeballs to build the building where we are now, and they needed to sell the old building and put all the money they could get out of it toward the note on the new building. Greater New Hope came up with the money to buy it cash on the barrelhead, and the church voted by an eight-vote margin to sell it to them. Harrington Baptist Church would've gone under financially if Greater New Hope hadn't bought their old building. Greater New Hope saved their hides, but instead of being thankful like they ought to've been, a lot of the people, even some who voted in favor of the sale, resented selling their old building to a black church."

"They needed to lynch somebody, and Franklin Seals was the most likely candidate," Karen added. "It's like they felt violated or something, like a white woman being raped by a black man, their sacred old building being taken over by black folks."

"That's exactly what it was," Wallace observed. "That old buildin' was the white woman who was supposedly raped, and Brother Seals became the nigger that had to be lynched on account of it. Same thing. Tryin' to talk sense with the people who ran Franklin Seals off would'a been like tryin' to talk to that lynch mob."

"You're right," Mike concurred. "Before Debbie was killed, and before the deacons got around to calling for his resignation, a lot of pressure was put on Brother Seals. They tried to starve him out. Some people started holding back their offerings or designating everything to the building fund so the church couldn't pay his salary. It wasn't just church people in on it, either. As you can see, the Harrington paper attacked him in editorials. The editor of the paper belonged to the Methodist church. He was close friends with Walter Holliday, a man in Harrington Baptist who was in the real estate business. Both of them were down on Brother Seals because he refused to come and pray over a meeting of the White Citizens Council, refused to have anything to do with it. Mrs. Seals was fired from her job at the bank for no apparent reason after she'd worked there five years. Neither of them had ever had a traffic ticket, all of a sudden it seemed like the Harrington Police had nothing else to do but lay in wait for them every time they got behind the steering wheel."

"Some of the ones who were already set to run Brother Seals off even used his daughter's death against him," Karen added. "I guess you read in Debbie's obituary that Dr. Martin Luther King had a part in her funeral…"

"Mmmhmm," Wallace acknowledged. "Were him'n Brother Seals friends?"

"No," Mike explained, "the first time Brother Seals met Dr. King was the night Debbie lay in state at the funeral home. Dr. and Mrs. King heard about it on the news the night Debbie was killed, and the news report said the killing was apparently related to Brother Seals' role in selling the building to the black church. Even though they didn't know the family, Dr. and Mrs. King came down to pay their respects. Nobody knew that they were coming until they walked into the funeral home. Eleanor Basden, the Methodist pastor, told me that she and her husband were at the funeral home when they came in. Dr. King came up to them and introduced himself and his wife. He asked Eleanor and Ben to take them over and introduce them to the Seals family. It meant so much to Brother Seals and his wife that they cared enough to come, and they asked Dr. King to say a few words at the funeral."

"Let me guess," Wallace responded. "The ones set on running Brother Seals off didn't have the decency to go to the funeral, but they were the experts on what Dr. King said, and they spread it all over town that Brother Seals brought Dr. King in to stir up trouble, acted just like that lynchin' party…"

"You got it," Mike answered. "The ones who were bent on runnin' Brother Seals off made an issue out of them having Debbie's funeral at a black church, asking Dr. King to have a part in the service, and burying Debbie in the black cemetery. They were gearing up to run him off anyway, but they turned Debbie's funeral into an excuse to do it sooner rather than later."

"And the truth did'n make any more difference than it did with the folks who lynched the young man in Riverton," Wallace surmised. "And they never charged anybody with killin' Debbie Seals?"

"Never did," Mike confirmed.

"They never tried to find out who killed her," Karen added. "It smells like a coverup to me. The law knew who did it or they could've found out with very little effort. There was a good witness, the pastor at the Church of God, who saw the person who fired the shot pulling the rifle back inside the car and saw the car speeding away. He tried to block them with his car, but they ran up on the sidewalk, hit his car and spun it around in the road, and kept on going. He told the police what he saw, but that was apparently the end of it."

"Is the Church of God preacher that saw it still here in Harrington?" Wallace asked.

"No," Mike responded, "he moved to another pastorate a year or so later. I don't know where he is now or, for that matter, whether he's still living. It's been twenty-six years, so a lot of people have died and took what they knew to the grave with them."

"Maybe so," Wallace acknowledged, "but twenty-six years is not a long time to a man who's lived eighty-six years and remembers stuff that happened sixty and seventy years ago like it was yesterday. I remember the flu epidemic of 1918. I remember Armistice Day at the end of World War One. My oldest brother was in the war. I remember when he shipped out an' when he come home. I told you about that lynchin' back around 1911 or '12. Like I told Asalee, I remember when they first put the river through Riverton, so don't tell me nobody's left that remembers somethin' that happened in 1964. I don't doubt that a lot of people've died since then, but they's a lot left that remember a whole lot more'n they're tellin'. There's still some men walkin' round this town'n actin' respectable that need to be held accountable for what they did. They'll give account when they come before God if they don't give account down here. Jesus said, *there is nothing covered that will not be revealed, and nothing hid that will not be known.* And then ol' Paul says over there in Romans that *God will judge the secrets of men through Christ Jesus.* Folks that think they can keep secrets and get by with stuff must not read the same Bible I read. They're like ol' John Ed McCormick, thinkin' he could cover up the smell'a Jack Daniels by eatin' wild onions. They's not enough wild onions in all creation to keep God from smellin' the truth. I recall a song we used to sing at church years ago, can't tell you how long it's been since I heard it, been thinkin' about it ever since you told me about the killin' of Debbie Seals. It says,

There's a God who's standing at heaven's door,
He's looking this universe o'er
And He sees each mortal with a searching eye,
You can't do wrong and get by.
You can't do wrong and get by, no matter how hard you may try,
Nothing hidden can be, ev'rything He doth see,
You can't do wrong and get by.

"Now if that ol' song's right, and I believe it is, they's one witness them boys wad'n countin' on. I know it'll be laid out'n the open when they come before God, but I believe it'll come out before then. It needs to be brought out'n the open, Brother Mike. The power'n blessin' of God's not gonna be on Harrington Baptist Church as long as people're keepin' dirty secrets'n coverin' up evil. Ol' David says over'n Psalms, *if I regard iniquity in my heart, Thou wilt not hear me.* People can't go on coverin' up a cold-blooded murder'n expect God to go on blessin' like nothin's a' matter. I'm not sayin' ever'body that knows the truth of the matter's in your church, Brother Mike, but I'd say they's some in the church who know a lot more'n they're tellin'. I don't know any of the answers myself. I'm just an old man, an' I prob'ly won't be around no whole lot longer, but I do know how to pray. You know ol' James says *the effectual fervent prayer of a righteous man availeth much.* I'm gonna pray for the Lord to pull the covers off'a this whole ugly mess'n bring it all to light." With a note of earnestness, Wallace added, "If I don't have but one more prayer answered 'fore the Lord calls me home, let that be it."

*   *   *   *   *   *   *   *   *   *   *

Wallace got up before five o'clock Monday morning to pack up his things in preparation for resuming his trip. By the time Deborah Estelle woke up and Karen got up to tend to her, Wallace had a pot of coffee made. He was sitting at the table, reading his Bible and drinking his second cup when Mike and Asalee came into the kitchen. Since finishing seminary and moving to Harrington, Mike had pretty much taken over as the breakfast cook in the Westover household. Asalee curled up in Wallace's lap while her father cooked breakfast.

"So where're you going to try to get to today, Wallace?" Mike asked.

"Gonna head straight up US 27 as far as Chattanooga. Not gonna get this close'n not go by Tennessee Valley Railroad Museum. They got the 630 up there, that's the last steam engine I ever run. One a' them K class Consolidateds like we had a bunch of. I got to run 'er some on steam excursions 'fore I retired. Whenever I had a crack at one of the steam excursions, I exercised my seniority. My seniority date's October 2, 1922, so I usually got what I wanted. By the time I retired, wad'n many men left that had experience on steam. One time we doubleheaded the 630 and the 4501, and I run the 630 that trip. Long train, nineteen cars, longest passenger consist I ever handled, heavy train. There's a rulin' grade of 'bout three percent comin' up through that cut north a' Ledford, 'tween Ledford'n Coley's Station. It started rainin' 'bout the time we got to Ledford. That's a mean grade any-way'n the engines were havin' to work harder on account'a the wet rails. Horace Whaley was runnin' the 4501. Both of us had the valve gear down in the last notch, throttle wide open, two men firin'. No tellin' how much sand we put down 'fore we got the train up onto the easy spot below Coley's Station. So, I want to kill some time at the railroad museum, climb up'n sit on the engi-neer's seat one more time while I can still mount an engine. Then, I mean to see Rock City and Ruby Falls 'fore the Lord calls me home. For the last sixty years, I've been seein' barns'n birdhouses an' I don' know what all else with 'See Rock City' or 'See Ruby

Falls' painted on 'em. I'm eighty-six years old, so I figure if I'm gonna see Rock City and Ruby Falls, I better do it this trip."

*   *   *   *   *   *   *   *   *   *   *   *

"Pastor, the phone's for you. It's Bob McKnight," Helen Walters called out from her office.

"Hey, Bob," Mike answered the phone in his office. "How're things going over at Lakeside? Haven't had a chance to talk with you in a while."

"The church is doing well. Ol' Roy Gilbert did a good job there, most of the people were sorry to see him go, of course there were a few that didn't like him, but you know how that goes. I always thought well of him myself, good preacher and a good pastor. He could've stayed as long as he wanted, I suppose, but that was a good opportunity for him up in South Carolina. They're treating us well, and I'm glad to have a place to preach for however long it takes them to call a pastor."

"That's good," Mike replied. "I trust everything is well with you and Susan."

"Well," Bob spoke, a note of hesitation in his voice, "that's what I called you to talk about. Something's been bothering me ever since the night you and Karen came over to work on the wedding plans, the way Susan reacted when y'all said that you were going to name your baby after Franklin Seals' daughter who was killed."

"We were kinda puzzled over her reaction. Karen and I talked about it on the way home and after we went to bed that night. Susan acted like we'd said something wrong, like we discovered some secret we weren't supposed to know about."

"Glad to hear you say that. You noticed the same thing I did. I called Susan after I got home that night and asked her what was up, and she said she'd rather not talk about it. I told her we were fixing to get married, and we needed to talk about anything that bothered her that much, told her this business of keeping secrets from each other wouldn't work if we were going to have any kind of a marriage. She said she'd tell me another time, just not right then, so I let it go and didn't say any more about it. Well, another time never came, so I asked her again after we stopped by to see the new baby, and all she'd say was that it was something horrible that happened a long time ago, and that she felt like she needed to try to put it out of her mind. Ever since then, Susan hasn't been sleeping well, and she's been having nightmares. Last night, she must've gotten up a half dozen times before deciding about 3:30 to stay up and read until it was time to get ready to go to her office. About five o'clock, I got up and told her, 'Susan, I love you, and it's killing me to see you like this. We've got to get at whatever it is that's bothering you that you can't talk about. It all started when Mike and Karen told us they were going to name their baby after Debbie Seals. Susan, honey, you know who killed that girl, don't you?' She said 'Yes' and then broke down and started crying, cried so hard she threw up. I just held her and let her cry. It was the better part of an hour before she could pull herself together enough for us to talk."

"So what'd she tell you?"

"She said she'd carried the burden as long as she could stand, that she knew all about who killed Debbie Seals. I asked her who it was, and she told me if I'd call you and Aaron Stewart and ask y'all to come over to the house tonight, she'd tell me, you, and Aaron everything she knows. Can you come over at 7:00?"

"I'll see you and Susan at 7:00."

* * * * * * * * * * * *

"Reverend, we've got to stop meeting like this," Aaron Stewart commented as he shook hands with Mike. They had arrived simultaneously at Susan and Bob's house, and they walked up the brick sidewalk together. "The first time I met you was at the scene of that accident when poor ol' Royce Green got killed. Now we meet when I'm coming to take a statement about a homicide from one of your members. Tell you what, meet me at the Lonesome Whistle tomorrow about 12:00 and I'll treat you to lunch, try not to be occupied with police business."

"You're on. I've heard good things about you, so I've been looking forward to getting to know you better." Changing the subject, Mike added, "This was a shock, getting the call from Bob about Susan knowing who killed Debbie Seals."

"I remember when she was killed. I was about thirteen years old, but I remember it like it was yesterday. It took me a while to find the case file. All the files from that far back are in boxes in a mini-warehouse the city rents, but I finally found it, such as it is for what it's worth. They didn't do much of an investigation. Barney Fife could've done better. What there is, is in my briefcase. It'll be good to close this case if we can."

"Hey, Pastor, Chief, come on in, have a seat. Can I get you a cup of coffee or something cold to drink?" Bob spoke softly.

"No thanks, I don't care for anything." Aaron replied. "How about you, Reverend?"

"Nothing for me either, I'm fine," Mike answered. He could not remember being in a more uncomfortable situation. Like dealing with the wreck that killed the two young people at Clear Springs, this had not been covered in any of his seminary classes.

Susan sat on the sofa. A box of Kleenex was on the end table beside her, and she had obviously been crying. "Thanks for coming over here instead of us coming down to the police station," Bob said. "This is hard for Susan."

"I understand," Aaron responded sympathetically. "It won't get any easier by putting it off."

Susan got up and hugged Mike and Aaron. "Thanks for coming. This is going to cause a lot of pain for a lot of people to bring this out, but I can't keep carrying this inside me. I've agonized over this, made myself sick over it, ever since Jim told me."

"Susan," Mike spoke up. "Look at me. You're not the one causing the pain by telling what you know. The people who killed Debbie are the ones causing whatever pain results from this coming to light."

"Brother Mike's right, Susan," Bob concurred. "Debbie's mother's still living. She's lived twenty-six years with the pain of not knowing who killed her daughter. Debbie's brother's still living. He's lived twenty-six years with the pain of not knowing who killed his sister. By telling what you know, you'll ease their pain a little bit. Whatever pain results for others from the truth coming out, the ones who killed Debbie are responsible for that, not you." With a note of firmness in his voice, he added, "The truth needs to come out, Susan."

"A crime was committed," Aaron added. "A homicide. There's no statute of limitations on that. Somebody shot a high-powered rifle into an occupied house, killed an innocent fourteen-year-old girl, and you know who did it. Anybody who'd do something like that needs to be held accountable. Susan, anything you can tell me that'll help solve this crime, please tell me, and tell me everything you know. Don't hold back anything to protect anybody. You need to do what's right." Taking a small cassette recorder from his inside coat pocket and placing it on the coffee table, he added, "I'd like your permission to record this conversation."

"Sure, Aaron, that's fine. Go ahead."

"I'm ready. The tape's running."

"I always felt like I knew, felt like Jim wasn't being truthful with me. Jim was a good man, just got in with the wrong bunch, and they were all drinking," Susan began, her voice breaking with emotion. "The first few years we were married, Monday night was Jim's night with the boys. There were four of them, they'd been friends since they were kids. It was him, Billy Ray Flint, Hoyt Lowery, and Junior Bazemore. They used to hunt and fish together. Junior's daddy was old man Bazemore that ran the *Harrington Courier* before Ted Coleman took it over. Billy Ray, works at the Chevrolet place, he's a brother to Carl Baxter's wife Joyce and Eleanor Flint Basden, the Methodist pastor. Their daddy ran Flint Furniture Company for years. Of course, you know Hoyt's daddy was Bud Lowery, the chief of police back then, and Hoyt was on the police force for years before he got elected sheriff. Junior was still single, had an apartment in the basement of his mother and daddy's house. They had a big pool table down there. They used to get together every Monday night to drink beer and shoot pool. Jim'd usually come stumbling in around one or two in the morning, knowing he had to get up and go to work at the bank in a few hours. The night Debbie was killed, Jim came in a little before ten o'clock. I asked him what was wrong, and he said nothing, he just needed to get up a little early the next morning to drop the car off at Jack Miller's body shop on his way to work, said somebody sideswiped it while it was parked on the street beside the bank. So, he got ready for bed. Our children were both preschoolers, and I didn't go back to work until after our youngest started to school. After Jim left the next morning, I turned the radio on to get the local news while I was washing up the breakfast dishes. That's when I heard about Debbie being killed. When the paper came out on Friday, I read what Preacher Garnett, the Church of God pastor, said about seeing the shot fired from a pink and white '58 Pontiac Catalina, and about the car hitting him when he tried to block it with his car. I confronted Jim about that, but he said it must've been a strange coincidence, that if I didn't believe him, he could show me the police report about the hit and run, and he did. He showed me the police report, saying our car'd been hit while it was parked on the street beside the bank between two and three that afternoon. It was signed by Hoyt Lowery. The time on the police report was 3:20 that afternoon if I remember right, close to five hours before Preacher Garnett's car was hit. I still had my doubts, but I tried to convince myself that Jim wouldn't be involved in anything like that and that he wouldn't lie to me. I tried to accept that it was just a coincidence and put it out of my mind. Jim quit his Monday nights with the boys after that night, started staying home with me and the girls. As far as I know, he never did drink anymore after that night, I know I never saw him drunk after that. I asked him why he'd given up his Monday nights with the boys, and he said he'd decided he was getting too old for such foolishness, said he'd finally figured out the connection between getting drunk on Monday night and having a rip-roaring headache Tuesday morning. Anyway, two days before he went into the coma, the home health care nurse had just left and Jim and I were the only ones in the house. Jim told me that he knew he was dying, and he said he had to get something off his chest before he could die in peace. He said I was the only person he could tell. He started crying, crying the way a child cries. I sat down on the bed beside him and held him, told him to tell me whatever he needed to tell me."

"So what'd he tell you?" Aaron inquired.

"Jim wasn't the one who fired the shot," Susan spoke haltingly. "He was driving the car. It was our car." As she opened the photo album on the coffee table and pointed to a picture, she continued, "You can see it clearly in this picture made on Easter Sunday 1963, right before we left for church. Jim was so proud of that car, kept it until 1968, traded it in on a new GTO. Jim always liked Pontiacs. We dated in that car, went on our honeymoon in it. It was a '58 Pontiac Catalina, Pepto-Bismol pink and white. I never saw another one in that pink and white two-tone. There wasn't another one like it in Mintz County, that's for sure."

"The pastor at the Church of God who witnessed the shooting got a good description of the car. Everything but a tag number, that is. He said it looked like a gunny sack or something was tied over the tag. But, like you said, it's not like every third car in the county was a pink and white '58 Pony. Did the police ever stop Jim or question him about the killing?"

"As far as I know, they never did. Jim drove that car around town every day for four years after Debbie was killed, until he traded it in on the GTO. If they ever asked him any questions, he never told me about it. Obviously, Hoyt falsified the police report about the car being hit while it was parked at the bank. I expect Bud Lowery knew the police report about the hit and run was fake, but of course that was evidence that the damage to our car wasn't from colliding with Preacher Garnett's car."

"And of course Jack Miller had that Pontiac fixed before any-body could look at it and Preacher Garnett's car together to see if the damage matched up, to see if there was paint off the Pontiac on the preacher's car and vice versa. If the police ever talked to Jim or any of the other guys, they never made any notes about it, or if they did, they're not in the case file. It took me most of the morn-ing to find the file. The original investigation notes say Jim Whitmire's pink and white '58 Pontiac had been ruled out as the car involved in the shooting. It makes reference to the accident report about the hit and run. It says Jim's Pontiac was hit on the left front, but the damage was sustained when somebody hit it while it was parked on the street beside the bank earlier in the day. The original case file's the nearest nothing I ever saw in my life. I was telling Reverend Westover as we were coming up the sidewalk, Barney Fife could've done better. Chief Lowery and both of the officers that worked the case are dead, so we can't talk to them. I was wondering whether they were protecting somebody or merely incompetent. You just answered that question for me. What else did Jim tell you? Did he tell you who fired the shot, or whose gun it was?"

"Jim said they were all drunk, but he wasn't as drunk as the others, and he had the fastest car, so they used his car. It was Billy Ray Flint's idea, and the others egged him on. Billy Ray told them while they were shooting pool over at the Bazemores that he had his 30.06 deer rifle and scope out in the car, and he thought it'd be fun to run by and shoot at Preacher Seals' house, just to scare him, maybe shoot out his porch light or shoot a couple of tires on his car. He and the other two boys didn't think Billy Ray was crazy enough to do it, and it got to be a dare. It was Hoyt's idea to tie the gunny sack over the tag. Anyway, Jim said, when they drove by the house and he slowed down, almost stopped, the draperies were open and he could see Debbie in the living room playing the piano. Billy Ray was sitting behind Jim and had his window rolled down. Jim said that Billy Ray said to Junior, 'You don't think I'll shoot the girl, do you?,' and Junior said he didn't think Billy Ray was that crazy. Jim said he heard the shot, and he floorboarded it and got out of there, didn't stop when he hit Preacher Garnett's car, kept going. He said Billy Ray was bragging like an idiot, "I got 'er, I got 'er! That oughta get that nigger-lover preacher outta Harrington!""

21

Mike's advise to Susan, that it was the people involved in the killing of Debbie Seals who were responsible for any pain that resulted from the truth coming to light, sounded good when he gave it. It sounded glib, overly facile, as he turned it over in his mind the next morning, but he was confident he had told her the right thing. It was cruel, selfish, unloving, and immoral for Jim to ask Susan to bear a horrible secret to her grave. The promise Susan made to Jim on his deathbed, extracted under duress, needed to be broken. The fact she had made the promise to Jim on his deathbed only made his manipulation all the more shameful. Jim had used the fact that he was dying to extract a promise she never would have made otherwise. If Jim had not been at death's door, Susan said, she did not know whether their marriage would have survived the disclosure. "All during the viewing and the funeral, here I am supposed to be the grieving widow," she said, "and part of what I'm feeling is revulsion toward the man I was married to for twenty-nine years. I was crying, all right, but not altogether for the reasons everyone assumed. Learning that Jim was involved in Debbie's murder was harder to bear than his death. I haven't been able to bring myself to tell the girls. They adored their daddy, and I don't want to tear down their image of him." Aaron told her that he didn't either, but it might be a good idea to find some way to tell them before they heard about it when she testified in court.

In the course of the three-hour conversation, Susan moved from excusing Jim's actions to venting all the rage she felt toward him and the other three occupants of the Pontiac on that long-ago February night. From the time Jim confided in her, Susan had borne an oppressive, crushing burden. With her degree in social work, she knew all of the things that Mike told her from her own professional training. She was also well-versed in the scriptural teachings that undergirded Mike's counsel. His advice was the same that she would have given anyone else in similar straits, but it helped to hear someone else confirm what she knew intellectually: that she was not responsible for the pain that resulted from the truth coming to light, that she had to face the fact that the man with whom she shared her life for twenty-nine years had committed unspeakable evil, and that it was morally wrong to ask anyone to carry the kind of secret that Jim had asked her to carry.

Nonetheless, a lot of pain had resulted in a very short time after the truth came to light, and Susan could not help feeling somewhat responsible. Billy Ray Flint was in jail, charged with first degree murder. His wife Judy, their children, and their grandchildren were devastated. His sister, Joyce Baxter, had taken it very hard. Joyce was vacillating between denial and acceptance of the hard truth, and her doctor had put her on an anti-depressant and given her some medication to help her sleep. She was so distraught at times that Carl feared that she might take an overdose. Billy Ray's other sister, Eleanor Flint Basden, was sickened by the revelation, but she told Mike she had always had a gut feeling that her brother was involved one way or another. District attorney Emily Turner, a member of Harrington United Methodist Church, was coming to terms with the unpleasant prospect of prosecuting her pastor's brother. She and Eleanor were friends, so Emily agonized over whether to change churches to make things easier. Eleanor told her that she abhorred what her brother did and understood that she was obligated to do her job. Eleanor assured Emily that she would harbor no ill feelings toward her. They embraced, and the two women prayed with and for each other. With Eleanor's encouragement, Emily decided not to change churches. Mintz County sheriff Hoyt Lowery abruptly resigned from office, and he and video store owner Junior Bazemore were charged as accessories to the murder of Debbie Seals.

Under questioning, Lowery and Bazemore told what they knew and agreed to testify against Billy Ray, hoping to save their own hides in the process. Lowery admitted writing the phony accident report to account for the damage to Jim Whitmire's car. Chief Stewart and the two GBI agents questioned Lowery and Bazemore separately. Both told the same story, that Billy Ray did not take a random shot into the house. The draperies were open, and he saw Debbie in the living room playing the piano, her back to the picture window. Using the scope on his 30.06 Winchester Model 70, he took careful aim, not at a porch light or a tire on Franklin Seals' car, but at the back of Debbie's head, and he hit his mark. When he saw her body slump forward onto the piano, he boasted of his marksmanship the way he would if he had brought down a deer.

Billy Ray steadfastly denied having anything to do with the crime, so it became necessary for the Harrington Police and the GBI to attempt a proper criminal investigation twenty-six years after the fact. Aaron was appalled to discover that no autopsy was done. Granted, the cause of death was obvious. Aaron had no quarrel with old Dr. Walters on that point. He had seen the grisly crime scene photos, clearly showing the entry wound in the back of Debbie's neck at the base of her skull. From his paramedic training, he knew that such a wound would destroy the part of the brain that controls the heartbeat and breathing, causing instant cardiac and respiratory arrest. Nonetheless, Aaron thought, it would have been right considerate of Dr. Walters, in his role as county medical examiner, to perform the autopsy required by law and remove the bullet from her body in case it might be needed for evidence someday. The police, along with Dr. Walters, concluded from the hole in the window and the wound to Debbie's neck that she had been felled by a single shot from a 30.06. Debbie was buried with the bullet embedded in her brain.

The next afternoon, superior court judge John Briscoe signed the order to exhume Debbie's body. By mid-morning Thursday, the rusty metal casket was in the back of a van headed to the state crime lab in Atlanta. Junior and Hoyt told the investigators they were pretty sure Billy Ray still had the rifle he used to kill Debbie, because they were with him on the first day of deer season when he felled an eight point buck with the same rifle or one identical to it. The investigators obtained a search warrant, quickly retrieved the vintage Winchester, and sent it to the crime lab for ballistics testing. Aaron couldn't help thinking how much the case against Billy Ray would have been strengthened if the police had recovered the rifle moments after the crime with Billy Ray's fingerprints all over it and gunpowder residue on Billy Ray's right hand.

Before it was over, Aaron was thankful that Debbie was buried with the fatal bullet still in her. That way, the projectile was preserved until it could be retrieved by a competent forensic pathologist. Aaron realized, if old Dr. Walters had possessed the foresight to retrieve it, it would have been lost long before he became police chief. Or, if it had not been lost, it might as well have been, because sloppy procedures for handling evidence would have given some defense lawyer a wide-open door to question where the bullet had been for twenty-six years and whether it was the same one that had been removed from Debbie's body.

Chief Stewart tried to push aside all thoughts of what might have been. Everyone in the four-room house that served as Harrington's police station heard a shout of "Thank you, Jesus!" from his office when he received the call from the crime lab in Atlanta, telling him that the ballistics tests were positive. A GBI ballistics expert was prepared to testify that the bullet the pathologist removed from Debbie's body was fired from the Winchester 30.06 that Aaron and the GBI agents seized from Billy Ray's house.

After hearing from the crime lab, the first call Aaron made was to district attorney Emily Turner. While wanting to see those responsible for Debbie's death tried and convicted, she had misgivings about whether it could be done. She knew that successful prosecution of a first-degree murder case is difficult enough when the events are fresh. While there is no statute of limitations on first degree murder, prosecuting a case that had been cold for more than a quarter of a century would be fraught with all kinds of problems. Emily was as pleased as Aaron had been with the ballistics test. It was Emily who pointed out that old Dr. Walters had unwittingly helped their case by not removing the bullet from Debbie's body before she was buried. Aaron called Jane Seals the morning after he took the statement from Susan to tell her about the break in the case and to tell her that they would have to exhume Debbie's body. The thought of exhuming her daughter's body was distressing to Mrs. Seals, but she understood the necessity of it. As soon as he got off the phone with Emily Turner, Aaron called Mrs. Seals again to tell her that the pathologist had recovered the fatal bullet, that ballistics had matched it with Billy Ray's 30.06, and that Emily would seek a first-degree murder indictment against Billy Ray when the grand jury convened in October.

*   *   *   *   *   *   *   *   *   *   *   *

Mike felt very good about the prospect of ordaining Eric Latham as a deacon, but he had serious misgivings about Bill Gentry. His feelings about both men were confirmed when the ordination council met. The questions of a spiritual nature were as difficult for Bill as questions about heating and air conditioning systems would have been for Eric. When asked about his Christian experience, Bill said that he was baptized and joined the church when he was seven years old, but he didn't remember much about it, and he told about the time the spot showed up on one of his lungs when he had a chest x-ray. The biopsy, he said, indicated the spot was not malignant, but it was enough to scare the living daylights out of him and make him decide that he had better quit smoking and start going to church, something he had rarely done as an adult. Mike was glad that Bill had quit smoking and started going to church, but he could not help noticing the absence of any mention of an awareness of sin, repentance, assurance of God's forgiveness, or the name of Jesus in Bill's testimony. After Bill's interview concluded and Mike dismissed him from the room, he told the council that he had serious reservations about Bill's readiness for ordination. All ordained deacons in the church, active and inactive, were invited to sit on the council for Bill and Eric, and they were all there. Brenda Coleman did not hesitate to express the reservations that Mike was feeling. "This is not about whether Bill's a nice guy or whether we like him," Brenda pointed out. "Bill's one of the nicest people I know, and we all like him. I'd recommend him very highly to anybody who needed heating or air conditioning work. He installed a new furnace in our house last year, did us a good job, treated us very fairly. But that doesn't mean that he should be ordained as a deacon. I'm not comfortable with ordaining Bill because I'm not sure he understands the gospel or has a clear concept of what it means to be a Christian." Jerry McWhorter nodded in seeming agreement with Brenda, but he also nodded understandingly when Rudy Blevins said his answers probably weren't any better at his ordination council and that he thought Bill would grow in his understanding after he was ordained. Mike did not say what he was thinking, but the thought crossed his mind that Rudy to this day might not be any better than Bill at fielding questions of a spiritual nature. Ted expressed concerns about Bill's understanding of what deacons were supposed to do, but his observations mostly fell on deaf ears. With all of the inactive deacons present, there was a clear majority of the old guard. The vote was seven to three in favor of ordaining Bill. The vote to ordain Eric was unanimous.

*   *   *   *   *   *   *   *   *   *   *   *

After breakfast Sunday morning, Mike called Heather Simmons at the home of her parents in McMillan, Tennessee. "Hello, Heather? Mike Westover down in Harrington, Georgia."

"Hey, Mike, great to hear from you!"

"Just thought I'd give you a call, make sure Wallace got there OK, let you know that we'll be praying for you and the new church this morning."

"Thanks, Mike. Wallace got here Friday. He's doing great, having the time of his life. He's staying with John and Becky Tant. He was over here last night for supper. Before that, he was out with us all day yesterday putting up posters and inviting people to church. After supper last night, he insisted on helping us set up the showroom for the church service this morning. He was dog-tired when we dropped him off at John and Becky's, but I've never seen him happier. I wish you could see how we've got the showroom set up. It's improvised, but it looks nice. Dad had the sign painter make a big sign to go in the window, right next to the sign about the new '91 Fords is this sign that says 'Providence Baptist Church meets here.' They've bought a hundred folding chairs. Jack and Ruth Harper donated their piano. Jack helped Lance Robinson build a pulpit and communion table last week. A church in Memphis heard about us and donated hymnals. The Presbyterian church here donated a beautiful silver communion service. While we were setting up last night, a guy from one of the florists delivered a floral arrangement from Pleasant Hope A.M.E. It looked so nice when we finished last night. Dad says that Simmons Ford is going to be the only car dealership in the country with a pulpit and piano in the showroom. I think Wallace must've taken two or three rolls of film of our improvised sanctuary. This morning, before I preach, Wallace and I are going to present a check for two thousand dollars from Clear Springs to Providence. It's a surprise. I haven't told Mom and Dad. The folks at Clear Springs feel sort of responsible for getting this new church started, so they wanted to help as much as they could."

"Sounds like something Clear Springs would do. I know it's going to be a wonderful service there this morning. Wish I could be there."

"We'll feel your presence because of your prayers for us. We've heard from so many who are praying for us. We covered up a big bulletin board with cards and notes that Wallace and I brought from people at Clear Springs. Carol and her kids called me last night. Soon as I hung up from talking to them, it rang again, and it was Wanda Halstead, or used to be Halstead, she's gone back to her birth name, Gonzales. She started a new job a couple of weeks ago, just got her own apartment and a phone in her name. I'm so proud of her! She's doing well, finally making a good life for herself after twenty-seven years of pure hell with Lester Halstead. The church has been so good to her, and she's been such a blessing to the church. I wish you could see and hear her playing her guitar and singing with the children. She talked about how much Clear

Springs has helped her, said we need more churches with the kind of spirit Clear Springs has. She promised to be praying for Providence and for me as I preach this morning. Then, as soon as I hung up from talking to Wanda, the phone rang again, and it was Rachel Minkins calling from way up there in British Columbia. It's incredible the prayer support we have. It feels like you're all right here with us. I'm so excited about preaching this morning and doing the baptism this afternoon. When Mom and Dad asked me about doing the baptism, they had four to baptize. When I got down here, there were three more, so I'm supposed to baptize seven this afternoon, four of them adults. It's going to be a wonderful day. You know Dr. Kerns at Mid-Atlantic retired at the end of the school year. He and Mrs. Kerns are moving down here this coming week, and the church has rented an apartment for them. He's agreed to be interim for up to a year until the church calls a permanent pastor. So, Providence is off to a great start. How're things in Harrington?"

"Good. We're ordaining two new deacons this morning and installing our first woman deacon. She was ordained at another church before they came to Harrington, and she was a member here for seven years before the church learned she was ordained. It's funny the way our bylaws are worded. The bylaws only permit the church to ordain men, but there's nothing in there to prohibit a woman ordained at another church from serving if the church elects her. Brenda's ordination came to light after I asked Carol to help serve communion when she and her kids were down here last summer. The bylaws require us to put the names of all ordained deacons and all men eligible for ordination on the ballot, Brenda's a sure-nuff genuine ordained deacon, we put her on the ballot, and the church elected her."

"It's like I tell the folks at Clear Springs, God has a sense of humor. I love that."

"We may get booted out of the association before it's over. Our director of missions is ticked off at me. I expect he'll get over it. Our association meets this Thursday, same day as Sanders County. I don't know what the outcome'll be, but I'm pretty sure there'll be a motion to take some kind of action against us. Wallace told us there's a possibility Clear Springs'll get the boot from the Sanders County Association."

"I hope it doesn't come to that. From the way things are shaping up, I expect it to get ugly, and they'll be able to muster the votes to do whatever they want. Billy Fite's let it be known that he's going to bring the motion to disfellowship us. I've never met this clown, never met Lester Halstead for that matter, but from what I gather they both must be bitter, mean-spirited men. We'll have our people there. If people act ugly, we won't act ugly back at them. The association will do whatever it decides to do, and the church is OK with that. If they throw us out, we'll go on doing what we're doing. The ones who've been our friends all along will still be our friends. John Bentley at First Baptist in Ledford called to tell me that he'll speak against the motion to disfellowship us, and he's going to tell the association that First Baptist intends to remain in fellowship with us no matter what the association does. Greg Nash and Claude Bradley are also going to tell the association that their churches intend to remain in fellowship with us. I was very well received when I preached the revival for Greg back in August. I've been in a couple of classes with him, but I'd never had occasion to talk with him all that much until he came to my ordination council. Greg's a good guy. I've really been impressed with ol' Claude Bradley, too. Such a humble, gracious man, a really sweet spirit. He invited me to preach a revival at Coley's Station in April. Mike, Clear Springs is doing so well, the Lord's blessing us, the church is growing. They're so good to me, it's overwhelming. I guess Wallace told you that the church voted to call me full-time when I graduate. Clear Springs is such a joyful place, and I love being their pastor. Anybody who wants to is welcome to share our joy and celebrate what God's doing. Everybody else can go sulk in their corner 'til they get over it."

"That's the only way you can look at it. All you can do fretting over it is just make yourself sick and not accomplish anything. By the way, who's preaching at Clear Springs today?"

"Oh yes, I meant to tell you about that!" Heather's voice rose to little-girl pitch. "There are so many good things happening at Clear Springs, it's hard to think of everything I want to tell you! Wesley Trimble's preaching his first sermon this morning, and Carol's leading the communion service. Linda's bringing her camcorder to tape it. I can't wait to watch the video. Of course, we're making a video of Providence's first service to take back to Clear Springs."

"And I want to see both of them. That's so good about Wesley. I can't say I'm surprised. He's really grown spiritually in the time I've known him. Wish I could be in three places at once. Thank the Lord for video. By the way, Heather, you were talking about how happy Wallace was last night. I need to give you a message to pass along that'll make him even happier, a very dramatic answer to prayer that happened right after he left here, and you'll want to tell Carol and her kids, especially Megan, because they've been involved in praying about the same thing..."

* * * * * * * * * * * *

The Sunday morning service at Harrington was well-attended. Mike was surprised to see Virgil Blackmon in the congregation after the unpleasant note on which their last conversation ended. Mike invited all ordained ministers and deacons to participate in the ordination service. Virgil took part, though he no doubt cringed when he found himself directly behind Brenda in the line of people waiting to lay hands on Eric and Bill. Mike had already asked Brenda to help serve communion on her first Sunday as an active deacon, so he did not put Virgil on the spot by asking him to help with communion, knowing how he felt about women deacons. Mike noticed that Brenda was the one who served the bread and cup to Virgil, and he was pleased that Virgil was able to put aside his objections to women deacons long enough to take communion.

"Brother Virgil, surprised to see you this morning," Mike called out when he saw him still standing around after the crowd thinned out.

"Thought I'd better come over to see what kind of trouble you're getting yourself into," Virgil responded in a jocular way that Mike did not know how to interpret. He did sound more pleasant than the last time Mike talked with him on the phone, and Mike had come to regard him as a decent enough fellow, but he still did not know what to make of Virgil's presence and light-hearted manner. "You brought a good ordination charge, Brother Mike. I jotted down some notes so I can borrow some of your thoughts the next time I do one," Virgil continued.

"Thanks, you're welcome to anything you can use."

Virgil finally got around to his purpose for being at Harrington. "Just wanted to let you know in person. Floyd Williams over't Freeman Valley's all overheated about y'all electing a woman deacon. As you'll find out when you get to know 'im, his thermostat's stuck and it don't take much to get him overheated. He's gonna bring a motion to disfellowship Harrington. I tried to talk him out of it, but he's gonna do it or bust. Ol' Floyd sees himself as a one-man orthodoxy patrol. You gotta have one like that in every association. Floyd likes to talk about the association's responsibility to police the churches that belong to it, that's the term he likes to use, 'police the churches.' I disagree with women deacons and women preachers as much as Floyd does, but I don't think we ought to make it a test of fellowship. Most of the pastors feel the same way I do. I don't think y'all are in any danger of getting turned out, but I expect it'll end up with some kind of resolution of reprimand, censure, whatever, to try'n pacify Floyd. They'll put something in the minutes saying the association didn't like what y'all did and y'all ought not to've done it, but the association respects y'all's autonomy. Floyd'll go home mad 'cause he did'n get all he wanted, but he'll cool down 'til he gets overwrought about something else. That boy's gonna end up havin' a stroke or heart attack one of these days. He'll give me grief about it at every executive committee meeting for a year or two because I did'n do more to crack down on that church with the woman deacon. Once again, I'll explain to him that I'm a Baptist director of missions, not the pope, and the only authority I have is through what little influence I have and what little persuadin' I'm able to do. Once again, I'll tell him that nobody but the Lord, sometimes nobody including the Lord, tells a Baptist church what to do. Once again, he'll gripe about what a liberal DOM we have. Then he'll gradually cool off, decide maybe I'm not goin' to hell after all, an' he'll get steamed up at somebody else, consume his energy there and not have any left for being mad at me. I know the drill."

* * * * * * * * * * * *

On Sunday, Mike wished he could be in three places at once. On Thursday, he was glad he could not. As it had been on Sunday, his mind was spread out over three places. At the Mintz County Courthouse in Harrington, the grand jury would be hearing the evidence against Billy Ray Flint and deciding whether to indict him for the murder of Debbie Seals. The grand jury deliberations were not open to the public, so Mike could not have been there if he had wanted to be. At Central Avenue Baptist Church in

Ledford, Virginia, the Sanders County Baptist Association would be meeting, and it would most likely be a replay of the 1988 meeting at Bolton's Chapel. The clerk would not get through the enrollment of messengers before Billy Fite would spring up like a Jack-in-the-box to challenge the seating of Clear Springs' messengers because the church had a woman pastor. Mike wondered whether Jerry Langley, the new moderator of the association, would handle Billy Fite as skillfully as Claude Bradley had. Mike was on his way to be physically present at the third of the three places where his thoughts were, Harmony Baptist Church, where the annual meeting of the Mintz County Baptist Association was to convene at 9:00. The meeting would be presided over by moderator Leroy Thacker, the pastor of Friendship Baptist Church. Mike remembered seeing the sign that read *Harmony Baptist Church 1 1/2 miles* pointing down a narrow blacktop that turned off Bailey's Mill Road when he had been out that way one evening to visit a family who had attended services and expressed an interest in church membership. After dropping Asalee off at school, Mike headed out of town on MLK Boulevard, which most people still call Monument Avenue, turned right onto Bailey's Mill Road, and found his way back there without difficulty. He pulled into the parking lot about twenty minutes early.

Harrington Baptist would have its full quota of messengers at the meeting, and Mike supposed that the ten the church elected were a good cross-section. Brenda had taken off from work to attend, and Ted was coming as well. Franklin A. Brinkley, Chairman of the Board of Deacons of Harrington Baptist Church and his wife Jean, That Woman, Miss Addie, Helen Walters, David and Cheryl Groves, and Joyce Baxter planned to be there. Mike pulled into the parking lot right behind Joyce, who had Miss Addie in the car with her.

"Hey, Brother Mike," Joyce called out as she got out of the car. As she came around to open the door for Miss Addie, she met Mike and gave him a hug. "Good to see you."

"Good to see you, Joyce. I wasn't sure you'd be here. I would've understood if you hadn't come, what with all that's going on with Billy Ray."

"I'm better off here than I'd be sitting at home. I can't help my brother by sitting at home and worrying, I'd just make myself worse. Besides, I knew it'd do me good to talk with Miss Addie. She's been a big help to me in dealing with all of this stuff with Billy Ray."

"I taught all three of the Flint children," Miss Addie commented. "It breaks my heart to know about Billy Ray. He was such a nice, well-mannered child when I taught him. All three of the Flint children were. Joyce has always been a delightful girl, and we've stayed close over the years."

"Miss Addie's shared every blessing and burden I've had from fourth grade onward," Joyce laughed. "When Carl and I got engaged, Miss Addie was the first person I told and she was the matron of honor at our wedding."

"Sounds like y'all go back a ways," Mike observed. "This is bound to be hard for you, Joyce, but I'm glad to know that you and Miss Addie are so close." Mike didn't have a brother being indicted for murder, but he knew the frustration of being unable to help people about whom he cared deeply. He had very little acquaintance with Billy Ray, but he had an embryonic pastoral relationship with his wife Judy. He felt somewhat responsible for the painful confrontation Heather and the messengers from Clear Springs would be facing at the Sanders County Association. There was nothing he could do to change either of those situations and very little he could do to change the situation where he was.

* * * * * * * * * * * *

Floyd Williams' abrasive manner and appetite for ugly confrontation had alienated even those who agreed with him theologically. His motion to refuse to seat Harrington's messengers never got off the ground. Floyd made his motion, and it was seconded by one of the men from his church. Bob McKnight, serving as a messenger from Lakeside where he was interim pastor, rose to speak against Floyd's motion. Bob spoke in his deep, resonant, God-speaking-from-Heaven voice, and he sounded so reasonable as he stood in contrast to the emotionally overwrought Floyd Williams. Bob focused the issue squarely on the autonomy of local churches and the right of each local congregation to choose its own leaders without interference from the association. Out of approximately a hundred and seventy-five messengers, no more that fifteen, including the men from Freeman Valley, voted in favor of Floyd's motion. Leroy Thacker seemed relieved to have the sticky mess off his hands and to be done with Floyd's embarrassing antics. When the meeting broke for lunch, he called on Deacon Brenda Coleman to offer the prayer of thanksgiving for the food.

When Mike came home during the break between afternoon and evening sessions, Karen told him that there had been two messages for him. Wallace had called to report that the Sanders County Association, by a twelve-vote margin, had disfellowshipped Clear Springs. The other message was from Judy Flint, who called to let him know that the grand jury returned a true bill, indicting her husband for first-degree murder.

22

Franklin A. Brinkley, Chairman of the Board of Deacons of Harrington Baptist Church, emerged from the October deacons meeting minus two-thirds of his name. He had taken it for granted that he would be unopposed for a second term as chairman. It was the first meeting attended by newly-elected deacons Brenda Coleman, Eric Latham, and Bill Gentry, and the first item on the agenda was the election of a chairman for the coming year. After Frank called the meeting to order and asked David Groves to open the meeting with prayer, he recognized Doc Walters to read the minutes of the previous meeting. Then, in his inimitable drone, he said, "We now move to our first item of business, the election of the chairman of the board of deacons for the 1990-91 church year. Do I hear nominations for chairman of the board of deacons?"

Doc Walters responded on cue, "I nominate Franklin Brinkley."

"Second," chimed Bill Gentry, following Doc's lead in monkey-see, monkey-do fashion.

Franklin A. Brinkley, Chairman of the Board of Deacons of Harrington Baptist Church, was opening his mouth to humbly declare his willingness to serve another term, if called upon to do so, for the glory of God and the good of the church, when David Groves spoke up. "And I nominate Ted Coleman."

Franklin A. Brinkley, Chairman of the Board of Deacons of Harrington Baptist Church, was momentarily stunned by the temerity of David nominating a challenger to his presumed right to another term. He quickly recovered enough to say, "Ted Coleman has also been nominated. Do I hear a second to the nomination of Ted Coleman?"

"Second," Eric Latham responded confidently.

With Frank and Ted abstaining, the vote was three to two in favor of Ted. Ted agreed to serve, and Mike was pleased to have a kindred spirit serving as chairman. He felt reasonably sure that Ted would not turn into Theodore E. Coleman, Chairman of the Board of Deacons of Harrington Baptist Church.

* * * * * * * * * * * *

After he got the results of the ballistics tests, Aaron Stewart called Jeremy Griffin at Baker Street Church of God to see if he knew the whereabouts of the church's former pastor, Cleon Garnett, who had seen the pink and white '58 Pontiac Catalina fleeing the scene of the crime and tried to block the killer's escape. Jeremy, who was five years old in 1964, did not know off the top of his head, but he promised to make some phone calls and find out. An hour later, Jeremy called Aaron back with the news he wanted. Garnett was still around, retired and living in Birmingham. Jeremy gave Aaron the phone number, and he called him immediately. The next day, Garnett, who had been gone from Harrington since 1966, drove back to meet with Aaron, district attorney Emily Turner, and two GBI agents. Emily found him to be the kind of witness for which she had hoped, cooperative and eager to help solve the long-ago killing. He was even-tempered, unlikely to be flustered by intense questioning from a defense attorney. Articulate and credible, his recall of that long-ago night was clear and detailed. In addition to his testimony, Emily had the testimony of the two surviving men who were in the car with Billy Ray, Susan's testimony about the damage to their '58 Pontiac and her late husband's deathbed confession, the murder weapon, the forensic pathologist's report, and the ballistics evidence. She was confident that she could win a conviction on first-degree murder.

Billy Ray's trial was scheduled to begin on Monday December 3 at the Mintz County courthouse. Although he had rarely attended any church as an adult, Billy Ray had been baptized when he was eight years old, and his name was still on the membership roll. His wife and younger sister were active members. It was one of those pastoral duties that Mike dreaded and would have preferred to avoid, but he went to see Billy Ray in jail the day after he was arrested. Mike found him dressed in jailhouse issue orange coveralls with *County Prisoner* stenciled across the back. Even when he factored in the influence of alcohol, it was hard for Mike to picture the affable fifty-six year old grandfather as the cold-blooded murderer who aimed a 30.06 at the back of Debbie's head as she was playing the piano, fired a bullet into her brain, and boasted of his marksmanship when her petite form slumped onto the keyboard. He would have found it easier to sort through his feelings if Billy Ray had seemed like a despicable specimen of humanity, but he didn't. Mike's effort to steer the conversation toward matters of the spirit were rebuffed as Billy Ray insisted, "Now Preacher, you don't need to be worried 'bout ol' Billy Ray. I'm all right. Me'n the Good Lord got it all worked out." Knowing Mike's background as an automotive machinist, Billy Ray kept trying to steer the conversation toward things automotive. He told him about the mint condition 1966 Chevelle SS 396 with 29,000 miles on the odometer that he had reluctantly signed over to his attorney. Bobby Joe Dean, who had lusted after that car for years and made many cash offers to buy it, accepted it as the first payment for defending Billy Ray against the murder charge. On each of Mike's visits, Billy Ray steadfastly denied any involvement in the death of Debbie Seals. "I don't know why'n the world they wanna dredge that mess up after twenty-six years. Franklin Seals, the girl's daddy, now that man was crazy, stirred up a lotta trouble in this town, I coulda understood if somebody'd shot him, but I sure did'n have nothin' to do with killin' that girl a' his. Hell, I had two kids a'my own at home back'n 1964. I ain't the kinda man that hurts kids. I would'n shoot a kid in the back'a the head just 'cause her old man was a damn fool. Wad'n the girl's fault her daddy was crazy. Did'n nobody much care for that highbrow music she played, but she was a good kid. I don't know who killed 'er, if I did I'd a' told 'em a long time ago, but whoever it was, they ain't much chance of 'em provin' it after she's been dead twenty-six years. Oughta let the poor girl rest in peace. They wad'n no sense in diggin' up her body. That was uncalled for. That nigger police chief needs to worry 'bout the criminals runnin' loose now, breakin' into people's houses, dealin' drugs, 'stead'a worryin' bout stuff that happened in 1964. Whoever shot that girl's liable to be dead'n buried by now. 'Sides, I don't think they's aimin' to kill nobody, they's just shootin' into the house to try'n scare some sense into that nigger-lovin' preacher, hopin' he'd take a hint'n move on down the road 'fore he caused more trouble. Whoever killed the girl, it was an accident, an' they oughta let it go at that." Billy Ray had plenty to say about hypocrites in the church, and he was not averse to naming names. He referred to his sister, Methodist pastor Eleanor Flint Basden, as a "religious nut," and declared that he thought it was ridiculous for a woman to be trying to preach and pastor a church. His speech was laced with profanity followed by profuse apology. He smoked and drank too much. He was an unrepentant racist who insisted that he had many black friends. One he mentioned was Troy Brumbelow, one of the mechanics at Groves Chevrolet. "Now that boy's a good mechanic, best automatic transmission man we got. His wife works at the bank right next to the Chevrolet place, comes over every day to bring him his lunch and eat with him. She's all right, too. They don't bother nobody, they ain't tryin' to join no white church, an' they ain't lazy, sittin' back'n drawin' welfare like most of 'em." Billy Ray was, in every respect, the quintessential good ol' boy.

When Mike first learned of the killing of Debbie Seals, when he had no idea who her killer might be, he told Karen that he thought whoever did it ought to get the electric chair. Now, the killer had a name and a face, and Mike had mixed feelings about that. He thought of Wallace Coggins' account of the lynching, and Wallace's observation about how seemingly decent people can commit unspeakable evil and then go back to being seemingly decent people as though nothing happened. Mike was repulsed by Billy Ray's racist attitudes, but the sentiments he expressed were no more vile than what Mike had heard his father verbalize in years past. Grady Westover, even before he became a Christian, or perhaps in the process of becoming a Christian, had begun to re-examine and reject his racial prejudices. Mike knew that most of the people who express such attitudes never commit any acts of violence, and most are a study in contradictions, expressing high regard for individual blacks while holding blacks as a group in contempt. Billy Ray had a long track record of marital infidelity, but Mike knew that most men who cheat on their wives never kill anybody. Billy Ray's affection for his children and his pride in each one was genuine, and he was a doting grandfather to his grandchildren. It was hard for Mike to understand how the like-able good ol' boy could have done it, how a man with two young children of his own at home could have killed someone else's child, but Mike felt certain that the right man was in jail. Though

Billy Ray's actions were no less despicable, he was not so easy to hate as he was when he was nameless and faceless. He was mostly an enigma that Mike tried to figure out. He found himself looking forward to subsequent visits with the man. On about the third or fourth visit, Billy Ray asked Mike to pray for him. Mike was never quite sure whether Billy Ray had done that for his benefit or if he saw himself in need of prayer.

Judy was at first unwilling to accept the possibility that her husband could be the killer, but she slowly came to terms with the truth and chose to believe the evidence rather than her husband. She had stood by her man through countless episodes of infidelity, a half dozen minor scrapes with the law, and innumerable drunken weekends, but she could not stand by him this time. "I won't be surprised if Bobby Joe gets him off the hook," Judy told Mike. "If there's any weakness in the case, Bobby Joe'll find it and play it up for all it's worth. That's what he's paid to do, he's good at it, makes good money doing it. But whether Bobby Joe gets him off the hook doesn't have anything to do with whether he did it. Bobby Joe's got plenty of people off the hook that ought to've been stuffed and mounted. Even if Bobby Joe gets him off the hook, there's no way I'll sleep in the same bed with a man that'd kill a fourteen year old girl. I stood by him for thirty-four years, probably more'n I should have, because I was raised to believe, if you marry somebody, you're supposed to stand by them no matter what. I still care about him. I don't hate him. I don't know what I feel. But I'll never live with him, never be a wife to him, never sleep with him again, never let him touch me again. Billy Ray's on his own this time. Good ol' Judy's not gonna stand by him on this one." Mike listened and made no effort to tell her what to do. She had divorce papers served on Billy Ray at the Mintz County jail three days later.

Joyce Baxter gave up the Sunday School class she had taught for ten years. Before her brother was arrested, she told the nominating committee that she would continue to teach her first and second graders. The day after Billy Ray's arrest, she called Sunday School director Jerry McWhorter to tell him that he and the nominating committee would need to get somebody else. Asalee liked her new teacher, Lori Pettit, but she missed Joyce. Mike and Karen were among many parents trying to explain to six and seven year olds why Miss Joyce would not be their teacher any more, and Asalee was not the only bewildered child wondering whether she did something to cause it. Samantha Baxter still came to the youth fellowship, but Joyce and Carl had not been in any of the worship services since Billy Ray's arrest. When Mike went to visit and encourage them to come back to church, Joyce told him they had been going to the Methodist church. "This has been the hardest thing we've ever had to deal with," Joyce explained. "I just can't face the people at church right now."

"Joyce, listen to me," Mike began. "No matter what Billy Ray may have done, you're not responsible for it. You and Billy Ray are two different people. Each of you is responsible for your own actions and no one else's. No matter what your brother did or didn't do, nobody thinks any less of you. You don't have anything to be ashamed of. All the church wants to do is to help you through this time."

"That's the same thing Miss Addie told me," Joyce acknowledged as she dabbed the tears from her eyes with a Kleenex and put her glasses back on. "And I know it's the truth. It's what I'd tell anybody else. I know it's not logical, but I can't help feeling the way I feel. Eleanor's having a hard time too, and she has to be up there in front of a whole congregation every Sunday."

"It's nothing against you, Brother Mike," Carl added. "I know it looks funny for the chairman of the pulpit committee that called you to start going to the Methodist church six months after you move onto the field. Some people're going to add two and two and get five, and I can't help that, but we're not mad at anybody. We think just as much of you and your family as we did the day we presented you to the church."

"And, like I said," Joyce continued, "this is hard for Eleanor, and I feel like I need to help her through it. Ben and the kids are very supportive, so is her church, but this is still hard for her. Maybe Carl and I can encourage her a little. We've both accepted that Billy Ray did it. Eleanor's felt like all along that Billy Ray had something to do with it, and deep down I guess I did too. It's just been hard to admit it to myself. You know El and I keep up Debbie's and Brother Seals' graves. We got some more crushed marble Saturday and fixed Debbie's grave back after they reburied her. I guess you could say we've been trying to atone for what Billy Ray did and for what the church did."

"Well, Joyce, it's very kind of you and Eleanor to care for the graves out of respect for Debbie and Brother Seals, but you don't need to atone for what your brother did or what the church did. Jesus' death on the cross is sufficient to atone for Billy Ray's sins, yours, mine, and everybody else's. Besides, you didn't have anything to do with killing Debbie."

"I know I didn't, but I always had that sick feeling about it, felt in my heart that my brother had something to do with it. Those four—my brother, Jim Whitmire, Hoyt Lowery, and Junior Bazemore—always got together on Monday night to shoot pool, drink beer, probably brag about who they'd slept with since last Monday night. I remember when it came out in the paper that the Church of God preacher saw a pink and white '58 Pontiac fleeing the scene with four men in it, I knew good and well who it had to be, and so did everybody else in Harrington. Police knew who did it, but they weren't going to do anything as long as Hoyt's daddy was police chief and Junior's uncle, his mother's brother, old man Ellis Snyder, was district attorney. That pink and white Catalina Jim Whitmire had was the only one like that I ever remember seeing around Harrington and Mintz County. Debbie was shot on a Monday night. A witness sees a pink and white '58 Catalina fleeing the scene with four guys in it. Jim Whitmire's car matched the description, and he was a part of that group of four that got together every Monday night. He took his car to Jack Miller's body shop the next morning to have Jack fix the damage on the left front. It looks to me like they had plenty of grounds to haul the four of them in for questioning, but the police never so much as looked at the damage to Jim's car to see if it matched the damage to Preacher Garnett's car."

"And, like you say," Mike observed, "what you knew was known by most of the people in Harrington, police included. If you could've given the police some information they didn't have, that would've been one thing, but that wasn't the case. It wouldn't have done any good to go to the police because they were involved in the coverup."

"I agree with Brother Mike, Joyce," Carl spoke up. "The police knew perfectly well the night it happened who was involved. Like I told you the other night, that's why I never voted for Hoyt Lowery when he ran for sheriff."

"Oh well," Joyce interrupted, "I didn't mean for us to get into all of that. Brother Mike, you came to see about us not being in church. I appreciate you caring about us and checking on us. We'll be back in time, just not right now. It's partly embarrassment, shame, whatever you want to call it. More than anything else, I feel like I need to be there for Eleanor..."

* * * * * * * * * * * *

Judy Flint, her daughter Angela Hutchison, and Angela and Bud's two boys, had not missed a Sunday since Billy Ray's arrest. Angela had started coming on Wednesday nights to practice with the choir. She could read music and sing quite well, so Eric was pleased to have her in the choir, in the alto section next to Brenda Coleman. Brenda could read music, and she had a good ear and a pleasant voice, but she lacked confidence as a singer. Placed next to a strong singer on the same part, she sang more confidently, so Eric really gained two good altos when Angela joined the choir. The third Sunday she was there, Angela presented herself as a candidate for baptism.

Judy, more reticent than her daughter, felt that some people looked harshly upon her. Her desire to be in church was sufficient to surmount any concern about what people might think of her, but she sat at the back of the church instead of her usual place. Karen had been sitting on the back pew to be near the newborn nursery, and babies are adept at facilitating conversations among women. Judy had taken to sitting with Karen every Sunday, and she ended up holding Deborah Estelle about as much as Karen did. Helping Karen with the baby seemed to soothe her spirit.

* * * * * * * * * * * *

Karen was changing Deborah Estelle when she heard Mike come in for lunch. "Hey, hon," she called out, "We got a letter from Wallace. It's on the kitchen table with the rest of the mail."

Mike gave Karen a hug and a kiss before picking up his freshly-diapered daughter and playing with her. Holding Deborah on his shoulder with one hand, he sat down at the table and picked up Wallace's letter.

Dear Bro. Mike and Family,

Thought I'd write and tell you how much I enjoyed the time I spent with you all. I'm glad I didn't let the girls talk me out of the trip just because I am old. Evelyn must have reminded me a dozen times that I'm 86 years old, and I told her there's no danger of me forgetting how old I am with her around to remind me. I got back home Tuesday. I took all of my film first thing Wednesday to that new one-hour photo place that just opened in Ledford so I'd have the pictures of Deborah Estelle to show off at church. I put some pictures up on the bulletin board and everybody sure does take on over what a pretty baby she is. Everybody says Asalee's really grown since y'all left Clear Springs. It means a lot to me that you remembered Estelle when you named your baby, and it was good that you remembered Bro. Seals' daughter that was killed.

I sure am thankful that the truth has come out on who killed Debbie Seals. The Lord answered my prayers and the prayers of a lot of other people. I hope some slick high-price lawyer don't get the one that did it off the hook. I'll be praying that don't happen. I heard a fellow say one time that a jury is 12 people who decide which side has the best lawyers. He had it pegged about right.

I've got the video tape of the service at the new church in Tennessee. It sure was a good service. We had 54 people for the first service, so the new church is off to a good start. Sister Heather preached one of the best messages I ever heard her preach, and she baptized 7 people Sunday afternoon. We got the baptism and Lord's Supper on the same tape with Sunday morning. We showed it Wednesday night at church. Wesley and Linda have got the machine that can copy video tapes and they are going making a copy to send to you. Linda said they'd make you a copy of the tape of Wesley preaching his first sermon and Carol leading the Lord's Supper.

It broke my heart what happened at the association meeting, but it didn't surprise me a whole lot. Sister Heather told us about the association over at Memphis turning a church out a couple of years ago for the same thing. I don't know if it could have been avoided if Claude Bradley had still been moderator or not. Bro. Claude would've had a hard time handling the meeting, but the moderator we have now, Bro. Jerry Langley from over at Mountain View, let things get out of hand. Bro. Billy Fite sure got a lot of people stirred up before the meeting. I never saw a meeting get so ugly. Clear Springs was in the association 144 years, supported the association right well for a small church, but I don't reckon that amounts to a hill of beans. I sure was proud of our pastor and all of our people, the way they handled their selves. When we left after the vote was taken, all the messengers from First Baptist in Ledford, Bolton's Chapel, Coley's Station, Bethlehem, and Heggie's Chapel walked out with us. I sure did hate to see a split in the association like that, but I believe Bro. Billy and Lester Halstead will have to answer for that. I don't know what we'll do. I think the Broad River Association over at Canfield might take us in, but some of the ones who left with us want to start a new association and call it the Clear Springs Association. Like I say, I don't know what we're going to do. Pray for us. The Lord's blessing our little church whether Lester and Bro. Billy like it or not. Sis. Heather says that the ones that don't like what the Lord's doing at Clear Springs can sulk 'til they get over it. That's the way I look at it too.

Got a letter from Bro. Dennis Palmer today. He's taking off the week of Thanksgiving, going to come up to Clear Springs and spend the whole week with me. I look forward to having his company, and I think it'll do him good. I sure hope so. Pray for Bro. Dennis. He needs your prayers. He's a good man that's been hurt bad. Pray that I'll know what to say to help him.

I put right at 3,000 miles on my truck making my big trip, and I sure am glad I did it. I've seen Rock City and Ruby Falls. I'm sending you a couple of pictures of me at the railroad museum in Chattanooga. They're closed during the week after Labor Day, *but some men were there doing some work. I showed them my Brotherhood of Locomotive Engineers card, told them I'd run the 630, the 722, and the 4501 on excursions. One of the fellows took my picture standing on the pilot of the 630 and another picture of me up in the cab sitting on the engineer's seat.*

I reckon that's all the news there is to tell you. I really enjoyed my time with you, and I pray God's blessing on you and the whole family and upon your ministry at Harrington.

Sincerely,
Wallace

* * * * * * * * * * * *

On her way home from work on the last day of November, three days before Billy Ray Flint's trial was to begin, Susan McKnight stopped by the Harrington police station, hoping to find Aaron Stewart there. She was relieved when Aaron saw her come in and invited her back to his office.

"I don't know how important this is or whether it'll help anything," Susan began as she handed Aaron a medium-sized brown envelope. "Jim was a fanatic about saving receipts, canceled checks, and such, never threw anything like that out, believed in keeping records forever. I don't know why I didn't think about this when you and Brother Mike were at the house. There's a box in the attic for every year, all the way back to when we first married in 1959. I went through the 1964 box to see what might be there. I found some things that might be helpful to you, so I brought them over."

"Thanks, Susan," Aaron replied as he sat down at the desk, put on his reading glasses, and opened the envelope. The first item was a copy of the phony police report of a hit and run accident that Hoyt Lowery had concocted to explain the damage to Jim

Whitmire's '58 Pontiac, dated February 10, 1964, the date of Debbie Seals' murder. The next item was an itemized estimate from Miller's Body Shop, describing the damage to the car in great detail, dated February 11, 1964 and signed by Jack Miller. The third item was the stub of the check from State Farm Insurance for the repairs to the car, less the deductible, and the final item was the canceled check for fifty dollars, dated February 14, 1964, payable to Miller's Body Shop and signed by James E. Whitmire. Aaron had a smile on his face as he picked up the phone and dialed Emily Turner's office at the courthouse. "Hey, Emily. Aaron Stewart here. Glad I caught you before you left for the day. Stop by my office on your way home. Susan McKnight just brought us a real nice early Christmas present..."

＊　＊　＊　＊　＊　＊　＊　＊　＊　＊　＊　＊

When Miss Addie learned that Mrs. Seals was coming up for Billy Ray's trial, she called and invited her to stay with her for the duration, and Mrs. Seals accepted the invitation. Her son, Dr. Michael Seals, an internist in Birmingham, had kept in touch with Prince Hammondtree ever since they left Harrington, and Mr. Hammondtree was another grandfather to Michael's children. Michael planned to take time off from his practice and stay with Mr. Hammondtree while the trial was in progress. Karen had wanted to have Jane and Michael over for dinner one night, but she and Mike did not know how they would feel about being entertained in the house that had once been their home, the house in which Debbie had died, the house from which they were evicted in the midst of their grief. Their dilemma over what to do was alleviated when Prince Hammondtree called Saturday morning to say that he was fixing dinner for Jane and Michael Monday evening. He said Miss Addie was coming, and he told Karen that she and Mike and the children were invited. "I got a big ol' dinner table from when Ophelia'n I had five children at home. I don't get many chances to cook for a crowd no more, an' that's the way I like to cook. Seems like it all turns out better if you fix a lot of it 'stead'a tryin' to fix a lil'a this'n a lil'a that for one or two people." Mike told Karen that his schedule was clear as far as he knew, and if it wasn't, he'd make it clear. Karen promised Mr. Hammondtree that she would bake a German chocolate cake and bring it for dessert.

*   *   *   *   *   *   *   *   *   *   *   *

Mike pulled the old blue Fairmount wagon into Prince Hammondtree's driveway and parked it behind a silver Lexus with a Jefferson County, Alabama tag. Asalee had been excited when Karen told her they were going to Mr. Hammondtree's for dinner. As soon as Mike stopped in the driveway, Asalee sprang from the car and ran toward Mr. Hammondtree, leaving her parents to deal with her baby sister and the German chocolate cake. She remembered his visit to her home, and she remembered seeing him at the service at Greater New Hope the day Deborah Estelle was born. She and her mother ran into him in the grocery store a couple of weeks earlier, and he bent down to speak to her and called her by name. Asalee hugged Mr. Hammondtree and went right on into the house just like she would at her grandparents' or at Papa Wallace's.

"Rev'ren Westover, Mrs. Westover, y'all come on in. Oh, and let me see Miss Deborah Estelle! Lord, this baby's growin'!" Mr. Hammondtree exclaimed as he held the screen door open. "So glad y'all could come this evenin'."

"It was so good of you to invite us," Mike responded. "We've been looking forward to coming over."

"My pleasure. Like I told you, Rev'ren, I like to cook for a crowd, and when it's a crowd of good folks who love the Lord, the pleasure's multiplied. Come on in, make yourselves at home. I want you to meet some folks you already know by reputation. Rev'ren, Mrs. Westover, this is Mrs. Jane Seals and her son, Dr. Michael Seals."

Michael bore a striking resemblance to the photo of his father that hung in the hallway at Harrington Baptist Church. Had his hair been cut in a flat top, and had he been wearing a 1960's vintage suit with narrow lapels and a skinny tie, the resemblance would have been uncanny. His mother was a small woman, not quite five feet tall, whose olive complexion, dark eyes, and coal-black hair bespoke her Choctaw Indian heritage.

"Pleased to meet you," Michael said as he stood to shake hands with Mike and Karen. "I've heard many good things about you. Glad I'm finally getting to meet you."

As she hugged Karen, Mike, and Asalee and bent down to admire the baby in the carrier that Mike was holding, Jane added, "Oh, and this must be the little girl you named after Debbie. My, she is so pretty! Look at her little hands! Long, slender piano fingers, just like my Deborah Jean had."

"And she may very well turn out to be a piano player," Karen commented. "She's used to hearing me play. I played a lot while I was pregnant. Now I put Deb in her cradle right by the piano while I'm playing. Sometimes that's the only way she'll go to sleep. My six year old was the same way. Now Az sits at the piano and picks out tunes by ear."

"Sounds just like my Deborah Jean. May I hold your baby?"

"Of course. Deb's used to being passed around at church, and we'd be honored for you to hold her."

Jane tenderly lifted Deborah Estelle from her carrier, carefully supporting her head, kissed her, and held her closely. Deb acted as though she was in familiar hands and seemed thoroughly content with Jane holding her. "It sure did make me happy," she said, "when I heard you named your baby after Debbie."

"It's strange, I suppose," Mike acknowledged, "but Karen and I feel a very special bond to Debbie even though she died a long time ago and we never knew her. About the time we found out for sure that we were having another girl, we learned about Debbie and what happened to her. From the time Mr. Hammondtree told us about your Debbie, what a lovely and gifted girl she was, and the horrible way she died, we knew that we wanted to remember her in naming our daughter. So, we named her Deborah after your daughter and Estelle after a really sweet older lady in my former pastorate who died right about the time she was conceived."

Asalee had attached herself like Velcro to her mother's right leg, so Karen continued the introductions, "And this is our older daughter, Asalee. She's six years old and in the first grade."

"Hello, Asalee," Michael responded. "We didn't mean to take on over your sister and ignore you. So you're in the first grade? Who's your teacher?"

"Mrs. Elrod. She's really nice."

"I wonder if she's the same Mrs. Elrod who taught me in the first grade?"

"One and the same," Miss Addie interjected. "Ruth's a lovely person. Of course, you know that, because you were in her class. She started teaching two or three years before I retired. The children who have her are most fortunate." With a demure smile, she added, "Ruth's one of my former students."

"Miss Addie's right, Asalee," Michael concurred. "You've got the best."

"I guess you've got all kinds of mixed feelings about coming back for the trial," Mike addressed Jane and Michael, searching for the right words.

"Yes, I do," Jane acknowledged. "I'm glad for the case to be solved, but going through the trial does bring back a lot of painful memories and reopen a lot of old wounds. I'd long since given up on justice being done in this life. The law knew who was involved when it happened, and they covered it up. It shocked the daylights out of me when Aaron called me about the break in the case."

"Me too," Michael added. "I was just nine years old when Debbie was killed, but I remember it like it was last night. I was sitting at the dining table doing my homework, and I saw the instant the bullet hit her. I was the first one to her, no more than two or three seconds after she was hit, but she was already dead. I feel the same way Mother does, glad to see the case solved, but processing a lot of old hurt and anger, a lot of emotions I don't know how to identify. I was with a patient when Mother called to tell me about the call from Aaron. She convinced my receptionist that it was urgent and it couldn't wait, insisted she get me on the phone right then. Mother was crying and laughing at the same time. I like to've never got her calmed down enough to tell me what she was calling about. After she told me, I was in about the same shape she was. The patient I was with is a homicide detective with the Birmingham Police Department, has a reputation of being one of the best. I told him about it, and he said it's not often you get a break in a case that's been cold that long."

"I can't say enough good things about Aaron Stewart," Jane commented. "He was just a young boy when we were here, about a year or two younger than Debbie. His younger sister Shaunice was one of the piano students Debbie taught. Aaron would walk her over to our house every Saturday for her piano lesson, wait for her, and walk her back home. Aaron thought the world of Franklin. He and Franklin used to sit and talk while Shaunice took her piano lesson. Even before we sold our old building to Greater New Hope, before Franklin spoke out against the Klan and the White Citizens Council, some of them were gearing up to run us off on account of Debbie teaching piano lessons to black children. Hilda Mae Snyder and her husband Ellis, who was the district attorney back then, bought the house across from the pastorium about the time we moved to Harrington. Hilda Mae never worked outside the home, never needed to, and didn't like it because I did. The woman just didn't have enough to occupy her mind, so she devoted all her time and energy to spying on us. I don't know if she still has those binoculars, but she used to sit at the living room window for hours, especially on Saturdays when Debbie taught her piano students, spying on us with those binoculars. I never will forget Debbie speaking to Hilda Mae at church one Sunday and saying to her, 'Mrs. Snyder, don't you ever get tired of watching us? We're about the most boring people in Harrington. There are lots of other families who'd be more interesting to watch.' Franklin was so proud of her, he gave her a five dollar bill! Hilda Mae got so incensed over what Debbie said that she ended up having a spell with her heart, had to be rushed to the hospital. Deb was a tenderhearted girl, and it upset her to think that we had caused Hilda Mae—we called her 'That Woman,' Franklin said he called her that to keep from calling her a lot worse…"

"I love it!" Karen exclaimed. "That's what we call her too!"

"Anyway," Jane continued, "it upset Deb to think she'd caused That Woman to have a spell with her heart. Deb was in tears when the ambulance took That Woman away. Franklin put his arms around her and told her, 'Deb, Honey, I'm still proud of you. You were not the least bit disrespectful to her, you told her the truth, and it was truth that needed to be told. If she gets worked up over that and has a spell with her heart, it's her own fault.' So Deb asked Franklin, 'But, Daddy! What if Mrs. Snyder dies?' Franklin told her, 'Deb, Honey, knowing That Woman, she probably won't, but if she does, I'll conduct her funeral, and you can play some of your high-falutin' piano music. Something by Chopin would be nice.' By then, they were both laughing hysterically as they kept on about music for That Woman's funeral. They planned a whole service for her. She was one of the main ones who griped about Debbie playing classical music in church."

"And you said Hilda Mae tried to stir up trouble over Debbie teaching piano lessons to black children?" Karen asked.

"She did more than try, she succeeded. Her brother, Roland Millican, was chairman of deacons, and her cousin Rudy Blevins was a deacon, too. That Woman reported everything she saw that she didn't like to Roland and Rudy. They buttonholed Franklin, demanded that he order Debbie to stop teaching the black children. Franklin told them that he'd do no such thing. He told them that Debbie earned her spending money teaching piano to younger children, that the black children wanted to learn to play the piano, and that Debbie was well qualified to teach them. Roland and Rudy brought up the fact that the church owned the house, and Franklin acknowledged that it did, but he pointed out that he was paying for the use of the house with his services as pastor, the same as if he was paying rent in cash. He told them, as long as he was pastor of Harrington Baptist Church, that house was his home, and that he and I would be the ones to say who was welcome in it. He told them we gave Debbie permission to teach her piano students at home, that we didn't put any restrictions on the color of her students, and that we weren't about to."

"So did they back down?" Mike asked.

"About that issue, they did. On Saturday, two days before she was killed, Deb taught her students in the morning and played for Mr. Aldridge's funeral that afternoon."

"And she played so beautifully!" Miss Addie exclaimed. "Debbie always played well, but she was quite fond of Mr. Aldridge and me, and she put her whole heart and soul into it. How I wish you could've heard her!"

"She and Daddy were two peas in a pod," Michael observed. "They'd finish each other's sentences, or they'd just look at each other and burst out laughing, and nobody else would even know what the joke was. Daddy died from a massive heart attack six months after Debbie was killed. Acute myocardial infarction, that's Latin for bad heart attack. Really, though, Daddy grieved and drank himself to death. I never knew him to touch alcohol before my sister was killed. Trying to take the edge off the pain, I guess. I don't know what I'd do if somebody killed one of my children, so I can't pass judgement on him. Daddy was killed by the same bullet that killed Debbie. It just took Daddy longer to die."

"From the time we moved back to Mississippi until he died, all Franklin did was work, cry, and drink," Jane elaborated. "I felt so helpless watching him. He was called to be a preacher and a pastor if ever any man was. I'm not just saying that because he was my husband. Franklin knew his career as a pastor was over. No church would call him because of his outspoken stand for racial justice. I never knew a man who enjoyed being a father more thoroughly than Franklin did. He delighted in both of our children. Losing Debbie on top of being forced out of the ministry was more than he could take. That's what killed him."

"It wasn't just Debbie and me, either," Michael added. "Daddy had room in his heart for any child who needed fathering. Daddy'd be so proud of Aaron Stewart. Aaron's father was killed in a car wreck when Aaron was three or four, so Daddy really took an interest in him. He and Daddy would talk while Shaunice took her piano lessons, and Daddy used to take Aaron and me fishing. I thought it was so neat that he took us at night. It made us feel so grown up. I was too naive at the time to know why. Daddy had this big ol' Coleman lantern, and he'd take Aaron and me fishing on Friday nights. We'd go as soon as it got good and dark, stay out 'til midnight or one o'clock in the morning. The place we used to fish was on Salyers Creek, above the dam at Bailey's Mill. We'd always come back with a nice mess of bluegills, sometimes something better. I never will forget one night, it was about midnight, and we were about to pack up and go home because it was starting to rain. Aaron hooked a largemouth bass, big ol' lunker, he must've been the granddaddy of all of 'em. That fish really put up a fight, took Aaron and Daddy both to pull it in. So now you know the reason Aaron's been willing to work so hard on such an old case. When Billy Ray killed Debbie, he killed Daddy, too. When he killed Daddy, he killed somebody who'd been like a father to Aaron. Even though they're not related, I can see a lot of my daddy in Aaron Stewart. Daddy'd be proud of him."

"So how'd the first day of the trial go?" Mike asked.

"OK," Michael responded. "I think we've got a good jury. Most of them are either too young to remember when it happened or they weren't living here at the time. One exception is Mr. Robinette, who was the principal for years at what used to be Florida Avenue Colored School. He's the foreman of the jury. Of course, he was here at the time and remembers when it happened. The jury is six men and six women, seven white and five black. Today, both sides made their opening statements, and the district attorney began presenting the prosecution's case. I'm trying to evaluate this thing objectively, which is hard to do when you're emotionally involved, and I'm neither a lawyer nor the son of a lawyer, but it looks to me like the case against Billy Ray is pretty tight. There's not much arguing that can be done with the report from the forensic pathologist or the ballistics tests. That's all hard evidence and straightforward science. Billy Ray's lawyer didn't try to cross-examine the pathologist or the ballistics guy. He did cross-examine Susan used-to-be Whitmire, Junior Bazemore, Hoyt Lowery, and Preacher Garnett, but he couldn't trip any of them up."

"I'm very impressed with the district attorney," Jane commented. "She's not loud and bombastic like Bobby Joe Dean. Very calm and methodical, barely raised her voice all day, just presented her case calmly and reasonably, no loose ends that I could see. It'll be interesting to see what kind of show Bobby Joe puts on tomorrow. All I'm praying for is that the jury'll follow the law, the evidence, and the testimony, and not be swayed by theatrics. If they do, they'll convict him, and I think they'll convict on first-degree murder."

"Everything's ready," Prince Hammondtree announced. "Y'all come on, gather 'round the table, let Rev'ren Westover say grace, then we can start fixin' our plates..."

＊ ＊ ＊ ＊ ＊ ＊ ＊ ＊ ＊ ＊ ＊ ＊

It was late, well past Asalee's normal bedtime, and she had school the next day. Mike had a full day lined up, and Jane and Michael wanted to be in court when it convened at nine the next morning. Karen had given Jane and Michael each a picture of Deborah Estelle. As Mike and his family were leaving, Jane reached into her purse, pulled out a framed five-by-seven print of an old black-and-white school picture, and handed it to Karen. "I want you to have this. You thought enough of Debbie to name your daughter after her, so I want you to have a picture of her. This is her eighth grade school picture, made just a few months before she was killed."

Mike and Karen hugged Jane and thanked her for the picture. "She was a beautiful girl," Karen commented, "and everyone who knew her tells us what a beautiful spirit she had."

"We'll always treasure this picture," Mike added. "I wish I could've heard Debbie play the piano. I can only try to imagine how much you must miss her even now. I hope that seeing her killer brought to trial brings you some comfort."

"It does in a way, I suppose," Jane acknowledged. "I just wish it wasn't somebody we knew. When Cleon told us he saw four men in a pink and white Pontiac, we knew who it was. It was just a question of which one pulled the trigger. I wish it'd been a stranger. Franklin conducted the funerals of all four of Billy Ray's grandparents. He married Billy Ray and Judy. He was at the hospital with them when their children were born. All night that night, we spent the night at the Garnetts', Franklin kept turning it over and over in his mind, saying he thought it had to be the Bazemore boy or Hoyt Lowery that shot her, because Jim would've been driving, and he didn't think Billy Ray was mean or crazy enough to do it. Of course, Billy Ray's parents were among the ringleaders trying to run us off, but Billy Ray's sister Eleanor and her husband were among our strongest supporters. With all Franklin did for Billy Ray and his family, as much as I wish I had him beside me right now, I'm thankful he didn't live to know that Billy Ray was the one who killed her. Franklin tried to believe the best about everybody. He always felt like they shot at the house to scare us and hit Debbie accidentally. That's what I believed too, or I did until I got the call from Aaron."

"When court recessed for lunch," Michael spoke up, "Mother, Miss Addie, and I took Judy to lunch. We really feel for her and the children and grandchildren. She's a decent person who can't help what Billy Ray did. As glad as I am for this case to be solved, I'm sorry to see the pain it's caused for innocent people. We wanted Judy to know we didn't hold anything against her." Motioning Mike toward the Lexus as he opened the trunk, Michael added, "Something I want you to see. This old lantern belonged to Daddy. It's the one he carried when he and Aaron and I went fishing at night. It means a lot to me, but I want Aaron to have it. I brought it up here so I could give it to him."

23

The jury received instructions from Judge Briscoe and retired to the jury room to begin deliberations at 3:40 Thursday afternoon. Unswayed by the theatrics of Bobby Joe Dean, they deliberated only an hour and five minutes before jury foreman Silas Robinette sent word to the judge's chambers that they had reached a verdict. A few minutes before 5:00, the judge reconvened court and directed Billy Ray and his lawyer to rise for the reading of the verdict. Turning toward the jury box, he asked, "Has the jury reached a verdict?"

Mr. Robinette, a tall, pencil-thin man of regal bearing, rose slowly and faced the bench. He adjusted his wire-rimmed glasses and cleared his throat. "Yes, your honor, we have. We, the jury, find the defendant, Billy Ray Flint, guilty of murder in the first degree in connection with the death of Deborah Jean Seals on February 10, 1964. So say we all."

"Order! Order in the court! There will be no outbursts of any kind in this court!" Judge Briscoe thundered as he rapped the bench with his gavel. He took the envelope containing the verdict from the bailiff and announced that sentencing would take place at 9:00 AM on Thursday, December 20. After ordering Billy Ray bound over to the Mintz County Jail to await sentencing, he adjourned court.

Judge Briscoe did not know the significance of the date that he set for sentencing. Jane Seals looked over at her son, who gently squeezed her hand to let her know that the date did not escape his notice. Billy Ray would be sentenced on Debbie's birthday.

Debbie's birth and death dates were etched into the minds of the two women who tended her grave as indelibly as they were etched into her headstone. Judy Flint was sitting between her estranged husband's sisters. When court was adjourned, the three women embraced and wept together. Jane Seals, sitting directly behind them, instinctively reached forward, put her arms around them, and comforted them. After they left the courtroom, Jane and Michael met Emily Turner and Aaron Stewart in the hallway, and the four of them locked arms in a long, tearful embrace.

Billy Ray had seemed confident, even cocky, throughout the trial. Before the trial began, Bobby Joe leveled with his client about the strength of the prosecution's case and tried to prepare him for the possibility that he would be convicted, but Billy Ray reasoned that he had always been able to weasel his way out of trouble before, so he did not take his lawyer's dire prediction too seriously. After the verdict was announced and Judge Briscoe ordered him bound over to the Mintz County Jail to await sentencing, he stood in stunned disbelief for what seemed like several minutes. He broke down and sobbed when the deputy handcuffed him, showing emotion for the first time since his arrest. The prosecution had not sought the death penalty, so he knew he would be facing life imprisonment in the Georgia State Penitentiary. He had expected to walk out of the courtroom a free, albeit much poorer, man. As two deputies led him out of the courtroom, he scanned the faces of the jury, his estranged wife, Susan McKnight, Cleon Garnett, and the two men who had been with him in Jim Whitmire's Pontiac on that long-ago February night. The look in his eyes demanded to know "How could you do this to me?"

* * * * * * * * * * * *

Mike, Karen, and Asalee enjoyed the festive spirit of the twenty
or so people who gathered to decorate the church for Advent.
With a twelve-foot Douglas fir lavishly decorated as a Crismon
tree, all of the greenery hung, and the bright red Advent banners
unfurled, even the tired seventies-vintage gold carpet did not look
all that bad. Mike remembered making a lame joke about his family
being able to enjoy the hanging of the greens since their name was
not Green.

The church did not take off like a rocket when Mike assumed
his pastoral duties, but things seemed to be going reasonably well.
During his first six months. the attendance and offerings had been
good, about ten percent better than the same period the previous
year. He had baptized five more since the Sunday he and Jerry
baptized Cassie. Three families, new residents of Mintz County,
had joined the church. Most of the church seemed receptive to his
ministry, and he was building some solid pastoral relationships.
Karen enjoyed her involvement in the music ministry. Since she
and Jenny Latham were both mothers of infants, and Judy Flint
was always eager to hold and tend to the babies, Karen and Jenny
were sharing piano-playing duties, with Jenny usually playing for
the morning service and Karen playing for the evening service.
Karen enjoyed leading Bible studies, and she was quite good at it.
She was eager to develop a ministry to meet the needs of mothers
who were at home with young children. She, Jenny, and Lori Pettit
started the Mothers Morning Out group that met at the church
every Tuesday. Asalee was doing well in school, and she enjoyed
her Sunday School class and the children's activities at church. She
made friends easily, and she seemed to be a happy child most of
the time. Mike and Karen had cultivated a network of friends outside the church. Prince Hammondtree, Aaron and Latisha
Stewart, Lonesome Whistle owners Brantley and Betty Jacobs,
and Eleanor and Ben Basden had been guests in the Westover

home, and they had all graciously received the Westovers in their homes. Latisha and her family remained active members at Greater New Hope, but she helped with the Mothers Morning Out group at Harrington Baptist, and she and Karen were developing a close friendship. Brantley still professed to be the town agnostic, but Betty had been coming to the Sunday morning worship service for the past month or more. Brantley had come with her a couple of times. Overall, things seemed to be going well.

Mike sensed an undercurrent of discontent, but he did not think too much of it. It seemed to be limited to the few chronic malcontents such as Franklin A. Brinkley, Former Chairman of the Board of Deacons of Harrington Baptist Church, the Millicans, Ben Basden's mother, and That Woman, the sort who will not be content in Heaven until they find something wrong with it.

After finishing his preparations for the service that night, Mike came home about 1:00 on Christmas Eve and sorted through the mail that Karen had left on the kitchen table. His attention was drawn to a plain white envelope with a computer-generated address label and no return address. He tore the envelope open, pulled out the letter, unfolded it, and read it. Disgusted, angry, and sick in the pit of his stomach, he refolded it, put it back in the envelope, and set it aside just as the phone rang.

"Sorry to call and bother you with this on Christmas Eve, Preacher," Ted apologized. "Did you get a copy of the anonymous letter that's making the rounds?"

"Yep, just got the mail and read it about a minute before you called. Who else got one?"

"Looks like all the deacons, active and inactive. About half of them have called me, so I figure they all got it. David's out of town, and the others I haven't heard from probably haven't gotten home and read their mail. Roland was the first one to call me.

Franklin A. Brinkley, Former Chairman of the Board of Deacons of Harrington Baptist Church, was next. We know what to expect from them. They think we ought to go ahead and make you the next Franklin Seals. Of course, Frank thinks we should follow the bylaws to the letter. Roland was less concerned about that."

"So what else is new, Ted?"

"Bill Gentry called me, pretty upset about it. Brenda and I had the same concerns you did about ordaining him, but he's with you on this one, thinking for himself instead of waiting to see what Doc says. Eric Latham said if they run you off that they'll have to run him and Jenny off with you. Brenda's normally a sweet, gentle woman, but right now I wouldn't want to get caught between her and the person who wrote that stupid letter if she knew who it was."

"How do you think we ought to respond to it?"

"I don't, and we won't while I'm chairman. One of my policies at the paper is that I don't publish unsigned letters. If the deacons were to respond to this thing, it'd be just like me printing it in the *Courier*. I can't speak for all the deacons, just telling you where I stand. If the deacons want to respond to this thing, they'll have to elect another chairman, because I won't present their response to the church. A person who won't sign his name doesn't deserve an answer. We don't even know whether this clown's a member of the church. That's what I've told all the ones who've called me about it."

"It seems like things have been going so well in the church," Mike spoke haltingly. "I know we've got our chronic malcontents, but overall I feel good about the church. I wonder how many people agree with the writer of this letter."

"Not many. Of course, this character is the self-proclaimed spokesperson for this great invisible multitude that thinks you and Karen ought to be strung up by your toes. This 'they, several, and some of 'em' business drives me crazy. Brenda can tell you, nothing gets my goat more than this kind of stuff. If we could find out who wrote it, some good old-fashioned church discipline would be in order, but I don't know how we could find out and prove it. The best thing is not to give people like this the recognition they want, not respond to it at all, and I don't think you need to respond to it. I know it's hard not to, because the letter attacks you and your wife. I'd want to come out swinging if somebody attacked Brenda like that. It's natural to want to get up and refute it point by point. I can't tell you what to do, but I hope you don't respond to it. I know you feel threatened, but try not to let it show. It's that old bit of wisdom, 'when around sharks, don't bleed.' You're not in any danger. Ignore it and go on pastoring the church."

"What about the next deacons meeting? Somebody's sure to bring it up."

"Somebody besides me. I'm not going to let anybody see me in a state of panic. We'll discuss it if somebody else brings it up. I'm not going to let it take up the whole deacons meeting, and there'll be no public response from the deacons while I'm chairman."

Mike thanked Ted for the affirming words and tried to heed his counsel, but he was stung by the letter and frustrated by his inability to respond to the person hiding behind it. He picked it up and read it again,

Dear Church Leader:

I am writing on behalf of a significant and growing number of church members who believe that our church made a grave mistake in calling Mike Westover as pastor. We believe that it is time to remove him, and we urge the deacons to call for his resignation for the good of the church.

The chairman of the pastor search committee and his wife have left the church. That in itself should tell us something. A number of other long-time members are ready to leave the church if the deacons fail to take action.

Rather than leading the church into the future, Mike Westover has opened old wounds by dredging up things that happened almost thirty years ago. He and Mrs. Westover named their new baby Deborah to remind the church of the unfortunate tragedy that occurred in 1964. Mike Westover has forced the issue of women deacons down our throats. Many of us believe that Mrs. Coleman has no business serving as a deacon. It is the position of the Southern Baptist Convention that women should not be ordained as deacons or ministers, which reflects the clear teaching of Scripture. If we are a Southern Baptist church—and we are— we have no right to go against the position of our denomination.

The abrasive manner of Mrs. Westover has deeply offended some long-time members of Harrington Baptist Church. Mrs. Westover is not submissive to her husband, and he has failed to assert his authority over her. He lets her do whatever she wants. The Westovers have tried to undermine the authority of the Board of Deacons and take total control of the church themselves. While the Westovers have found time to entertain Negroes at the parsonage, they have not found time to open their home to members of Harrington Baptist Church.

Quick and drastic action is needed to save our church. We who have belonged to Harrington Baptist Church for many years, supporting it generously with our time, money, and energy, we who have stood by the church in good times and bad, must not sit idly by while our church is taken from us. I speak for many who urge you to prayerfully seek God's guidance and take the appropriate action to save our church.

A Concerned Church Member

Mike must have read and re-read the letter a dozen times before he became aware of Karen looking over his shoulder. "Can you believe this?" he asked when he became aware of her presence.

"Yes, I can," she responded matter-of-factly. "This kind of stuff used to make the rounds at Luckett's Creek every couple of years. We had at least one pastor, Conley Bledsoe, the one who baptized me, get all panicked and leave because of a round of this garbage. I was ten when he baptized me, so I must've been eleven or twelve when he left. Daddy tried to shield us from it, but growing up in a deacon's family, you'd have to be dumber than a rock not to catch on. I heard you talking to Ted. What did he have to say?"

"He doesn't think it deserves a response, said there won't be a response from the deacons while he's chairman. He doesn't publish unsigned letters in the paper, and he's not going to give this clown any free publicity in the church."

"Well, I think we've got us a good deacon chairman, one in the same league with Wallace. Ted's trying to be a buffer between you and this kind of stuff, and I'd let him do it if I were you. I'm glad we're spending a couple of days with Mother and Daddy this week, get away from here and get our minds off this stuff." Gently massaging the back of Mike's neck, she continued, "I know this is upsetting, but Ted's right. Nothing's going to come of it. May I see the letter?"

Mike handed her the letter, thinking that she wanted to read it. He watched with a puzzled look as she carefully folded the top corners toward the center of the page to make a pointed shape and then made three precise parallel creases down the center to form the fuselage and wings. As she made the final crease and launched it into flight across the kitchen, she asked, "Mike, Hon, didn't anybody teach you how to make paper airplanes?"

*   *   *   *   *   *   *   *   *   *   *   *

About ninety people came to the service at 10:00 PM on Christmas Eve. Mike found it surprisingly easy to push aside thoughts of the anonymous letter and enjoy leading the service of carols, readings, and a candlelight communion observance. He was pleased to see Joyce and Carl Baxter and noticed that Judy Flint came with them. After the service, they went out of their way to speak to That Woman and Franklin A. Brinkley, Former Chairman of the Board of Deacons of Harrington Baptist Church. Roland and Geneva Millican were not there. Mike was pleased to see Brantley and Betty Jacobs, along with Aaron and Latisha Stewart and their two children. He knew the Stewarts were planning to come, and he had asked Aaron ahead of time to do one of the scripture readings. Miss Addie sat with the Stewarts, and most of the people spoke to them and welcomed them. After the service, Miss Addie took considerable pride in telling people that she had been Aaron's first grade teacher.

It was a few minutes past midnight when Brantley and Betty dropped Mike off at the parsonage, apologizing profusely for keeping him so late. Karen had long since taken the children home and put them to bed. Brantley and Betty had lingered after everyone else was gone to talk with Mike. Betty said she needed to confess something, that she had taken communion that night for the first time since she was nineteen years old, and she hoped she hadn't done anything wrong. She explained that she had never taken communion outside the Catholic church before, and she knew her Irish Catholic mother was turning over in her grave. "I wasn't planning to do it when I came here. I hesitated, didn't know if I ought to do it or not," she gushed, "but you said 'all who love the Lord Jesus Christ, all who look to Him for the forgiveness of their sins, all who desire to follow Him, are welcome at the Lord's table.' I do love the Lord Jesus Christ, He has forgiven my sins, and I want with all my heart to follow Him. So, when Brenda offered me the bread and the grape juice, I took you at your word."

Mike assured Betty that she had done the right thing. She and Brantley had a lot of stored-up questions. As the three of them talked in the dimly-lit sanctuary, Brantley's facade as the town agnostic crumbled. He apologized for not knowing much about the Bible, since he didn't grow up in the church. Mike told him that he didn't, either. Brantley explained that, after a stint in the Navy during the Korean War, he had gone into the restaurant business with his father and grandfather, and he had worked seven days a week all of his adult life until he sold the business in Atlanta and moved to Harrington. The usually articulate fifty-seven year old man searched for words with which to frame the same questions eleven year old Cassie McWhorter had asked. As Mike got out of the Jacobs' car and walked toward the house, he made a mental note to call Ted and Brenda the next morning to wish them a merry Christmas and ask them to help with the two baptisms on the first Sunday in January.

✳   ✳   ✳   ✳   ✳   ✳   ✳   ✳   ✳   ✳   ✳   ✳

Asalee picked up the phone when Wallace called a little before noon on Christmas day. They were about to leave for Williston to spend a couple of days with Karen's family. If Wallace had called ten minutes later he would have missed them. He almost convinced Asalee that he was Santa Claus, calling to make sure she found all of her presents, but she recognized his voice and said, "Papa Wallace! You're pulling my leg!"

After Mike and Karen picked up the phone, Wallace wished them a merry Christmas and said he didn't mean to be a gossip, but he wanted to pass along the news about the latest romantic development at Clear Springs. "The week Brother Dennis Palmer spent with me seemed to do him good, and it sure was nice to have his company," Wallace began the story. "Brother Dennis got up here the Saturday before Thanksgiving, went to church with me the next mornin'. First time any of 'em at church'd seen 'im in 'bout fifteen years. He ended up talkin' a long time with Carol after church that mornin', again that night, and again on Wednesday night. Friday night, Carol sent the kids up to her mother'n daddy's, and her'n Brother Dennis went out to dinner and a movie. Brother Dennis said it was the first time either one of 'em'd gone out with anybody since their divorces. Anyway, he drove back up here yesterday, spent the night with me last night, and he's spendin' the day today with Carol and her kids."

"Sounds serious," Mike observed.

"I think it is. Brother Dennis talked to me a long time last night, asked me what I thought about him'n Carol datin' each other. I told 'im Carol was a mighty good woman, 'course, he knew that. Some people might think I'm wrong, but I told 'im to go right ahead. Way I see it, they're both good people who love the Lord, both got good sense about 'em. Both been hurt pretty bad, did'n neither one of 'em deserve it, far as I can tell. I did'n never know Brother Dennis's first wife 'cause he did'n get married 'til after he left Clear Springs, but I did know Bill Richardson, an' I know he did'n do right by Carol and the children. A man'd be mighty blessed to have one child turn out as nice as all three of the Richardson kids have turned out, but Bill had'n had the time 'a day for the children he had with Carol since he got hooked up with that woman up at Blacksburg. Carol and those children of hers deserve a lot better, if you ask me."

"Did Brother Dennis and his first wife have any children?"

"No children. His ex-wife is done married to somebody else. Carol's kids sure have taken to Brother Dennis, Little Bill especially. Lord willin', I hope it works out for 'em. Brother Dennis is already talkin' 'bout movin' back up this way'n lookin' for work up here."

"Well," Mike observed, "if they keep seeing each other, it'll be interesting to see how the church deals with it. We talked a lot about Linda and Carol being the first women deacons in the history of the church, but Carol's also the first divorced deacon in the history of the church, as far as I know."

"Far as I know, too," Wallace concurred. "She was the first'n in my time, so I'd say she was the first. I'm pretty sure she was the first one in the Sanders County Association."

"Kind of ironic that ol' Lester Halstead'll be the second one," Mike noted. "That is if Brother Billy and True Gospel let him keep on serving."

"Had'n thought about it, but you're right. The church'll be fine about it if Carol'n Brother Dennis get married, in fact, the church'd be right happy for 'em. Since we're not in the association any more, we don't have to worry about what ol' Lester'n Brother Billy have to say about it. Oh yeah, I meant to tell you something else. When Brother Dennis spent Thanksgiving week with me, went to church with me the Sunday before Thanksgiving, Sister Heather asked 'im if he'd stay over to the next Sunday and preach for us. He did, and you could tell it was hard for him, but he sure did bring a good message. First time he'd preached since he got chewed up at the church down in North Carolina."

"I hope he'll have the opportunity to pastor again," Karen commented.

"Me too," Wallace agreed. "He sure would make some church a good pastor. I've about decided that church that hurt Brother Dennis so bad must've been a lot like ol' Bill Richardson, not havin' sense enough to appreciate the blessin' the Lord gave 'em. Hard for me to understand, but some churches use preachers the way some men use women. Comin' up here seemed to do Brother Dennis good, and I sure did enjoy his company."

Karen told Wallace and Mike that she couldn't help thinking about the stanza of "Rescue the Perishing" that goes,
Down in the human heart, crushed by the tempter,
Feelings lie buried that grace can restore.
Touched by a loving heart, wakened by kindness,
Chords that were broken will vibrate once more.

* * * * * * * * * * * *

"You know something, Mike?" Karen asked as Mike headed the car out of town toward the Alabama line.

"What's that?"

"Other than the one night I spent in the hospital when Deb was born, this'll be our first night away from home since we've been in Harrington, and we've been there seven months now."

"Hadn't thought much about it, but you're right."

"I'm glad we're getting away for a few days, even if it's just to hang loose with family. Don't get me wrong. I like Harrington for the most part, but I'm ready to come up for air. Did you leave Mother and Daddy's phone number with somebody?"

"Only Ted and Brenda. Ted said it'd be a sure enough emergency if he called us, said it'd take more than That Woman having a spell with her heart.

"She's not going to have a spell with her heart while we're out of town. She wouldn't have her audience, and you wouldn't be able to go rushing across the street. My heart'll quit before hers does."

* * * * * * * * * * *

Karen's two brothers and their families had gone home. Harold carried Asalee upstairs and put her to bed after she went to sleep in the floor watching a cartoon video on the big screen TV that had been Harold's and Margaret's Christmas present to each other. Karen had changed into flannel pajamas, and she covered herself with an afghan as she curled up at one end of the big over-stuffed sofa to nurse Deborah Estelle. Margaret was sitting next to Karen, eagerly waiting to hold her four-month-old granddaughter.

"Y'all want anything else to eat?" Harold asked. "Plenty of leftovers in the Frigidaire."

"Thanks, Pop, I'm stuffed," Mike responded. "Couldn't eat another bite if my life depended on it."

"Same here," Karen concurred.

"So how are things at Harrington, Mike?" Harold probed. "Seemed like some nice people, had a right good attendance the Sunday we were over there last month."

"OK, I guess. We had about ninety for the Christmas Eve service. Attendance and offerings have been pretty good. No surplus to speak of, but we're meeting budget. Deacons meetings are more productive and less stressful now that Ted Coleman's chairman."

"Ted's the young guy that runs the newspaper?"

"Right."

"I sure did like him and his wife the little bit I got to talk to them at the hospital when Deb was born and the Sunday we were in church with you."

"Ted's a good guy, vast improvement over ol' Franklin A. Brinkley, Former Chairman of the Board of Deacons of Harrington Baptist Church. Ted's on the same page with me, helping me shift the focus of the deacons away from being a board of directors toward helping with the pastoral care ministry."

"That's a hard thing to do, and you can get yourself killed real easy. A collision between a young preacher and a *board of* deacons is like a collision between a Honda Civic and a Mack truck. Glad you've got a good chairman to take some heat off of you."

"So how long've you been a deacon, Pop?"

"I was ordained in '61, about a month after Karen was born, back when Leonard Haley was pastor. You know, the hardest thing for me when I became a deacon was that I had all these idealistic notions about deacons being spiritual leaders, but it didn't take me but a couple of deacons meetings to figure out they picked me to be a deacon because of my business experience. If it was business sense they wanted, they ought to've made Margaret a deacon, and I told 'em so. I'm a good enough pharmacist, but Margaret was the business manager as long as we had the store. If I'd been trying to run the business part, we'd've folded the first year we were open. Other than serving the Lord's supper, a man doesn't even need to be a Christian to do most of the stuff we do as deacons at Luckett's Creek. I mean, there's no difference between fixing the leaky faucet at the church and fixing the leaky faucet at Joe's Tavern. And, for all the talking we do about not being the preacher's bosses, it sure is easy to fall into the routine of doing just that. Now I remember when I had my heart attack and bypass surgery, Wayne and June Ethridge drove all the way down from Virginia, drove all night long, to see me and pray with me before my surgery, and they stayed with Margaret and the kids 'til I was out in recovery. Now, to me, that's what being a deacon's all about, and it sure meant a lot to me. They did it because they wanted to, not because anybody expected 'em to. I don't mean this as a criticism of Brother Woodrow, but Wayne and June were more help to me that Brother Woodrow was, especially since Wayne had been through the same thing."

"Doesn't surprise me," Mike commented. "Their presence sure meant a lot to Karen, I know that, especially since we hadn't been at Clear Springs very long when all of that happened. The deacons at Clear Springs have always done most of the day-to-day pastoral ministry, since they've always had student pastors who were thirty miles away at the seminary. The only thing unusual about what

Wayne and June did was that they drove further than usual to do it. The deacons at Clear Springs are as good at crisis ministry as a lot of pastors, better than some."

"So how are your deacons at Harrington handling this change of direction? They're used to having a full-time pastor, and they're used to running the church."

"It's an adjustment. Some are more ready than others. David Groves, the Chevy dealer, was a big help back when Royce Green got killed. Royce had family coming from out of town, and David took up a lot of time, picking them up when they flew into Dobbins and helping them while they were in Harrington for the funeral. It was the toughest situation he ever had to deal with. I think he surprised himself how well he did and how much his ministry meant to Royce's family. Ted and Brenda came from a church in Macon with a strong deacon family ministry program, so they're more geared to that understanding of deacon ministry. Eric Latham grew up in a church with a board about like Luckett's Creek, but he's a people person, one of the most compassionate men I know. He's the band director at Harrington High School, very popular with his students. Last year, one of the girls in the band got pregnant. She was scared to death, worried about how she was going to tell her parents. She confided in Eric. Eric and Jenny met with her and her parents, helped her break the news to them. They handled that as well as anyone could have, and that whole family's in our church now. So, I've got some people on board who have the same vision I do, but I've also got Doc Walters and Franklin A. Brinkley, Former Chairman of the Board of Deacons of Harrington Baptist Church, trying to pull us back to the old ways—duplicating the work of the committees, endless discussions about the logistics of taking the offering and serving communion."

"Believe me, I know the drill," Harold groaned sympathetically.

"We've got a couple of other deacons who aren't active, but they still have a lot of influence in the church, and they're very much into the board mentality. Then there's ol' Bill Gentry, new deacon, just ordained in October. Bless his heart, good guy, but he was chosen for his knowledge of heating, air conditioning, plumbing, and electrical systems. But, as I recall, most of the ones Jesus picked for disciples were guys I'd hesitate to ordain. Bill's got a tendency to ride Doc's coattails because he doesn't know what else to do, but he can be influenced. So, to answer your question in a round-about way, yes, it can be turned around; no, I don't expect it to be easy. We'll always have those trying to pull us back to the old ways. I like your observation, Pop, about the board mentality being the default mode for deacons. It's the path of least resistance."

"Anything new since the last issue of your newsletter?" Margaret asked.

"We gained two more by profession of faith last night, though the church won't know it 'til Sunday. You remember Brantley and Betty Jacobs, the ones who have the restaurant in the old depot?"

"Sure," Harold responded, "we met them when you took us out to dinner on Saturday night when we were up there. Nice folks."

"I'll be baptizing both of them the first Sunday in January. They hung around to talk to me last night after everybody was gone, and we talked 'til after midnight. They've been catering our Wednesday night dinners for a couple of months, so the folks in the church know them. Betty grew up Catholic, been away from the church since she was a teenager. Brantley's the third generation of his family in the restaurant business. He worked seven days a week his whole adult life until he came to Harrington a few years ago. He really had no church background at all. Betty started coming to church first, and then he started coming with her some. Last night, he was asking the same kinds of questions ten and eleven year old kids would ask. To make a long story short, I'll be presenting them this coming Sunday. I called Ted and Brenda this morning to wish them merry Christmas and tell them about Brantley and Betty."

"I'm enjoying my Mothers Morning Out group," Karen injected. "We've got about a dozen moms now, and we've got one couple, Lori and Daniel Pettit, who joined the church after Lori connected with Mothers Morning Out. Things are OK," Karen continued as she burped Deborah Estelle and handed her over to Margaret. "Still, it feels good to come up for air for a few days before we plunge back in. I don't think we realized how stressed we were from everything coming to light about the killing of Debbie Seals and then the murder trial."

"How did that come out?" Margaret asked as she cuddled her youngest grandchild.

"As good as it could, I guess. Billy Ray was convicted on first degree murder, and they sentenced him to life. The whole trial business was hard on the church. I'm glad it's over."

"It's a wonder they got a conviction on a case that old," Harold observed.

"Yeah, I wasn't counting on it," Karen concurred. "It sort of surprised me, too. Aaron Stewart, our police chief, took a personal interest in the case when they got their big break. His sister was one of Debbie's piano students, and Brother Seals used to take him fishing when he was a kid. The district attorney put in a lot of hard work on the case and prosecuted it herself. Looks like they did everything right. Jury deliberated about an hour before they returned a guilty verdict. Mike and I had no idea the can of worms we were opening when we named our baby after Debbie Seals, but I'm still glad we did. We met Debbie's mother and brother when they came up for the trial, seem like really good people. Mrs. Seals gave us a picture of Debbie that was made not long before she was killed."

"Did you bring it with you?" Margaret asked.

"No, it's in a frame, sitting on the piano. Seemed like the obvious place. Debbie was a very talented pianist. From the time she was eleven or twelve, her parents took her to one of the music profs at West Georgia College for her piano lessons. She was too advanced for any of the teachers in Harrington. She was teaching piano to about a half dozen younger kids at the time she was killed. That's one of the reasons they ran Brother Seals off. Two of her students were black. The deacons told Brother Seals to make her stop teaching the black kids, or at least make her stop teaching them at the pastorium, and he refused."

"I hope I'd have the integrity he had if I were in the same situation," Mike added. "It's hard for me to believe the church ran him off right after he buried his daughter."

"I can believe it," Harold stated flatly. "I hate to break the news to you, Son. Some of these churches can be meaner'n Hell. The ones who are ring leaders running off preachers can seem like nice people 'til they get ready to do their dirty work, and then they go right back to being nice as soon as they're done. Luckett's Creek's chewed up a couple of good pastors, Karen can tell you. Conley Bledsoe, the one who baptized Karen, was one of our casualties. Somebody sent out a bunch of anonymous letters claiming he was running around on his wife. Brother Conley told the deacons he hadn't done any such thing. I thought he was telling the truth, still do, never saw any evidence to indicate that he wasn't, but some of the deacons said 'where there's smoke, there's fire,' thought there had to be something to it just 'cause somebody who wouldn't sign their name said so. His wife stood by him, though I know she had to be awful hurt and humiliated."

"So what'd they have against the man?"

"Some of 'em didn't like it because his wife worked outside the home. Didn't want to pay him enough to live on, but they griped about her not being home all the time. Far as I was concerned, his wife working was between the two of them and none of the church's business. The church did him dirty, and it took him about two years to get called to another church. It made me so mad when I was on the pulpit committee, the way most of 'em didn't want to consider anybody who didn't have a church. It was OK for us not to have a pastor because we'd just run off a good one for no good reason, but it wasn't OK for a preacher not to have a church. If a preacher wasn't in a pastorate, they wouldn't even talk to him. Marvin Grayson was another good one our church didn't do right by."

"Tell me something, Pop. There are plenty of good people in every church. Why do they allow a handful to run off preacher after preacher? Why doesn't the church deal with the trouble-makers instead of running the preacher off?"

"Because preachers come and go, and those people are here to stay. We have to live with them, or we think we do. If we stood up to them, they'd get upset and leave the church, go cause trouble somewhere else, or that seems to be the way most of the people see it. It's not the way I look at it. If they're that unhappy, let 'em leave. We'd be better off without them. Funny thing, they wouldn't have any trouble getting another church to take them in as members, but let a pastor leave without a call to another church, and he has an awful time getting another church to consider him. Far as I'm concerned, there's something wrong with that picture."

"I wish everybody looked at it that way," Karen injected. "but they don't. Most of the church is with us, and I don't think we're about to get run off, but we've just had our first round of anonymous letters. They came on Christmas Eve. A lovely touch I thought, almost as nice as canning Franklin Seals before his daughter's body was cold. Mike's never seen that kind of garbage before, and it floored him."

"I'm OK about it," Mike said, his voice registering more than a little irritation at Karen for mentioning the letter to her parents. "It mostly made me mad, frustrated me because I couldn't identify the person, go see 'em, choke the living daylights out of 'em—in a loving, redemptive, pastoral way, of course."

"Have you talked to your deacons about it?" Harold asked.

"Just Ted. He's as mad about it as I am, Brenda too. Ted said he'd hate to get caught between Brenda and the person who wrote that letter if she knew who it was. Ted said he doesn't publish unsigned letters in the paper, and the deacons won't make any public response to it while he's chairman."

"Sounds like you've got a good chairman. Wish we had one like him at Luckett's Creek. Tell me why some churches like Clear Springs don't have this garbage?"

"The short answer is two words, Wallace Coggins. The long answer is that stuff like this only happens where there's a climate of tolerance for it. People don't stoop to dirty tricks unless they have some cause to think they'll work. People don't try this stuff at Clear Springs because they know it wouldn't work. Clear Springs doesn't welcome people who want to play those games. Anybody who was into that kind of stuff would find out quickly that the church isn't willing to play their game, and they'd give up and go somewhere else. If somebody tried that foolishness at Clear Springs, the church would hold them accountable."

"One other thing," Karen added, "Clear Springs isn't afraid of losing members. People can't hold the church hostage by threatening to leave. We had one family, the Kelseys, who left when we ordained Carol and Linda. Mike and I didn't know them all that well, because they left about the time we got there, but the church let them go in peace and didn't try to hold onto them. The church wouldn't have reached a lot of the people it's reached since then if they'd bent over backwards to hold onto the Kelseys. They joined

Bethany, which is closer to where they live anyway, they're still friends with people at Clear Springs, and everybody is better off."

* * * * * * * * * * * *

"Mike, it's for you," Harold called out after he answered the phone. They had just gotten up from eating a late breakfast on the morning after Christmas. As he handed the receiver to his son-in-law, he added, "it's Carol Richardson."

"Hey, Carol, what's up?" a bewildered Mike asked as he took the phone.

"Hey, Mike. I tried to call your house, got the message on the voice mail with Ted and Brenda's number. I called them, and they gave me the number where I could reach you."

"Is something wrong?" Mike felt his stomach knotting up as he asked the question.

"I'm sorry to be the one to have to call you with this." Carol's voice broke with emotion. "Mike, it's Wallace. Matt and Sarah Beth's boys found him last night. He was supposed to eat supper with Matt and Sarah Beth and spend the night at their place. When he didn't show up and they couldn't get him on the phone, the boys went to check on him. They found him in his recliner, tried to revive him, but he was gone. Looks like he kicked back in his recliner, dozed off, and didn't wake up."

24

"I can't believe Wallace is gone." Karen must have uttered those words a half dozen times. Her eyes red from crying, feeling numb, she sat at the kitchen table slowly sipping another cup of coffee, trying to absorb the news of Wallace's death. "We all talked to him right before we left home yesterday. We may've been the last ones to talk to him. I could accept it more easily if he'd been sick or lying bedfast in a nursing home somewhere, but Wallace seemed to be feeling fine when we talked to him. Asalee answered the phone, and Wallace tried to pull her leg, make her think he was Santa Claus. If it'd been Maude or Arthur Sessions, it'd be easier to accept. It'd be a blessing for their suffering to be over, but Wallace…"

Asalee was crying hard, great heaving sobs. Harold pulled his granddaughter close, gently rubbed her back, and let her cry. "It's OK to cry, Az. Sit up here in Paw Paw's lap and cry as much as you need to." Asalee accepted the invitation, curled up in his lap, buried her face in his shoulder, and wept.

"I feel like I should be able to dial his number and hear him answer on the first or second ring, 'Hello, Wallace Coggins,' the way he always did. Retired twenty years, still answered the phone like he thought it might be the dispatcher calling him for one more run," Mike reminisced. Hot tears trickled down his cheeks as he held Deborah Estelle and played with her. "I sure am glad he got to make his big trip, see all the people he saw, spend the time he spent with us, and make the trip over to McMillan to help with the new church. Not many people his age could've done what he did. He talked about seeing Rock City and Ruby Falls, said he'd been seeing those signs painted on barns for sixty years, and he figured he'd better see Rock City and Ruby Falls if he was ever going to. Maybe he had a premonition."

"Wouldn't surprise me," Margaret Owen observed. "I know Granny Kemp did. Bless her heart, she loved to play her piano, but the arthritis in her hands got so bad it hurt too much for her to play, and her eyes were so bad she couldn't see the music. She played at church, played for opening assembly before Sunday School and filled in when they needed her until she was well up in her eighties, 'til she got to where she couldn't do it any more. She knew her time was near. Karen, remember how she loved to hear you play her piano? Y'all were down here that weekend, and she called and asked if you'd come over and play her piano for her..."

"Oh, I'll never forget that. It was a Saturday. Asalee was about two, and Ma really took on over her. We had the best time. She kept pulling out tons of old sheet music, awful maudlin stuff from around World War I up into the 20's and 30's. I played through some of it, making fun of the music and lyrics the whole time, really hamming it up. Ma was laughing so hard tears were running down her face and she had to sit down and catch her breath. I played until I thought my fingers were going to fall off! I don't think I ever saw Ma happier than she was that day, and she kept telling us how much she enjoyed our visit as we were leaving. Sunday morning, she got up and went to Sunday School and church. Sunday night, she went to bed and died in her sleep. I know it's awful to laugh at a funeral, but all through her funeral, I kept getting tickled, thinking about how she laughed and clapped when Asalee started dancing around while I was playing *Redwing*. She lived to be ninety-two and died happy. I contributed to her happiness, and that's what I kept thinking about. I'm so glad we've got her old piano. I know she's looking over my shoulder when I get in the mood to pull out that arrangement of *Redwing*."

"Wallace was like Ma Kemp," Mike observed. "He'd done just about everything he ever wanted to do and seen just about everything he ever wanted to see. After ordaining Heather, making his big trip, and helping constitute the new church at McMillan, he was like ol' Simeon saying *"Now Lord, Thou dost let Thy bond-servant depart in peace, according to Thy word..."* He lived a good long life and died happy, which is all anybody could ask for. He'd been ready for the Lord to take him ever since Estelle died. He was lost without her. Wallace said the only thing he missed out on was getting a song written about him, said he reckoned an engineer'd have to get himself killed before anybody'd write a song about him. He had us cracking up one night, talking about all the songs written about engineers who got killed on account of their own carelessness, said nobody ever wrote a song about an engineer who retired with forty-seven years service and a flawless safety record."

"Yeah," Karen laughed through her tears, "Wallace said if he'd been a better poet, he'd've done something about that, but as far as he could get was *Come and listen to my story of an old-time engineer who always took the time to get his orders clear...*He said being found in the wreck with your hand on the throttle is not what it's cracked up to be, and if that's the only way to be famous, he'd just as soon live out his years in obscurity."

"I'm glad he lived out his years in obscurity at Clear Springs," Mike commented. "glad he was there for us and for Heather."

"And he was there twice for Dennis Palmer," Karen noted, "first when he pastored Clear Springs and again after he got chewed up at the church in North Carolina. Speaking of Dennis, wasn't he supposed to've spent the night with Wallace Christmas Eve?"

"He did," Mike responded. "Carol said Dennis got to Wallace's about nine o' clock Christmas Eve. Wallace usually goes to bed about dark-thirty'n gets up with the chickens, but he was waiting up for him when he got there. They talked a while, went to bed a little after ten. Dennis woke up about six-thirty, and Wallace was already shaved and dressed, sitting at the kitchen table, drinking coffee and reading his Bible. Wallace cooked breakfast for them. Dennis said Wallace seemed fine. They talked a good while over breakfast and cleaned the kitchen up together. Dennis left about nine to go over to Carol's, and Wallace was getting ready to go over to Ledford to visit a couple of children who had to spend Christmas day in the hospital. Wallace told Dennis that he was going over to Matt and Sarah Beth's later in the day for dinner with all the family, said he'd never locked the doors in the fifty-six years he'd lived there, told Dennis to come on in when he got back. Wallace said he'd spend the night at Matt and Sarah Beth's since he didn't drive after dark, but he'd be coming home at sunup, told Dennis to make himself at home 'til he got back. Dennis is torn up pretty bad over Wallace's death. Carol sounded overwhelmed, too. Dennis surprised her with an engagement ring and asked her to marry him, just a month after their first date. Carol thought that was all she could process in one day, and then to have Wallace die the same day—she said she was praying, 'Lord, please don't hit me with anything else today!'"

"So did Carol accept the ring and the proposal?" Karen asked.

"She did. Dennis asked her right in front of the kids, Carol said he like to've stopped her clock. They haven't set the date, probably be sometime this summer, of course the wedding'll be at Clear Springs."

"I want to go back for Wallace's funeral. I guess you do, too. Do you know the funeral arrangements?"

"Viewing's tomorrow night at Gresham Brothers in Ledford, funeral's Friday at 2:00 at the church. Wallace had everything pre-arranged. Carol said we're welcome to stay with her. We can go by the house, pack clothes for the funeral, spend the night at Mother and Daddy's tonight, and get on the road early in the morning. The viewing's not 'til tomorrow evening because of all the people coming from out of town. Some of the Tennessee bunch who came up for Heather's ordination are coming. Wallace used to say he wanted everybody to go easy on the lamentations when he died, said he'd lived so long his friends in Heaven were wondering if he made it, so the service will be a celebration. You know we'll sing *I'll Fly Away.* Heather'll have the main funeral message, and Matt told Carol they want anybody who wants to say a word to feel free to do so. One more thing, Karen. The family wants you to do the committal like you did for Estelle, and they want us to sing *God Be With You 'Til We Meet Again* at the graveside, just like we did when Estelle died."

"I'll do it. Probably be a gazillion preachers there, but if they want me to, I will."

"How come Papa Wallace died?" Asalee asked as she snubbed back tears and rubbed her eyes.

"Because we all have to die, Az," Karen answered. "We're sad because he died, but Papa Wallace lived a long, long time. He was almost eighty-seven. Remember you and Papa Wallace had the same birthday. You were born on his eightieth birthday. I'm glad he lived long enough for you to know him, long enough to see Deborah Estelle and hold her."

"Is Papa Wallace with Jesus up in Heaven now?"

"Of course he is, Az."

"Neat," Asalee responded as a slight smile broke across her tear-streaked face, "that's where Mama Stell is. Papa Wallace missed Mama Stell a lot. Now he won't be lonesome any more."

"That's right, Az. They're together with Jesus forever. And we'll be there too, someday, and we'll get to see them again."

"I'm going to miss Papa Wallace."

"We all are, Az. But it won't always hurt as bad as it hurts right now, and we can always think about the good things we remember about him, the funny stories he loved to tell, the way he liked to pull your leg..."

"Yeah, trying to make me think he was Santa Claus..."

"That was just like Wallace," Mike acknowledged. "My favorite was the time he had you believing he could remember back before they put the river through Riverton."

"Don't forget his excuse for not having a knee replacement on that left knee that bothered him so much," Karen added, "said he was so old they couldn't get the parts."

*   *   *   *   *   *   *   *   *   *   *   *

"Come on in," Carol called out as she stood on the deck of her double-wide mobile home, holding the storm door open. She hugged Mike, Karen, and Asalee as soon as they got within arm's reach. "Sorry it's a funeral that brings you back up here, but it sure is good to see you all. Oh, and this must be Deborah Estelle. She's so pretty! I can't wait to hold her! I'm so glad you could come. Come on in, I want you to meet my fiancee, Dennis Palmer, the man who put me into full cardiac arrest Christmas morning. Dennis, this is one of our former pastors, Mike Westover, his wife Karen, daughter Asalee, and new baby Deborah."

"Pleased to meet you," Mike said as he shook hands with Dennis. "We've heard good things about you. Wallace sure did speak well of you."

"Not surprised," Dennis responded with a self-effacing chuckle, "a man'd have to be a real scoundrel before you'd hear Wallace say anything bad about him. Never heard him or Estelle say anything unkind about any preacher they ever had. I sure did appreciate him going to the trouble to look me up when he made his trip. Did me good to see him, first time I'd seen him since I left Clear Springs in '75. I'm glad I took him up on the invitation to come up here and stay with him—'come rest your soul' was the way he put it, and that's pretty much what I did."

With Little Bill Richardson tagging along, Dennis went with Mike to help bring in the luggage. Karen lifted Deborah Estelle out of her carrier and placed her in Carol's waiting arms. Carol sat in the recliner cuddling the baby while her daughters hovered close, awaiting their turns to hold her. "I can't believe how fast things are coming together for Dennis and me," Carol said as she put Deborah up on her shoulder and gently rubbed her back. "Dennis followed Kevin Stone in '72, the year I graduated from high school and went away to college. I didn't always get home on weekends when I was in college, didn't always make it to church when I did, so I didn't know Dennis all that well back then. When he left in '75, I was engaged to Bill. I never thought I'd see Dennis again, and here we are engaged! Christmas morning, after we opened all the presents, Dennis said, 'Carol, I've got one more present for you,' and he handed me this little ring box. I opened it, saw it was an engagement ring, tried to open my mouth to say something and no sound would come out! Right there in front of my kids, he got down on his knees and asked me to marry him. The kids're all jumping up and down, cheering and saying, 'Say yes, Mom! Say yes, Mom!' Dennis and I really hit it off when we renewed our acquaintance the week of Thanksgiving, and we both enjoyed ourselves so much when we went out together. I haven't had that much fun on a date since I was a teenager. We've been writing and calling back and forth ever since, and I was definitely interested in continuing the relationship, but I had no idea he was going to pull an engagement ring on me and pop the question, at least not this soon. As soon as I got my heart restarted and got my breath back, I threw my arms around him, kissed him, and said 'yes.'"

Mike caught the tail end of the conversation between Carol and Karen as he and Dennis came in and set the suitcases down. "I wish Wallace could've known about the engagement ring. Wallace told us when we talked to him Christmas day that he didn't mean to be a gossip, but he told us y'all were seeing each other, said he'd given his blessing, but apparently he didn't know about the ring."

"Wallace knew all about it," Dennis interjected. "I showed him the ring at breakfast, told him I was going to ask Carol to marry me. He said 'go for it,' laughed and said he wished he could be a fly on the wall so he could see the look on Carol's face. He told me how he shocked the daylights out of Estelle proposing to her in the cab of the engine at Coley's Station the day before her nineteenth birthday, showed me a picture of the engine they were on when he proposed to her. So Wallace knew. Other'n the guy at the jewelry store in North Carolina who sold me the ring, he was the only one who knew. Wallace didn't tell you because he wanted you to hear it from us."

"Karen, Mike, y'all go ahead and put your things in my room," Carol directed. "I'll sleep on the sofa bed tonight, Dennis is going to spend the night at Mom and Dad's. Put Asalee's things in Megan and Jessica's room. I need to check on the roast in the oven. We've got so many coming from out of town that we're spreading supper at the church for everybody before we go to the funeral home. Claude Bradley, pastor over at Coley's Station, called me this morning, said his church and Bethlehem are fixing dinner after the funeral tomorrow for the family, our whole church, and all the people coming from out of town, because they knew this was like a death in the family for our whole church."

"Are the ones coming up from Tennessee here yet?" Mike asked.

"Got here about two hours before you did, set up the motor home over at Wayne and June's. Heather left after church Sunday to go down and spend Christmas with her family, so she rode back up here in the motor home. She's staying with Wanda used-to-be-Halstead, Wanda Gonzales, at her apartment in Ledford since the dorm's closed for the holidays. Heather's taking it hard. Wallace was such an encouragement to her, just like he was to you and every other pastor we've had. I know how she feels. You know Wallace stepped down as chairman of deacons in October, and I'm chairman now. Wallace said he wanted to turn it over to some-body else before he died at the throttle. I wouldn't've accepted it if Wallace hadn't had so much confidence in me. So, we've all had a death in the family. Of course, Wallace and I were related by mar-riage. Estelle was my great-aunt, but even the ones that aren't kin to him feel the loss. Tycina's going to sing at the funeral. Wallace loved to hear her sing. You know she graduates this year. Did I tell you? She just auditioned and won a scholarship to study voice at Peabody in Baltimore. She thought the world of Wallace. She's going to say something at the funeral about Wallace making the motion to receive her the Sunday she joined the church."

"Oh Lord, yes, I remember that Sunday!" Karen said. "We'd never had a black person presented for membership, and I didn't know how some of the church might react, but ol' Wallace, bless his heart, didn't hesitate, rolled out '*Movewereceiver*,' there'll never be anybody else who can say it like he could, sounded like God speaking from Heaven. Then Kim's mother seconded the motion. After that, nobody would've dared to object."

* * * * * * * * * * * *

"Hey, Mike, Karen, Az, glad y'all could come," Heather called out as she rushed over to hug the Westovers when they entered the fellowship hall at Clear Springs. "This is a shock about Wallace. He was such a vigorous, active man to the very last, seemed like he'd always be here."

"Well, I know how much you're going to miss him," Mike replied. "I went straight from Wallace to Franklin A. Brinkley, Chairman of the Board of Deacons of Harrington Baptist Church, sure did miss Wallace."

"He was so encouraging and helpful, couldn't do enough for me. "I guess you know the church called me full-time as soon as I graduate, which won't be a day too soon to suit me. Mid-Atlantic's getting worse by the day. I won't get into that except to say that knowing I'll soon be full-time at Clear Springs is the only thing that's getting me through this last year. That, and I want an M. Div. from Mid-Atlantic just to spite Sturgill. Does my heart good to know how much he'll agonize over signing an M. Div. with a woman's name on it. Coming down here on weekends and Wednesday nights is my sanity break. When I'm dealing with the craziness, I remind myself I can get in my little red Escort, drive thirty miles, and be in a rational universe. Sure is hard to leave here and go back to the Twilight Zone. This church never ceases to amaze me, how good they are to me, how progressive they are. It's been Wallace's influence more than anything."

"You've got that right. The church was doing something nice for us every time we turned around. Most of the time, Wallace was behind it one way or the other."

"Like the Christmas card Wallace handed me on his way out of church Sunday. I gave him a hug and thanked him and stuck the card in my Bible. When I got out to my car and opened it, there was a hundred-dollar bill inside and the sweetest note saying how much he appreciated my ministry and telling me to spend the money on something nice I can use."

"Sounds just like him. Wallace told us about deeding his house over to the church for a parsonage," Karen said.

"I'm going to enjoy living in Wallace and Estelle's house. Of course, Estelle died before my time, but I feel like I knew her from hearing Wallace and others talk about her. Like Wallace said, there's been a lot of love in that old house. It made him happy to be able to give it to the church, and the same spirit's rubbed off on their kids. On what would've been Wallace and Estelle's sixty-fourth anniversary, right after the church voted to call me full-time, they gave a generous gift to furnish a pastor's study. Dr. Corrie's building the bookcases, solid cherry to match the frame he made for my ordination certificate. Wallace didn't live to see it finished, but he knew it was in the works. They surprised him making the presentation on his and Estelle's anniversary."

"Having a full-time pastor is going to be a big adjustment after a hundred-plus years of student pastors from Mid-Atlantic," Mike observed, "but it's a good move for the church. I think it'll be necessary to sustain the growth y'all are having."

"I agree. I love pastoring Clear Springs, but right now I'm run ragged with work, school, and pastoring the church. Plenty here to keep a full-time pastor busy. We'll miss Wallace. He did as much visiting as a lot of full-time pastors, enjoyed it, said he'd still do it if I was full-time. Even with Wallace gone, we still have a good group of deacons, and Carol's as good a chairman as anybody could want. It's still frustrating, though, seeing plenty of work for a full-time pastor and not having time to do it."

"I know the feeling. It was starting to get that way during our time, and the church has really taken off since you've been there."

"Which surprised me more than anybody. The Lord's doing it, Mike. I'd be afraid to take credit, afraid it would stop cold if I did, but I'm enjoying being caught up in it. Y'all go ahead and fix your plates. I expect there'll be a huge crowd at the funeral home."

*   *   *   *   *   *   *   *   *   *   *   *

Nobody minded the length of Wallace's service. It was, as he had wished, a celebration. More than two hundred people packed into the white-clapboard auditorium. Wallace would have said that people were taking on over him too much, but he would have been pleased that so many thought so well of him. He would have liked the singing. *I'll Fly Away* never sounded better, with two hundred voices singing parts and Tycina Nichols soaring high above them all as she improvised a soprano descant on the chorus. Mike Westover, Dennis Palmer, and retired Knoxville Division road foreman Isaiah Mathis III were among those who shared personal recollections. Megan Richardson and Wesley Trimble read scripture, Carol offered a prayer, and Tycina sang a medley of Wallace's favorite hymns before Heather preached. It was after 4:00 when Heather pronounced the benediction. Karen took her place beside Heather, and the two of them began the slow walk ahead of the casket, leading the procession out the front door of the church to the Coggins plot in the cemetery.

When they arrived at the graveside, the funeral director guided Wallace's immediate family to the four rows of chairs under the tent. The Corries saved a seat for Heather. She took her seat with the family, and Karen took her place at the head of the casket to do the committal. "It startled me," she began, "when Wallace asked me to do the committal at Estelle's funeral. I told him that I wasn't a preacher, I wasn't ordained, and I'd never done anything like that before. Wallace said he knew all of that and it didn't make any difference. He thought it would please Estelle for me to do it, so I did. When Carol called to tell us Wallace had died, she said the family wanted me to do the committal for Wallace, too. It is a sad privilege for me to honor that request as we stand at the graveside of a kind, gracious, godly man who leaves his fingerprints on the soul of every one of us. We will place Wallace's body in the ground. For Christians, that is an act of faith in God's promise of the resurrection. We will carry Wallace's legacy with us for generations to come. Let us hear the word of the Lord..."

＊ ＊ ＊ ＊ ＊ ＊ ＊ ＊ ＊ ＊ ＊ ＊

"Brother Dennis, my name's Becky Tant, and this is my husband John," Becky said as she and John sat down across the table from Dennis and Carol in the fellowship hall at Coley's Station Baptist Church. "We're from McMillan, Tennessee, got acquainted with Wallace when we were up here last spring for Heather's ordination. Carol, it's good to see you again, and congratulations to both of you on your engagement."

"Thanks, Becky, John," Dennis replied. "Pleased to meet you. So you know Heather?"

"Since the day she was born," Becky responded. "I was her Sunday School teacher when she was in the first and second grades, remember her telling me when she was seven years old that she was going to be a preacher."

"And she made a good one," Carol added. "We're so fortunate to have her as our pastor, even if we did get kicked out of the association for calling her. The Lord's blessing the church, and Heather's doing a wonderful job as pastor. As soon as she graduates, she'll become our first full-time pastor. A couple of months ago, Wallace deeded his house over to the church to be used as a pastor's residence after his death. We had no idea Wallace would be taken from us so soon, but the house'll be ready for Heather to move in when she graduates. It's a nice old house, very convenient to the church, about a quarter mile down Clear Springs Road. We need Heather on the field full-time with the growth we're experiencing."

"That's wonderful. Doesn't surprise me, though," John Tant responded. "Like Becky said, we've known her all her life. She's a very gifted young lady, and a powerful preacher to be so young. She brought a fine message at the funeral, though you could tell it was hard for her. We're thankful she's here. All the way up here, she was talking about how good this church is and how much she's enjoying being your pastor."

"Brother Dennis," Becky continued, "there's another church that needs a full-time pastor, Providence Baptist Church in McMillan, Tennessee. I'm chair of the pastor search committee, and two other members of the committee are here. Heather's daddy, Roy Simmons, is one of them, and Lance Robison is the other one who's here. There're two more who didn't make the trip up here. I hope I'm not getting ahead of myself. We just elected the committee a week ago, but I've talked to Roy and Lance, and they're thinking the same thing John and I are thinking. We were impressed by what you said at Wallace's funeral, and Heather told us a lot about you on the way up here. If it's agreeable with you, we want you and Carol to come down to McMillan, meet with the committee, preach for us, and look over the situation. We're a new church, don't have a building yet. Heather's dad owns the Ford dealership, and that's where we're having services. Roy says he's got the only showroom in the country with a pulpit and a piano in it. Heather's sister said we should've named it Ford Place Baptist Church. Dr. Kerns, just retired from Mid-Atlantic, is our interim pastor. If it's OK with you, we want to talk to the other two members of the committee and then call to set up a weekend that you and Carol could come down and meet with us."

"If it were just me, I'd say yes in a heartbeat. Only thing, Carol and her kids are rooted pretty deeply here. Carol's been teaching fifteen years at Sanders County High School, and she's chairman of deacons here at Clear Springs. That, and all her family's here."

"What do you teach, Carol?" John Tant asked.

"High school biology, and I want to keep teaching wherever Dennis and I live."

"Well, Carol, it looks like the Lord could be killing two birds with one stone. I'm principal at McMillan High School, and the head of my biology department is retiring at the end of this year. I talked to the superintendent last week. We've got a couple of applications, but we haven't hired anybody yet. Ward Tidwell's shoes will be hard to fill, good man, one of the best teachers we've ever had at McMillan High School. I've been praying for the Lord to send us somebody of the same caliber." Handing Carol his business card, he continued, "Here's my address. Get a resume to me as soon as possible. I'll set it up for you to tour the school, and I'll arrange for you to meet our superintendent and interview with her when you and Dennis come down."

* * * * * * * * * * * *

"Brother Mike, there's a message for you on the answering machine. Ted Coleman called about 3:30 while we were at the funeral. Needs you to call him as soon as possible," Carol came outside to report as Mike and Dennis were loading the Westovers' luggage into the car.

"Did he say what was up?"

"No, but it sounded urgent. Go ahead and use my phone."

"Thanks, Carol. Glad we got the message before we left. Ted said he wouldn't call us unless it was a genuine emergency."

Mike had an uneasy, queasy feeling as he picked up the phone to dial Ted and Brenda's number. "Hello," Ted answered on the second ring.

"Hey, Ted. This is Mike. Got your message on Carol's answering machine. We were at the church when you called. Huge crowd for Wallace's funeral, service lasted better'n two hours, and we had dinner at the church afterward. Just got back to Carol's place. What's up?"

"It's That Woman, Preacher. She had a spell with her heart this morning about 11:00, had to be rushed to the hospital..."

"Must be pretty serious, Ted. You told me when we talked Christmas morning that it'd take more than That Woman having a spell with her heart for you to call us, so I take it she's not pulling our leg. How serious is it?"

"Pretty serious, Preacher. She's dead."

"You're kidding."

"'Fraid not. They tried to get her stabilized at the hospital here in Harrington, thought she was stable enough to transport to Carrollton, but she died in the ambulance on the way. That Woman's been threatening or promising, depending on how you look at it, for years, finally did it, and it really was her heart."

"Do you know anything about the funeral arrangements?"

"Tommy Sheridan up at Webster Funeral Home faxed them over to me right before I left my office. Viewing's tomorrow, seven to nine, funeral's 2:00 Sunday afternoon at the church, burial at Oak Hill, you've got the service. The Brinkleys and Millicans are bent out of shape because you were off up there in Virginia when it happened."

Mike told Ted that they were just about to get on the road and that he would call Jean Brinkley and talk to her before they left. He told Ted of their plans to drive as far as his parents' home in Denham, catch a few hours' sleep, eat breakfast, and pick up Wallace the Dog. "Should be home around noon, so I can meet the family at the funeral home for the private viewing before the public viewing starts at seven."

"Sounds good. Y'all be careful on the way home."

"What's wrong, Hon?" Karen asked as Mike hung up the phone in the kitchen and came back into the living room, doing his best to keep from laughing.

"Well, it looks like you finally did it this time, Karen," Mike managed to say with a straight face.

"Did what, Mike?"

"Killed That Woman. She's dead. You might as well take credit, because you're gonna get the blame."

"What happened to her?"

"Heart attack, just like she's been threatening, or promising, depending on how you look at it. She wasn't bluffing this time."

Mike gave Karen a puzzled look as she pressed the fingers of her right hand against the artery in her left wrist. "Why are you checking your pulse?"

"I can't believe it. I could've sworn my heart'd quit before hers did."

Mike dialed the number of Frank and Jean Brinkley to talk to Jean and offer their condolences in the death of her mother. He breathed a sigh of relief when he got the answering machine, and he left a brief message assuring Jean that he would meet them for the private viewing at the funeral home Saturday evening.

25

"I feel like such a hypocrite going to the funeral home with you," Karen confessed as Mike headed the car toward Webster Funeral Home, "but it was nice of Kristin to watch the kids so we could both go and not have to drag the kids along. First time we've been anywhere, just the two of us, since Deb was born, and we're going to a funeral parlor!"

"Yeah, I know, but considering who's dead, you shouldn't complain."

"I'm not complaining, Mike. Ordinarily, I wouldn't be thrilled about going on a date to a funeral home, but I'll make an exception for That Woman, provided we don't stay any longer than we have to, just long enough to give our condolences to the family and make sure she's dead. Then you're taking me out to dinner."

"Sounds good to me," Mike concurred as he parked the car. "We're the first ones here. I don't see the Brinkleys' car or the Millicans' car. They should be impressed, considering we were in Virginia when she died. Try to look sad, Karen."

＊ ＊ ＊ ＊ ＊ ＊ ＊ ＊ ＊ ＊ ＊ ＊ ＊

"Hey, Pastor, Mrs. Westover, come on in," funeral director Tommy Sheridan said as he held the door open. "Y'all are the first ones here, so make yourselves at home while you wait for the family. I understand y'all just got back from Virginia. How was your trip?"

"OK," Mike replied. "We were up there for the funeral of a man we were really close to in my former pastorate. We were about to start home when we got the call from Ted telling us Hilda Mae was dead."

"I'm sorry to hear about your friend. Was it sudden or had he been sick a while?"

"Very sudden, just up and died. Wallace was eighty-six but didn't look it, retired Southern Railway engineer, he was just down to see us in September. He was our chairman of deacons at Clear Springs. Good man, and a real help to me in my first pastorate. He kicked back in his recliner Christmas afternoon, dozed off, and didn't wake up."

"Sounds like a fine man. Wish I could've known him. At least he didn't suffer," Tommy sympathized. Then, in his most solemn, funereal tone, he added, "It was a shock, rather sudden, wasn't it? About Mrs. Snyder, I mean."

"It really was," Karen replied in a tone of voice matching the solemnity of the funeral director. "I didn't think That Woman ever would die. I could've sworn my heart'd quit before hers did."

Tommy glanced around to be sure none of Hilda Mae's family had arrived. Seeing that they had not, he released a gale of pent-up laughter and allowed a big grin to break across his face as he regaled Mike and Karen with war stories about That Woman from the days when the funeral home ran ambulance service. "Back then, we didn't have an ambulance. When I started in '63, we had a '60 Cadillac hearse with a siren and red light on it and a gurney in the back. Just what an eighteen-year-old boy needs to be driving, vehicle with a four-hundred'n-something cubic inch motor, big ol' Quadrajet carburetor, and a siren and red lights. Gas hand on that sucker'd drop a quarter tank when you showered down on it. We carried a small tank of oxygen and a first aid kit, that was it. None of us were trained as paramedics. All we knew to do was give 'em oxygen and a fast ride to the hospital. That Woman rode more miles in the back of our hearse than any other living person. I started here when I was eighteen, making ambulance runs and picking up bodies at night'n on weekends, and she was the first'n I hauled. Good Lord willin', I'll haul 'er once more for old times' sake tomorrow, a little slower this time."

Karen excused herself on the pretense of going to the restroom and slipped away, leaving Mike talking to Tommy. She cracked open the door of the room where Hilda Mae lay in state, sneaked inside, pulled the door to behind herself, and tiptoed over to the casket. That Woman looked rather peaceful in her expensive solid cherry casket, laid out in an attractive gray wool suit with a white silk blouse and an elegant pearl necklace, hands folded demurely at her waist. The mortician had somehow managed to put a slight, almost angelic smile on her face in place of the usual scowl, and the beautician brought in by the funeral home did a better job than the one who usually fixed her hair.

Karen must have spent a couple of minutes studying That Woman's uncharacteristically peaceful countenance before she said, "Hilda Mae, I know you did this to make us feel bad for being out of town. Mike and I feel no remorse whatsoever. I hate to have to do this, but I don't trust you, and I have to be sure." Karen rested her hand on That Woman's chest, feeling for the slightest motion that would suggest respiration or a heartbeat, and she detected none. She checked the artery in That Woman's wrist and then her carotid artery. A smile came to Karen's face when she ascertained that there was no pulse. Remembering how That Woman greeted her on the day of the trial sermon, she taunted her in a sing-song, *"I'm gonna mess with your nursery! I'm gonna mess with your nursery! You are dead and you can't stop me!*" Then she tiptoed out of the room and found Mike sitting in the lobby, waiting for the family to arrive.

"You sure were gone a long time. Where'd you go?"

"I sneaked into the parlor where they've got her laid out. I don't trust her, Mike. I had to make sure she's dead. You know this was her last hurrah."

"So you're satisfied she's really dead?"

"I'm encouraged. She doesn't seem to be breathing, and I couldn't find a pulse on her, but I won't trust That Woman 'til she's in the ground."

Karen had barely finished speaking those words when the door opened and Jean Brinkley came in, followed by Franklin A. Brinkley, Former Chairman of the Board of Deacons of Harrington Baptist Church, Roland and Geneva Millican, and the Brinkleys' daughter Rhonda and her husband and two sons from Atlanta. As Mike and Karen rose to greet them, Mike breathed a quick silent prayer that he and Karen would be genuinely sympathetic and that neither of them would reveal their true feelings about That Woman. Some people, Mike reminded himself, were sad about her demise.

"Hello, Jean," Mike said in his most pastoral tone. "I certainly was sorry to hear about your mother's death, and very sorry that we were out of town when it happened. We were just about to start home when we got Ted's call, and we got home as quickly as we could."

"Thanks, Pastor. I got your message on the answering machine. I appreciate you being here. Hey, Karen, thanks for coming." Jean reached out to hug Karen as Mike proceeded to greet Franklin A. Brinkley, Former Chairman of the Board of Deacons of Harrington Baptist Church, Roland, Geneva, and the rest of the family.

"Ted Coleman said you were up in Virginia for a funeral at your former church," Roland commented, "which would be fine if you didn't have responsibilities here." Geneva was nodding her agreement with her husband, either that or she was indicating that Roland was saying exactly what she had coached him to say.

Mike hated being put on the defensive by the man who engineered the demise of Franklin Seals before his daughter's body was cold. He told himself that That Woman would still be just as dead if he had been in town. He reminded himself that Roland had not been an active deacon for a long time because the church had not seen fit to elect him and that Roland and Geneva were just two chronically discontented church members with one vote apiece and very little following, but Mike allowed this man and the woman who pulled his strings to intimidate him, and he heard himself gushing profuse apologies for being out of town and explaining the closeness of their friendship with Wallace Coggins.

"I'm very sorry about the death of your sister," Karen lied through her teeth as she spoke firmly to Roland, "but she would've died if we had been here. We all know she's had a bad heart for years. We've been in town far more than we've been gone. We can't help her dying during one of the rare times we were away. Like Mike said, Wallace's death really has been like a death in the family for us."

"And you owe our pastor and his wife an apology, Roland," Jean spoke sharply to her uncle. Her husband, uncle, and aunt were aghast. "You ought to be ashamed of yourself. I think they've got as much right to have a death in the family as we do. Brother Mike's just one man, and he can't be everywhere at once."

＊　＊　＊　＊　＊　＊　＊　＊　＊　＊　＊　＊

"Is this everyone who's coming for the family viewing?" Tommy asked, having recovered his solemnity enough to speak in funereal tones again. His question broke the awkward silence that followed Jean's confrontation of her uncle. When Roland indicated that they were all there, Tommy continued, "Follow me, right this way. Mrs. Snyder is in repose in Parlor B. Y'all just take your time by yourselves, and if you see anything that needs to be fixed differently, just let me know. I'll be in my office across the hall."

Mike and Karen stood by the head of the casket as the family viewed the body. For reasons Karen did not understand, Jean Brinkley, in the midst of her grief, was reaching out to her. As Jean viewed her mother's body in the casket, Karen stepped close to her and put an arm around her shoulder, and Jean reached for Karen's free hand. Mike pondered the strange sight of Jean Brinkley being embraced simultaneously by Karen Westover and Franklin A. Brinkley, Former Chairman of the Board of Deacons of Harrington Baptist Church. Feeling compassion for Jean but no sorrow over the demise of her mother, Karen prayed silently for the right words to say at that inevitable moment when she would have to say something.

"It's hard to believe Mother's gone, isn't it?" Jean finally said to Karen.

"It really is," Karen concurred with the utmost sincerity. "It seemed like she would always be with us."

*   *   *   *   *   *   *   *   *   *   *

"We got her in the ground, so you can relax," Mike announced as he came in from the funeral, carrying a gift-wrapped package that Jean gave him at the cemetery. Deb seemed to be taking a cold, and Karen welcomed the excuse to stay home with the children and not drag them along to a funeral on a dreary late December Sunday afternoon. "I watched the Wilbert Vault guys put the lid on that vault," Mike continued, "one seriously heavy piece of concrete. She won't be going anywhere."

"Sounds good to me. Who's the present for?"

"It's for us. I don't know what's going on, but Jean said for us to open this together. It's some things that belonged to her mother, and she wanted us to have them. The curiosity is killing me. Here, Karen. Hurry, open it."

Karen pressed an ear to the box and listened intently. "I don't hear it ticking. I suppose that's a good sign."

"Jean seemed sincere and appreciative. I think it's safe to open it."

"I know. I'm kidding, Mike. I'm starting to think Jean may be a halfway decent person in spite of whose daughter she is and who she married, especially after the way she stood up to Roland at the funeral home last night." Karen tore off the wrapping paper, ripped open the package, and began laughing hysterically when she pulled out the wadded-up newspapers with which Jean had packed her mother's binoculars and police scanner. Both items were expensive, top-of-the-line models, and the binoculars came with a fine leather case. "Can you believe this, Mike?"

"Looks like a peace offering, at least from Jean. Don't know about Frank. When Jean was giving it to me, Frank shook his head disapprovingly, rolled his eyes, and went over and talked to Roland and Geneva until I was gone."

"There's a note in the box," Karen said as she handed Mike a pale blue vellum stationery envelope. "It's addressed to both of us. Here, you open it. I did the honors on the box."

Mike opened the envelope, unfolded the note, and began reading aloud,

Dear Pastor and Mrs. Westover,

Thank you so much for your ministry to me and my family during our time of bereavement. You were especially kind, considering how unkind Mother was to you. She was my mother, and I loved her, but she was a difficult person. It wasn't just you. She was a thorn in the flesh to every pastor we've had in the last thirty years.

*I apologize for all that she put you through, and I was proud of
the way you stood up to her about the key to the parsonage.*

*I felt terrible about what Uncle Roland said to you at the
funeral home last night. He was out of line, and he had no right to
say what he said. I can understand you being close to Mr.
Coggins. I remember meeting him when he was here, and he certainly impressed me as a fine man. You have my sympathy in your
time of sorrow. I am glad that you could go to Virginia for his
funeral. That is where you needed to be. I deeply appreciate you
rushing back to be with our family when you received the news of
Mother's death.*

*I suppose it seems strange to give you Mother's binoculars and
scanner, but it somehow seems appropriate. Perhaps your children
will enjoy using the binoculars to look at birds and squirrels. The
scanner has only been turned on and off one time. Mother turned
it on the day she bought the thing, and I turned it off after she
died. I don't know how she could stand to listen to that thing
squawking day and night.*

*Again, thank you for your kindness to me and my ungrateful
family. I think you have been very good for our church, and my
prayer is that you will be with us for a long time.*

Sincerely,
Jean S. Brinkley

"Whoa! What do you make of that?" Mike asked.

"Amazing. Obviously, Jean thinks for herself and doesn't go
along with Frank. It's encouraging to know she has a mind of her
own, and to see her using it."

"What're we going to do with the binoculars and scanner?"

"Well, Jean's right about the binoculars being educational and
fun for the girls. Asalee's big enough to enjoy them now. As for the
scanner, I don't have any plans to turn the stupid thing on.

It goes on the mantleboard, my trophy for outliving That Woman."

* * * * * * * * * * * *

Brantley and Betty Jacobs' two sons, their wives, and the grandchildren all came down from Atlanta for the baptismal service. Brantley and Betty had been full of excitement about their upcoming baptism, and they had invited everyone they knew. All of the restaurant employees came. Under lead-gray skies on a cold, blustery first Sunday in January, Harrington Baptist Church recorded the largest number of visitors since Mike became pastor.

Miss Addie said it was the first time in her memory that the church had not sung *Shall We Gather at the River* and *On Jordan's Stormy Banks I Stand* at a baptismal service. "They sang those two songs the Sunday I was baptized in Salyers Creek in 1908," she reminisced, "and neither one has a blessed thing to do with baptism. I'm glad we sang something different." Eric and Mike thought that a baptismal service on the first Sunday of the new year was as good a time as any to make the change. Jean Brinkley had been at the organ, and Franklin A. Brinkley, Former Chairman of the Board of Deacons of Harrington Baptist Church, Jack Miller, and Doc Walters had all been sitting on the back row of the choir at rehearsal on Wednesday night, and not one of them uttered a squeak of protest when Eric announced that there would be a change in the baptismal hymns. Eric had served as a pallbearer for That Woman, and he and Jenny sang at the funeral, so Eric thought it wise to cash in whatever good will he had accumulated while his good deeds were fresh in everyone's minds. It was the church's first time to sing *Baptized in Water*, one of the newer hymns in the new *Baptist Hymnals* the church had recently purchased, and after that they sang *I Have Decided to Follow Jesus*. On the final refrain, *no turning back, I'll follow Him,* Brenda Coleman came down the steps and joined Mike in the baptistry.

Although she eagerly agreed to do it when Mike asked her Christmas morning, Brenda was a little apprehensive about helping with the baptismal service, and she became more nervous when she came into the auditorium from Sunday School and spotted her parents sitting in the congregation. Lauretta, Ted and Brenda's older daughter, thought it was awesome that her mother was going to help with baptism. She surreptitiously placed a call to her grandparents to tell them about it. Brenda's parents said they wouldn't miss it. They got up early and made the two-and-a-half hour trek from Macon. It was Brenda's first time in a baptistry since her own baptism at age nine, and she breathed a sigh of relief when she made it all the way down the steps without missing a step and immersing herself face-first.

Betty had been at church the Sunday that Cassie McWhorter was baptized, and she had witnessed a couple of baptisms since, so she had some idea of what to expect. An attractive woman of fifty-four, Betty had never allowed herself to be seen in public with a single hair out of place. The congregation would soon see her looking like a drowned rat, and her willingness to be seen in that condition bespoke the seriousness of her Christian commitment. It was not martyrdom, but it was close enough.

Brenda took Betty's hand as she came down into the water, and Betty turned to face the congregation, with Mike on her left and Brenda on her right. "Elizabeth Ann O'Shaughnessy Jacobs," Brenda began, "do you believe that Jesus is the Son of God, do you look to Him alone for the forgiveness of your sins, and do you intend to follow Him as long as you live?"

"Yes, I do," Betty declared confidently as she made eye contact with all of her family members who had come to see her baptized.

"In obedience to the command of our Lord Jesus Christ," Mike began the baptismal formula, "and upon your profession of faith in Him, we baptize you, our sister Betty, in the name of the Father, the Son, and the Holy Spirit."

"Buried with Him in baptism," Brenda added as she covered Betty's mouth and nose with a handkerchief. She and Mike locked arms behind Betty's back, lowered her gently into the water, and brought her back up.

"Raised to walk in the newness of life in Christ Jesus," Mike concluded as Betty dried her face on the towel draped around his shoulders. Brenda made her way back up the steps to the dressing room, but Betty remained in the water as her husband came down into the baptistry. Before baptizing Brantley, Mike spoke to the church, "It's not every day that I get to baptize a husband and wife together. Brantley and Betty have become delightful friends of ours, and it's been a joy to see them both come to faith in Jesus Christ. It is a happy privilege to baptize them both in the same service. Many people influenced them toward faith in Christ. The spiritual struggle that led to this baptismal service started with Betty. Brantley once considered himself an agnostic, but Betty's time of searching stirred up questions in his mind as well. Brantley found himself drawn to the same love of God to which Betty was drawn, and the Holy Spirit convinced him of the truth of the Gospel message. Like Andrew bringing his brother to Jesus, Betty brought her husband."

As Betty moved closer to her husband's side, Mike continued, "When I asked Brenda and Ted about helping with baptism today, they gladly agreed, but Ted suggested that Brenda help me baptize Betty and then, since Betty played such a significant role in leading her husband to Christ, let Betty help baptize Brantley. There's nothing in the Bible that says you have to be ordained to help with baptism. Brantley comes now to confess his faith in Jesus Christ through believer's baptism, and Betty, still dripping from her own baptism, will help me baptize him."

Though she was addressing only her husband, Betty spoke in a strong, clear voice, and the microphone suspended over the baptistry easily picked up what she said and projected her words to the whole congregation. "Brantley," she said, "I love you. We've been blessed with a very good marriage, and we've done just about everything together, but this is one thing that we must do as individuals. We can stand by each other and encourage each other, but we must each make the commitment for ourselves. Brantley Edward Jacobs, do you believe Jesus is the Son of God, do you look to Him alone for the forgiveness of your sins, and do you intend to follow Him as long as you live?"

No one could have missed the deep, resonant baritone that answered, "Yes, I do."

"In obedience to the command of our Lord Jesus Christ," Mike began, "and upon your profession of faith in Him, we baptize you, our brother, Brantley Jacobs, in the name of the Father, the Son, and the Holy Spirit."

"Buried with Him in baptism," Betty added as she locked arms with Mike behind her husband's back and helped Mike lower him into the water and bring him back up.

"Raised to walk in the newness of life in Christ Jesus," Mike concluded as they brought Brantley up out of the water. Betty and Brantley had tears running down their faces as they embraced each other and then drew Mike into their embrace.

＊   ＊   ＊   ＊   ＊   ＊   ＊   ＊   ＊   ＊   ＊   ＊

The Christmas Eve service and the late-night conversation with Brantley and Betty that followed, Christmas Day with Karen's family, the trip back to Clear Springs for Wallace's funeral, the hurried trip home to Harrington to bury That Woman, and the baptism of Brantley and Betty on the first Sunday of the new year had been more than enough to crowd the anonymous letter out of Mike's mind. If Karen had thought about it at all in the past week and a half, she had kept it to herself and said nothing about it. They had not mentioned it since the conversation with Karen's parents on Christmas Day. True to his word, Ted had not put it on the deacons' meeting agenda that he left in Mike's box at the church on the Sunday of That Woman's funeral. Nobody else had called or said anything about it. Mike was not thinking about it at all when he arrived at the church Sunday afternoon a little before 4:30 for the deacons' meeting.

So far, this had been one of the better Sundays since their arrival in Harrington. After church, Mike cooked dinner while Karen tended to Deb. He kept it simple—spaghetti, meatballs, a big jar of Ragu sauce, and garlic bread. Afterward, full stomachs and a gray, overcast day conspired to put everyone in the mood for a nap. Deb dropped off to sleep as soon as Karen put her down. Asalee actually admitted being sleepy and asked her mother if it was OK for her to take a nap. She never knew when her head touched the pillow. When Wallace the Dog saw Asalee stretch out on her bed, he went through his canine ritual of circling a couple of times before collapsing in a pile on his throw rug beside her bed. Mike set the alarm for 3:45. With both children and the dog sound asleep, he and Karen snuggled up in bed, and their lips met in a long passionate kiss. They had made love the night before, and the closeness on a sleepy Sunday afternoon put them both in the mood for more. If Mike had been thinking at all about the anonymous letter, the afternoon of leisurely lovemaking would have been more than enough to banish it from his mind.

*   *   *   *   *   *   *   *   *   *   *   *

"Is there anything else we need to discuss before we adjourn?" Ted asked. It was 5:20 when he posed the question, knowing what the answer would be. He had hewed the line, running the meeting by the printed agenda. Ted knew that Doc or Frank would bring up the letter, and his strategy was to leave them as little time as possible in which to do it. Both of them had their copies in hand, fiddling with them, folding and unfolding them, all through the meeting. Ted fairly enjoyed watching them gnaw at the bit as he allowed no departure from the printed agenda.

"Brother Chairman, we need to discuss the letter we all received," Frank spoke up.

"Why?" Brenda asked bluntly.

"In order to formulate a response from the board of deacons to present to the church," Doc answered. "The deacon board needs to acknowledge this letter and respond to it."

"Why?" Brenda reiterated.

"We just do," Frank shot back, the irritation registering clearly in his voice.

"There'll be no public response from the deacons as long as I'm chairman," Ted declared firmly. "If you vote to respond to it, you'll have to elect yourselves another chairman to present your response. As long as I'm chairman, there will be no acknowledgment from the deacons that this letter was received. I don't print unsigned letters in the *Courier*, and I don't print letters from people claiming to speak for some invisible multitude. We get a fair number of letters like that from time to time, and I feed them to the shredder and watch them come out in little strips about an eighth of an inch wide. As an editor, I make it my business to know the laws concerning libel, and I don't publish letters full of unsubstantiated allegations. All of those letters go in the shredder, too. If this letter had been written about the mayor, the chief of police, or a member of the city council and sent to me at the paper, it would never see print. This letter meets none of my criteria for publication and all of my criteria for shredder food."

"Ted, I agree with you," Bill Gentry spoke up. "Doc, Frank, I usually go along with y'all, but not this time. Since I'm married to the mayor, I'm glad Ted looks at this kind of stuff the way he does. I'd be right perturbed if somebody went after Sue like that, especially some coward who wouldn't sign his name. It doesn't bother me that people disagree with Sue over some of her decisions as mayor or some of her ideas about how to spend the city's money. I don't always agree with her myself, that's reasonable and it's to be expected. But stuff like this is just plain wrong. If we respond to it, we're giving 'em what they want, playing right into their hands."

"We don't even know that the person who wrote this is a member of the church," David Groves added. "I think this great invisible multitude the letter writer claims to speak for—I like Ted's term, 'the great vague they'—could meet in the broom closet. Brother Mike, I'm very pleased with the direction you're leading us. The church seems to be doing well and responding to your ministry. I think it's clear that the Lord brought you and your family to us, and I'm glad you're here. I'm against any response to this letter, though I'd personally like to choke the living daylights out of whoever wrote it."

"If we respond," Eric concurred, "we'll add legitimacy to accusations that are either false or a whole lot of nothing. I'm Carl and Joyce's son-in-law. I assure you they haven't left the church and they have nothing against the pastor or his wife. Joyce and Carl went to the Methodist church for a while because Joyce wanted to be there for her sister while their brother was up on murder charges. That's all there ever was to that. Carl and Joyce came to the Christmas Eve service, and they've been in church here the last two Sundays. The rest of the accusations are a whole lot of nothing. Mike and Karen have a right to name their daughter after anyone they wish. The church elected Brenda to serve as a deacon;

Brother Mike didn't appoint her. This church has a right to disagree with the Southern Baptist Convention's position on women
deacons or anything else, and we're not bound by what the SBC
says about the ordination of women. Yes, Karen Westover has a
backbone and a mind of her own, and thank God she does! So
does my wife. That's probably the reason Karen and Jenny are
such close friends. I'm glad they're both the way they are. I never
did like to see a woman be a doormat. Jenny and I are equal partners
in our marriage. I wouldn't have voted to call a pastor who didn't
treat his wife as an equal. As for the Westovers undermining the
authority of the board of deacons, whoever wrote that stupid letter
needs a crash course in Baptist polity. The deacons are not a
governing board. The governing body of a Baptist church is the
congregation."

Eric paused momentarily to watch Doc Walters and Franklin A.
Brinkley, Former Chairman of the Board of Deacons of Harrington
Baptist Church, squirm before he continued, "As far as who the
Westovers invite into their home, that's none of the church's business. I don't expect them to entertain church members all the time,
especially since they have a new baby in the house. I'm glad they
have friends outside the church. This church'd run them crazy if
they didn't. I'm glad they don't limit their friendships to people
with the same color skin. The way I look at it, that's a positive
Christian witness. It sets a good example for their children—and
the church, for that matter. All this letter writer did was make me
angry and make me more determined than ever to support our
pastor. It's been my pleasure to work with him, and I want him to
stay here a long time."

"Amen," Bill and David said in perfect unison, as though they
had rehearsed it.

"We do need to pray for the person who wrote this letter," Brenda
spoke thoughtfully. "I'm quite concerned about the spiritual

condition of a person who would write such a letter. I wonder whether this person knows the Lord at all. This person has little regard for the truth and a heart full of hate and prejudice. That's scary."

"I think you're right, Brenda," Ted said as he guided the meeting to a close at fifteen minutes before six. "The consensus of the deacons seems to be that we will not acknowledge or respond to this letter, but that we will pray for the person who wrote it. It's almost time for the evening service. Brother Frank, dismiss us in a word of prayer."

Franklin A. Brinkley, Former Chairman of the Board of Deacons of Harrington Baptist Church, stammered his way through a perfunctory prayer. He was hardly in the mood to pray, since he was still working steam for the two other items on his agenda: the fact that the pastor was way off up in Virginia and unavailable when his mother-in-law died, and a report that a lot of people had called him all upset because the pastor allowed a woman who was not ordained to help with baptism.

Mike caught up with Ted as he walked outside to catch a breath of fresh air and greet people who were arriving for the evening service. As he put his hand on Ted's shoulder, he said, "Good job running that meeting, Ted. As ol' Wallace Coggins would've said, you ran that meeting as smooth as Isaiah Mathis running an engine."

"Thanks, Preacher. I hated to be heavy-handed, but I wasn't about to let Frank and Doc take over the meeting with that stupid letter. If I were a betting man, I'd bet good money they know who wrote it. For what it's worth, I was right impressed with ol' Bill Gentry. He's thinking for himself instead of echoing Doc."

"Yeah, you noticed that, too. At the risk of sounding like a Bartles and Jaymes commercial, I need to thank him for his support."

26

Toward the end of February, Mike went over to help Daniel Groves put up a Red Carpet Realty sign in front of That Woman's house. About two weeks earlier, the auctioneer had come from Carrollton to sell off the furniture and household goods. Jean Brinkley was not overly sentimental about her mother's things. She kept the 1903 vintage Estey pump organ that had belonged to her grandmother. She divided up the family pictures with her Uncle Roland. Rhonda, Jean and Frank's daughter, took the antique cherry bedroom suite, some quilts, and her grandmother's good china, silver, and table linens. Jean, Rhonda, and Geneva divided up the jewelry. Jean and her mother were the same size, so Jean kept a couple of her mother's nicest dresses. Her mother's bed linens and the rest of her clothes went to the Salvation Army. Everything else was auctioned off one bitterly cold Saturday morning in early February.

Mike and Karen had saved a little over six hundred dollars—money their parents had given them at Christmas plus honoraria from Bob and Susan's wedding and several funerals—toward the purchase of a dining room suite. "I don't think there's a chance in the world I can get it, that it'll be in our price range," Karen commented to Mike a couple of nights before the auction, "but did you get a look at That Woman's dining room suite when we were over there having it out with her about the key?"

"Can't say that I did. I remember noticing that her house was very nicely furnished, but I don't remember the dining room suite in particular."

"Well, I did. Granted, I was mad enough to kill her, which I would've done if the old biddy had provoked me any more than she already had, but I wasn't too mad to notice that dining room suite. I put Deb in her carrier and walked back over there one day last week when Jean was there going through her mother's stuff, just to get another look at the dining room suite. Jean said that she and her friends referred to the living room and dining room as 'the museum' when they were growing up, because those two rooms were kept pristine and rarely used. That dining room suite's a museum piece, all right. Solid walnut, big table, eight chairs, china cabinet, buffet, and a custom-made pad for the table, no telling how old it is but it looks like it's never been used. Probably not a chance in the world we could get it. Some antiques dealer'll grab it in a heartbeat, pay big bucks for it..."

"But you want it so bad you can taste it, and if there's a chance in the world you can get it for the money we've got, you want it? Go ahead'n get the money out of the bank, buy it if you can. We'd pay a lot more at a furniture store for something not nearly as nice. I doubt you'll get it with the money we've got, but you'll never know unless you bid on it."

Mike had to make a hospital visit in Carrollton the morning of the auction. He returned to find Karen as giddy as a thirteen-year-old on laughing gas. As she threw her arms around him and kissed him, she exclaimed, "Oh, Honey, I'm so glad That Woman's heart quit before mine did! I spent most of the money, but I got the dining room suite and some other neat stuff. Jerry McWhorter's coming over with his truck about 2:30 to help you move it."

"Well," Mike searched for words, "as Asalee would say, cool. What'd you have to give for the dining room suite?"

"You won't believe it. There weren't many there, and the auctioneer started the bidding at $400. Nice as it is, nobody wanted it because it's so big, but it's perfect for that fellowship hall of a dining room. The bids went to $450 and stopped. I yelled out '$460!' Nobody else bid after that, and the auctioneer said 'going once, going twice, SOLD for $460 to the young lady who's jumping up and down and squealing!' Then I got a beautiful matching set of coffee table and end tables for $90."

"Anything else?"

"A million lacy little doilies, enough to put one under every object in our house. I just wanted two, one for the binoculars and one for the scanner, but I had to buy the whole box. If That Woman's scanner and binoculars are going to sit on our mantle board, they should be on lacy little doilies."

"So how much do we have left?"

"Forty-six dollars. You'll need to offer Jerry something for helping you move stuff, though I doubt he'll take it, and I thought we could have pizza delivered for supper."

* * * * * * * * * * * *

"Well, Preacher, you'n your wife oughta be happy now," Roland Millican spoke bitterly. He and Geneva waited until most of the congregation was gone before he launched his verbal assault on Mike in the foyer of the church where he stood to speak with the departing congregation. Geneva, a few steps behind Roland, nodded approvingly.

Mike decided to play dumb in order to make Roland say what he meant. "You're right, Roland. Karen and I are very happy. The Lord's blessed us far beyond what we deserve. Karen's a fine woman, and we're quite happy in our marriage. We have two beautiful, healthy children. I'm pastoring a fine church with great potential, and the Lord's blessing our ministry. We like Harrington. The parsonage is spacious and comfortable. Asalee's doing well in school. She has an excellent teacher, and she's made friends easily. We've made a lot of friends outside of church. We have enough to meet our needs. We have every reason to be happy, and it's so kind of you to ask about our happiness." Mike could see Roland's blood pressure escalate with each pulse, and he decided to let up before he caused him to have a stroke.

"You know good and well what I'm talking about, Preacher!" Roland barely vented his wrath in time to keep himself from exploding. "I suppose y'all are tickled to death to have coloreds moving in on our street, my sister's house, right across the street from you. I got nothing against coloreds, but they don't belong in the middle of a white neighborhood."

"Oh, you're talking about the Stewarts," Mike responded calmly. "Yes, we're very happy about them moving to our neighborhood. Mrs. Stewart told Karen Tuesday at Mothers Morning Out, said she and her husband had a contract on Hilda Mae's house. I hope it works out for them. They're good people. I met Chief Stewart when Royce Green got killed, got better acquainted with him when the break came in the murder of Debbie Seals. Fine man, deacon at Greater New Hope. His grandfather was pastor there before Reverend Conway. Of course, you know Mrs. Stewart helps Karen with Mothers Morning Out. She's a freelance photographer, does some nice work. She did Bob and Susan McKnight's wedding pictures. She's from South Carolina, of course you know Chief Stewart was raised in Harrington. They met while he was stationed at Fort Jackson. They've got a daughter in first grade and a son in third grade at Harrington Elementary. It'll work out great for us. We can help each other out taking kids to school and picking them up, and Asalee'll have somebody her age to play with."

"First the government says we gotta let coloreds and whites go to school together," Roland shot back, "and you see the shape our schools are in. I fought that long as I was on the school board. Now we got 'em teachin' white children, we got one of 'em for a police chief, and now you got 'em movin' in to what's always been white neighborhoods. You'd think that was enough, without voluntarily associatin' with 'em. Y'all've done been socializing with coloreds, havin' 'em in your home. Y'all've visited'n et dinner at colored folks' houses. You'n your wife're gonna let your little girls play with colored children like there's no difference. 'Fore it's over, you'll end up with a colored son-in-law'n a bunch 'a mulatto grandkids."

"Roland, wait a minute." Mike spoke in calm, measured tones, trying not to let Roland see how angry he was, but he could not completely suppress the indignation in his voice. He did well to restrain the urge to punch Roland in the mouth. "Asalee won't be seven until the twenty-seventh of this month. Karen and I aren't worried about her getting married and having babies real soon. She's a child, Roland. She watches Sesame Street and Saturday morning cartoons, plays with dolls, kisses the dog good night, and sleeps with forty stuffed animals. We're less worried about who she might marry than we are about bringing her up to be a Christian and a decent human being. The Stewarts are Christians, and they're trying to raise their children the same way we're trying to raise ours. It'll be nice to have them as neighbors."

"All of that sounds well and good, Preacher, but you watch what happens to property values on our street when one of 'em moves in. Pretty soon the whole street'll go colored. That's what happened over 'round Atlanta where Geneva's brother used to live. Him'n his wife've had to sell their house'n move twice on account'a niggers movin' in an' takin' over. You watch it. Let one of 'em move in, and before you know it, the whole neighborhood'll go colored."

"I'm sorry you feel that way, Roland, but the Stewarts are our friends. If they buy Hilda Mae's house, we'll welcome them as our neighbors. If you're thinking about selling and moving, Idaho is the state with the lowest percentage of blacks in the population. Some places out there are so sparsely populated, you wouldn't have to live within ten miles of anybody."

Jean Brinkley walked up as Mike and Roland were speaking, in time to get the gist of their conversation. Before Roland could gather his thoughts for another rejoinder, Jean said, "Plan on making them welcome, Pastor. Get used to it and get over it, Uncle Roland. I accepted the Stewarts' contract yesterday, should settle in about two weeks. Like the pastor was saying, Uncle Roland, it's nice to have neighbors who uphold the same values you're trying to teach your children. Children today need all the positive influences they can get."

✶   ✶   ✶   ✶   ✶   ✶   ✶   ✶   ✶   ✶   ✶   ✶

Helen Walters reminded Mike at the last church council meeting that he needed to be thinking about who to invite to preach the annual revival in August. "The church is used to having revival the third week of August," she said. "We missed having it last year because you were new on the field and there wasn't time to plan it. The church is really counting on doing it this year."

"Believe on the Lord Jesus Christ during the third week of August and thou shalt be saved?" Mike quipped.

"Something like that," Helen snapped back. "It's what the people are used to. This used to be a lot more of an agricultural area than it is now, farms right up to the edge of town. Third week of

August was laying by time. Nobody in the church who farms any more, but the older ones still think revival has to be the third week of August. Also, the third Sunday in August is the anniversary of the church's founding."

Mike was thinking about a revival meeting, though he had not been thinking about that particular week. Eric said the third week of August was a no-go if they expected him to lead the music, since he had marching band camp that week. They settled on the second week, and Ted, who represented the deacons on the church council, said the church always left it up to the pastor to secure a revival preacher. Mike called Heather Simmons that night, and she accepted the invitation.

"I hope I don't get you in hot water," Heather said only half-jokingly. "Remember I split one church and caused another one to get kicked out of the association before I turned twenty-five. If you're crazy enough to invite me, I'm crazy enough to come. I'll send you a mug shot and bio for publicity."

"Great. I'll watch the mail for it. What's happening at Clear Springs?"

"We elected five new deacons. With the growth we're having, we needed them. We needed to fill the vacancy left by Wallace's death, and poor old Arthur'll never be able to serve actively again. On top of everything else, he's got Alzheimer's, doesn't even recognize Maude or Mary Kate half the time. All the new deacons are good ones, I think. Wesley Trimble, Wanda used-to-be Halstead, Wanda Gonzales now, Marie Jernigan, and Matt and Sarah Beth Coggins.

"I'll bet ol' Lester blew a gasket when he heard his ex-wife was going to be ordained a deacon!" Mike cackled.

"I'm told that he did, and ol' Billy Fite said some nasty stuff about us from the pulpit. If the Lord keeps blessing Clear Springs like He's been doing, He's going to end up killing those two ol' boys. Their hearts can't take much more. Of course, we're losing

Carol and her kids. Carol's a super deacon chairman, and I love her kids to death, really hate to see them leave us. It'll be hard to let them go, but they'll do a lot of good where they're going. Providence called Dennis as pastor. He's been down there since February. He and the church seem to be a good match. I'll be doing my first wedding, tying the knot for Dennis and Carol on Friday night before I start the revival in Harrington."

"Wow, sounds like things are happening up there."

"That's only the beginning. There's so much to tell you. I'm here, and it's all I can do to stay on top of it. As soon as we finish talking, I'll think of something else I should've told you. Let's see—the five new deacons'll be ordained April 7. The church licensed Wes Trimble and Megan Richardson to preach. Getting kicked out of the association was a wakeup call, the way they beat us over the head with that resolution against women ministers the SBC adopted in '84, really woke the church up to what's happened to the SBC and got us taking a close look at whether we want to be a part of it any more. I'm excited about the formation of the Cooperative Baptist Fellowship. Six of us—me, Wesley and Linda, Matt and Sarah Beth, and Wanda are going down to Atlanta for the CBF meeting. The Sunday we're gone, the youth'll be in charge of the service, and Meg's going to preach her first sermon. I let her be in charge of prayer meeting one Wednesday night last summer, and I was impressed with how well she did. She brought an excellent devotional, very well prepared. I don't want to push her too fast, but I do want to encourage her."

"I remember her reading the Scripture at Wallace's funeral. "I know it was hard for her, but she did well."

"That was Wallace's request. The first time Meg read Scripture in church, Wallace had tears in his eyes when he complimented her on how well she read, said it did his heart good to hear somebody read Scripture so well. Like Wallace said, you can tell she loves the Bible by the way she reads it. She practices ahead of time to be sure she knows how to pronounce all the words. She projects well, a lot of expression in her voice. It really is a pleasure to hear the Bible read by one who loves it."

"Y'all sure are going to miss Carol and her family, but they'll be a big boost to Providence. I guess y'all are planning a big sendoff for them."

"Sunday August 4. We'll present them with a gift from the church, and I'm sure there'll be many individual gifts. The wedding's that Friday night, and then I'll be at your place Sunday morning to start the revival."

* * * * * * * * * * * *

"Pastor, I don't mean to speak unkindly of anyone," Miss Addie said apologetically when she called Mike the morning the newsletter arrived in the mailboxes of most church members, "but I don't trust Roland and Geneva as far as I could throw them. They're up to no good!"

"What makes you say that, Miss Addie? I know they're not members of my fan club, but it sounds as though you know something I don't."

"Pastor, it's been a long time since Roland ran for public office, but he still knows how to run a dirty campaign. You'll meet some of our members for the first time at the business meeting Wednesday night. Roland and Geneva are on the warpath because of the deacons' recommendation to amend the bylaws so the church can ordain women, divorced people, and single people as deacons. That, and Roland's having a hissy fit over you inviting the young woman to preach the revival. They're calling members who haven't attended or supported the church in thirty years, trying to get them to come and vote down the recommendation. If they can vote that down, Roland's going to make a motion to cancel the revival."

"Thanks for letting me know. Does Ted know about it?"

"Clarence and Lunell called him. They're the ones who called to tell me what the Millicans were up to. Roland and Geneva know better than to call me with their foolishness. Bless his heart, Roland should've had more sense than to try to get Clarence on his side. Clarence has had no use for Roland since Roland and his cronies ran Brother Seals off. Clarence started coming to church when Brother Seals was our pastor, and he was saved and baptized under Brother Seals' ministry. He was very active in the church, good worker, president of the brotherhood until the deacons asked Brother Seals to resign. Since then, he's only attended once in a while on special occasions. I was so pleased to see him the day his granddaughter Cassie was baptized."

"So what did Clarence tell Roland?"

"He told him, 'Yes, I'm still a member of the church, and I'll most definitely be at the business meeting. We've got a fine young pastor and some good deacons. I'll be there to support them and oppose whatever trouble you're trying to stir up. Lunell and I'll try to get as many others there as we can to support our pastor.' Clarence said, as far as the women deacons and the woman revival preacher are concerned, he doesn't see what the problem is, and he figures anything Roland's against is a good idea. Clarence and Lunell are going to make some calls, and I'll make some calls, too. I'm so pleased with my new pushbutton phone with the great big numbers. I showed it to you the last time you were at my house. It's much easier to use than my old telephone. We might get some of these people started back to church while we're at it. It's like Clarence told Roland, Pastor. This business of calling people back from the dead to vote in a business meeting is a game two sides can play."

"Do you think that Roland'll be able to get the votes to do what he wants?"

"I doubt it, Pastor. A lot of the ones who quit coming to church years ago quit because of the way Roland and his bunch ran the church. The church was doing well under Brother Seals before Roland and his bunch started all the trouble. We led the association in baptisms four consecutive years, which is the reason we outgrew our old building. Brother Seals was the third pastor Roland and his cronies ran off. Roland was chairman of deacons back then. He was the main one responsible for running off Lawrence Carson and Jim Decker, both of whom were fine pastors. Roland and Geneva were down on Brother Seals long before the issue came up about selling our old building. That was the ugliest thing I ever saw. Roland got his way, but a lot of people have come to see that the way the church did Brother Seals was wrong. We had a number of people who moved to other churches or quit going to church altogether because of the way Brother Seals was treated."

*   *   *   *   *   *   *   *   *   *   *   *

Business meetings had been much better attended since the church started the catered meals. Before that, it was often necessary to count heads to be sure the necessary quorum of twenty members was present. Since the church started the Wednesday night suppers, forty-five or fifty adults was an average turnout for business meetings.

That there was an unusual degree of interest in the March business meeting, Mike knew. He began to appreciate just how much interest when Helen Walters told him that eighty-four adults, half again the usual number, had made reservations for supper on business meeting night. *Roland and his bunch won't come to dinner,* Mike reasoned. *They'll just show up for the business meeting.*

Most of the ones signed up for dinner are with us. Roland and Geneva disapproved of the Wednesday night suppers as much as Royce Green would have, so they never came for the meal and attended on Wednesday night only when it was business meeting night. Roland would question some item in the treasurer's report every month. Last month, it was a payment of $63.75 to Tabor Piano Company for tuning the piano in the sanctuary. Roland ranted about how the church used to get its pianos tuned for $15. Joyce Baxter gently reminded him that, when the church got its pianos tuned for $15, gasoline was twenty-five cents a gallon, bread was a dime a loaf, and the minimum wage was $1.25 an hour. She pointed out that the regular rate was $75 and that Mr. Tabor gave a fifteen percent discount to all of the churches.

Mike hated thinking in terms of *them* and *us* as he contemplated who might show up, but there was a very real and palpable division. Clarence Bishop had spoken eloquently of the division when he said that he figured anything Roland was against was a good idea. Mike scanned the list of people who had made reservations for supper on business meeting night and counted seventy-five of *us* and nine of *them*. It was anybody's guess as to how many more in each camp would arrive after supper in time for the business meeting.

*   *   *   *   *   *   *   *   *   *   *   *

"We will now move to the next item on our agenda, the report from the deacons," Mike proceeded. "I recognize deacon chairman Ted Coleman to present his report."

"Thank you, Brother Mike." Ted paused a moment to scan a crowd that included about thirty more who had arrived after supper. Some of them he had never seen before. Others he recognized, although he had no previous inkling that they were members of

Harrington Baptist Church. Glancing down at his notes, he began, "The deacons have one recommendation, an amendment to the bylaws. As required, a copy of the present reading and the proposed amendment was printed in this month's newsletter and in the bulletin the past two Sundays. Printed copies were distributed along with the other reports you received at the beginning of the meeting. Is there anyone who does not have a copy? It's printed on light blue paper. I have extra copies if anyone needs one." Seeing no one who did not have a copy, he continued, "At present, Article II 'Church Officers,' Section B 'Deacons,' paragraph two, the second and third sentences read *Ordained deacons holding membership in Harrington Baptist Church who have not served actively for a period of one year, along with men eligible to be ordained as deacons, shall be eligible to be elected for service as active deacons. Those eligible to be ordained are active resident male members of Harrington Baptist Church, at least twenty-one years of age, who are married or widowed and who have never been divorced.* The deacons recommend that the word *men* in sentence two be replaced with the word *those*, and we recommend that the third sentence be stricken in its entireity and replaced with this sentence: *Active resident members of Harrington Baptist Church who are at least twenty-one years of age shall be eligible to be ordained as deacons.* We further recommend that sentence four, which reads, *The pastor and deacons shall cause to be published in the August issue of the church newsletter each year a list of all ordained deacons holding membership in Harrington Baptist Church who have not served actively in the past year, along with a list of men eligible for ordination as deacons,* be amended by replacing the word 'men' with the word 'those.' Brother Moderator, on behalf of the deacons, I move the adoption of this amendment."

"Thank you, Ted. A recommendation from the deacons, like a recommendation from a committee, does not require a second. I will now open the floor for discussion. We will alternate between someone speaking for and someone speaking against. I'll begin by recognizing our deacon chairman, Brother Ted Coleman, to explain the rationale for this recommendation and speak in favor of it. Brother Ted…"

"Thank you, Pastor. The purpose of this amendment is to resolve an inconsistency in our bylaws. If a woman, divorced person, or single person is ordained as a deacon in another Baptist church and subsequently joins this church, that person is eligible to be elected as an active deacon. That's how Brenda was eligible even though she could not be ordained by this church. However, a woman, divorced person, or single person who was baptized in this church and who has been a devout Christian and a faithful member of this church for many years cannot be ordained as a deacon by this church. Our pastor and deacons believe we should correct this inequity so women, divorced people, and single people will not be automatically excluded as candidates for ordination."

"Thank you, Ted." Mike pondered the coup of providence that had brought this motion to the floor. Franklin A. Brinkley, Former Chairman of the Board of Deacons of Harrington Baptist Church, had been sick with a terrible case of bronchitis that forced him to miss the deacons meeting in which this recommendation was drafted. Doc Walters was against it, but without Frank to lead the charge, and after Bill Gentry said the idea made a lot of sense to him, he realized that he would be alone in his opposition. Doc said nothing and meekly caved in to the will of the majority. "The floor is open," Mike continued, "for someone to speak against the recommendation. I recognize Brother Roland Millican to speak against the recommendation."

"This is the most wrong-headed, anti-Scriptural foolishness I've ever seen in my life!" Roland blurted out, not pausing for any courtesies before he began his tirade. "My wife and I've been members of this church since I got saved in 1939, and I've been a deacon since 1945, but we're ready to leave if this passes. When I was ordained, a man served on the deacon board for life, there wad'n none of this foolishness of rotatin' off the board after three years'n havin' to stay off for a year before you could come back on. I guarantee you, if I was still on the deacon board, this never would'a seen the light of day, and we'd'a got shed of any pastor that was for such foolishness..."

"Brother Roland!" Mike interrupted with some trepidation, though there was a discernable note of sternness in his voice. He knew it was largely up to him to keep the meeting from turning into a shouting match. "Brother Roland, please confine your remarks to the issue at hand. We're not discussing deacon rotation. You have the floor to speak against the proposed amendment."

"I'm gettin' to that, Preacher!" Roland shot back angrily. "Like I was saying before I was interrupted, it all started with this deacon rotation foolishness, actin' like we need to keep ordaining new deacons every year when we already had plenty of good men serving. We had seven good men that ran this church, but we went'n elected a bunch a' new deacons, some that wad'n even from Harrington, did'n grow up in this church. We been goin' down a slippery slope ever since. Our pastor let a woman deacon from another church, somebody we did'n know from the man in the moon, serve communion. Used to, we would'n even let a visitor from another church take communion, let alone serve it. It was strictly a local church ordinance. Come to find out, the lady from the other church is divorced, and our pastor had a part in ordainin' her. They's some churches and preachers that'll ordain anything. They don't care what the Bible says. If that wad'n bad enough, it comes to light that Mrs. Coleman was ordained by some liberal church over't Macon where her'n her husband used to belong, so her name gets put on the ballot'n she gets elected to the deacon board'n our pastor's been showcasin' her, lettin' 'er help with baptizin'n servin' the Lord's Supper ever chance he gets, like havin' a woman deacon was somethin' to be proud of. If this thing passes, 'fore you know it, women'll take over the deacon board and we won't be able to get men to serve. God meant for women to take care of the home and children, and He meant for men to run the church. When I was growin' up, the church had business meetin' on Saturday before communion Sunday an' hit was just the men that come. We did'n have none of this foolishness of women holdin' office in the church like we got now, wad'n no women church clerks or treasurers, and they wad'n no women speakin' or votin' in the business meetin'. The men ran the church and we'd be better off if they still did. Over there in Acts, chapter six, verse three, the apostles told the people—I'm readin' from the King James Version, I don't know what some a' them translations they got now say and I don't much care, this is what the Bible says: *Wherefore brethren, look ye out among you seven men of honest report, full of the Holy Ghost and wisdom, whom we may appoint over this business.* They told 'em to choose men, not women, and they told 'em to put 'em in charge of the business of the church so the apostles could tend to spiritual things. Then, over there in I Timothy, it says a deacon's got to be the *husband of one wife.* Now, I don't see how in the world a woman, or a divorced man, or a single man can be the husband of one wife. This is the most wrong-headed thing this church has considered in the forty-one years I've been a member," Roland concluded as he wiped sweat from his brow and tears from his eyes, "and I hope to God we vote it down."

As Roland sat down, there was a brief, eerie silence that ended with the *thump* of Miss Addie's cane as she hoisted herself to her full height. "Brother Pastor," she began, still punctuating her words with the occasional *thump* of her cane, "I'd like to speak in favor of this recommendation."

"I recognize Miss Addie to speak for the recommendation."

"Thank you, Pastor." Miss Addie's voice belied her advanced age and small stature, "I am so thankful our deacons have brought this recommendation, and I intend to vote for it. We ought to've done this long ago. Spare me any foolishness about our people not being ready for it. If Moses had waited until everybody was ready, the Israelites would still be in Egypt! I'll be ninety-four years old if the Good Lord lets me live until July 26. I'm so weary of people threatening to leave the church every time they don't get their way about something. I've been a member of this church since 1922, and I've noticed that the people who try to blackmail the church by threatening to leave never actually do. It's absolutely shameful for a church to cave in to such manipulative behavior. Many good people quietly left this church because they didn't agree with a handful of men meeting behind closed doors running the church as though they owned it. There are people here tonight who stopped coming to this church because they got tired of a handful of men running pastors off at the drop of a hat. Starting deacon rotation was a step in the right direction. This recommendation is yet another step in the right direction. Brenda Coleman's a very good deacon, and we have many other women just as capable. From my own Bible study, I believe that women as well as men should serve as deacons—and pastors too, for that matter. When I was in college, we had to take Greek so we could read the classics in the original language. I purchased a Greek New Testament when I was nineteen years old because I wanted to read the New Testament in the original language, and I still use it for Bible study and devotional reading. In Romans 16, verse one, Phoebe is referred to as a deacon of the church at Cenchrea. I know the King James Version calls her a 'servant' of the church, but the Greek word is *diakonos*, the very same word translated 'deacon' in I Timothy chapter three. In verse seven, Paul refers to a woman named Junia as an apostle—he says that she's an outstanding apostle. Roland, you'll find that verse translated correctly in the King James, so you can read it for yourself. If a woman can be an apostle, she can serve as a deacon or preach a revival. As for the 'husband of one wife' part, that doesn't have a blessed thing to do with divorce. Paul's not talking about whether a man has ever been divorced. He's talking about a man being faithful to his wife, unlike some deacons we've had over the years. The Bible says a deacon is supposed to be sober. Roland, the only thing I detest more than the smell of whiskey is the smell of whiskey and breath mints! The Bible says a deacon mustn't be double-tongued, but I remember how some deacons in this church resorted to every kind of lie and subterfuge imaginable when they got ready to run off a pastor. Now, let's look at verse 11 of I Timothy chapter three. The King James makes that verse into a list of qualifications for deacons' wives, but the Greek says 'women' rather than 'their wives.' Verse 11 is talking about women deacons, not deacons' wives. I have my Greek New Testament with me if anyone wishes to debate Scripture. Looking at it from a purely pragmatic standpoint, women couldn't do any worse than some of the men." Miss Addie paused, punctuating the silence with with a *thump* of her cane on the hard tile floor. "I know how much it bothers some people for a woman to speak in a business meeting, so I shall soon be finished. One more thing and I shall sit down. It's always bothered me to see only men serve the Lord's Supper. It bothered me when I was a little girl. Having only men serve the Lord's Supper sends a message to every woman and girl that she can never be more than a second-class member of the church. I'm ninety-three years old, and the first time I ever saw a woman serve the Lord's Supper was when Deacon Carol Richardson from Clear Springs Baptist Church was here last summer. After the service, I tried to tell her how much it meant to me, but all I could do was hug her and cry. Our deacons have brought a fine recommendation, and I urge you all to join me in voting for it."

As Miss Addie sat down, David Groves rose from his seat. He was trembling, his voice was shaky, and hot tears were coursing down his cheeks. "Brother Pastor, I need to tell the church something."

"I recognize Brother David Groves for a point of personal privilege," Mike said, not knowing what David had on his mind.

"Thank you, Pastor. Pray for me. This is something that's hard to talk about. Right now, Cheryl and our two sons are the only people in Harrington who know what I'm about to tell you. It's been pointed out that we already have a woman deacon serving, and Brenda's a fine deacon, one of the best in my book. We also have a divorced and remarried deacon already serving. I'm talking about myself." A hush fell over the meeting as David composed himself again and continued. "My first marriage and divorce took place before I became a Christian. I was a nineteen year old Marine stationed at Camp Lejeune, North Carolina. My first wife was barely eighteen when we married. I met her in a bar on a weekend pass, and we were married a month later. It lasted about six months. She was the one who left, but I don't blame her. Neither one of us was grown up enough to be married to anybody. It was as much my fault as hers, and I don't hold any bitterness toward her. I met my present wife, Cheryl, not long after I became a Christian, and we'll soon celebrate our twenty-fourth anniversary. Cheryl's a fine woman, better than I deserve, and we have a very good marriage. We plan to stay married 'til the Lord takes one of us home. Even though I could not have been ordained by this church, I was eligible to serve for the same reason Brenda was. I was ordained by Downing Memorial Baptist Church in Atlanta. I was a deacon there for six years before we moved to Harrington. That church was fully aware of my situation when it ordained me. When we moved to Harrington, we joined this church, the church Cheryl grew up in. About a year later, I was asked to serve as a deacon. The church accepted my ordination at face value and never asked any questions. The fact that I married Walt Holliday's granddaughter probably helped. If anyone had asked me whether I'd been married before, I would have told them the truth, but nobody asked. I didn't see any need to volunteer it at the time. Tonight, though, I think it might help you decide how to vote on this recommendation." David sat down, tears still streaming down his face. Cheryl put her arm around him and kissed him gently on the cheek.

"I call for the question!" The booming voice that broke the silence belonged to Clarence Bishop. At eighty, he was still vigorous and active, a ramrod-straight six-feet-two with a thick shock of snow-white hair.

"I hear a call for the question," Mike responded. "Do I hear a second?"

"Second," Jean Brinkley called out as Franklin A. Brinkley, Former Chairman of the Board of Deacons of Harrington Baptist Church, grimaced.

"We have a motion and a second to call for the question. That means we're voting on whether to vote. If you vote 'yes,' you're voting to cut off debate and bring the recommendation from the deacons to a vote. If you vote 'no,' you're voting to allow more debate about this recommendation before we vote it up or down. All in favor of calling for the question, indicate by saying 'Aye.'" After a clear majority responded in the affirmative, Mike continued, "All opposed, indicate by saying 'No.'" After a small rumble of dissent, Mike declared, "The motion carries. We will now vote on the recommendation to amend the bylaws. The church constitution requires a two-thirds majority to amend the bylaws, and it stipulates that the vote must be taken by secret ballot. Deacons Bill Gentry and Brenda Coleman are distributing the ballots and pencils. If you favor the recommendation, check "Yes' on your ballot. If you are opposed, check 'No.' Then, fold your ballot and pass it to the right so Bill and Brenda can collect the ballots and count them."

Karen played the clunky out-of-tune fellowship hall piano and Eric led the group in singing *Amazing Grace* while the ballots were being counted. As the people were singing about *no less days to sing God's praise than when we first begun,* Brenda made her way up to the podium. "We have the results of the vote on the bylaw change. There were one hundred and thirty-one ballots cast, which means that eighty-seven votes would be needed for the recommendation to pass. One hundred and nine who voted 'yes' and twenty-two who voted 'no.'" Mike declared that the recommendation had passed, and Roland didn't try to bring his motion to cancel the revival.

27

"Delicious meal, Karen," Aaron Stewart commented, "and so kind of you to fix for us."

"It was a lot better than we would've had at home," Latisha concurred. "With us in the middle of moving and my kitchen still in boxes, I'd've been sending Aaron out for a sack of hamburgers if we'd eaten at home."

"Glad y'all enjoyed it," Karen replied, "and glad you're going to be our neighbors. We were so happy when we heard you'd put a contract on That Woman's house. It's still hard to believe she's gone. I didn't think That Woman ever would die. It's a miracle I'm not behind bars right now. Aaron, you don't know how close you came to having a homicide at 723 Alabama Avenue the first week we were here. When I found out she had a key to the parsonage, I made Daddy and Mike change the locks before I'd spend a single night in this house. Then, Asalee and I come back from the grocery store to find a key broken off in the front door. It was all Mike could do to talk me out of calling the police and pressing charges. Anyway, she's dead and buried now."

"Yeah," Mike picked up the thread, "we got to the funeral home before the family, and Karen sneaked into the parlor where

Hilda Mae was layin' a corpse and checked her pulse to make sure she was dead. When she came back out and told me where she'd been, I asked her if she was satisfied that Hilda Mae was dead. Karen said she was encouraged, but she wouldn't trust That Woman 'til she was in the ground."

"He's not kidding," Karen admitted. "I really did check her for a pulse when she was lying in her casket. Anyway, after six months of That Woman, it'll be nice to have y'all over there. Two things I prayed for when we were getting ready to move here: One, that we'd develop friendships outside the church, and two, that there would be children in the neighborhood close to Asalee's age. Maybe God was testing me those first six months. I think my prayers have been answered. We're already friends. Your children are close to Asalee's age, and they get along well. It's going to be great to be able to help each other taking kids to school and picking them up."

"Praying is risky business," Aaron commented in a serious tone. "You can get more'n you ask for sometimes, *exceeding abundantly above all that we ask or think*, to use the Apostle Paul's words. Go ahead'n tell 'em, Latisha."

"I'm pregnant again, went to the doctor the same day we closed on the house. She figures my due date's November 24, so Deb'll have somebody to play with, too."

Mike and Karen congratulated Latisha and Aaron, the two women hugged, and the two men exchanged a hearty handshake. As they did, Asalee and Rosa emerged from Asalee's room, dressed in each other's clothes. "Mommy," Asalee appealed in her most plaintive voice, "can Rosa spend the night with me tonight?"

"You'll have to ask her mom."

Before Asalee could ask, Latisha said, "it's fine with me if you don't mind, Karen."

"OK," Karen agreed. "Tomorrow's Saturday. Rosa, you can borrow one of Asalee's gowns to sleep in."

As the girls went outside where nine-year-old Jordan Stewart was playing with Wallace the Dog, Aaron said, "Mike, Karen, I have to ask about the police scanner and binoculars. I know a lot of people own scanners, and a lot of people own binoculars. I just don't know anybody who keeps them on the mantleboard on lacy little doilies…"

* * * * * * * * * * * *

"Lunell and I'd like to have the revival preacher stay in our home if you haven't made other arrangements," Clarence Bishop said when he spoke to Mike after church on the Sunday following the business meeting. "It's just the two of us in that big old house since our kids're grown. We'd enjoy her company, she can have as much privacy as she wants, and it'll save the church having to spend for lodging and meals."

"That's very kind of you and Lunell, and we haven't made any other plans. Heather's a delightful person, very down to earth. You'll enjoy having her."

"It'll be a pleasure for us. Lunell or I one'll call you at the church office tomorrow to get Preacher Simmons' address and phone number so we can get in touch with her and extend the invitation."

* * * * * * * * * * * *

Clearly, Roland's effort to stack the business meeting had blown up in his face. Not only did Clarence come to the business meeting to vote for anything Roland was against, he had not missed a church service, Wednesday night supper, or business meeting since. Much to Roland's chagrin, Clarence went out of his way every Sunday to speak to him, shake his hand, and thank him for encouraging him to start back to church.

Easter Sunday, as people were making their way from their Sunday School classes to the sanctuary, Karen just about swallowed her tongue to keep from laughing out loud when Roland ducked into a broom closet trying to avoid Clarence. Fortunately or unfortunately, depending upon one's perspective, Clarence saw him. Clarence opened the closet door, shook Roland's hand, patted him on the shoulder, and—in a booming voice that everyone could hear—proclaimed, "Brother Roland! It's so good to see you! I look forward to seeing you every Sunday. If I haven't already told you this, I want to thank you from the bottom of my heart for encouraging me to come back to church. Lunell's been after me for the longest to come back, but you know how we stubborn men are about listening to our wives. I don't think I ever would've come back if it hadn't been for you coming by the store that day to get me to come to that business meeting." After laying it on thick and watching Roland turn several colors not found in nature, Clarence added softly, "I apologize for disturbing you, Roland. I know you were doing what the Bible says, entering into your closet and shutting the door so you can pray. I'll let you get back to praying now." With that, he closed the door in Roland's face, leaving him in the dark closet surrounded by brooms, mops, buckets, paper goods, and the overwhelming smells of ammonia and Pine Sol. Roland stayed there until the sound of footsteps in the hall disappeared and he heard the congregation start singing *Christ the Lord is Risen Today.* He then sheepishly made his way outside, around to the main entrance and into the sanctuary where he took his seat beside his scowling wife.

Although he was genuinely glad to be back in church, Clarence drew the line at going back into the Senior Men's Bible Class after trying it one Sunday. He told Lunell that Doc Walters was as boring with a Bible as he was with a dental drill and that, if he hadn't already read the Bible for himself, Doc would have turned him against ever reading it. Doc had taught the class for men fifty-five to glory for the past twelve years, reading the lesson straight from the teacher's quarterly Sunday after Sunday, leaving little room for questions or discussion. Clarence knew his Bible better than most people, and he had a penchant for raising tough questions and playing devil's advocate. Clarence had a probing question on the tip of his tongue when Doc droned his way directly from the last sentence of the printed lesson into "that's all I have for today, gentlemen, and it looks like our time's about gone. Brother Jack Miller, dismiss us in a word of prayer." The next Sunday, Clarence found a more hospitable climate in the class taught by Cheryl Groves, a group of married and single adults ranging widely in age. Cheryl's class used an advanced Bible study curriculum. She was well-prepared every Sunday, and her class was known for lively repartee. Clarence liked being in the same class with Lunell. Lunell, like Miss Addie, had long since given up on the fifty-five to glory women's class that Geneva Millican taught.

*   *   *   *   *   *   *   *   *   *   *

Roland had another dying duck fit at the April business meeting when the church council presented the recommendation about Vacation Bible School. It all started with Mike's coversation with Henry Conway, pastor of Greater New Hope, at the February meeting of the Mintz County Ministerial Association. Mike shared his frustrations over VBS with Conway, telling him that he wanted to have the school in the morning so more children would come, but a shortage of teachers would probably force them to have it in the evening or not at all, since most of the younger women in the church worked full-time jobs during the day.

Conway said he was up against the same thing, not wanting to do VBS in the evening because the children would start out tired and end up out of sorts before the end of the evening's activities.

Mike suggested a combined VBS sponsored by both churches, which would make it possible to have enough workers to do it in the morning. Mike found his church council as amenable to the idea as Conway had been. Roland's dying duck fit and the objection of Franklin A. Brinkley, Former Chairman of the Board of Deacons of Harrinton Baptist Church, that the recommendation was not run past the deacons, notwithstanding, the church voted by a substantial majority to do the joint VBS with Greater New Hope. The school would be held at Harrington Baptist, which had more classroom space. It would be staffed by teachers and workers from both churches. Both pastors would be present and involved. The two churches would split the cost of literature and supplies, and the missions offering would be divided equally between Southern Baptist and Progressive National Baptist missions endeavors. After the business meeting, Mike handed Helen Walters an announcement to put in the bulletin, that the first planning meeting would be held the following Saturday morning at Greater New Hope.

"I want to help out with VBS," Joyce Baxter told Mike after the business meeting. "I know I gave up my first and second graders when all the trouble was going on with my brother. Lori's doing a great job with them now, so I don't want to rock that boat, but I do miss teaching children at church…"

"Well, Brenda Coleman and Latisha Stewart are the VBS directors. Brenda's here, so talk to her before she gets gone. I expect she'll tell you to come to the meeting at Greater New Hope, and we'll put you to work somewhere doing something. At the first meeting, we'll see who we've got available to work and decide who we'll put where doing what. If you're willing to help, there'll be a place for you."

As Mike concluded the conversation with Joyce, he turned to face the insistent sound of a cane thumping the hard tile floor. "I've already talked to Brenda," Miss Addie announced, "and I don't need anybody to remind me that I'll soon be ninety-four years old. I'm not able to teach a class all morning like I'd like to do, but I can come in and teach the Bible lesson for one of the classes each day. I do find it refreshing to be around young children." As she reached up with her free hand, beckoning Mike to bend over for a hug, she continued, "I am so pleased that the Good Lord let me live to see this day."

In his dying duck fit at the April business meeting, Roland declared that the church just wasn't ready for all of this race-mixing and solemnly warned about where it would all lead. Miss Addie's cane thumped the floor vigorously as she reminded Roland and the church where the Israelites would be today if Moses had waited until everybody was ready. Brenda spoke up and told Roland he was misinformed. "You've got it all wrong, Roland. There's not going to be any race-mixing. All the children we enroll will be members of the human race. Besides, the children are not coming to VBS to look for their future marriage partners. In my experience as a fourth grade teacher, most elementary school children are not entirely sure the opposite sex is human. I've always had a harder time getting boys and girls to coexist peacefully than I've had getting black and white kids to get along."

* * * * * * * * * * * *

"Are you available Saturday morning at ten?" It was Ted Coleman's voice on the phone Tuesday morning two weeks before the start of Vacation Bible School. "We're doing a feature story about the joint VBS, and I want a picture of you, Reverend Conway, Latisha, and Brenda in front of the church holding up the VBS banner."

"Sounds good, Ted. I'll be there."

"This is more than the usual church news. I think it's signifi-cant, given this town's history, that a black church and a white church are cooperating like this. I'm going to give it some good coverage, plus some good ink on the editorial page, suggest that the other churches *go thou and do likewise*. Preacher, I've never seen Brenda this excited about anything, and I've been married to her sixteen years, known her since third grade. She and Latisha have been talking on the phone or in person just about every day. They've really connected, and they're going to be a super team on this Vacation Bible School. Of course, I know Karen and Latisha are close, too."

"They are. Got a lot in common. Deb's starting to crawl and get into everything, and Latisha's four months pregnant. Karen's mar-ried to a preacher, and Latisha's a preacher's kid."

"So she was telling me last week, said her dad pastors a church in Columbia, South Carolina, thirty-six years at the same church. Latisha's like Brenda and Karen, very creative. She's been teaching children at church since she was a teenager."

"Latisha's the one who sold everybody on the idea of offering Vacation Bible School for the high school kids. I know a lot of the kids have summer jobs and other things that'll conflict, but it looks like we'll have a half dozen or so from each church at the very least. Karen suggested a hands-on missions project in the daytime, followed by supper, Bible study, and recreation at Greater New Hope in the evening. Of course, all the kids are acquainted with each other from school, especially the ones involved with band or sports. I know Coretta Brinkley, the drum major for the band, is active at Greater New Hope, she and all her family. Hudson Westbrooks, plays football, is president of the youth group over there."

"Oh, I know Hudson. Believe me, I know Hudson! He's the one who kicked that forty-one yard field goal with three seconds on the clock to win the game against Hansonville 17-14. Wildest high school game I ever saw! Ol' Derek Elliott was in the right place at the right time, nailed a spectacular photo, perfect camera angle. It shows Hud's foot still up in the air, the ball sailing over the goalpost, the clock showing one second, and the referee with his arms up like he was charismatic. I gave Derek a hundred-dollar bonus for that picture, put in on the front of the sports section, made prints for him, Hudson, Coach Middleton, made another print for the high school yearbook, got one hanging in my den. Georgia Press Association prize for best sports photograph. Hudson's still got another year of high school, and the college scouts have their eyes on him. Coretta's a sharp kid, too, straight superior drum major ratings in every band festival the band's marched in. I know all of her family. Her grandfather, Cleon Brinkley, died a couple of years ago, owned a garage down on Florida Avenue, first black elected to public office in Mintz County, served three terms on the school board, fine man, deacon at Greater New Hope. Coretta's dad has the garage now, her mother drives a school bus, drives for all of the band trips. Lauretta, my fifteen-year-old, thinks the world of Eloise Brinkley, tries to get on her bus any time the band goes out of town."

"I talked to Lauretta last Sunday, also talked to David and Cheryl's boys. They're really excited about the missions projects. They'll be dividing into two teams, with kids from both churches on each team. One team'll do some minor repairs, painting and fixing up, at the domestic violence shelter. Being on the board now, I know what the needs are over there. Their budget's pretty tight, so they have to rely on volunteers and donations to get things done. Hutton Builder's Supply is donating the paint, which is a big help. The other team's going to do backyard Bible clubs at the mobile home park over there off Boundary Street."

"I'm going to run Derek Elliott's legs off between now and September when he starts at the University of Georgia," Ted commented. "He'll be the one coming out to get pictures of the kids working at the shelter and the trailer park."

"Speaking of Derek, I saw in the paper that he's the valedictorian for his graduating class."

"I'm proud of him," Ted acknowledged. "First one in his family to graduate from high school, and he did it up right. Top of his class, headed to the University of Georgia on a full scholarship to major in journalism. I've already called a guy I know at the Athens paper about letting him do some freelancing for them while he's up there in school. We're really going to miss him. I told Derek last week that I sure do wish he had a younger brother or sister with the same interest in journalism."

*   *   *   *   *   *   *   *   *   *   *   *

David Groves made Mike and Karen an unbeatable deal on a new Chevy Astro minivan, and they took delivery on Thursday afternoon of Vacation Bible School week. When Mike mentioned trading the Fairmount wagon, David said to keep it, since he could give them a better deal on a straight sale. "That way," David pointed out, "y'all'll have two vehicles and no arguments over who needs the car the worst. You'll just argue over who gets to drive the new van with air conditioning." Asalee and Deb rode home with their mother in the van, and Mike followed at a respectable distance in the Fairmount. He was actually glad they had not traded it. It would, as David suggested, end the arguments over which one had the most urgent need for the car, and the Fairmount was a solid old car even if it wouldn't win any beauty contests.

Mike did get to drive the new van Thursday night when he went over to Greater New Hope for the youth Bible study. The van had a great sound system, and the cold air conditioning felt good on a muggy summer night. Karen had asked him to pick up a gallon of milk on the way home, and he wanted to see if the *Courier* was out yet. The paper carried Friday's date, but Ted always got the rack copies out to the convenience stores by 7:30 or 8:00 on Thursday night. Mike and Karen would receive a copy in Friday's mail, but Mike wanted some extras. He pulled into the Phillips 66 Stop'n Shop and returned to the van with a gallon of milk and five copies of the *Courier* that still smelled of fresh ink. He turned on the map light and unfolded the front section of one of the papers.

The coverage was even better than he had anticipated, filling the bottom half of the front page with pictures, captions, and an article under Derek Elliott's byline. The headline proclaimed *CHURCHES PARTNER IN BIBLE SCHOOL, MISSIONS.* One photo showed Hudson Westbrooks leading outdoor recreational activities for younger children. Another showed Miss Addie sitting in a rocking chair surrounded by third and fourth graders hanging on every word she said. The third photo showed young people from both churches leading a Backyard Bible Club at Whispering Pines Mobile Home Park, and the final scene was a group of happy, paint-spattered teens pausing from their missions project at My Sister's Place for a group photo. Mike took time to read the caption under that one: *MISSIONS PROJECT AT MY SISTER'S PLACE:* "We'll all be the same color by the time we finish painting," quipped Coretta Brinkley, 17, of Greater New Hope, "Robin's egg blue, Sherwin-Williams interior flat latex." Mike smiled, folded the paper, and drove home where he would have better light for reading Derek's article.

* * * * * * * * * * * *

"Well, Preacher, you seen the paper?" the voice on the phone demanded. "I've done had about ten people call me all upset about it, and everybody had'n got their paper yet, so there'll be more." Mike recognized the raspy voice as belonging to Roland Millican.

"I'm fine, Roland, and you?" Mike responded sarcastically. "I know you meant to ask and just forgot. Karen and the girls are fine, too. Yes, I've seen the paper. I picked up some extra copies on the way home last night, just finished putting the article and pictures, along with Ted's editorial, on the bulletin board. I thought it was the best publicity the church has had in a long time."

"I expect you're real happy about that picture of David Groves' oldest boy with his hands all over some colored girl."

"Your paper must have a picture that's not in mine. I've got a copy of the paper in front of me as we speak, and there's no picture of Daniel with his hands all over anybody." Mike studied the picture again, eleven teenagers and three adults, wearing matching Sherwin-Williams painter's caps, posing for a group photo at My Sister's Place. "Roland, there's one picture in this paper with Daniel Groves in it, and I'm looking at it. The young lady in front of Daniel is Coretta Brinkley from Greater New Hope. Nice girl, Christian, comes from a good family. She's an honors student, drum major for the high school band. Yes, Daniel does appear to have his hand resting on her shoulder, but you've got eleven kids and three adults squeezing in close for a group photo, and I think that's all there is to that. The woman to the right of Daniel is Coretta's mother, Eloise Brinkley. She's been there every day while the kids worked at the shelter. She and Mr. Brinkley both have been at Greater New Hope every night when the kids met for Bible study. The kids've been well-supervised, and I don't think they had a chance to do anything improper if they wanted to."

"Well, it's like I said, Preacher. There's a lot of folks upset, and there'll be more by the time everybody gets their paper. You know how I feel about all this race mixin'. If God'd meant for us to mix, he'd'a made us all the same color."

"And you know how I feel about it, Roland. Race is a man-made distinction invented in the seventeenth century. There's never been any scientific agreement on a definition of race or how many races there are, and most scientists have abandoned the concept of race altogether. People have migrated all over the globe and intermarried for thousands of years, so if there ever was such a thing as a pure race, it's too late to worry about it now."

"I don't know where you learnt that hogwash! You go back'n read your Bible, get a King James Version 'stead'a one'a them translations. Read that ninth chapter'a Genesis, 'bout the sons of Noah'n the curse on Ham an' his descendants, right there in the Bible, plain as can be."

"I know the passage, Roland. I've got my Bible open to it. King James Version. I keep one for reference, just for discussions like this. It was Noah, not God, who pronounced the curse, and Noah was drunk at the time. God's not bound by what Noah said when he was drunk." Mike wanted to add *just as God is not bound by stuff you say when you're drunk, like you were at the March business meeting,* but he resisted the urge. "Roland, this passage has nothing to do with the origin of different races, and it doesn't say that God meant for one race to be superior to another. That interpretation goes back to a preacher in Richmond, Virginia in the 1840's who was trying to come up with a Biblical defense of slavery. It's a perfect example of somebody starting with their own ideas and then trying to find something in the Bible to support them."

"You'n keep believin' that lib'ral crap if you want to, but you're not gonna last long here if you do. I'm warnin' you, Preacher, you had'n heard the last'a this. We got shed'a one preacher for preachin' this integrationist business. You ain't satisfied with race-mixin', you gotta go bring a woman preacher in for revival. Mark my words, Preacher, your days in this church are numbered. We got shed'a that nigger-lovin' Franklin Seals, an' we'n get shed'a you!"

"Roland, I'm not going to be intimidated by your threats. If you're worried about how things look, what's in the paper looks a lot better than what y'all did to Franklin Seals, calling for his resignation before his daughter's body was cold. If I were you, I'd be trembling in my boots at the prospect of facing God in judgement. You've got a lot to answer for. I'm ending this conversation before I say something I'll regret. It's 8:40, opening assembly starts in twenty minutes, and some of the children and workers are arriving. Goodbye, Roland." Mike hung up the phone and tried to compose himself. Although he was angry, he had felt in control while talking to Roland. Now, he was shaky, nauseous, and fighting back tears. When he felt sufficiently composed, he opened the door and stepped out into the hallway. He narrowly missed being creamed by Asalee and Rosa, who were racing down the hall hand-in-hand with Molly Coleman on their heels. Henry Conway came in just as Mike was gently reminding the girls to walk, not run, inside the building. As he gave the girls a group hug, he said, "Conway, wouldn't it be nice to have this much energy?"

"Nope, not in this old frame. That'd be like puttin' a jet engine in a Model A Ford."

✳   ✳   ✳   ✳   ✳   ✳   ✳   ✳   ✳   ✳   ✳

After opening assembly, when the children had adjourned to their classes, Mike suggested to Conway that they go back to the kitchen for some coffee. "I made it about 8:00 and then got tied up on the phone, never got to drink any. Get yourself a mug out of the upper cabinet. Those little styrofoam cups don't hold enough to do any good. Cream's in the refrigerator, sugar and Sweet'n Low's in the canister behind the coffee pot."

"Thanks, Reverend. I could use a cup after the conversation I had with Deacon Brinkley 'fore I came over here."

"That's interesting. I just got off from a very unpleasant phone conversation right before you came in. Let's go back to my office to drink our coffee."

As Mike closed the door to the outer office where Helen was finishing the bulletin for Sunday, Conway picked up where he had left off. "Deacon Brinkley, Arthur Brinkley, called me this morning about 6:30, asked me to stop by his garage on my way over here, said he needed to talk with me about something. He sounded upset, and I asked him what the problem was, and he said he'd rather talk face-to-face. When I got there, he told me that his daughter Coretta and one of the boys from your church, Daniel Groves, had taken a liking to each other while they were working together at the shelter and having Bible study at our church. Daniel asked Coretta to go out with him to dinner and a movie in Carrollton tomorrow night, and Coretta wants to go. He asked me what I thought he and Mrs. Brinkley ought to do."

"So what did you tell him?"

"I told him I thought they ought to let her go. Told him, in the first place, we're talking about two seventeen year olds going on a date, not a man and woman about to get married, and it's best we don't blow it out of proportion. Let's take this for what it is, a boy and girl, seventeen years old, both Christians from good families, spending money they earned, going out to dinner and a movie and enjoying each other's company. I think that's all there is to it. They're not doing anything on the sly. Coretta's talkin' about meetin' the boy in the living room, not going out the window. Both of 'em told their parents about their plans. They're talking about going to public places together, so he doesn't mind being seen with her and doesn't care who might see them together. All we've got is two nice kids going on a date, and we ought not make it into more than what it is or something besides what it is."

"I agree, but what'd Mr. Brinkley say to that?"

"He asked me, "spose it does turn into more than that. Suppose they end up going steady, decide they want to get married?' He asked me what I'd say then."

"And you told him…"

"I said, 'Deacon Brinkley, let's talk about something we don't talk about much.' I told him most if not all of us've already got white kinfolks, never mind that we don't claim 'em and they sure don't claim us. I worked at the post office twenty years, mail carrier. Soon's I got my twenty years in, back'n '87, I took early retirement to devote full time to the church. Now, ol' Cliff Fuller, white man, delivers the route you're on, is my cousin. I don't know if he knows it, but he is. My grandmother told me not long 'fore she died. Cliff's granddaddy, ol' man Oscar Fuller, raped my grandmother and got her pregnant. The baby Mama Tatum had by Oz Fuller was my mother. Cliff's daddy and my mother're half-brother and sister. That makes me'n Cliff first cousins. Now Cliff and I always got along fine, worked together twenty years. I was the first black mail carrier to work out of the Harrington post office, Cliff started carrying mail about three years before I did. He helped train me, and nobody could've treated me any better. I never said anything about us being kin, 'cause I don't know how he'd take it. Like I said, I don't know if he knows. 'Course, he may know all about it and wonder if I know. I always thought it best not to say anything. We're friends, and I don't want to change that. Besides, he can't help what his granddaddy did in 1920. I remember ol' man Oz Fuller from when I was a kid. He was sheriff of Mintz County, mean as a rattlesnake, at least he was to black folks. Cliff and ol' man Oz're as different as night'n day."

"Like Miss Addie told me, a lot of black folks and white folks have common ancestors much more recent than Adam and Eve. Don't know if you know it, but the Brinkleys in your church are kin to the Brinkleys in my church."

"They are?"

"Mmmhmm, all the Brinkleys around here are kin, and I mean *all* the Brinkleys. You know Franklin A. Brinkley, Former Chairman of the Board of Deacons of Harrington Baptist Church—Karen said she wonders if all of that's on his driver's license—the one who has Brinkley Insurance Agency. I doubt he'd admit it, but he and Coretta's daddy are cousins. Miss Addie told me that old preacher Joshua Brinkley, Frank's great-grandfather, kept a black woman as his mistress and had several children by her. All of the black Brinkleys are descended from ol' Josh Brinkley and his mistress. Joshua Brinkley'd be Mr. Arthur's great-great-grandfather, Coretta's three-times-great-grandfather. Miss Addie'll be ninety-four in August, been around here all her life, knows what she's talking about."

"That may be a useful bit of information before this is over."

"Pastor, can you pick up the phone?" Helen Walters' voice crackled over the intercom.

"It's David Groves. Says it's urgent..."

* * * * * * * * * * * * *

"I never thought we'd need to deal with anything like this," Cheryl Groves said as she and David sat in Mike's office that afternoon. "Daniel's always been a good kid, him and Luke both. Since Dan's had his driver's license, he's been a big help to me, delivering contracts, putting up signs and taking them down, helps at the dealership, too."

"Yeah," David concurred, "Dan can detail a car as well as any professional shop, better than some of them, and I don't mind paying him what I'd pay a detail shop. He makes decent grades. Never gave us any trouble to speak of, so this has floored us, him telling us he has a date with a black girl."

"I don't want to sound prejudiced," Cheryl searched for words. "Coretta's a lovely girl."

"Cheryl," Mike began, "are you more concerned with sounding prejudiced or actually being prejudiced? How things sound is less important that how things really are."

"Brother Mike, in my real estate business, I follow the law on equal housing opportunity to the letter. It's a good law and it ought to be enforced. Monica Lewis is black, been with my company five years, one of my best agents. I'd fire any agent who discriminated against a client because of race. We've got blacks and whites living in our apartments, and I'd be the first to tell you there's no correlation between skin color and who makes a good tenant. Good and bad tenants come in all colors. But there's a difference between treating people fairly and dating them."

"Cheryl, Daniel's not talking about dating a whole race of people. Last I heard, he was only talking about dating Coretta. I've met Coretta and her parents, gotten pretty well acquainted with them this week, seem to be good people."

"I know they are," David agreed. "As far as liking people goes, the black Brinkleys are generally more likeable than the white ones. But doesn't the Bible say something about not taking strange wives?"

"When's the wedding?" Mike asked. "I thought they were planning their first date."

"They are, but it could lead to that."

"It could, but it probably won't. I didn't marry any of the girls I dated in high school. You didn't either."

"Yeah, but what if it should lead to that? Doesn't the Bible say something about not taking strange wives?"

"I haven't noticed anything strange about Coretta. She seems pretty normal as far as I can tell. David, the passage you're talking about is in the tenth chapter of Ezra, but it doesn't have a thing in the world to do with this situation. The Jewish people had returned from captivity after the Persians conquered Babylon. A lot of Jewish men had married Babylonian women while they were in exile, and these women brought Babylonian religious beliefs and practices with them. The issue wasn't skin color, it was the influence of the Babylonian religions."

"I don't know," Cheryl stammered, "this just goes against the way we were raised."

"Now we're talking," Mike injected. "This isn't about what the Bible says, it's about what we're used to and what we're comfortable with, and we need to deal with it on that level. I'd be a lot more comfortable if this hadn't come up, not because Daniel and Coretta are doing anything wrong, but because I'm going to have people upset with me no matter what I say or don't say. But, as far as it being something that goes against Scripture, it's not. The Bible never mentions race, because people were never classified into races on the basis of skin color until the seventeenth century. Race is a man-made distinction."

"It's hard to change the way we feel, though," David objected.

"It sure is," Mike agreed. "It's a lot easier to work on behavior than feelings."

"So what do you think we ought to do?" Cheryl asked.

"What would you do if Daniel wanted to go out with a white girl who was as decent a person as Coretta?"

"I'd slip him a few extra bucks, tell him to be careful and have a good time," David replied sheepishly.

"Then my suggestion is to let them go out together and do what you just said. One more thing…"

"What's that?" Cheryl asked.

"Reverend Conway was telling me that Mr. and Mrs. Brinkley have the same concerns you do, and Conway's concerned about being on the hot seat over this, just as I am. It might be good to talk things out face-to-face with the Brinkleys, maybe invite them over tomorrow night while Daniel and Coretta are out together. It might be awkward at first, but I don't see how it could hurt, and it might help. The Brinkleys are good parents who want the best for their children just like you want the best for yours."

Cheryl looked at David, squeezed his hand gently, and said "I'll call the Brinkleys."

28

"Brother Mike, you're on your own if you have the woman preacher in for revival," director of missions Virgil Blackmon's voice on the phone warned Mike when the announcement came out in the newsletter. Virgil repeated his warning after the pastors conference a month later, with the added caveat, "Same goes if y'all bring any more women deacons on board. I had a lot of ruffled feathers to smooth over y'all bringing that woman onto the deacon board."

Mike resisted the urge to tell Virgil that That Woman, now dead and buried, never did serve as a deacon (for that divine favor, he would be eternally grateful), and that the woman elected last time was Brenda Coleman. The humor would have been wasted on Virgil. "Then I guess I'm on my own," Mike replied. "I'm not going to break the commitment to Heather or the church. As for who the church elects as deacons, that's up to the church. I've got one vote, just like any other member of the church."

"Like I said, there'll be trouble in the association if y'all go ahead with the woman preacher or any more women deacons. You're not in the shadow of Mid-Atlantic Seminary anymore. This is Mintz County, Georgia, Son. People down here aren't ready for such as that. Now, I can appreciate what y'all did, doin' the Vacation Bible School with the black church, but there's a lot of folks not ready for that, either. I had some of your folks call me all upset about that. I know you mean well, Son, but you gotta understand where you are. You're gettin' yourself into more trouble than you can get out of. I don't have a problem workin' with colored folks, though I don't believe in intermarryin' with 'em. As for the woman preacher and women deacons, you're going against Scripture the way I see it, and I do have a problem with that. Now, I might be wrong, and the way I was raised has prob'ly got a lot to do with the way I interpret Scripture. Whether it's right or wrong, you're gonna get yourself in trouble over it. There's a lot of people in your church like me, just not ready for such as that."

"I look at it the same way Miss Addie does, Virgil. If Moses had waited until everybody was ready, the Israelites would still be in Egypt."

* * * * * * * * * * * *

"Mike, Honey, you need to go ahead'n come in, take a shower and get cleaned up," Karen announced as Mike put up the lawnmower and came in from cutting the grass. "Clarence and Lunell just called. Heather's at their house. It's a little after 3:30 now. Lunell said supper'll be ready between 5:30 and 6:00, but to come on over whenever we can get there. I talked to Heather. She had a good trip, says she can't wait to see all of us. She's got a lot to tell us about Carol and Dennis's wedding and lots of other news from Clear Springs. Eric and Jenny are coming over for dinner, so you'n Eric and Heather can get your heads together about the service in the morning."

* * * * * * * * * * * *

"Y'all come on in," Clarence called out cheerily as he held the screen door open for the Westovers. "Eric and Jenny are in the den with Preacher Simmons. We've been talking her ears off ever since she got here. We sure are going to enjoy having her this week. I can't wait to hear her preach."

"She's good," Mike acknowledged. "Clear Springs has really done well since she's been there. They love her to death up there."

"And I can see why," Lunell said as she emerged from the kitchen to join the conversation.

"We feel like we've known her forever, and she just got here. The ham'll be ready in about twenty minutes, then I've got to brown the rolls, and we'll be ready to eat."

"Can I help you in the kitchen?" Karen asked.

"Oh no, Karen. It's under control. There's no kitchen big enough for two women anyway. Y'all go on in the den, make yourselves at home."

"Preacher Heather!" Asalee squealed as she ran excitedly toward her, arms stretched up for a hug.

"Hey, Azzie!" Heather hugged Asalee and swung her off the floor. "Girl, you're getting tall! You've grown so much since the last time I saw you! Oh, and look at you, Miss Deborah Estelle! Walking already! Come here and give me a hug!"

"Asalee's getting ready to start second grade," Karen commented, "and Deb'll be a year old a week from Monday. Doesn't seem possible. I don't know where the time goes. They're growing up."

"Great to see you," Mike said as he and Karen hugged Heather and greeted Eric and Jenny. "How was the trip?"

"Good, no problems, made good time. I'm an early morning person anyway, always have been. I ate breakfast with Wayne and June before I left. That's gotten to be a standing appointment since I moved into Wallace's house, to walk across the road at sunup on Saturday morning for breakfast with Wayne and June. You know

Wallace used to eat with them every Saturday morning after Estelle died. Wayne says Saturday's the one day a week June cooks all the good stuff he's not supposed to eat since the heart attack and bypass surgery, says he eats bran flakes and grapefruit six days a week to get a real breakfast on Saturday. So I had enough for a barn raising, got on the road about 7:00. Clarence gave me good directions, drove right to their door. The Bishops are really sweet. I'm going to enjoy staying with them."

"So what's it like being full time at Clear Springs?" Mike asked as Asalee climbed over the side of the recliner and squeezed in beside Heather.

"It's different, for me and for the church, but it's going to be good. The church has never had a full-time pastor, so they don't know what to expect from one. That gives me a lot of freedom. It's easier in some ways, don't know how in the world I was able to live on campus, carry a full load at the seminary, and pastor the church. I love living in Wallace and Estelle's house. It's got lots of character, still got a lot of their furniture. The only furniture I owned was my bedroom suite from home. My parents brought that up for me, and they took me to a furniture store in Canfield and told me to pick out a sofa and chair. Everything else is Wallace and Estelle's stuff the family gave me, right down to the pots, pans, dishes, and silverware. I love that big front porch. It's so peaceful to sit in the swing early in the morning and watch the deer walk right up in the yard, very conducive to prayer and meditation."

"How was the wedding last night?" Karen asked.

"You would've loved it! We were all wishing you could've been there. I was telling Eric and Jenny about it before you got here. I was nervous as a cat, it being my first wedding. The church was packed. Carol was a beautiful bride, and Dennis looked like the happiest man I ever saw. Tycina sang *Joyful, Joyful, We Adore Thee*. Megan and Jessica served as ushers and read Scripture.

Little Bill was the best man. Russ and Joan walked Carol down the aisle. Sharon, Linda, and Mary Kate were bridesmaids. Sheila Hampton, music teacher at Sanders County High School, played the violin, did the wedding march and recessional. Everybody who has rose bushes brought roses and helped decorate the church. And—this could only happen at Clear Springs—we had dinner on the grounds for the reception!"

"You're kidding," Mike responded.

"Nope, serious. We had the wedding at 6:00 so we'd have plenty of daylight. People brought food like it was homecoming. If you can picture the usual homecoming spread with a big wedding cake in the middle of the table, you've got it. I thought Carol was pulling my leg when she suggested it. Come to find out, it started as Linda's idea. I should have suspected as much. She was being face-tious, typical Linda Trimble wisecrack, but Carol and Dennis went for it. It was so neat, and it was a lot better than the usual reception fare. I want to do mine the same way when I get married..."

"Speaking of which," Karen probed, "Carol told us that you were dating someone..."

"Yeah, I figured she'd tell the world," Heather blushed demurely. "His name's Joel Moore, good guy whether I marry him or not. He's twenty-six, teaches English and drama at Sanders County High School. Carol introduced us, and we've been dating about three months. I'm not rushing into anything. I went through a bad breakup with a guy at seminary a couple of months before I was called to Clear Springs, don't want to go through that again. Joel's a member of First Baptist in Ledford, but he's been at Clear Springs just about every Sunday since we started dating, won't surprise me if he moves his letter soon. He volunteered to take Carol's Sunday School class for the time being. The church loves him to death. They're all set to do another big wedding, dinner on the grounds, the whole nine yards, whenever we're ready. Joel'd like for things to move faster, but he's patient, understands my need to go slow. My parents met him when they came up to help me move, and they really like him. I talked to Granny Becker on the phone a couple of weeks ago, told her all about Joel and me. She said he sounds like a good one, said I'd better not let him get away."

"Sounds like what my father told me the first time I took Karen to meet my parents," Mike commented. "Dad took me aside and said, 'Son, this'n's a keeper. You'd better marry her 'fore she changes her mind.' Dad's a good judge of women," Mike added as he gave Karen a playful squeeze.

"Everything's ready," Clarence announced. "Let's all join hands around the table. As we give thanks for the food, we want to thank the Lord for bringing Preacher Simmons safely to us and pray the Lord's blessing on her ministry here this week. Brother Mike, offer our prayer for us…"

* * * * * * * * * * * *

"So who's preaching at Clear Springs tomorrow?" Mike asked as everyone settled in the living room after dinner.

"Dr. Corrie. He hasn't preached at Clear Springs since my ordination, so I thought it'd be good to invite him down. Now that he's retired, he stays busy with interim work and pulpit supply. I was lucky to get him. He's starting an interim at Calvary Baptist in Riverton next Sunday, and he'll be there a while. That church has a lot of healing to do before they're ready to call anybody."

"Corrie'll be good for them. We're talking about Dr. Gordon Corrie, Old Testament prof at Mid-Atlantic for about forty years," he explained to the others in the room. "Y'all remember Wallace Coggins from Clear Springs who came to see us last fall and then died on Christmas day. Dr. Corrie is Wallace's son-in-law."

"So how long have you all been members at Harrington?" Heather directed the question first to Lunell Bishop, who was sitting beside her on the sofa.

"Me? Since 1935, the year Clarence and I married. I grew up in Freeman Valley Baptist Church, about five or six miles out in the county, baptized there when I was twelve years old, joined Harrington Baptist when John Leland Walters was pastor."

"I grew up in Columbus," Clarence picked up the thread, "came to Harrington in '34 when I got out of pharmacy school, came to work for old Doc Gowin, who was trying to do what I'm trying to do now, halfway retire but keep one hand in the business. I worked for him twelve years, eventually bought him out. I met Lunell right after I came to Harrington, married her the next year. We had two sons and a daughter. My father was Methodist, Mother was Episcopalian, but we weren't much of a church-going family. I'd go to church with Lunell and the kids on special occasions, didn't become a Christian and get involved in the church regularly 'til I was forty-nine years old, 1960. Franklin Seals baptized me, one of the kindest and most patient men I ever knew. Brother Mike puts me in mind of him a lot. The Good Lord knew it'd take somebody like that to win me over. I was real active for about the next four years, until the bunch that ran the church back then decided to get rid of Brother Seals. I was right put out with the church for years. I started back a few months ago because the same man who was the ringleader in running Brother Seals off was trying to make trouble for Brother Mike..."

"Clarence, Hon, let's not get into all of that right now," Lunell chided.

After an awkward silence, Jenny spoke up. "I grew up in this church, baptized when I was ten, never belonged anywhere else."

"And I'm the new kid on the block," Eric said. "Been here about five years, originally from up at Villa Rica, met Jenny at

Jacksonville State. I'm band director at Harrington High School, been doing the music at church for the past three years."

"Neat," Heather commented. "I was in the band all through high school and college, clarinet player. It was no great loss to the music world when God called me to preach."

"Well, Eric observed, "you're obviously doing what you're supposed to be doing, and I think I'm doing what the Lord wants me to do. I couldn't do what you do. I felt like I knew you before I met you today, just hearing so much about you. The folks who've visited here from Clear Springs speak well of you, too. Just talking to you today, I can tell it's going to be a pleasure to work with you. I'm eager to hear you preach."

"Thanks, Eric. I've been looking forward to this week. We're going to be a good team. I'm not saying this just because Mike is sitting here—I have tremendous respect for your pastor, and I feel honored that he's invited me here. I wouldn't've had the opportunities I've had, wouldn't be where I am now, if Mike hadn't been willing to stick his neck out for me. There were plenty of guys at the seminary Mike could've asked to preach at Clear Springs those two Sundays he was in the process of being called here. There are plenty of men he could have invited to preach this revival. A lot of preachers say they're all for women in ministry, but they won't invite one to their pulpit."

"Well," Mike laughed, "I didn't think I was taking that much of a risk inviting you to Clear Springs. I invited you the first time because I'd heard you preach in class and in chapel, interacted with you in some classes, and I was impressed with you. I invited you the second time, and the church called you as pastor, because they were as impressed with you as I was. I suppose I did take a risk inviting you here, but anybody who doesn't take some risks is not much of a leader. I think the risk is worth it. You'll do this church good."

"The music's going to be good this week," Jenny commented. "Our choir's been working hard to get ready. Pretty good for a small church choir, I think. Sunday night, the choir from Greater New Hope's going to sing. Greater New Hope's the black church we partnered with for Vacation Bible School. The Methodist choir's singing Tuesday night. My aunt, Eleanor Flint Basden, Mother's sister, is the pastor there. Aunt El grew up in Harrington Baptist, so did her husband. She was a nurse for about twenty years, made a mid-life career change, went to Candler after her kids were in high school, became a Methodist minister..."

"Oh Wow!" Heather injected, "I can't wait to meet her."

"Eleanor and Ben are good people," Lunell commented. "I taught both of them in the second grade and taught them in Sunday School. I was really sad when they left our church, but I understood them doing what they needed to do. She knew it'd just cause a big stink if she told our church she was called to preach, so they quietly went and joined the Methodists. She was right to do what the Lord called her to do, and I was so proud of Ben and their two boys for supporting her the way they did. She made the Methodists a fine pastor, and they really love her over there. She's a good preacher. Clarence and I went to hear her the first Sunday she preached at Harrington Methodist, and we heard her at the Easter sunrise service last year."

"That reminds me, Heather," Jennie spoke up. "Mother and Aunt El have lunch together every Tuesday at the Lonesome Whistle, neat little restaurant in the old railroad depot. Mother wanted me to ask if you'd join her and Ellie for lunch on Tuesday."

"As far as I know, I can and I'd love to. What's our schedule, Mike?"

"Nothing that would interfere with the lunch plans. We're pretty flexible."

"Then we're on. Jen, if you'll make sure I get introduced to your mother tomorrow...now, you were telling me about the music for the revival..."

"Yes, now where was I? Oh, yes, our choir's singing Sunday morning, Monday night, and Wednesday night, Greater New Hope choir Sunday night, and the Methodist choir Tuesday night. Eric and I, along with David and Cheryl Groves, another couple in our church, sing together as a quartet, do a lot of *a cappella* stuff. Eric's got perfect pitch, and the rest of us blend in. We're singing Thursday night, doing a couple of pieces out of the *Sacred Harp*. Friday night, the combined youth choirs from our church and Greater New Hope are going to sing."

"Sounds like a lot of people have been working hard to get ready for this week, working and praying, too," Heather commented. "Clear Springs is committed to praying for the revival here. There'll be prayer meetings at Clear Springs every night at the same time the services are going on here. I imagine you've got some who're not thrilled about a woman coming in to preach a revival..."

"You won't be the first woman to preach at Harrington Baptist," Clarence commented.

"I won't?" The note of surprise was evident in Heather's voice. "Who was the first?"

"Miss Addie," Lunell answered. "Addie Jane Peyton Aldridge, just turned ninety-four. I'm eighty years old, and she was my first grade teacher back in 1917, the first year she taught, at a one-room school out in Freeman Valley. I taught forty-one years at Harrington Elementary, she and I taught there together about twenty-some-odd years. She's the oldest member of our church and the most forward-thinking of the bunch."

"Pastor asked her to tell about her baptism in the creek back in 1908 on the Sunday our granddaughter Cassie was baptized last summer," Clarence continued the story. "She did that, all right, and then she went on to preach one of the best sermons I ever heard. She talked about how remembering her baptism had helped her with the hard decisions in her life, helped her find the courage to do the right thing when it wasn't easy. She told Cassie to remember her baptism whenever she was torn between obeying God and giving in to her fears. 'Just close your eyes and feel the water, and you'll know what you need to do,' she said. It meant a lot to our granddaughter, and it was a good sermon for the whole church."

"Both of our girls love her to death," Karen added, "and she's excited about meeting you, Heather, can't wait to hear you preach. Miss Addie said she was happy to be the first woman to preach at Harrington Baptist Church, but she didn't want to be the last one."

"As for some of them in the church not being ready for a woman revival preacher," Mike observed, "I look at it the same way Miss Addie does. If Moses had waited until everybody was ready, the Israelites would still be in Egypt!"

"I like that!" Heather laughed. "I've got to meet this woman. That line of hers is going to find its way into a sermon at Clear Springs, perhaps as soon as next Sunday."

"You probably don't know it, Heather," Mike continued, "but some people at Clear Springs were a little skeptical about a woman preacher the first time I invited you to supply for me. But, they came on to church anyway and heard you. Some came out of curiosity, I guess they'd never met a woman preacher and wanted to see what one looked like. Some of them figured you couldn't do any harm in one Sunday, and they came on out of a sense of duty. I won't tell you who the skeptics were, maybe they'll tell you someday, but they're among your strongest supporters now."

"I know who two of them were. I ate breakfast with them this morning. We laugh about it now."

"You'll win over some of our skeptics before this week's over," Mike commented.

"I hope I do," Heather observed, her voice taking a serious tone, "but that's not what I came to do. I'm here to preach the gospel and do what I can to help this church. If anybody's mind is changed about women preachers, that'll be icing on the cake."

∗   ∗   ∗   ∗   ∗   ∗   ∗   ∗   ∗   ∗   ∗   ∗

"Come on, Roland," Geneva Millican barked as she nabbed her husband the moment he emerged from the fifty-five-to-glory Men's Bible Class. "I dismissed my class a little early so we'd have time to get home before Charles Stanley comes on," she announced in a voice loud enough for all in the vicinity, especially Heather, to hear. Mike was in the hallway with Heather, in front of the pictures of the Beloved Former Pastors, greeting people as they came out of their Sunday School classes. Mike and Heather spoke to Geneva and Roland as they passed by, but their greetings were not returned. Like a police officer taking some miscreant off to jail, Geneva marched Roland past Mike's and Heather's out-stretched hands. As the Millicans started out the door, Roland commented to Franklin A. Brinkley, Former Chairman of the Board of Deacons of Harrington Baptist Church, "I'm not about to stay and listen to no woman preacher."

"I reckon I'm staying," Frank replied sheepishly. "Jean brought food for the dinner after church. She said if I left after Sunday School to plan on going to McDonald's, said she wasn't about to bring me a plate from the dinner or fix for me when she got home."

Mike turned to Heather to apologize for the rudeness of the Millicans. Before he could say anything, she spoke up. "It's all right, Mike. Really, I've got thicker hide than that." The tears that welled up in her eyes contradicted her words. Before Mike could make any further effort to apologize for the Millicans, Heather turned to face the sound of a cane thumping the floor.

"You must be Preacher Simmons," Miss Addie said as she reached out to hug Heather.

"I'm Addie Jane Aldridge, the oldest member of this church. I look forward to hearing you preach."

"Oh, Miss Addie, I'm so glad to meet you!" Heather exclaimed as she reciprocated the hug. "I've heard so much about you! The Bishops tell me you were the first woman to preach at this church. Clarence said you preached the glory down the Sunday their granddaughter was baptized."

"That's the good thing about being ninety-four years old. I can preach whenever I want, and nobody dares to tell me I can't. Honey, don't be upset about Roland and Geneva. They enjoy hearing Dr. Stanley so much. I wonder whether they know that he was converted under the ministry of a woman Pentecostal preacher?" With a demure, mischievous grin, she added, "I must remember to tell them that."

* * * * * * * * * * * *

Mike surveyed the Sunday morning congregation as he got up to introduce Heather. A few people had left after Sunday School. Franklin A. Brinkley, Former Chairman of the Board of Deacons of Harrington Baptist Church, realized that Jean—who had been in Miss Addie's class in fourth grade—was not bluffing, and he decided he didn't want McDonald's for Sunday dinner. The revival announcement in the *Courier* with Heather's picture had apparently been effective in bringing in the curious, including director of missions Virgil Blackmon. Mike noticed a fair number of visitors, and a good contingent of those who came only sporadically. Bob McKnight had kept his calendar clear, and he and Susan were there. It was a better-than-average crowd for the first service of the revival. Heather appeared poised and comfortable as she sat in one of the pulpit chairs, holding her Bible on her lap with one finger marking her text.

"I am pleased to welcome to our pulpit for this week of revival services Pastor Heather Simmons of the Clear Springs Baptist Church near Ledford, Virginia," Mike began the introduction. "I know Heather from our days at Mid-Atlantic Baptist Theological Seminary. As I had opportunities to interact with her in classes, I was impressed by her abilities and her strong sense of calling to be a pastor. We were in the same preaching class with Dr. Emory Leggs. Hearing her in class, and again in chapel when she was presented the James Towers Memorial Award for excellence in preaching, I was in awe of her ability in the pulpit. I invited her to preach at Clear Springs the Sunday I was in Alabama preaching for the committee from this church. The church was as impressed with her as I was. They wanted to hear her again, so I invited her back the Sunday I preached the trial sermon here. When I resigned to come here, Clear Springs—without considering any other candidates—unanimously called her to be their pastor. Heather was ordained by Clear Springs, and it was my privilege to preside at her ordination. Under her leadership, Clear Springs has experienced the greatest growth in its history. For over a century, the church was served by student pastors. That tradition ended in May when Heather graduated from seminary and became the first full-time pastor of Clear Springs Baptist Church. It is because of the obvious blessing of God on Heather's ministry that I invited her here this week. Heather is a gifted communicator of the gospel who will be as good for this church as she has been for Clear Springs. After the anthem by our choir, we will hear her prayerfully..."

* * * * * * * * * * * *

"Well, Brother Mike," Virgil Blackmon commented as the crowd was dispersing after dinner, "I have to admit the young lady can preach. She preached as sound a message as you'll hear anywhere, and she knows how to communicate. Still, it's like I told you, Brother Mike, there's going to be trouble in the association over this, and I don't like anything that causes trouble in the association. Ol' Floyd Williams out at Freeman Valley called me at home Friday night after he saw the writeup about the revival in the paper. That boy's gonna keel over dead one of these days, the way he gets himself worked up over stuff like this. He was demandin' to know what *I'm* going to do about *your* church havin' a woman revival preacher. I told him I was going to get over to hear her, beyond that I wasn't going to do anything, told 'im if anything was done, it'd be the association doin' it'n not me. Lord, I wish that boy could comprehend the difference between a Methodist district superintendent and a Baptist director of missions."

"He called our house Friday night, don't know if it was before or after you had the pleasure of talking to him. I was gone to buy groceries, so Karen answered the phone, and he started in on her, which was a serious mistake on ol' Floyd's part. Karen's a sweet woman, but she won't back down from anybody. Karen asked him if he'd like for me to call him back when I got home, but he just kept on, so Karen spoke the truth in love with both barrels."

"This is gonna be good," Virgil laughed, "What'd she tell 'im?"

"She reminded him that half of his ancestors were women, and then she hung up on him. She was playing the piano furiously when I came in."

* * * * * * * * * * * *

"Hey, Preacher, good message this morning, might preach it myself sometime," Virgil commented to Heather as he shook hands with her.

"Thanks," Heather acknowledged the compliment. "You're welcome to it if you can use it. I think it was Spurgeon who said, 'He who never quotes will never be quoted.'"

Heather was polite to Virgil, but she was obviously thinking *Who is this clown, and am I supposed to know him?* so Mike made the introduction, "Heather, this is Virgil Blackmon, director of missions for the Mintz County Association."

"Just came over to see what kind of trouble Brother Mike's getting himself into," Virgil quipped.

"Well, you've got to have at least one lightning rod in every association," Heather rejoined wryly as she moved on to speak to Bob and Susan McKnight.

* * * * * * * * * * *

"Come on in, Heather," Mike called out from his office as he heard Heather come in. "Eric just got here. Coffee's on back in the kitchen if you want some, help yourself."

"No thanks, already had my caffeine quota," Heather laughed as she took one of the burnt-orange waiting room chairs in Mike's office. "Lunell put on a big breakfast. There's no telling how many cups of coffee I drank. My cup never got all the way empty before Clarence or Lunell one would top it off."

"Sounds just like them. So they're taking good care of you?"

"They are, and they're very understanding of me needing a lot of time alone to read, pray, and think. I told them not to feel like they need to get up if they hear me stirring before the crack of dawn. Their front porch faces due east just like mine, so I sat out there in my pajamas and robe and watched the sun come up this morning, just like I do at home. Lunell got up about 6:30 and saw me out there reading my Bible, so she just let me be. I came in when I smelled breakfast cooking. I thought I'd be too wound up to sleep last night, but I never knew when my head touched the pillow. The phone was ringing when we came in last night. It was Joel, calling to check on me and find out how the revival's going. Talking to him helped me unwind enough to go to sleep. We talked a long time. I'm getting serious with him in spite of myself. Enough about my love life. I'm glad we're having these meetings every morning to debrief. It's going to help me to have the feedback. I feel like we're off to a good start. How about y'all?"

"You brought two excellent messages yesterday," Eric began. "I know we've got a half-dozen or so who're staying home because the preacher is a woman, but the way I look at it, it's their loss, and we've got that many or more who're here for the same reason. I'm glad Mike invited you. It wouldn't've been right to deprive the rest of the church of your ministry just because a few people want to act like jerks. I'm more concerned with reaching people who haven't heard the gospel than I am with placating negative people. Some of our skeptics had the decency to come and hear you in spite of their reservations. If they reserved judgement until they heard you and if they judged you on the quality of your preaching, they shouldn't have any problem with you."

"I agree with Eric," Mike said, "just one thing I'd add. We had at least one who was here because his wife would've given him fits otherwise. I'm talking about ol' Franklin A. Brinkley, Former Chairman of the Board of Deacons of Harrington Baptist Church."

"Oh yes," Heather laughed, "the one who told Roland that his wife told him to plan on eating at McDonald's if he didn't stay for preaching. At the dinner yesterday, Jean came up to me, hugged me, and said, 'I'm Jean Brinkley, Frank's wife. I'm glad you're here, and Frank'll get over it.'"

"That's good," Mike concurred. "I thought our choir sounded good yesterday morning, and Greater New Hope had the place rocking last night. We had a pretty full house, and it looked like about as many of our folks Sunday night as there were Sunday morning. I think we'll have good attendance the rest of the week."

"Tell me about the two who made professions of faith yesterday, the little girl Sunday morning and the teenage boy last night, and tell me about the couple that moved their membership yesterday morning," Heather inquired.

"The little girl's name is Molly Coleman. She'll be starting third grade when school opens. Her parents, Ted and Brenda, are deacons. Ted's chairman of deacons and editor of our local paper. Brenda teaches fourth grade at Harrington Elementary, teaches the same age group in Sunday School," Mike answered. "Luke Groves, the one who came forward last night, is going in eighth grade. His father, David, is a deacon, owns the Chevrolet dealership. His mother, Cheryl, owns Red Carpet Realty. Nice kid, shy until you get to know him, computer whiz."

"Sounds like they're both plugged in to the church pretty well, lots of support at home,"

Heather observed. "And the couple who joined by letter?"

"Paul and Alice Lassiter. They've been visiting for a couple of months now, new to Harrington. Alice said they decided to check us out after they saw the writeup in the paper about the combined VBS with Greater New Hope. Paul's a pediatrician, just opened a practice here. Alice is an RN but not practicing for now, being a stay-at-home mom while the kids are little. They're from Philadelphia, came by letter from an American Baptist church up there. Paul told me, when he saw the statue of Captain Cicero Mintz in front of the courthouse and the stars and bars in the Georgia flag, he wondered if it might not be a little too soon after the war for them to settle down here, but he said they've been well received. Cheryl Groves helped them find a house to rent while Carl Baxter builds them a house out in Freeman Valley. They've been pleased with their dealings with Cheryl and Carl, so that's helped them connect with the church, too."

"That's good," Heather commented. "I ended up talking a good bit over dinner with Charlene, don't remember her last name, not sure she ever told me, but she needed a hug and needed to talk. She's got a daughter named Amy, looks to be eleven or twelve, sweet kid. They've been through a lot, she was telling me some of it, but it looks like things are getting better for them. Charlene said they started coming here after y'all did the backyard Bible club at their mobile home park."

"Oh yes," Mike acknowledged. "This place has its frustrations. There are things about this church that make me want to pull my hair out, or pull somebody's hair out, but working with folks like Charlene and Amy makes me want to stick around. I wish I could say everybody's welcomed them, but they haven't. We've got a few who go out of their way to avoid them. I've heard snide remarks about 'trailer trash,' and the same handful have said ugly things behind their backs about Amy being biracial. I was worried, didn't know how the church would react, two Sundays ago when I gave the invitation and they came forward, both of them on profession of faith as candidates for baptism. I shouldn't have been worried. Ol' Clarence Bishop is about as good as Wallace was at saying "Movewereceive'em.' About a dozen people said 'second' in perfect unison, sounded like they'd rehearsed it. Like I said, not everybody's welcomed them, but nobody voted against them."

"Then they adjourned to the parking lot where they said what they really thought?" Heather quipped.

"Something like that," Mike agreed. "I'm glad Roland and Geneva picked that Sunday to be mad enough at me to go home after Sunday School. They were at home sulking and watching Charles Stanley on TV when Charlene and Amy joined the church."

"It's like I keep telling you, Mike," Heather commented. "God has a sense of humor. That's not as good as ol' Lester Halstead getting mad, tearing out of the church parking lot, and nearly colliding with a state trooper, but it's close. That happened back when Logan Clark was pastor, but every once in a while somebody brings it up and people still crack up over it. Wanda says the nicest thing about being divorced from Lester is being able to laugh at that story, says she wouldn't have dared to crack a smile over it as long as she was living with him—which brings me back to Charlene and Amy. Charlene told me that she moved down here from Chattanooga to get out of an abusive relationship. Said she packed herself, her daughter, and what they could get into her station wagon and hit the road while he was at work. A preacher in Hansonville put them in touch with My Sister's Place. From there, Charlene got a job at a warehouse in Hansonville, rented the mobile home, and they settled here."

"Did Charlene tell you about her new job?" Mike queried.

"She did," Heather answered excitedly, "said David Groves hired her to manage the parts department at his dealership."

"Yeah, it was so neat the way that worked out," Eric added. Jenny's uncle, the one who was convicted of killing Debbie Seals, was the parts department manager at the Chevrolet place. You'll be having lunch with his two sisters tomorrow. Billy Ray's ex-wife Judy got to talking with Charlene and Amy the first Sunday they were here, found out that Charlene grew up around her grandfather's auto parts store in Chattanooga, so she knows the parts business. She has good computer skills, and she was doing inventory control at the warehouse. Judy's the receptionist for the dealership, so she knew the man David hired to replace Billy Ray was quitting to take a job at a dealership in Columbus. Judy called David, and he called Charlene that afternoon. David and Cheryl went over and met her at the dealership, and David hired her on the spot. David says she's great, said it took the mechanics about a day to see that she knows her stuff, and she won their respect. David said, not only has she been doing a good job, some of the mechanics have cleaned up their language on account of her being back there."

"Charlene told me it's a good job, good insurance and benefits, and the most money she's ever made," Heather added. "She's working with Cheryl on buying a house for herself and her daughter. Puts me in mind a lot of Wanda used-to-be-Halstead, Wanda Gonzales, starting over with next-to-nothing. Wanda just bought a house. Cute little house, emphasis on little, but it's in good shape, comfortable enough for one person who doesn't have a lot of stuff. It's up on Cotton Avenue in Ledford."

"That's great," Mike commented. "Charlene and Amy should be getting a place of their own soon. Cheryl's working hard to find something decent and affordable for them. The new job expands the definition of affordable, so that should help things along. She's going to do all right, and I expect Wanda will, too. I've got a lot of respect for both of them."

"By the time I learn the whole cast of characters here, it'll be time for me to go home," Heather prefaced her question, "but I did want to ask you about one couple I saw last night, looked to be high school age, he was white and she was black..."

"You're talking about Daniel Groves and Coretta Brinkley," Eric replied. "Daniel is David and Cheryl's older boy. Coretta's a member of Greater New Hope. Both good kids. Coretta's my drum major. They'll both be seniors when school starts back."

"They've been dating since back in June after Vacation Bible School," Mike elaborated. "When we partnered with Greater New Hope on VBS, the high school kids worked on missions projects as well as doing Bible study. Daniel and Coretta were acquainted from school but really got to know each other that week. They took a liking to each other, wasn't long after their first date they were going steady. Both sets of parents have had a hard time coming to terms with it. They're getting better about it. David and Cheryl took Daniel and Coretta to a dinner theater in Atlanta a couple of weeks ago to celebrate Coretta's birthday, and Daniel's become a regular for Sunday dinner at the Brinkleys'. It'd be a stretch to say either set of parents is thrilled about the relationship, but they're not looking at it as the end of the world, and they're acting like Christians."

"Sometimes," Heather observed, "making up your mind to be kind and behave as a Christian is the best you can do until you can do better. Give them credit for that."

"Believe me, I do," Mike responded, "thanking the Lord all the time that they're doing as well as they are. David and Cheryl have come a long way in accepting Coretta. They both hugged her and talked with her after church last night. That's major progress from where they were a couple of months ago. I was telling David last Sunday that Charlene said she knew the Lord led her and Amy to Harrington and to our church. David had tears trickling down his face, and he said maybe the Lord led them here as much for his benefit as theirs, and not just because he got a cracker-jack good parts department manager out of the deal. David said he'd been turning it over and over in his mind for a couple of weeks, waking up at night worrying about what if Daniel did end up married to Coretta some day and they had children. All of a sudden, he said, Charlene and Amy show up at church, and you can tell by looking at Amy that her father was black, and she's a beautiful girl, sweet as she can be, just a normal child. David said Amy helped him see that, if Daniel and Coretta did marry and have children, having a biracial grandchild would be far from the worst thing that could happen, said he knew he'd love and be proud of those children just like any other grandchildren he might have."

"Reminds me of a sermon Mike preached one Sunday night from Matthew 24 where Jesus prophesied the destruction of the temple in Jerusalem," Eric commented. "The disciples jumped straight from that to asking about the end of the world. They assumed that the destruction of the temple would mean the end of the world. The point of Mike's message was that most of the things we think would be the end of the world turn out not to be."

"That's good," Heather observed. "That'll get preached at Clear Springs. It does sound like God was saying something to David and Cheryl, and to the whole church, bringing Charlene and Amy here. How is the church responding to Daniel and Coretta dating each other?"

"Most of them have the same reservations the parents do," Mike answered, "but they're too nice to say anything unkind, at least to their faces. Greater New Hope doesn't have a Sunday night service, so Coretta's been here with Daniel just about every Sunday night. She comes with him to the youth fellowship on Friday nights. The kids've probably accepted her better than the church as a whole. Most of the people are getting used to her being here and the two of them sitting together, and they're acting civil if not Christian."

"It's a tough thing for the church," Eric acknowledged. "I've had a hard time coming to terms with it, and I've always prided myself on being pretty openminded. Seeing them together, seeing Daniel with his arm around Coretta, stirred up some old attitudes I thought I'd dealt with and put to rest. With me being band director and Coretta being drum major—one of the best in the state, I think—I need to maintain a good relationship with her to get the band through marching season. As a Christian, as a deacon, as a friend of both families, I need to maintain a good relationship with both kids and both sets of parents. They're good kids from good families, both Christians, and my gut-level reaction to them dating is my problem. I've got some old prejudices that aren't pleasing to God, and I need to get rid of them. Above all, I want to stay close to the Lord, and I know I can't do that as long as I consciously harbor sin."

"Putting it on the table, confessing it, calling it what it is, seeking God's forgiveness," Heather commented, "is the only way you'll ever get rid of it. That, and you've chosen to act according to what you know is right instead of your prejudice. It's a lot easier to change actions than feelings, and our feelings usually change once we change our actions. You want to get rid of the old prejudices because they're not consistent with who you are as a Christian, and you will get rid of them because you put supreme value on your relationship with God."

"Heather, I just wish everybody who's uncomfortable with Daniel and Coretta dating had the same outlook Eric does. If they did, it wouldn't be a problem," Mike injected. "We had a pretty ugly confrontation over it in the July deacons' meeting."

"What happened?"

"Ol' Franklin A. Brinkley, Former Chairmain of the Board of Deacons of Harrington Baptist Church..."

"Mr. Personality himself? The great stone face?"

"Yeah, him."

"Kind of curious that Frank and Coretta have the same last name, isn't it?"

"I'm coming to that. It's a long story," Mike continued. "Frank jumped David Groves and me, demanding to know what action we were going to take about this miscegenation—that was the term he used—going on between Daniel and Coretta."

"And you told him?"

"I told him I wasn't going to take any action because I didn't see any action I needed to take. I told him that Coretta wouldn't be here today if his great-grandfather, Reverend Joshua Brinkley, had been all that opposed to miscegenation. I told him what Miss Addie said about ol' Josh Brinkley having several children with his black mistress, and how that made him and Coretta distant cousins."

"Did you have to do CPR?"

"Thought I was going to have to. As I was waiting to see whether Frank's body and soul were going to part company, David spoke up. He said, 'Brother Frank, Coretta's a decent, respectable young lady, and that's the way Cheryl and I are going to treat her. As far as what action we plan to take, Cheryl and I are taking Daniel and Coretta somewhere really nice for Coretta's birthday next week.' Then he said, 'Brother Frank, it sure is a good thing I'm a Christian and the Lord's helped me deal with my temper. If we'd had this conversation before I was saved, you'd either be unconscious or in a lot of pain right now.' David said that so calmly, it was plumb eerie. Frank got a lot quieter after that."

"Whoa!" Heather exclaimed, "At least ol' Stone Face'll have second thoughts about crawling down David's throat again. How'd the other deacons react?"

"Well, I can usually count on Doc Walters going along with Frank and backing him up, but he didn't this time. I don't know if he didn't want to antagonize David or what, but he just sat there like a bump on a log. Ted Coleman's our deacon chairman and a good one. He's a nice guy and usually pretty easy-going, but he can be as stern as he needs to be to keep things from getting out of hand. Ted told Frank he was out of line and told him to stay in his seat and on his side of the table. The rest of the deacons just looked at Frank like he was a complete idiot. They left Frank out on a limb by himself, and he backed down when nobody rallied to his cause."

"Sounds like you've got a pretty good group of deacons," Heather observed, "and a good chairman. That's been one of the best things we've had going for us at Clear Springs. It'd be hard to say whether Wallace or Carol was the best chairman. They had different strengths but both were good. With Carol leaving to go to Tennessee with Dennis, we elected Linda Trimble chairman, and I think she'll do well. Our deacons at Clear Springs make me look better than I really am. I often think of the story in Exodus 17 of Aaron and Hur holding up Moses' hands! I started to say I miss Wallace. In a way I do. There are times I wish I could talk with him and draw on his wisdom or just be entertained by some of the great stories he could tell. But, in another way, I don't miss him because it doesn't really feel like he's gone. His spirit permeates the place. I've often thought about what Dennis Palmer said at the funeral, that Wallace never tried to run the church, but he shaped the character of the church. A lot of times when I'm preaching, I'll look over to where Wallace used to sit, and I know it's a projection of my imagination, but he's there. I'll never forget the first time somebody joined the church after Wallace died. Ol' Matt Coggins, bless his heart, rolled out "Movewereceive'em,' all one word, sounded just like his daddy. People were laughing and crying at the same time, and I said, 'Matt, was that you or did Wallace just speak from Heaven?' and Matt laughed and said, 'Some of both, Preacher.'

"I'm glad I got to start my ministry at Clear Springs," Mike commented, "and I'll always be glad I got to work so closely with Wallace. It was like pulling eye teeth to leave. Heather, you remember the Sunday the church voted to call you, when we led the communion service together. We were reading the church covenant, and we came to the part that says,

We moreover engage that when we remove from this place, we will as soon as possible unite with some other church where we can carry out the spirit of this covenant and the principles of God's word.

I got so choked up, I couldn't get the words to come out. You put your arm around my shoulders and you led that part of the reading. Then, when you were riding with Karen and me over to the Corries' for Sunday dinner, I commented on that, said that I got choked up because I realized that I'd never find another place like

Clear Springs. Do you remember what you told me? It was a word from the Lord for me that day."

"I told you," Heather replied, "that the covenant didn't say anything about finding another place like Clear Springs. It says 'some other church where we can carry out the spirit of this covenant and the principles of God's word.' The question is, can you carry out the spirit of Clear Springs' covenant and the principles of God's word in partnership with the people at Harrington Baptist Church?"

"And I told you then that I didn't know the answer to that question, but I do know now, and the answer is 'yes'."

About the Author

Lamar Wadsworth, a native of Rockmart, Georgia, is a Baptist minister and writer. A graduate of Jacksonville State University and The Southern Baptist Seminary, he has pastored churches in Alabama, Kentucky, Georgia, and Maryland. He also studied creative writing with the late Dr. Jesse Stuart at Murray State University.

Lamar has had articles published in *Baptists Today* and *Priscilla Papers*. He writes an occasional column for his hometown paper, *The Rockmart Journal*, which is published faithfully once a week whether anything happens or not. His first novel, *The Spirit of This Covenant*, is set in the world he knows best, rural and small-town Baptist churches in the deep south, which offer enough plot lines and fascinating characters to keep a writer busy for a lifetime.

Lamar and his wife Marilyn have three grown daughters and one grandchild. He, Marilyn, and daughter Missy live in Baltimore.

Made in the USA
Lexington, KY
01 December 2014